Along the
INFINITE
SEA

A graduate of Stanford University with an MBA from Columbia, Beatriz Williams lives with her husband and four children near the Connecticut shore, where she divides her time between writing and laundry.

Visit her online at
www.beatrizwilliams.com
Facebook.com/BeatrizWilliamsAuthor
Twitter @BCWilliamsBooks

BY THE SAME AUTHOR

Overseas
A Hundred Summers

Coming soon
The Secret Life of Violet Grant
Tiny Little Thing

Along the INFINITE SEA

BEATRIZ WILLIAMS

HARPER

Harper
HarperCollins*Publishers*
1 London Bridge Street
London SE1 9GF

www.harpercollins.co.uk

First published by Berkley, Penguin Group (USA) 2015

This paperback edition published by *Harper* 2015
1

A catalogue record for this book
is available from the British Library

ISBN: 978-0-00-813495-2

This novel is entirely a work of fiction.
The names, characters and incidents portrayed in it are
the work of the author's imagination. Any resemblance to
actual persons, living or dead, events or localities is
entirely coincidental.

Set in Adobe Garamond Pro by Palimpsest Book Production Limited,
Falkirk, Stirlingshire

Printed and bound in Great Britain by
Clays Ltd, St Ives plc

MIX
Paper from
responsible sources
FSC www.fsc.org **FSC™ C007454**

FSC™ is a non-profit international organisation established
to promote the responsible management of the world's forests.
Products carrying the FSC label are independently certified
to assure consumers that they come from forests that are managed
to meet the social, economic and ecological needs
of present and future generations, and other controlled sources.

Find out more about HarperCollins and the environment at
www.harpercollins.co.uk/green

To those who escaped in time
and those who did not
and those who risked their lives to help

Overture

"To see all without looking;
to hear all without listening."

CÉSAR RITZ
King of Hoteliers, Hotelier of Kings

ANNABELLE

Paris • 1937

All you really need to know about the Paris Ritz is this: by the middle of 1937, Coco Chanel was living in a handsome suite on the third floor, and the bartender—an intuitive mixologist named Frank Meier—had invented the Bloody Mary sixteen summers earlier to cure a Hemingway hangover.

Mind you, when I arrived at Nick Greenwald's farewell party on that hot July night, I wasn't altogether aware of this history. I didn't run with the Ritz crowd. Mosquitoes, my husband called them. And maybe I should have listened to my husband. Maybe no good could come from visiting the bar at the Paris Ritz; maybe you were doomed to commit some frivolous and irresponsible act, maybe you were doomed to hover around dangerously until you had drawn the blood from another human being or else had your own blood drawn instead.

But Johann—my husband—wasn't around that night. I tiptoed in through the unfashionable Place Vendôme entrance on my brother's arm instead, since Johann had been recalled to Berlin for an assignment of a few months that had stretched into several. In those days, you couldn't just flit back and forth between Paris and Berlin, any more than you could flit between heaven and hell; and furthermore, why would you want to? Paris had everything I needed, everything I loved, and Berlin in 1937 was no place for a liberal-minded woman nurturing a young child and an impossible rift in her marriage. I stayed defiantly in France, where you could still attend a party for a man named Greenwald, where anyone could dine where he pleased and shop and bank where he pleased, where you could sleep with anyone who suited you, and it wasn't a crime.

For the sake of everyone's good time, I suppose it was just as well that my husband remained in Berlin, since Nick Greenwald and Johann von Kleist weren't what you'd call bosom friends, for all the obvious reasons. But Nick and I were a different story. Nick and I understood each other: first, because we were both Americans living in Paris, and second, because we shared a little secret together, the kind of secret you could never, ever share with anyone else. Of all my brother's friends, Nick was the only one who didn't resent me for marrying a general in the German army. Good old Nick. He knew I'd had my reasons.

The salon was hot, and Nick was in his shirtsleeves, though he still retained his waistcoat and a neat white bow tie, the kind you needed a valet to arrange properly. He turned at the sound of my voice. "Annabelle! Here at last."

"Not so very late, am I?" I said.

We kissed, and he and Charles shook hands. Not that Charles paid the transaction much attention; he was transfixed by the black-haired beauty who lounged at Nick's side in a shimmering silver-blue dress that matched her eyes. A long cigarette dangled from her fingers. Nick turned to her and placed his hand at the small of her back. "Annabelle, Charlie. I don't think you've met Budgie Byrne. An old college friend."

We said *enchantée*. Miss Byrne took little notice. Her handshake was slender and lacked conviction. She slipped her arm through Nick's and whispered in his ear, and they shimmered off together to the bar inside a haze of expensive perfume. The back of Miss Byrne's dress swooped down almost to the point of no return, and her naked skin was like a spill of milk, kept from running over the edge by Nick's large palm.

Charles covered his cheek with his right hand—the same hand that Miss Byrne had just touched with her limp and slender fingers and said that bastard always got the best-looking women.

I watched Nick's back disappear into the crowd, and I was about to tell Charles that he didn't need to worry, that Nick didn't really look all that happy with his companion and Charles might want to give the delectably disinterested Miss Byrne another try in an hour, but at that exact instant a voice came over my shoulder, the last voice I expected to hear at the Paris Ritz on this night in the smoldering middle of July.

"My God," it said, a little slurry. "If it isn't the baroness herself."

I thought perhaps I was hallucinating, or mistaken. It wouldn't be the first time. For the past two years, I'd heard this voice everywhere: department stores and elevators and street corners. I'd seen its owner in every possible nook, in every conceivable disguise, only to discover that the supposed encounter was only a false alarm, a collision of deluded molecules inside my own head, and the proximate cause of the leap in my blood proved to be an ordinary citizen after all. Just an everyday fellow who happened to have dark hair or a deep voice or a certain shape to the back of his neck. In the instant of revelation, I never knew whether to be relieved or disappointed. Whether to lament or hallelujah. Either way, the experience wasn't a pleasant one, at least not in the way we ordinarily experience pleasure, as a benevolent thing that massages the nerves into a sensation of well-being.

Either way, I had committed a kind of adultery of the heart, hadn't I, and since I couldn't bear the thought of adultery in any form, I learned to ignore the false alarm when it rang and rang and rang. Like the good wife I was, I learned to maintain my poise during these moments of intense delusion.

So there. Instead of bolting at the slurry word *baroness*, I took my deluded molecules in hand and said: *Surely not.*

Instead of spinning like a top, I turned like a figurine on a music box, in such a way that you could almost hear the tinkling Tchaikovsky in my gears.

A man came into view, quite lifelike, quite familiar, tall and just so in his formal blacks and white points, dark hair curling into his forehead the way your lover's hair does in your wilder dreams. He was holding a lowball glass and a brown Turkish cigarette in his right hand, and he took in everything at a glance: my jewels, my extravagant dress, the exact state of my circulation.

In short, he seemed an awful lot like the genuine article.

"There you are, you old bastard," said Charles happily, and *sacré bleu*, I realized then what I already knew, that the man before me was no delusion. That the Paris Ritz was the kind of place that could conjure up anyone it wanted.

"Stefan," I said. "What a lovely surprise."

(And the big trouble was, I think I meant it.)

First Movement

"Experience is simply the name
we give our mistakes."

OSCAR WILDE

PEPPER

Palm Beach • 1966

1.

The Mercedes-Benz poses on the grass like a swirl of vintage black ink, like no other car in the world.

You'd never guess it to look at her, but Miss Pepper Schuyler—that woman right over there, the socialite with the golden antelope legs who's soaking up the Florida sunshine at the other end of the courtyard—knows every glamorous inch of this 1936 Special Roadster shadowing the grass. You might regard Pepper's pregnant belly protruding from her green Lilly shift (well, it's hard to ignore a belly like that, isn't it?) and the pastel Jack Rogers sandal dangling from her uppermost toe, and you think you have her pegged. Admit it! Lush young woman exudes Palm Beach class. What the hell does she know about cars?

Well, beautiful Pepper doesn't give a damn what you think about her. She never did. She's thinking about the car. She slides her gaze along the seductive S-curve of the right side fender, swooping from the top of the tire to the running board below the door, like a woman's voluptuously naked leg, and her heart beats a quarter-inch faster.

She remembers what a pain in the pert old derrière it was to repaint that glossy fender. It had been the first week of October, and the warm weather wouldn't quit. The old shed on Cape Cod stank of paint and grease, a peculiarly acrid reek that had crept right through the protective mask and into her sinuses and taken up residence, until she couldn't smell anything else, and she thought, *What the hell am I doing here? What the hell am I thinking?*

Thank God that was all over. Thank God this rare inky-black 1936 Mercedes Special Roadster is now someone else's problem, someone willing to pay Pepper three hundred thousand dollars for the privilege of keeping its body and chrome intact against the ravages of time.

The deposit has already been paid, into a special account Pepper set up in her own name. (Her own name, her own money: now, that was a glorious feeling, like setting off for Europe on an ocean liner with nothing but open blue seas ahead.) The rest will be delivered today, to the Breakers hotel where Pepper is staying, in a special-delivery envelope. Another delightful little big check made out in Pepper's name. Taken together, those checks will solve all her problems. She'll have money for the baby, money to start everything over, money to ignore whoever needs ignoring, money to disappear if she needs to, forever and ever. She'll depend on no one. She can do whatever the hell she pleases, whatever suits Pepper Schuyler and—by corollary—Pepper Junior. She will toe nobody's line. She will fear nobody.

So the only question left in Pepper's mind, the only question that needs resolving, is the niggling Who?

Who the hell is this anonymous buyer—a woman, Pepper's auction agent said—who has the dough and the desire to lay claim to Pepper's very special Special Roadster, before it even reaches the public sales ring?

Not that Pepper cares who she is. Pepper just cares who she *isn't*. As long as this woman is a disinterested party, a person who has her own reasons for wanting this car, nothing to do with Pepper, nothing to do with the second half of the magic equation inside Pepper's belly, well, everything's just peachy keen, isn't it? Pepper will march off with her three hundred thousand dollars and never give the buyer another thought.

Pepper lifts a tanned arm and checks her watch. It's a gold Cartier, given to her by her father for her eighteenth birthday, perhaps as a subtle reminder to start arriving the hell on time, now that she was a grown-up. It didn't work. The party always starts when Pepper gets there, not before, so why should she care if she arrives late or early? Still, the watch has its uses. The watch tells her it's twenty-seven minutes past twelve o'clock. They should be here any moment: Pepper's auction agent and the buyer, to inspect the car and complete the formalities. *If* they're on time, and why wouldn't they be? By all accounts, the lady's as eager to buy as Pepper is to sell.

Pepper tilts her head back and closes her eyes to the white sun. She can't get enough of it. This baby inside her must have sprung from another religion, one that worshipped the gods in the sky or gained nourishment from sunbeams. Pepper can almost feel the cells dividing in ecstasy as she points herself due upward. She can almost feel the seams strain along her green Lilly shift, the dancing monkeys stretch their arms to fit around the ambitious creature within.

Well, that makes sense, doesn't it? Like father, like child.

"Good afternoon."

Pepper bolts upright. A small and slender woman stands before her, dark-haired, dressed in navy Capri pants and a white shirt, her delicate face hidden by a pair of large dark sunglasses. It's Audrey Hepburn, or else her well-groomed Florida cousin.

"Good afternoon," Pepper says.

The woman holds out her hand. "You must be Miss Schuyler. My name is Annabelle Dommerich. I'm the buyer. Please, don't get up."

Pepper rises anyway and takes the woman's hand. Mrs. Dommerich stands only a few inches above five feet, and Pepper is a tall girl, but for some reason they seem to meet as equals.

"I'm surprised to see you," says Pepper. "I had the impression you wanted to remain anonymous."

Mrs. Dommerich shrugs. "Oh, that's just for the newspapers. Actually, I've been hugely curious to meet you, Miss Schuyler. You're even more beautiful than your pictures. And look at you, blooming like a rose! When are you due?"

"February."

"I've always envied women like you. When I was pregnant, I looked like a beach ball with feet."

"I can't imagine that."

"It was a long time ago." Mrs. Dommerich takes off her sunglasses to reveal a pair of large and chocolaty eyes. "The car looks beautiful."

"Thank you. I had an expert helping me restore it."

"You restored it yourself?" Both eyebrows rise, so elegant. "I'm impressed."

"There was nothing else to do."

Mrs. Dommerich turns to gaze at the car, shielding her brows with one hand. "And you found it in the shed on Cape Cod? Just like that, covered with dust? Untouched?"

"Yes. My sister-in-law's house. It seemed to have been abandoned there."

"Yes," says Mrs. Dommerich. "It was."

The grass prickles Pepper's feet through the gaps in her sandals. Next to her, Mrs. Dommerich stands perfectly still, like she's posing for a portrait, *Woman Transfixed in a Crisp White Shirt*. She talks like an American, in easy sentences, but there's just the slightest mysterious tilt to her accent that suggests something imported, like the Chanel perfume that colors the air next to her skin. Though that skin is remarkably fresh, lit by a kind of iridescent pearl-like substance that most women spend fruitless dollars to achieve, Pepper guesses she must be in her forties, even her late forties. It's something about her expression and her carriage, something that makes Pepper feel like an ungainly young colt, dressed like a little girl. Even considering that matronly bump that interrupts the youthful line of her figure.

At the opposite end of the courtyard, a pair of sweating men appear, dressed in businesslike wool suits above a pair of perfectly matched potbellies, neat as basketballs. One of them spots the two women and raises his hand in what Pepper's always called a golf wave.

"There they are," says Mrs. Dommerich. She turns back to Pepper and smiles. "I do appreciate your taking such trouble to restore her so well. How does she run?"

"Like a racehorse."

"Good. I can almost hear that roar in my ears now. There's no other sound like it, is there? Not like anything they make today."

"I wouldn't know, really. I'm not what you'd call an enthusiast."

"Really? We'll have to change that, then. I'll pick you up from your hotel at seven o'clock and we'll take her for a spin before dinner." She holds out her hand, and Pepper, astonished, can do nothing but shake it. Mrs. Dommerich's fingers are soft and strong and devoid of rings, except for a single gold band on the telling digit of her left hand, which Pepper has already noticed.

"Of course," Pepper mumbles.

Mrs. Dommerich slides her sunglasses back in place and turns away.

"Wait just a moment," says Pepper.

"Yes?"

"I'm just curious, Mrs. Dommerich. How do you already know how the engine sounds? Since it's been locked away in an old shed all these years."

"Oh, trust me, Miss Schuyler. I know everything about that car."

There's something so self-assured about her words, Pepper's skin begins to itch, and not just the skin that stretches around the baby. The sensation sets off a chain reaction of alarm along the pathways of Pepper's nerves: the dingling of tiny alarm bells in her ears, the tingling in the tip of her nose.

"And just how the hell do you know that, Mrs. Dommerich? If you don't mind me asking. Why exactly would you pay all that money for this hunk of pretty metal?"

Mrs. Dommerich's face is hidden behind those sunglasses, betraying not an ounce of visible reaction to Pepper's impertinence. "Because, Miss Schuyler," she says softly, "twenty-eight years ago, I drove for my life across the German border inside that car, and I left a piece of my heart inside her. And now I think it's time to bring her home. Don't you?" She turns away again, and as she walks across the grass, she says, over her shoulder, sounding like an elegant half-European mother: "Wear a cardigan, Miss Schuyler. It's supposed to be cooler tonight, and I'd like to put the top down."

2.

At first, Pepper has no intention of obeying the summons of Annabelle Dommerich. The check is waiting for her when she calls at the front desk at the hotel, along with a handwritten telephone message that she discards after a single glance. She has the doorman call her a taxi, and she rides into town to deposit the check in her account. The clerk's face is expressionless as he hands her the receipt. She withdraws a couple hundred bucks, which she tucks into her pocketbook next to her compact and her cigarettes. When she returns to the hotel, she draws herself a bubble bath and soaks for an hour, sipping from a single glass of congratulatory champagne and staring at the tiny movements disturbing the golden curve of her belly. Thank God she hasn't got any stretch marks. Coconut oil, that's what her doctor recommended, and she went out and bought five bottles.

The water turns cool. Pepper lifts her body from the tub and wraps herself in a white towel. She orders a late room-service lunch and stands on the balcony, wrapped in her towel, smoking a cigarette. She considers another glass of champagne but knows she won't go through with it. The doctor back on Cape Cod, a comely young fellow full of newfangled ideas, said to go easy on the booze. The doctor also said to go easy on the smokes, but you can't do everything your doctor says, can you? You can't give up everything, all at once, when you have already given up so much.

And for what? For a baby. *His* baby, of all things. So stupid, Pepper. You thought you were so clever and brave, you thought you had it all under control, and now look at you. All knocked up and nowhere to go.

The beach is bright yellow and studded with sunbathers before a lazy surf. Pepper reaches to tuck in her towel and lets it fall to the tiled floor of the balcony. No one sees her. She leans against the balcony rail, naked and golden-ripe, until her cigarette burns to a tiny stump in her hand, until the bell rings with her room-service lunch.

After she eats, she sets the tray outside her door and falls into bed. She takes a long nap, over the covers, and when she wakes up she slips into a sleeveless tunic-style cocktail dress, brushes her hair, and touches up her lipstick. Before she heads for the elevator, she takes a cardigan from the drawer and slings it over her bare shoulders.

3.

But the elevator's stuck in the lobby. That was the trouble with hotels like the Breakers; there was always some Greek tycoon moving in, some sausage king from Chicago, and the whole place ground to a halt to accommodate his wife and kids and help and eighty-eight pieces of luggage. Afterward, he would tell his friends back home that the place wasn't what it was cracked up to be, and the natives sure were unfriendly.

Pepper taps her foot and checks her watch, but the elevator is having none of it. She heads for the stairs.

On the one hand, you have the luxurious appointments of the Breakers, plush carpets and mirrors designed to show you off to your best advantage. On the other hand, you have the stairwell, like an escape from Alcatraz. Pepper's spindly shoes rattle on the concrete floors; the bare incandescent bulbs appear at intervals as if to interrogate her. She has just turned the last landing, lobby escape hatch in sight, when a man comes into view, leaning against the door. He's wearing a seersucker suit—a genuine blue striped seersucker suit, as if men actually wore them anymore—and his arms are crossed.

For an instant, Pepper thinks of a platinum starlet, sprawled naked on her bedroom floor a few years back. *Killed herself, poor bimbo,* everyone said, shaking the sorrowful old head. *Drugs, of course. A cautionary Hollywood tale.*

"Nice suit," says Pepper. "Are they making a movie out there?"

He straightens from the door and shoots his cuffs. "Miss Schuyler? Do you have a moment?"

"I don't think so. Certainly not for strangers who lurk in stairwells."

"I'm afraid I must insist."

"I'm afraid you're in my way. Do you mind stepping aside?"

In response, Captain Seersucker stretches his thick candy-stripe arm across the passage and places a hand against the opposite wall.

"Well, well," says Pepper. "A nice beefy fellow, aren't you? How much do they hire you out for? Or do you do it just for the love of sport?"

"I'm just a friend, Miss Schuyler. A friend of a friend who wants to talk to you, that's all, nice and friendly. So you're going to have to come with me."

Pepper laughs. "You see, that's the trouble with you muscle-men. Not too much in the noggin, is there?"

"Miss Schuyler—"

"Call me Pepper, Captain Seersucker. Everyone else does." She holds out her hand, and when he doesn't take it, she pats his cheek. "A big old lug, aren't you? Tell me, what do you do when the quiz shows come on the TV? Do you just stare all blank at the screen, or do you try to learn something?"

"Miss Schuyler—"

"And now you're getting angry with me. Your face is all pink. Look, I don't hold it against you. We can't all be Einstein, can we? The world needs brawn as well as brain. And the girls certainly don't mind, do they? I mean, what self-respecting woman wants a man hanging around who's smarter than she is?"

"Look here—"

"Now, just look at that jaw of yours, for example. So useful! Like a nice square piece of granite. I'll bet you could crush gravel with it in your spare time."

He lifts his hand away from the wall and makes to grab her, but Pepper's been waiting for her chance, and she ducks neatly underneath his arm, pregnancy and all, and brings her knee up into his astonished crotch. He crumples like a tin can, lamenting his injured manhood in loud wails, but Pepper doesn't waste a second gloating. She throws open the door to the lobby and tells the bellboy to call a doctor, because some poor oaf in a seersucker suit just tripped on his shoelaces and fell down the stairs.

4.

"I thought you wouldn't come," says Mrs. Dommerich, as Pepper slides into the passenger seat of the glamorous Mercedes. Every head is turned toward the pair of them, but the lady doesn't seem to notice. She's wearing a wide-necked dress of midnight-blue jacquard, sleeves to the elbows and hem to the knees, extraordinarily elegant.

"I wasn't going to. But then I remembered what a bore it is, sitting around my hotel room, and I came around."

"I'm glad you did."

Mrs. Dommerich turns the ignition, and the engine roars with joy. *Cars like this, they like to be driven,* Pepper's almost-brother-in-law said, the first time they tried the engine, and at the time Pepper thought he was crazy, talking about a machine as if it were a person. But now she listens to the pitch of the pistons and supposes he was probably right. Caspian usually was, at least when it came to cars.

"I guess you know how to drive this thing?" Pepper says.

"Oh, yes." Mrs. Dommerich puts the car into gear and releases the clutch. The car pops away from the curb like a hunter taking a fence. Pepper notices her own hands are a little shaky, and she places her fingers securely around the doorframe.

Just as the hotel entrance slides out of view, she spots a pair of men loitering near the door, staring as if to bore holes through the side of Pepper's head. Not locals; they're dressed all wrong. They're dressed like the man in the stairwell, like some outsider's notion of how you dressed in Palm Beach, like someone told them to wear pink madras and canvas deck shoes, and they'd fit right in.

And then they're gone.

Pepper ties her scarf around her head and says, in a remarkably calm voice, "Where are we going?"

"I thought we'd have dinner in town. Have a nice little chat. I'd like to hear a little more about how you found her. What it was like, bringing her back to life."

"Oh, it's a girl, is it? I never checked."

"Ships and automobiles, my dear. God knows why."

"You know," says Pepper, drumming her fingers along the edge of the window glass, "don't take this the wrong way, but I can't help noticing that you two seem to be on awfully familiar terms, for a nice lady and a few scraps of old metal."

"I should be, shouldn't I? I paid an awful lot of money for her."

"For which I can't thank you enough."

"Well, I couldn't let her sit around in some museum. Not after all we've been through together." She pats the dashboard affectionately. "She belongs with someone who loves her."

Pepper shakes her head. "I don't get it. I don't see how you could love a car."

"Someone loved this car, to put it back together like this."

"It wasn't me. It was Caspian."

"Who's Caspian?"

Pepper opens her pocketbook and takes out her compact. "We'll just say he's a friend of my sister's, shall we? A very good friend. Anyway, he's the enthusiast. He couldn't stand watching me try to put it together myself."

"I'm eternally grateful. I suppose he knows a lot about German cars?"

"It turns out he was an army brat. They lived in Germany

when he was young, right after the war, handing out retribution with one hand and Hershey bars with the other."

Mrs. Dommerich swings the heavy Mercedes around a corner, on the edge of a nickel. Pepper realizes that the muscles of her abdomen are clenched, and it's nothing to do with the baby. But there's no question that Mrs. Dommerich knows how to drive this car. She drives it the way some people ride horses, as if the gears and the wheels are extensions of her own limbs. She may not be tall, but she sits so straight it doesn't matter. Her scarf flutters gracefully in the draft. She reaches for her pocketbook, which lies on the seat between them, and takes out a cigarette with one hand. "Do you mind lighting me?" she asks.

Pepper finds the lighter and brings Mrs. Dommerich's long, thin Gauloise to life.

"Thank you." She blows a stream of smoke into the wind and holds out the pack to Pepper. "Help yourself."

Pepper eyes the tempting little array. Her shredded nerves jingle in her ears. "Maybe just one. I'm supposed to be cutting back."

"I didn't start until later," Mrs. Dommerich says. "When my babies were older. We started going out more, to cocktail parties and things, and the air was so thick I thought I might as well play along. But it never became a habit, thank God. Maybe because I started so late." She takes a long drag. "Sometimes it takes me a week to go through a single pack. It's just for the pure pleasure. It's like sex, you want to be able to take your time and enjoy it."

Pepper laughs. "That's a new one on me. I always thought the more, the merrier. Sex *and* cigarettes."

"My husband never understood, either. He smoked like a chimney, one after another, right up until the day he died."

"And when was that?"

"A year and a half ago." She checks the side mirror. "Lung cancer."

"I'm sorry."

They begin to mount the bridge to the mainland. Mrs. Dommerich seems to be concentrating on the road ahead, to the flashing lights that indicates the deck is going up. She rolls to a stop and drops the cigarette from the edge of the car. When she speaks, her voice has dropped an octave, to a rough-edged husk of itself.

"I used to try to make him stop," she says. "But he didn't seem to care."

5.

They eat at a small restaurant off Route 1. The owner recognizes Mrs. Dommerich and kisses both her cheeks. They chatter together in French for a moment, so rapidly and colloquially that Pepper can't quite follow. Mrs. Dommerich turns and introduces Pepper—*my dear friend Miss Schuyler,* she calls her—and the man seizes Pepper's belly in rapture, as if she's his mistress and he's the guilty father.

"So beautiful!" he says.

"Isn't it, though." Pepper removes his hands. Since the beginning of the sixth month, Pepper's universe has parted into two worlds: people who regard her pregnancy as a kind of tumor, possibly contagious, and those who seem to think it's public property. "Whatever will your wife say when she finds out?"

"Ah, my wife." He shakes his head. "A very jealous woman. She will have my head on the carving platter."

"What a shame."

When they are settled at their table, supplied with water and crusty bread and a bottle of quietly expensive Burgundy, Mrs. Dommerich apologizes. The French are obsessed with babies, she says.

"I thought they were obsessed with sex."

"It's not such a stretch, is it?"

Pepper butters her bread and admits that it isn't.

The waiter arrives. Mrs. Dommerich orders turtle soup and sweetbreads; Pepper scans the menu and chooses mussels and canard à l'orange. When the waiter sweeps away the menus and melts into the atmosphere, a pause settles, the turning point. Pepper drinks a small sip of wine, folds her hands on the edge of the table, and says, "Why did you ask me to dinner, Mrs. Dommerich?"

"I might as well ask why you agreed to come."

"Age before beauty," says Pepper, and Mrs. Dommerich laughs.

"That's it, right there. That's why I asked you."

"Because I'm so abominably rude?"

"Because you're so awfully interesting. As I said before, Miss Schuyler. Because I'm curious about you. It's not every young debutante who finds a vintage Mercedes in a shed at her sister's house and restores it to its former glory, only to put it up for auction in Palm Beach."

"I'm full of surprises."

"Yes, you are." She pauses. "To be perfectly honest, I wasn't going to introduce myself at all. I already knew who you were, at least by reputation."

"Yes, I've got one of those things, haven't I? I can't imagine why."

"You have. I like to keep current on gossip. A vice of mine."

She smiles and sips her wine, marrying vices. "The sparky young aide in the new senator's office, perfectly bred and perfectly beautiful. They were right about that, goodness me."

Pepper shrugs. Her beauty is old news, no longer interesting even to her.

"Yes, exactly." Mrs. Dommerich nods. Her hair is cut short, curling around her ears, a stylish frame for the heart-shaped, huge-eyed delicacy of her face. A few silver threads catch the light overhead, and she hasn't tried to hide them. "You caused a real stir, you know, when you started working in the senator's office last year. I suppose you know that. Not just that you're a walking fashion plate, but that you were good at your job. You made yourself essential to him. You had hustle. There are beautiful women everywhere, but they don't generally have hustle. When you're beautiful, it's ever so much easier to find a man to hustle for you."

"Yes, but then you're stuck, aren't you? It's his rules, not yours."

The skin twitches around Mrs. Dommerich's wide red mouth.

"True. That's what I thought about you, when I saw you. I saw you were expecting, pretty far along, and all of a sudden I understood why you fixed up my car and sold it to me for a nice, convenient fortune. I understood perfectly."

"Oh, you did, did you?" Pepper lifts her knife and examines her reflection. A single blue Schuyler eye stares back at her, turned up at the corner like the bow of an especially elegant yacht. "Then why the hell were you still curious enough to invite me out?"

The waiter arrives solemnly with the soup and the mussels. Mrs. Dommerich waits in a pod of elegant impatience while he sets each dish exactly so, flourishes the pepper, asks if there will be anything else, and is dismissed. She lifts her spoon and smiles.

"Because, my dear, I can't wait to see what you do next."

6.

Pepper lights another cigarette after dinner, while Mrs. Dommerich drives the Mercedes north along the A1A. *For air,* she says. Pepper doesn't care much about air, one way or another, but she does care about those two men hanging around the entrance of the hotel before they left. She can handle one overgrown oaf in a stairwell, maybe, but two more was really too much.

So Pepper says okay, she could use some air. Let's take a little drive somewhere. She draws the smoke pleasantly into her lungs and breathes it out again. Air. To the right, the ocean ripples in and out of view, phosphorescent under a swollen November moon, and as the miles roll under the black wheels Pepper wonders if she's being kidnapped, and whether she cares. Whether it matters if Mrs. Dommerich acts for herself or for someone else.

He was going to track her down anyway, wasn't he? Sooner or later, the house always won.

Pepper used to think that *she* was the house. She has it all: family, beauty, brains, moxie. You think you hold all the cards, and then you realize you don't. You have one single precious card, and he wants it back.

And suddenly three hundred thousand dollars doesn't seem like much security, after all. Suddenly there isn't enough money in the world.

Pepper stubs out the cigarette in the little chrome ashtray. "Where are we going, anyway?"

"Oh, there's a little headland up ahead, tremendous view of the ocean. I like to park there sometimes and watch the waves roll in."

"Sounds like a scream."

"You might try it, you know. It's good for the soul."

"I have it on good authority, Mrs. Dommerich—from a number of sources, actually—that I haven't got one. A soul, I mean."

Mrs. Dommerich laughs. They're speaking loudly, because of the draft and the immense roar of the engine. She bends around another curve, and then the car begins to slow, as if it already knows where it's going, as if it's fate. They pull off the road onto a dirt track, lined by reeds a yard high, and such is the Roadster's suspension that Pepper doesn't feel a thing.

"I'm usually coming from the north," says Mrs. Dommerich. "We have a little house by the coast, near Cocoa Beach. When we first moved here from France, we wanted a quiet place where we could hide away from the world, and then of course the air-conditioning came in, and the world came to us in droves." She laughs. "But by then it didn't seem to matter. The kids loved it here too much, we couldn't sell up. As long as I could see the Atlantic, I didn't care."

The reeds part and the ocean opens up before them. Mrs. Dommerich keeps on driving until they reach the dunes, silver and black in the moonlight. Pepper smells the salt tide, the warm rot. The car rolls to a stop, and Mrs. Dommerich cuts the engine. The steady rush of water reaches Pepper's ears.

"Isn't it marvelous?" says Mrs. Dommerich.

"It's beautiful."

Mrs. Dommerich finds her pocketbook and takes out a cigarette. "We can share," she says.

"I've already reached my limit."

"If we share, it doesn't count. Halves don't count."

Pepper takes the cigarette from her fingers and examines it.

Mrs. Dommerich settles back and stares through the windshield. "Do you know what I love most about the ocean? The way the water's all connected. The bits and pieces have different names, but really it's all one vast body of salt water, all the way around the earth. It's as if we're touching Europe, or Africa, or the Antarctic. If you close your eyes, you can feel it, like it's right there."

Pepper hands back the cigarette. "That's true. But I don't like to close my eyes."

"You've never made an act of faith?"

"No. I like to rely on myself."

"So I see. But you know, sometimes it's not such a bad thing. An act of faith."

Pepper snatches the cigarette and takes a drag. She blows the smoke back out into the night and says, "So what's your game?"

"My game?"

"Why are you here? Obviously you know a thing or two about me. Did *he* send you?"

"He?"

"You know who."

"Oh. The father of your baby, you mean."

"You tell me."

Mrs. Dommerich lifts her hands to the steering wheel and taps her fingers against the lacquer. "No. Nobody sent me."

Pepper tips the ash into the sand and hands back the cigarette.

"Do you believe me?" Mrs. Dommerich asks.

"I don't believe in anything, Mrs. Dommerich. Just myself. And my sisters, too, I guess, but they have their own problems. They don't need mine on top of it all."

Mrs. Dommerich spreads out her hands to examine her palms. "Then let me help instead."

Pepper laughs. "Oh, that's a good one. Very kind of you."

"I mean it. Why not?"

"Why not? Because you don't even know me."

"There's no law against helping strangers."

"Well, I certainly don't know a damned thing about you, except that you're rich and your husband died last year, and you have children and love the ocean. And you drove this car across Germany thirty years ago—"

"Twenty-eight."

"Twenty-eight. And even if that's all true, it's not much to go on."

"Isn't it? Marriages have been made on less knowledge. Happy ones."

That's an odd thing to say, Pepper thinks, and she hears the words echoing: *an act of faith*. Well, that explains it. Maybe Mrs. Dommerich is one of those sweet little fools who thinks the world is a pretty place to live, filled with nice people who love you, where everything turns out all right if you just smile and tap your heels together three times.

Or maybe it's all an act.

A little gust of salt wind comes off the ocean, and Pepper snuggles deeper into her cardigan. Mrs. Dommerich finishes the cigarette and smashes it out carefully into the ashtray, next to Pepper's stub from the ride up. She reaches into the glove compartment and draws out a small thermos container. "Coffee?" she asks, unscrewing the cap.

"Where did you get coffee?"

"I had Jean-Louis fill it up for me before we left."

Pepper takes the small plastic cup. The coffee is strong and still hot. They sit quietly, sipping and gazing, sharing the smell of the wide Atlantic. The ocean heaves and rushes before them, unseen except for the long white crests of the rollers, picked out by the moon.

Mrs. Dommerich asks: "If I were to guess who the father is, would I be right?"

"Probably."

She nods. "I see."

Pepper laughs again. "Isn't it hilarious? Who'd have thought a girl like me could be so stupid? It isn't as if I didn't have my eyes open. I mean, I knew all the rumors, I knew I might just be playing with a live grenade."

"But you couldn't resist, could you?"

"The oldest story in the book."

The baby stirs beneath Pepper's heart, stretching out a long limb to test the strength of her abdomen. She puts her hand over the movement, a gesture of pregnancy that used to annoy her, when it was someone else's baby.

Mrs. Dommerich speaks softly. "Because he was irresistible, wasn't he? He made you think there was no other woman in the world, that this thing you shared was more sacred than law."

"Something like that."

Mrs. Dommerich pours out the dregs of her coffee and wipes out the cup with a handkerchief. "I'm serious, you know. It's the real reason I wanted to speak to you. To help you, if I can."

"You don't say."

Mrs. Dommerich pauses. "You know, there are all kinds of heroes in the world, Miss Schuyler, though I know you don't believe in that, either. And you're a fine girl, underneath all that cynical bluster of yours, and if this man wasn't what you hoped, I assure you there will be someone else who is."

Pepper looks out at the ocean and thinks about how wrong she is. There will never be someone else; how could there be? There will be men, of course. Pepper's no saint. But there won't be someone else. The thing about Pepper, she never makes the same mistake twice.

She folds her arms atop her belly and says, "Don't hold your breath."

Mrs. Dommerich laughs and gets out of the car. She stretches her arms up to the night sky, and the moon catches the glint in her wedding ring. "What a beautiful night, isn't it? Not too cool, after all. I can't bear the summers here, but it's just the thing to cheer me up in November."

"What's wrong with November?"

Mrs. Dommerich doesn't answer. She goes around the front of the car and settles herself on the hood, tucking up her knees under her chin. After a moment, Pepper joins her, except that Pepper's belly sticks out too far for such a gamine little pose, so she removes her sandals, stretches her feet into the sand, and leans against the familiar warm hood instead.

"Are we just going to sit here forever?" Pepper asks.

Mrs. Dommerich wraps her arms around her legs and doesn't speak. Pepper wants to tap her head like an eggshell, to see what comes out. What's her story? Why the hell is she bothering with Pepper? Women don't usually bother with Pepper, and she doesn't blame them. Look what happens when you do. Pepper fertilizes her womb with your husband.

"Well?" Pepper says at last, because she's not the kind of girl who waits for you to pull yourself together. "What are you thinking about?"

Mrs. Dommerich starts, as if she's forgotten Pepper is there at all. "Oh, I'm sorry. Ancient history, really. Have you ever been to the Paris Ritz?"

Pepper toes the sand. "Once. We went to Europe one summer, when I was in college."

"Well, I was there in the summer of 1937, when the Ritz was the center of the universe. Everybody was there." She stands up and dusts off her dress. "Anyway. Come along, my dear."

"Wait a second. What happened at the Ritz?"

"Like I said, it's ancient history. Water under the bridge."

"You were the one who brought it up."

Mrs. Dommerich folds her arms and stares at the ocean. Pepper's toe describes a square in the sand and tops it off with a triangular roof. She tries to recall the Ritz, but the grand hotels of Europe had all looked alike after a while. Wasn't that a shame? All that effort and expense, and in a week or two they all blurred together.

Still, she remembers a bit. She remembers glamour and a glorious long bar, a place where Pepper could do business. What kind of business had sweet, elegant Mrs. Dommerich done there?

Just as Pepper gives up, just as she reaches downward to thread her sandals back over her toes, Mrs. Dommerich turns away from the ocean, and you'd think the moon had stuck in her eyes, they're so bright.

"There was this party there," she says. "A going-away party at the Ritz for an American who was moving back to New York. It was the kind of night you never forget."

1.

But long before the Ritz, there was the Côte d'Azur.

My father had used the last of Mummy's money to lease his usual villa for the summer, perched on a picturesque cliff between Antibes and Cannes, and such was the lingering glamor of his face and his title that everybody came. There were rich American artists and poor English aristocrats; there was exiled Italian royalty and ambitious French bourgeoisie. To his credit, my father didn't discriminate. He welcomed them all. He gave them crumbling rooms and moderately fresh linens, cheap food and good wine, and they kept on coming in their stylish waves, smoking cigarettes and getting drunk and sleeping with one another. Someone regularly had to be saved from drowning.

Altogether it was a fascinating summer for a young lady just out of a strict convent school in the grimmest possible northwest corner of Brittany. The charcoal lash of Biscay storms had been replaced by the azure sway of the Mediterranean; the ascetic nuns had been replaced by decadent Austrian dukes. And there was my brother, Charles. I adored Charles. He was four years older and terribly dashing, and for a time, when I was young, I actually thought I would never, ever get married because nobody could be as handsome as my brother, because all other men fell short.

He invited his own guests, my brother, and a few of them were here tonight. In the way of older brothers, he didn't quite worship me the way I worshipped him. I might have been a pet lamb, straying in my woolly innocence through his fields, to be shooed gently away in case of wolves. They held their own court (literally: they gathered in the tennis courts at half past eleven in the morning for hot black coffee and muscular Turkish cigarettes) and swam in their own corner of the beach, down the treacherous cliff path: naked, of course. There were no women. Charles's retreat was run along strictly fraternal lines. If anyone fancied sex, he came back to the house and stalked one or another of my father's crimson-lipped professional beauties, so I learned to stay away from the so-called library and the terrace (favored hunting grounds) between the hours of two o'clock in the afternoon and midnight, though I observed their comings and goings the way other girls read gossip magazines.

Which is all a rather long way of explaining why I happened to be lying on the top of the garden wall, gazing quietly toward the lanterns and the female bodies in their shimmering dresses, the crisp drunk black-and-white gentlemen, on the moonless evening they brought the injured Jew to the house.

At half past ten, shortly before the Jew's arrival, I became aware of an immense heat taking shape in the air nearby. I waited for this body to carry on into the garden, or the scrubby sea lawn sloping toward the cliffs, but instead it lingered quietly, smelling of liquor and cigarettes. Without turning my head, I said, in English, "I'm sorry. Am I in your way?"

"I beg your pardon. I did not wish to disturb you." The English came without hesitation, a fluid intermingling of High German and British public schools, delivered in a thick bass voice.

I told him, without turning my head, that he hadn't. I knew how to kick away these unwanted advances from my father's accidental strays. (The nuns, remember.)

"Very good," he said, but he didn't leave.

He occupied a massive hole in the darkness behind me, and that—combined with the massive voice, the hint of dialect— suggested that this man was Herr von Kleist, an army general and Junker baron who had arrived three days ago in a magnificent black Mercedes Roadster with a single steamer trunk and no female companion. How he knew my father, I couldn't say; not that prior acquaintance with the host was any requirement for staying at the Villa Vanilla. (That was my name for the house, in reference to the sandy-pale stone with which it was built.) I had spoken to him a few times, in the evenings before dinner. He always sat alone, holding a single small glass of liquor.

I rose to a sitting position and swung my feet down from the wall. "I'll leave you to yourself, then," I said, and I prepared to jump down.

"No, please." He waved his hand. "Do not stir yourself."

"I was about to leave anyway."

"No, you mistake me. I only came to see if you were well. I saw you steal out here and lie on the garden wall." He gestured again. "I hope you are not unwell."

"I'm quite well, thank you."

"Then why are you here, alone?"

"Because I like to be alone."

He nodded. "Yes, of course. This is what I thought about you, when you were playing your cello for us the other night."

He was dressed in a precise white jacket and tie, making him seem even larger than he did by day, and unlike the other guests he had no cigarette with him, no glass of some cocktail or another to occupy his hands, though I smelled both in the air surrounding him. The moon was new, and I couldn't see his face, just the giant outline of him, the smudge of shadow against the night. But I detected a slight nervousness, a particle of anxiety lying between me and the sea. I'd seen many things at the Villa Vanilla, but I hadn't seen nervousness, and it made me curious.

"Really? Why did you think that?"

"Because—" He stopped and switched to French. "Because you are different from the others here. You are too young and new. You shouldn't be here."

"None of us should be here, really. It is a great scandal, isn't it?"

"But you particularly. Watching this." Another gesture, this time at the terrace on the other side of the wall, and the shimmering figures inside it.

"Oh, I'm used to that."

"I'm very sorry to hear that."

"Why should you be sorry? You're a part of it, aren't you? You came here willingly, unlike me, who simply lives here and can't help it. I expect you know what goes on, and why. I expect you're here for your share."

He hesitated. There was a flash of light from the house, or perhaps the driveway, and it lit the top of his head for an instant. He had an almost Scandinavian cast to him, this baron, so large and fair. (I pictured a Viking longboat invading some corner of Prussia, generations ago.) His hair was short and bristling and the palest possible shade of blond; his eyes were the color of Arctic sea ice. I thought he was about forty, as old as the world. "May I sit down?" he asked politely.

"Of course."

I thought he would take the bench, but instead he placed his hands on the wall, about five feet down from me, and hoisted his big body atop as easily as if he were mounting a horse.

"How athletic of you," I said.

"Yes. I believe firmly in the importance of physical fitness."

"Of course you do. Did you have something important to tell me?"

He stared toward Africa. "No."

Someone laughed on the terrace behind us, a high and curdling giggle cut short by the delicate smash of crystal. Neither of us moved.

Herr von Kleist sat still on the brink of the wall. I didn't know a man that large could have such perfect control over his limbs. "My friend the prince, your father, I saw him quite by chance last spring, at the embassy in Paris. He told me that I must come to his villa this summer, that I am in need of sunshine and *amitié*. I thought perhaps he was right. I am afraid, in my inexperience, I did not guess the meaning of his word *amitié*."

"Your inexperience?" I said dubiously.

"I have never been to a place like this. Like the void left behind by an absence of imagination, which they are attempting, in their wretchedness and ignorance, to fill with vice."

"Yes, you're right. I've just been thinking exactly the same thing."

"My wife died eleven years ago. *That* is loss. That is a void left behind. But I try to fill that loss with something substantial, with work and the raising of our children."

What on earth did you say to a thing like that? I ventured: "How many children do you have?"

"Four," he said.

I waited for him to elaborate—age, sex, height, education, talents—but he did not. I stared down at the gossamer in my lap and said, "Where are they now?"

"With my sister. She was the one who insisted I go, and so I did. I regretted it the instant I walked through the door. There was a woman in the hall, a dark-haired woman, and she was smoking a cigarette and using the most unkempt language."

"Probably Mrs. Henderson. She's desperately rich and miserable. An American. She sleeps with everybody, even the servants."

"It grieves me to hear this."

"I'm afraid it's true."

"No, not that it's true. I do not give a damn—pardon, Mademoiselle—about Mrs. Henderson. It grieves me that you know this about her. That your family would allow you under the same roof as such a woman as that."

"Oh, it's not as bad as that. My father doesn't allow me to mingle very much with his guests, except to entertain them with my cello after dinner. He doesn't know what to do with me at all, really, since I left Saint Cecilia's, and I'm too old for a governess."

"He ought to send you to live with a relative."

"I would run away. I'd return here."

"Why? You will pardon my curiosity. Why, when you are not like them?"

"Why not? I'm like a scientist, studying bugs. I find them fascinating, even if I don't mean to turn into a mosquito myself."

Herr von Kleist had placed his hands on his knees, and as large as his knees were, his hands dwarfed them. "Mosquitoes. Very good," he said gravely. "Yes, this is exactly what I imagined about you, when I saw you lying on the garden wall just now, observing the mosquitoes."

We had switched back into English at some point, I couldn't remember when.

I said, "Really, you shouldn't be here. You should go home to your children."

He made another one of his sighs, weary of everything. "*You* are the one who should leave. There is not much hope for us, but you can still be saved. This is not the place for you."

I jumped down from the wall and dusted the grit from my hands. "I'd say there's plenty of hope for you. You seem like a decent man. Anyway, this is the only place I know, other than the convent."

"Then go back to your convent."

I was about to laugh, and I realized he was serious. At least his voice was serious, and his eyes, which were sad and invisible in the darkness. "But I don't want to go back."

"No, of course you do not. You want to live. You are how old?"

"Nineteen."

He made a defeated noise and slid down from the wall. "You think I am ancient."

"No, not at all," I lied.

"I'm thirty-eight. But that does not matter." He picked my hand from my side and kissed it. "It is you who matter."

He was drunk, of course. I realized it now. He was one of those lucky fellows who held it perfectly, without slurring a single word, but he was drunk nonetheless. There was the slightest waver in his titanic frame as he stood before me, engulfing my fingers between his two leathery palms, and there was that waft of liquor I'd noticed from the beginning. Who could blame him? It took such an unlikely amount of moral resolve to remain sober at the Villa Vanilla.

When I didn't speak, he moved his heavy head in a single nod. "Yes. It is better this way. Nothing valuable is ever gained in haste."

"Quite true," someone said, but it wasn't me. It was my brother, Charles, coming up behind me like a cat in the night, and before either of us had time to reflect on the silent surprise of his appearance, he had pried my hand from the grasp of Herr von Kleist and begged the general's forgiveness.

An urgent matter had arisen, and he needed to borrow his sister for a moment.

2.

"Borrow me?" I jogged to keep up as my brother's long legs tore the scrubby grass between the garden and the cliffs. "Are you short for poker?"

"Of course not." He yanked the cigarette stub from his mouth and tossed it on the ground, into a patch of gravel. "What the hell were you doing with that Nazi?"

"Nazi? He's a Nazi?"

"They're all Nazis now, aren't they? Pay attention, it's the cliff."

I wasn't dressed for climbing. I gathered up my skirts in one hand. We started down the path, over the lip of the cliff, and the sea crashed in my ears. I followed the flash of Charles's shoes just ahead. "What's the hurry?" I asked.

"Just be quiet."

The last of the light from the house had dissolved, and I began to stumble in the absolute blackness of the night. I had only the faint ghostliness of Charles's white shirt—he had somehow shed his dinner jacket—to guide me, as it jerked and jumped about and nearly disappeared in the space before me. The toe of my slipper found a rock, and I staggered to the ground.

"What's the matter with you?" Charles said.

"I can't see."

He swore and fumbled in his pockets, and a second later a match struck against the edge of a box and hissed to life. "My God," I said, staring at Charles's face in the tiny yellow glow. "Is that blood?"

He touched his cheek. "Probably. Look around. Get your bearings."

I looked down the slope of the cliff, the familiar path dissolving into the oily night. "Yes. All right."

The match sizzled out against his fingers, and he dropped it into the rocks and took my hand. "Let's go. Try to keep quiet, will you?"

I knew exactly where I was now. I could picture each stone, each twist in the jagged path. Inside the grip of Charles's hand, my fingers tingled. Something was up, something extraordinary—so extraordinary, my brother was actually drawing me under the snug shelter of his confidence. Like when we were children, before Mummy died, before we returned to France and went our separate ways: me to the convent, my brother to the École Normale in Paris. That was when the curtain had come down. I was no longer his co-conspirator.

But I remembered how it was. My blood remembered: racing down my limbs, racing up to my brain like a cleansing bath. *Come down to the beach, I've found something,* Charles would say, and we would run hand in hand to the gritty boulder-strewn cove near the lighthouse, where he might show me an old blue glass bottle that had washed up onshore and surely contained a coded message (it never did), or a mysterious dead fish that must—equally surely—represent an undiscovered species (also never); and once, best of all, there was a bleached white skeleton, half articulated, its grinning skull exactly the size of Charles's spread hand. I had thought, *We're in trouble now, someone will find out, someone will sneak into the house and kill us, too, to eliminate the witnesses*; at the same time, I had cast about for the glimpse of wood that must be lying half hidden in the nearby sand, the treasure chest that this skeleton had guarded with his life.

Now, as I stumbled faithfully down the cliff path in Charles's wake, and my eyes so adjusted to the darkness that I began to pick out the white tips of the waves crashing on the beach, the rocks returning the starlight, I wondered what bleached white skeleton he had found for me tonight.

And then the path fell into the sand, and Charles was tugging me through the dunes with such strength that my slippers were sucked away from my feet. We made for the point on the eastern end of the beach, where the sea curled around a finger of cliff and formed a slight cove on the other side. There was just enough shelter from the current for a small boathouse and a launch, which the guests sometimes used to ferry back and forth to the yachts in Cannes or Antibes. I saw the roof now, a gray smear in the starlight. Charles plunged straight toward it, running now. The sand flew from his feet. Just before he ducked through the doorway, he stopped and turned to me.

"You *did* say you nursed in a hospital, right? At the convent? I'm not imagining things?"

"What? Yes, every day, after—"

"Good." He took my hand and pulled me inside.

There were four of them there, Charles's friends, two of them still in their dinner jackets and waistcoats. An oil lantern sat on the warped old planks of the deck, next to the nervously bobbing launch, spreading just enough light to illuminate the fifth man in the boathouse.

He sat slumped against the wall, and his bare chest was covered in blood. He lifted his head as I came in—the chin had been tucked into the hollow of his clavicle—and he said, in deep German-accented English, much like the voice of Herr von Kleist, only more slurred and amused: "*This* is your great plan, Créouville?"

3.

But his chest wasn't injured. As I cried out and fell to my knees at his side, I saw that he was holding a thick white wad to his thigh, around which a makeshift tourniquet had already been applied, and that the white wad—a shirt, I determined—was rapidly filling with blood, like the discarded red shirts next to his knee.

"Actually, it seems to be getting better," he said.

I adjusted the tourniquet—it was too loose—and lifted away

the shirt. A round wound welled instantly with blood. I said, incredulous: "But it's a—"

"Gunshot," he said.

I pressed the shirt back into the wound and called for whisky.

"I like the way you think," said the wounded man.

"It's not to drink. It's to clean the wound. How long ago did this happen?"

"About twenty minutes. Right, boys?"

There was a general murmur of agreement, and a bottle appeared next to my hand. Gin, not whisky. I lifted away the shirt. The flow of blood had already slowed. "This will sting," I said, and I tilted the bottle to allow a stream of gin on the torn flesh.

I was expecting a howl, but the man only grunted and gripped the side of the leg. "He needs a doctor, as quickly as possible," I said to the men. "Has someone telephoned Dr. Duchamps?"

There was no reply. I put my fingers under the injured man's chin and peered into his eyes. His pupils were dilated, but not severely; he met my gaze and followed me as I turned my face from one side to the other. I glanced back at Charles. "Well? Doctor? Is he on his way?"

Charles crouched next to me. "No."

"Why not?"

"Too much fuss. There's someone meeting you on the ship."

"Ship? What ship?"

The injured man said, "My ship."

"You're going with him," said Charles. "You can still drive the launch, can't you?"

"*What?*"

"You're the only one who can do it. The rest of us have to stay here."

"What? Why?"

"Cover," said the injured man, through his gritted teeth.

I looked back down at the wound, which was now only seeping. Probably the bullet had only nicked the femoral artery, otherwise he would have been dead by now. He was a large man—not as large as Herr von Kleist, but larger than my brother—and he had plenty of blood to spare. Still, it was a close thing. My brain was sharp, but my fingers were trembling as I pressed the shirt back down. Another fraction of an inch. My God. "I don't have the slightest idea what you mean," I said, "and why not one of you perfectly able-bodied men can help me get this man to safety, but we don't have a minute to waste arguing. Give him a fresh shirt. If he can hold it to his leg himself, I can take him to his damned yacht. It *is* a yacht, isn't it?"

"Yes, Mademoiselle," the man said humbly.

"Of course it is. And if the police catch up with us, what am I to say?"

"That you know nothing about it, of course."

I took the fresh shirt from Charles's hand and replaced the old; I took the man's large limp hand and pressed it to the makeshift bandage. "I'll take the gin. Charles, you put him in the launch."

"You see?" said Charles. "I told you she was a sport."

4.

On the launch, I took pity on the man and gave him the bottle of gin, while I steered us around the tip of the Cap d'Antibes and west toward Cannes, where his yacht was apparently moored.

He took a grateful swig and tilted his head to the stars. The lantern sat at the bottom of the boat, so as not to be visible from shore.

"You are very beautiful," he said.

"Stop. You're *not* flirting with me, please. You came three millimeters away from death just now." The draft was cool and salty; it stung my cheeks, or maybe I was only blushing.

"No, I am not flirting. But you *are* beautiful. A statement of fact."

I peered into the dark sea, seeking out the distant harbor lights, smaller than stars on the horizon. The water was calm tonight, only a hint of chop. As if God himself were watching over this man.

"Am I allowed to ask your name?" I said.

He hesitated. "Stefan."

"Stefan. Is that your real name?"

"If you call me Stefan, Mademoiselle, I will answer you."

"I see. And what sort of trouble gets a nice man shot in the middle of a night like this, so he can't see a doctor onshore? Argument at the casino? Is the other man perhaps dead?"

"No, it was not an argument in the casino."

He tilted the bottle back to his lips. I thought, I must keep him talking. He has to keep talking, to stay conscious. "And the other man?"

"Hmm. Do you really wish to know this, Mademoiselle?"

"Oh, priceless. I'm harboring a criminal fugitive."

"Do not worry about that. You will be handsomely rewarded."

"I don't want to be *rewarded*. I want you to live."

He didn't reply, and I glanced back to make sure he hadn't fainted. I wouldn't have blamed him, lighter as he was of a pint or two of good red blood. But his eyes were open, each one containing a slim gold reflection of the lantern, and they were trained on me with an expression of profound . . . something.

I was about to ask him another question, but he spoke first.

"Where did you learn to treat a wound from a gun, Mademoiselle de Créouville?"

"I've never even seen a wound from a gun. But the sisters ran a charity hospital, and the men from the village got in regular brawls. Sometimes with knives."

"The sisters? You are a nun?"

"No. I was at a convent school. I've only just escaped. Anyway, they made us all work in the charity hospital, because of Christ tending the feet of the poor. Hold on!" We hit a series of brisk chops, the wake of some unseen vessel plowing through the night sea nearby. Stefan grunted, and when the water calmed and I could relax my attention to the wheel, I glanced back again to see that his face was quite pale.

He spoke, however, without inflection. "You have a knack for it, I think. You did not scream at the blood, as most girls would. As I think most men might."

"I have a brother. I've seen blood before."

"Ah, the dashing mademoiselle. You tend wounds. You drive a boat fearlessly through the dark. What sort of sister is this for my friend Créouville? He said nothing about you before."

"He has successfully ignored me for the past half decade, since we were sent back to France after our mother died."

"I am sorry to hear about this."

I tightened my hands on the wheel and stared ahead. The pinpricks were growing larger now, more recognizably human. I hardly ever ventured into Cannes, and certainly not by myself, but I'd passed the harbor enough to know its geography. "Where is your ship moored?" I asked.

He muttered something, and I looked back over my shoulder. His eyes were half closed, his back slumped.

"Stefan!" I said sharply.

He made a rolling motion and braced his hand on the side of the launch. His head snapped up. "So sorry. You were saying?"

I couldn't leave the wheel; I couldn't check his pulse, his skin, the state of his wound. A sliver of panic penetrated my chest: the unreality of this moment, of the warm salt wind on my face, of the starlight and the man bleeding in the stern of my father's old wooden launch. Half an hour ago, I had been lying on a garden wall. "Stefan, you've got to concentrate," I said, but I really meant myself. Annabelle, you've got to concentrate. "Stefan. Listen to me. You've got to stay awake."

His gaze came to a stop on mine. "Yes. Right you are."

"How are you feeling?"

"I am bloody miserable, Mademoiselle. My leg hurts like the devil and my head is a little sick. But at least I am bloody miserable with *you*."

I faced the water again and turned up the throttle. "Very good. You're flirting again, that's a good sign. Now, tell me. Where is your ship moored? This side of the harbor, or the other?"

"Not the harbor. The Île Sainte-Marguerite. The Plateau du Milieu, on the south side, between the islands."

I looked to the left, where a few lights clustered atop the thin line between black water and blacker sky. There wasn't much on Sainte-Marguerite, only forest and the old Fort Royal. But a ship moored in the protected channel between Sainte-Marguerite and the Île Saint-Honorat—and many did moor there; it was a popular spot in the summer—would not be visible from the mainland.

"Hold on," I said, and I began a sweeping turn to the left, to round the eastern point of the island. The launch angled obediently, and Stefan caught himself on the edge. The lantern slid across the deck. He stuck out his foot to stop its progress just as the boat hit a chop and heeled. Stefan swore.

"All right?" I said.

"Yes, damn it."

I could tell from the bite in his words—or rather the lack of bite, the dissonance of the words themselves from the tone in which he said them—that he was slipping again, that he was fighting the black curtain. We had to reach this ship of his, the faster the better, and yet the faster we went the harder we hit the current. And I could not see properly. I was guided only by the pinprick lights and my own instinct for this stretch of coast.

"Just hurry," said Stefan, blurry now, and I curled around the point and straightened out, so that the Plateau de Milieu lay before me, studded with perhaps a dozen boats tugging softly at their moorings. I glanced back at Stefan to see how he had weathered the turn.

"The western end," he told me, gripping the side of the boat hard with his left hand while his right held the wadded-up white shirt against his wound. Someone had sacrificed his dinner jacket over Stefan's shoulders, to protect that bare and bloody chest from the salt draft and the possibility of shock, and I thought I saw a few dark specks on the sleek white wool. But that was always the problem about blood. It traveled easily, like a germ, infecting its surroundings with messy promiscuity. I turned to face the sleeping vessels ahead, an impossible obstacle course of boats and mooring lines, and I thought, We have got to get that tourniquet off soon, or they will have to remove the leg.

But at least I could see a little better now, in the glow of the boat lights, and I pushed the throttle higher. The old engine opened its throat and roared. A curse floated out across the water behind us, as I zigzagged delicately around the mooring lines.

"I see you are an expert," said Stefan. "This is reassuring."

"Which one is yours?"

"You can't see it yet. Just a moment." We rounded another boat, a pretty sloop of perhaps fifty feet, and the rest of the passage opened out before us, nearly empty. Stefan said, with effort: "To the right, the last one."

"What, the great big one?" I pointed.

"Yes, Mademoiselle. The great big one."

I opened the throttle as far as it could go. We skipped across the water like a smooth, round stone, like when Charles and I were children and left to ourselves, and we would take the boat as fast as it could go and scream with joy in the briny wind, because when you were a child you didn't know that boats sometimes crashed and people sometimes drowned. That vital young men were shot and sometimes bled to death.

Stefan's yacht rose up rapidly before us, lit by a series of lights along the bow and the glow of a few portholes. It was long and elegant, a sweet beauty of a ship. The sides were painted black as far as the final row of portholes, where the white took over, like a wide neat collar around the rim, like a nun's wimple. I saw the name *Isolde* painted on the bow. "Ahoy!" I called out, when we were fifty feet away. "*Isolde* ahoy!"

"They are likely asleep," said Stefan.

I pulled back the throttle and brought the boat around. We bobbed on the water, sawing in our own wake, while I rummaged in the compartment under the wheel and brought out a small revolver.

"God in heaven," said Stefan.

"I hope it's loaded," I said, and I pointed the barrel out to sea and fired.

The sound echoed off the water and the metal side of the boat. A light flashed on in one of the portholes, and a voice called out something outraged in German.

I cupped my hands around my mouth. "*Isolde* ahoy!"

"*Ja, ja!*"

"I have your owner! I have—oh, damn."

The boat pitched. I grabbed the wheel. Behind me, Stefan was moving, and I hissed at him to sit down, he was going to kill himself.

But he ignored me and waved the bloodstained white shirt above his head. He brought the other hand to his mouth and yelled out a few choice German words, words I didn't understand but comprehended perfectly, and then he crashed back down in his seat as if the final drops of life had been wrung out of him.

"Stefan!" I exclaimed. The boat was driving against the side of the ship; I steered frantically and let out the throttle a notch.

A figure appeared at the railing above, and an instant later a rope ladder unfurled down the curving side of the ship. I glanced at the slumping Stefan, whose eyes were closed, whose knee rested in a puddle of dark blood, and then back at the impossible swinging ladder, and I yelled frantically upward that someone had better get down here on the fucking double, because Stefan was about to die.

1.

Mrs. Dommerich leans back on her palms and stares at the moon. "Isn't it funny? The same old moon that stood above the sky when I was your age. It hasn't changed a bit."

"I don't do moons," says Pepper. "Who was this American of yours? The one having the party?"

"He was a friend. He was living in Paris at the time. A very good friend."

"What kind of friend?"

Mrs. Dommerich laughs. "Not *that* kind, I assure you. He might have been, if I hadn't already fallen in love with a friend of his." Without warning, she slides off the hood of the car to stand in the sand, staring out into the ocean. "We should be going."

"Going where?"

She doesn't answer. Unlike Pepper, she didn't follow her own advice and wear a cardigan, and her forearms are bare to the

November night. She crosses them against her chest, just beneath her breasts. The material falls gently from her body, and Pepper decides she isn't quite like Audrey Hepburn after all. She's slender, but she isn't skinny. There is a soft roundness to her, an inviting fullness about her breasts and hips and bottom, which she carries so gracefully on her light frame that you almost don't notice, unless you're looking for it. Unless you're a man.

She turns to Pepper. "I have an idea. Why don't you come back with me to Cocoa Beach? We have a little guest cottage in the back. You can stay there until you're ready to make some decisions. A little more private than the Breakers, don't you think?"

"Are you serious?"

"Of course. I'd love the company. To tell the truth, it's a bit lonely, now that my husband's gone and the children are grown. And you need me."

Pepper opens her mouth to say that she doesn't need anyone.

"Yes, you do," says Mrs. Dommerich, before the words come out.

"You're just nuts, do you know that?"

"No, you're nuts. You think—what? That I'm involved in some vast conspiracy to keep all this out of the public notice?" She waves her hand at Pepper's belly. "That I'm in cahoots with the great man himself?"

"I'd be crazy not to consider it."

Mrs. Dommerich narrows her eyes to consider Pepper's point of view. "I suppose that's fair enough," she says. "But you're already here. You've trusted me this far."

"I haven't trusted you a bit. I'm just trying to figure out your game."

"Figure it out at my place, then." Mrs. Dommerich walks around the left fender and opens the door. "It's a hell of a lot more comfortable, for one thing. What have you got to lose?"

"My luggage. For one thing."

Mrs. Dommerich swings into her seat and starts the engine. She calls out, over the throaty roar: "We'll ring up the Breakers in the morning and have it sent over."

Pepper stands there in the beam of the headlights, arms still crossed, trying to find Mrs. Dommerich's heart-shaped face in the middle of all that glare. Mrs. Dommerich gives the horn an impatient little toot.

"All right," Pepper says at last, walking back to her door and climbing inside. The leather seat takes her in like an old friend. "After all, I don't suppose I have any choice."

Mrs. Dommerich turns the car around and starts back down the dirt track to the highway, chased by the moon.

"Honey, you always have a choice," she says. "The trick is making the right one."

2.

"I suppose you can call me Pepper now," she says, as they bounce elegantly back down through the parting in the reeds, "since I'm going to be your houseguest, and not a very good one."

Mrs. Dommerich changes gears and accelerates down the dirt track.

"You'll be a wonderful houseguest, Pepper. Better than you think. And you can call me Annabelle."

3.

They are back on the highway, roaring north under the moon. The landscape passes by, dark and anonymous. Pepper yawns in the passenger seat. "Tell me about this lover of yours."

"I thought you weren't interested in romance."

"I'm just being polite. And I don't like silence."

Annabelle shakes her head. "Tell me something. What *do* you believe in, Miss Pepper Schuyler?"

"Me? I believe in independence. I believe in calling the shots and keeping your eyes wide open. Because in the end, you know, he just wants to get into bed with you. That's what they're after. They'll kiss you in the sunset, they'll carry you upstairs, they'll gaze into your eyes like you might disappear if they stop. They might even tell you they're in love. But the point is to seduce you."

Annabelle taps her thumbs on the steering wheel and considers this. "Do you know, though, I think I was the one who seduced him, in the end."

"Well, that's how they do it, the best of them. They make you think it was your idea."

The draft whistles around them. Pepper checks her watch. It's half past eleven o'clock, and she's getting sleepy, except that the baby is pressing on a nerve that tracks all the way down her foot and turns her toes numb. She shifts her weight from one leg to the other.

"Do you know what I think, Miss Schuyler?"

"Call me Pepper, I said."

"Is that your real name?"

"Pepper will do. But really. Tell me what you think about me, Annabelle. I'm dying to know."

"I think you really *are* a romantic. You're longing for true love with all your tough little heart. It's just that you're too beautiful, and it's made you cynical."

"That doesn't make any sense."

"Yes, it does. Any unearned gift makes you cynical, unless you're a psychopath."

"Beauty hasn't made *you* cynical."

"But I'm not beautiful. I suppose I'm attractive, and I have a few nice features. My eyes and skin. My figure, if you like your women petite. But I was never beautiful, certainly not compared to someone like you."

"Don't sell yourself short. Look at those cheekbones of yours."

"Not like *yours*. I could hang my hat on yours. No, there were just two men in my life who thought I was beautiful, and I think they thought I was beautiful because they loved me, because they were attracted to something inside me, and not the other way around."

Pepper laughs. "Trust me, it was the other way around."

"How can you say that? You don't know either man."

"I know men."

"You think you know men, but you only know cads, because the cads are the only ones brash enough to take you on. You don't know the first thing about a man capable of a great love."

"Because there's no such thing. It's just the sex instinct, the need for reproduction, and the more attractive the man, the more women he wants to reproduce with."

"All right, Miss Schuyler. That's quite enough. You just shut that steely old mouth of yours and hear me out."

"So you're feisty, after all!"

"When I have to be. So be quiet and listen up, and you might actually learn something, my so-wise friend with the prize-winning cheekbones and the knocked-up belly." Annabelle taps her long fingers against the steering wheel. "In fact, I'll make you a bet."

A bet. Pepper's heart does the old flutter.

"I don't know," she says, poker-faced. "What're the stakes?"

"Stakes?"

Pepper shrugs. "It's got to be interesting, that's what my mother says. The only true crime is boredom."

Annabelle laughs. "My, my. The apple doesn't fall far. Well, then. Let's see. You're an unwed mother on the run, in need of a little extra insurance. I'll bet my black pearl necklace to your gold Cartier watch that I'll have you believing in true love by the time that baby of yours sees daylight."

"I don't know." Pepper brushes her lap. "I haven't seen this pearl necklace of yours."

"My husband gave me that necklace as a Christmas present in 1937, from the Cartier shop on rue de la Paix, because he could not find another jeweler in Paris who was skilled enough to satisfy him."

Pepper makes a few rapid calculations, carries the eight, adds a zero or two. The old heart flutters again.

"True love, you said?"

"True blue, faithful and everlasting."

"In that case," Pepper says, "you're on."

4.

Annabelle asks if there is any more coffee. Pepper reaches for the thermos and gives it a jiggle.

"Not much." She pours what's left into the plastic cup and hands it to Annabelle.

"Thank you."

"You're not getting sleepy, are you? I can always take a turn at the wheel."

"Not on your life." Annabelle hands back the empty cup. "Not that you're not perfectly capable, I'm sure. But I'd like to drive her myself."

Pepper tucks the thermos back into the glove compartment and latches the polished wooden door. "Because you have history, don't you?"

"Yes, we do." Annabelle pats the dashboard.

"I'd ask how it happened, but I'd rather stay awake."

"I can't really tell you, anyway. Too many lives involved."

"My God, what a relief. I bore so easily, you understand."

Annabelle laughs. "Do you, now? Have you ever been in love, Miss Schuyler?"

"It's Pepper, remember?"

"Pepper, then. Tell me the truth. I'm taking you home with me, so you've got to be honest." She pauses, and when Pepper doesn't speak, she adds: "Besides, it's one o'clock in the morning. No secrets after midnight."

"I don't know." Pepper looks out the side, at the shadows blurring past. "Maybe."

"Were you in love with the father of your baby, or someone else?"

"I was very deeply in lust with him, if that's what you mean."

"That's not at all what I mean, but it can be very hard to tell the difference. Do you still want him?"

Pepper's hand finds the neck of her cardigan. She thinks of

the last time she saw the father of her baby, the day before she left Washington. "No. Not anymore. I'm cured."

"If you say so. We're very good at pretending, we women. And the heart is such a complicated little organ."

A light flashes in the rearview mirror, and Pepper jumps in her seat. Annabelle glances into the mirror and slows the car a fraction. The light grows larger and brighter, resolving into two headlamps, and the drone of an engine undercuts the noise of their own car, their own draft. Annabelle glances again into the mirror and says something under her breath.

Pepper's fingernails dig into the leather seat next to her leg. "What is it?" she says.

There is a flash of bright blue, followed instantly by red, and the shriek of a siren sails above their heads. Annabelle swears again—loudly enough that Pepper recognizes the curse as French—and slows the car.

"What are you doing?"

"What else can I do?"

The car drifts to the shoulder, and the siren reaches a new pitch behind them. The red and blue lights fill the air, throwing a lurid pattern on Annabelle's cheeks and neck. She brakes gently, until the car comes to a stop. The siren screams in Pepper's ears. She clenches her hands into balls of resistance against the authority of the roaring engine drawing up behind them, the unstoppable force that has found them here, of all places, in the middle of the night, on a deserted Florida highway next to the restless Atlantic. Two well-dressed women inside a car of rigid German steel.

The steel vibrates faintly. The lights and the roar increase to gigantic proportion, drenching the entire world, and then everything hurtles on to their left. The siren begins its Doppler descent, and the world goes black again, except for the flashing lights that narrow and narrow and finally disappear around a curve in the road, and the moon that replaces them.

"Holy God," says Pepper, and she opens the car door and vomits into the sand.

ANNABELLE

Isolde • 1935

1.

The doctor arrived over the side of the boat just after I laid Stefan out on the deck and loosened the tourniquet.

"Why did you loosen this?" he demanded, dropping his bag on the deck and stripping his jacket.

"Because it had been on for well over half an hour. I wanted to save the leg."

"There is no use saving the leg if the patient bleeds to death."

At which point Stefan opened one eye and told the esteemed doctor he wanted to keep his fucking leg, and if the esteemed doctor couldn't speak with respect to the woman who had saved Stefan's life, the esteemed doctor could walk the fucking plank with a bucket of dead fish hanging around his neck to attract the sharks.

The doctor said nothing, and I assisted him right there on the deck as he dug into the hole and extracted the bullet, as he cleaned and stitched up the wound and Stefan drifted in and out of consciousness, always waking up with a faint start and a mumbled apology, as if he had somehow betrayed us by not remaining alert while the forceps dug into his raw flesh and the antiseptic was poured over afterward.

"You are a lucky man, Silverman," said the doctor, dropping the small metal bullet into a towel, and I thought, Silverman, Stefan Silverman, that's his name, and wiped away the gathering perspiration on his broad forehead.

The doctor asked for the sutures, and I rooted through the bag and laid everything out on the towel next to Stefan's arm: sutures, needle, antiseptic. "What's your blood type, nurse?" the doctor asked as he worked, as I silently handed him each suture, and I said I was O negative, and he replied: "Good, what I hoped you would say. Can you spare a pint, do you think?" and I said I could, of course, of course. I was glowing a little, in my heart, because he had called me *nurse*, and no one had ever called me anything useful before. And because I had brought Stefan Silverman safely to his ship through the dark and the salt wind, and the doctor was efficiently fixing him, putting his leg back together again, and the ball of terror was beginning to drop away from my belly at last.

The doctor stood at last and told me that he was finished, and I should dress the wound. "Not too tight; you nurses are always dressing a wound too tight. I will have to come back with the transfusion equipment. It may take an hour or two. Can you stay awake with him?"

Yes, I could.

"Then we will put him in his bed." He signaled for one of the crew, who were hovering anxiously nearby, and somehow made himself clear with gestures and a few scant words of German. Two of the men hoisted Stefan up—he was out cold by now, his dark head turned to one side—and the doctor yelled at them to be careful. He turned to me. "Don't leave his side for a second. You know what to look for, I think? Signs of shock?"

"Yes. I will watch him like a child, I promise."

2.

He *did* look like a child, lying there on his clean white bed, when I had tucked the sheets around his bare chest, and his face was so pale and peaceful I checked his pulse and his breathing every minute or so to make certain he hadn't died. I turned off the electric light overhead and kept only the small lamp burning next to his bed, just enough to see him by. His skin was smooth, only a few faint lines about the eyes, and his hair was quite dark, curling wetly around his ears and forehead. He was about my brother's age, I thought, twenty-three or -four. His lashes were long and dark, lying against his cheek, and I wondered what color his eyes were. Stefan Silverman's eyes. When I touched his shoulder, his lids fluttered.

"Shh," I said. "Go to sleep."

He opened those eyes just long enough for me to decide that they were probably brown, but a very light brown, like a salt caramel. He tried to focus and I thought he failed, because his lids dropped again and his head turned an inch or two to the side, away from me.

But then he said, almost without moving his lips: "Stay, Mademoiselle."

I smoothed the sheets against his chest, an excuse to touch

him. He smelled of gin and antiseptic. I thought, It's like waiting forever for the film to start, and then it does.

"As long as you need me," I told him.

3.

At half past eight o'clock in the morning, Stefan's mistress arrived.

Or so I assumed. I could hear a woman on the other side of the cabin door, shrill and furious like a mistress. She was remonstrating with someone in French (of course), and her opponent was speaking back to her in German. Stefan opened his eyes and stared, frowning, at the ceiling.

"I think you have a visitor," I said.

He sighed. "Can you give us a minute or two, Mademoiselle?"

"You shouldn't see anyone. You have lost so much blood. You need to rest."

"Yes, but I'm feeling better now."

I wanted to remind him that he was feeling better only because he had a pint of Annabelle de Créouville coursing through his veins. I rose to my feet—a little carefully, because a pint of blood meant a great deal more to me than it did to him—and went to the door.

The woman stopped shrilling when she saw me. She was dressed in a long and shimmering evening gown, and her hair was a little disordered. There was a diamond clip holding back a handful of once-sleek curls at her temple, and a circle of matching diamonds around her neck. Her lipstick was long gone. Her eyes flicked up and down, taking me in, exposing the line of smudged kohl on her upper lid. "And who are you?" she asked, in haughty French, though I could tell from her accent that she was English.

"His nurse."

"I must see him."

I stood back from the door. "Five minutes," I said, in my sternest ward sister voice, "and if you upset him even the smallest amount, if I hear so much as a single *word* through this door, I will open your veins and bathe in your blood."

I must have looked as if I meant it, for she ducked through the door like a frightened rabbit, and when six minutes had passed without a single sound, I knocked briefly on the door and opened it.

Stefan lay quite still on the bed. His eyes were closed, and the woman's hand rested in his palm. She was curled in the armchair—*my* armchair, I thought fiercely—and she didn't look up when I entered. "He is so pale," she said, and her voice was rough. "I have never seen him like this. He is always so vital."

"As I said, he has lost a great deal of blood."

"May I sit with him a little longer?"

She said it humbly, the haughtiness dissolved, and when she tilted her head in my direction and accepted my gaze, I saw a track of gray kohl running down from the corner of her eye to the curve of her cheekbone. She had dark blond hair the color of honey, and it gleamed dully in the lamplight. Her gown was cut into a V so low, I could count the ribs below her breasts. I looked at Stefan's hand holding hers, and I said, "Yes, a little longer," and went back out the door and down the narrow corridor to the stern of the ship, which was pointed toward the exposed turrets of the Fort Royal on the Île Sainte-Marguerite, where the Man in the Iron Mask had spent a decade of his life in a special isolated cell, though no one ever knew who he was or why he was there. Whether he had a family who mourned him.

4.

I had sent a note for Charles with the departing doctor, in the small hours of the morning, and I expected my brother any moment to arrive on the yacht, to assure himself of Stefan's survival and to bring me home.

But lunchtime came and went, the disheveled blonde departed, and though someone brought me a tray of food, and a bowl of hot broth for Stefan, Charles never appeared.

Stefan slept. At six o'clock, a boat hailed the deck and the doctor's head popped over the side, followed by his bag. The day had been warm, and the air was still hot and laden with moisture. "How is our patient this evening?" he asked.

"Much better." I turned and led him down the hallway to Stefan's commodious stateroom. "He's slept most of the day and had a little broth." I didn't mention the woman.

"Excellent, excellent. Sleep is the best thing for him. Pulse? Temperature?"

"All normal. The pulse is slow, but not alarmingly so."

"To be expected. He is an active man. Well, well," he said, ducking through the door, "how is our intrepid hero, eh?"

Stefan was awake, propped up on his pillows. He shot the doctor the kind of look that parents send each other when children are present, and listening too closely. The doctor glanced at me, cleared his throat, and set his bag on the end of the bed.

"Now, then," he said, "let us take a look at this little scratch of yours."

On the way back to the boat, the doctor gave me a list of instructions: sleep, food, signs of trouble. "He is quite strong, however, and I should not be surprised if he is up and about in a matter of days. I shall send over a pair of crutches. You will see that he does not overexert himself, please."

"I don't understand. I had no expectation of staying longer than a day."

The doctor stopped in his tracks and turned to me. "What's this?"

"I gave you a message, to give to my brother. Wasn't there a reply? Isn't he coming for me?"

He pushed his spectacles up his nose and blinked slowly. The sun was beginning to touch the cliffs to the west, and the orange light surrounded his hair. The deck around us was neat and shining, bleached to the color of bone, smelling of tar and sunshine. "Coming for you? Of course not. You are to care for the patient. Who else is to do it?"

"But I'll be missed," I said helplessly. "My father— You must know who I am. I can't just disappear."

The doctor turned and resumed his journey across the deck to the ladder, where his tender lay bobbing in the *Isolde*'s lee. "My dear girl, this is nothing that young Créouville cannot explain. He is a clever fellow. No doubt he has already put about a suitable story."

"But I don't understand. What's going on? What sort of trouble is this?"

"I don't know what you mean," he said virtuously.

"Yes, you do. What sort of trouble gets a man shot in the

night like that, everything a big secret, and what . . . what does my *brother* have to do with any of it? And why the devil are you smiling that way, like a cat?"

"Because I am astonished, Mademoiselle, and not a little filled with admiration, that you have undertaken this little adventure with no knowledge whatever of its meaning."

We had reached the ladder. I grabbed him by the arm and turned him around. "Then perhaps you might begin by explaining it to me."

He shook his head and patted my cheek. His eyes were kind, and the smile had disappeared. "I cannot, of course. But when the patient is a little more recovered, it's my professional opinion that you have every right to ask him yourself."

5.

The next day, Stefan roared for his crutches, an excellent sign, but I wouldn't let him have them. I made him eat two eggs for breakfast and a little more beef broth, and he grumbled and ate. I told him that if he were very good and rested quietly, I would let him try out the crutches tomorrow. He glared with his salt caramel eyes and directed me to go to the *Isolde*'s library and bring him some books. He wrote down their titles on a piece of paper.

The weather was hot again today, the sun like a blister in the fierce blue sky, and every porthole was open to the cooling breeze off the water. I passed along the silent corridor to the grand staircase, a sleek modern fusion of chrome and white marble, filled with seething Mediterranean light, and the library was exactly where Stefan said it should be: the other side of the main salon.

It was locked, but Stefan had given me the key. I opened the door expecting the usual half-stocked library of the yachting class: the shelves occupied by a few token volumes and a great many valuable *objets* of a maritime theme, the furniture arranged for style instead of a comfortable hours-long submersion between a pair of cloth covers.

But the *Isolde's* library wasn't like the rest of the ship. There was nothing sleek about it, nothing constructed out of shiny material. The walnut shelves wrapped around the walls, stuffed with books, newer ones and older ones, held in place by slim wooden rails in case of stormy seas. A sofa and a pair of armchairs dozed near the portholes, and a small walnut desk sat on the other side, next to a cabinet that briefly interrupted the flow of shelving. I thought, Now, here is a room I might like to live in.

I looked down at the paper in my hand. Goethe, *Die Leiden des jungen Werthers*; Locke, *Some Thoughts Concerning Education*; Dumas *père*, *Le vicomte de Bragelonne, ou Dix ans plus tard*.

When I returned to Stefan's cabin a half hour later, he was sitting up against the pillows and staring at the porthole opposite, which was open to the breeze. The rooftops of the fort shifted in and out of the frame, nearly white in the sunshine. It was too hot for blankets, and he lay in his pajamas on the bed I had made expertly underneath him that morning, tight as a drum. "Here are your books," I said.

"Thank you."

"How are you feeling?"

"Like a bear in a cage."

"You are certainly *acting* like a bear."

He looked up from the books. "I'm sorry."

"I've had worse patients. It's good that you're a bear. Better a bear than a sick little worm."

"Poor Mademoiselle de Créouville. I understand your brother has ordered you to stay with me and nurse me back to health."

"Not in so many words." I paused. "Not in any words at all, really. He sent over a few clothes and a toothbrush yesterday, with the doctor, but there was no note of any kind. I still haven't the faintest idea who you are, or what I'm doing here."

He frowned. "Do you need one?"

I folded my arms and sank into the armchair next to the bed. His pajamas were fine silky cotton and striped in blue, and one lapel was still folded endearingly on the inside, as if belonging to a little boy who had dressed himself too hastily. The blueness brought out the bright caramel of his eyes and, by some elusive trick, made his chest seem even sturdier than before. His color had returned, pink and new; his hair was brushed; his thick jaw was smooth and smelled of shaving soap. You would hardly have known he was hurt, except for the bulky dressing that distended one blue-striped pajama leg. "What do you think?" I said.

He reached for the pack of cigarettes on the nightstand. "You are a nurse. You see before you an injured man. You have a cabin, a change of clothes, a dozen men to serve you. What more is necessary for an obedient young lady who knows it is impertinent to ask questions?"

I opened my mouth to say something indignant, and then I saw the expression on his face as he lit the cigarette between his lips with a sharp-edged gold lighter and tossed the lighter back on the nightstand. The end of the cigarette flared orange. I said, "You *do* realize you're at my mercy, don't you?"

"I have known that for some time, yes. Since you first walked into that miserable boathouse in your white dress and stained it with my blood."

"Oh, you're flirting again. Anyway, I returned the favor, didn't I?"

"Yes. We are now bound at the most elemental level, aren't we? I believe the ancients would say we have taken a sacred oath, and are bound together for eternity." He reached for the ashtray and placed it on the bed, next to his leg, and his eyes danced.

"If that's your strategy for conquering my virtue, you'll have to try much harder."

Stefan's face turned more serious. He placed his hand with the cigarette on the topmost book, the Goethe, nearly covering it, and said, "What I mean by all that, of course, is *thank you*, Mademoiselle. Because there are really no proper words to describe my gratitude."

I leaned forward and turned the lapel of his pajamas right side out. "Since we are now bound together for eternity," I said, "you may call me Annabelle."

6.

Of course, my full name was much longer.

I was christened Annabelle Marie-Elisabeth, Princesse de Créouville, a title bought for me by my mother, who married Prince Edouard de Créouville with her share of the colossal fortune left to her and her sister by their father, a New England industrialist. Textiles, I believe. I never met the man who was my grandfather. My father was impoverished, as European nobility generally was, and generously happy to make the necessary bargain.

At least my mother was beautiful. Not beautiful like a film star—on a woman with less money, her beauty would be labeled *handsome*—but striking enough to set her apart from most of the debutantes that year. So she married her prince, she gave birth to Charles nine months later and me another four years after that, and then, *ooh la la,* caught her husband in bed with Peggy Guggenheim and asked for a divorce. (*But everybody's doing it,* my father protested, and my mother said, *Adultery or Peggy Guggenheim?* and my father replied, *Both.*) So that was the end of that, though in order to secure my father's co-operation in the divorce (he was Catholic and so was the marriage) my mother had to leave behind what remained of her fortune. *C'est la vie.* We moved back to America and lived in a modest house in Brookline, Massachusetts, summering with relatives in Cape Cod, until Mummy's appendix burst and it was back to France and Saint Cecilia's on the storm-dashed Brittany coast.

"But that is medieval," said Stefan, to whom I was relating this story a week later, on a pair of deck chairs overlooking a fascinating sunset. He was still in pajamas, smoking a cigarette and drinking a dry martini; I wore a lavender sundress and sipped lemonade.

"My father's Paris apartment was hardly the place for an eleven-year-old girl," I pointed out.

"True. And I suppose I have no right to complain, having reaped the benefit of your convent education. But I hate to think of my Annabelle being imprisoned in such a bitter climate, when she is so clearly meant for sunshine and freedom. And then to have lost such a mother at such an age, and your father so clearly unworthy of this gift with which he was entrusted. It enrages me. Are you sure you won't have a drink?"

"I *have* a drink."

"I mean a real one, Annabelle. A grown-up drink."

"I don't drink when I'm on duty."

"Are you still on duty, then?" He crushed the spent cigarette into an ashtray and plucked the olive out of his martini. He handed it to me.

I popped the gin-soaked olive into my mouth. "Yes, very much."

"I am sorry to hear that. I had hoped, by now, you were staying of your own accord. Do you not enjoy these long hours on the deck of my beautiful ship, when you read to me in your charming voice, and then I return the favor by teaching you German and telling you stories until the sun sets?"

"Of course I do. But until you're wearing a dinner jacket instead of pajamas, and your crutches have been put away, you're still my patient. And then you won't need me anymore, so I'll go back home."

He finished the martini and reached for another cigarette. "Ah, Annabelle. You crush me. But you know already I have no need of a nurse. Dr. Duchamps told me so yesterday, when he removed the stitches." He tapped his leg with his cigarette. "I am nearly healed."

"He didn't tell *me* that."

"Perhaps he is a romantic fellow and wants you to stay right here with me, tending to my many needs."

Suddenly I was tired of all the flirting, all the charming

innuendo that meant nothing at all. I braced my hands on the arms of the deck chair and lifted myself away.

"Where are you going?" asked Stefan.

"To get some air."

The air at the *Isolde*'s prow was no fresher than the air twenty feet away in the center of the deck—and we both knew it—but I spread my hands out anyway and drew in a deep and briny breath. The breeze was picking up with the setting of the sun. My dress wound softly around my legs. I wasn't wearing shoes; shoes seemed pointless on the well-scrubbed deck of a yacht like this. The bow pointed west, toward the dying red sun, and to my left the water washed against the shore of the Île Saint-Honorat, a few hundred yards away.

I thought, It's time to go, Annabelle. You're falling in love.

Because how could you not fall in love with Stefan, when he was so handsome and dark-haired, so well read and well spoken and ridden with mysterious midnight bullets—the highwayman, and you the landlord's dark-eyed daughter!—and you were nursing him back to health on a yacht moored off the southern coast of France? When you had spent so many long hours on the deck of his beautiful ship, in a perfect exchange of amity, while the sun glowed above you and then fell lazily away. And it was August, and you were nineteen and had never been kissed. This thing was inevitable, it was impossible that I *shouldn't* fall in love with him.

For God's sake, what had my brother been thinking? Did he imagine I still wore pigtails? I thought of the woman who had visited Stefan that first day, who had held Stefan's hand in hers, tall and lithe and glittering. She hadn't returned—women like her had little to do with sickrooms—but she would. How could you not return to a man like Stefan?

Time to go home, Annabelle. Wherever that was.

I closed my eyes to the last of the sun. When I turned around, Stefan's deck chair was empty.

7.

I didn't have much to pack, and when I finished it was time to bring Stefan his dinner, which I had formed the habit of doing myself. He wasn't in his room, however. After several minutes of fruitless searching, I found him in the library, with his leg propped up on the sofa.

He waved to the desk. "You can put it there."

"Oh, yes, my lord and master." I set the tray down with a little more crash than necessary.

Stefan looked up. "What was that?"

I put my hands behind my back. "I'm leaving tomorrow morning. The wound is healing well, and you're well out of danger of infection. You don't need me."

He placed his finger in the crease of the book and closed it. "What makes you think that?"

"Because the flesh has knit well, there's no sign of redness or suppuration—"

"No, I mean thinking that I don't need you."

I screwed my hands together. "I'm going to miss this flirting of yours."

"I am not flirting, Annabelle."

His face was serious. A Stefan without a smile could look very severe indeed; there was a spare quality to all those bones and angles, a minimum of fuss. My hands were damp; I wiped them carefully on the back of my dress, so he wouldn't see. "I've already packed," I said. "It's for the best."

He went on looking at me in his steady way, as if he were waiting for me to change my mind. Or maybe not: Maybe he was eager for me to leave, so his mistress could return. Nurse out; mistress in. The patient's progress. For everyone's good health and serenity, really.

"Well," I said. "Good night, then."

"Good night, Mademoiselle de Créouville," he said softly, and I turned and left the room before I could cry.

8.

I woke up suddenly at three o'clock in the morning and couldn't go back to sleep. The wind had changed direction, drawing the yacht around on her mooring; you started to notice these things when you'd been living on a ship for a week and a half, the subtle tugs and pulls on the architecture around you, the various qualities of the air. My legs twitched restlessly. I rose from my bed and went out on deck.

The night was clear and dry and unnaturally warm. I had been right about the change in wind: the familiar shape of the Île Sainte-Marguerite now rose up to port, lit by a buoyant white moon. I made my way down the deck, and I had nearly reached the railing when I realized that Stefan's deck chair was still out, and Stefan was in it.

I spun around, expecting his voice to reach me, some comment rich with *entendre*. But he lay still, overflowing the chair, and in the pale glow of the moon it seemed as if his eyes were closed. I thought, I should go back to my cabin right now.

But my cabin was hot and stuffy, and while it was hot outside, here in the still Mediterranean night, at least there was moving air. I stepped carefully to the rail, making as little noise as possible, and stared down at the inviting ripples of cool water, the narrow silver path of moonlight daring me toward the jagged shore of the island.

If I were still a girl on Cape Cod, I thought, I would take that dare. If I hadn't spent seven years at a convent, learning to subdue myself, I would dive right off this ship and swim two hundred yards around the rocks and cliffs and the treacherous Pointe du Dragon to stagger ashore on the Île Sainte-Marguerite, where France's most notorious prisoner spent a decade of his life, dreaming over the sea. I had been like that, once; I had taken dares. I had swum fearlessly into the surf. When had I evaporated into this sapless young lady, observing life, living wholly on the inside, waiting for everything to happen to me? When had I decided the risk wasn't worth the effort?

I looked back over my shoulder, at Stefan's quiet body. He wasn't wearing his pajamas, I realized. He was wearing something else, a suit, a dinner jacket. As if he were waiting to meet someone, at three o'clock in the morning, on the deck of his yacht; as if he had a glamorous appointment of some kind, and the lady was late. The blood splintered down my veins, making me dizzy, the kind of drunkenness that comes from a succession of dry martinis swallowed too quickly.

You should wake him, I thought. You should do it. You have to be kissed by someone, sometime. Why not him? Why not here and now, in the moonlight, by somebody familiar with the practice of kissing?

"Good evening," he said.

I nearly flipped over the railing, backward into the sea. "I didn't realize you were here."

"I'm here most nights. The cabin's too stuffy for me." He sat up and swung his left foot down to the deck, next to a silver bucket, glinting in the moonlight. "Join me. I have champagne."

"At this hour?"

"Can you think of a better one?"

"I don't drink on duty."

"But you're not on duty, are you? You have tendered your resignation to me, and rather coldly at that, considering what we have shared." He rested his elbow on his left knee and considered me. I was wearing my nightgown and my dressing gown belted over it, like a Victorian maiden afraid of ravishment. My hair was loose and just touched my shoulders. "Is something the matter?" he said.

"No."

"There must be something the matter. It's not even dawn yet, and here you are, out on deck, looking as if you mean to do something dramatic."

I laughed. "Do I? I can't imagine what. I don't do dramatic things."

"Oh, no. You only wrap tourniquets around the legs of dying men—"

"You weren't dying, not quite, and anyway, I wasn't the one who put the tourniquet on you."

He waved his hand. "You carry him in a boat across the sea—"

"Across a *harbor*, a very still and familiar harbor."

"Toward an unknown destination, a yacht, and you nurse him back to health. All without knowing who he is, and why he's there, and why he's been shot through the leg and nearly killed. Whether you've just committed an illegal act and are now wanted by a dozen different branches of the police."

"Am I?"

"I doubt it. Not in France, in any case."

"Well, that's a relief."

He reached into his inside jacket pocket and drew out his cigarette case. "So I've been lying here, day after day, and wondering why. Why you would do such a thing."

"You might just have asked me."

"I was afraid of your answer."

I watched him light the cigarette and replace the case and the lighter in his pocket. The smoke hovered in the still air. Stefan waved it away, observing me, waiting for me to reply.

"There's nothing to be afraid of," I said. "It's simple. My brother asked me to."

"You trust your brother like that?"

"Yes. He would never ask me to do something dishonorable."

He muttered something in German and swung himself upright.

"You should use your crutches," I said.

"I am sick of fucking crutches," he said, and then, quickly, "I beg your pardon. I find I am out of sorts tonight."

I gripped the rail as he limped toward me. "I suppose I am, too."

"Ah. Now, this is a curious thing, a very interesting thing. Why, Annabelle? Tell me."

"Surely you know already."

"I know very well why *I* am out of sorts. I am desperate to know why *you* are out of sorts."

The water slapped against the side of the ship. I counted the glittering waves, the seconds that passed. I pressed my thumbs together and said: "I don't know. Just restless, I suppose. I've been cooped up for so long. I'm used to exercise."

He leaned his elbow on the railing, a foot or so from mine. I felt his breath as he spoke. "You are bored."

"Not bored."

"Yes, you are. Admit it. You have had nothing to do except fetch and carry for a grumpy patient who does not even thank you as you deserve."

I laughed. "Yes, that's it exactly."

"There is an easy cure for your boredom. Do something unexpected."

"Such as?"

"Anything. You must have some special talent, besides nursing. Show it to me." He transferred his cigarette to his other hand and reached into his pocket. "Do you draw? I have a pen."

"I don't have any paper."

"Draw on the deck, if you like."

"I'm not going to ruin your deck. Anyway, I'm hopeless at drawing."

"A poem, then. Write me a poem."

I was laughing, "I don't write, either. I play the cello, quite well actually, but my cello is back at the Villa Vanilla."

"The Villa Vanilla?"

"My father's house."

Stefan began to laugh, too, a handsome and hearty laugh

that shivered his chest beneath his dinner jacket. "Annabelle. Am I just supposed to let you slip away?"

"Yes, you are." His hand, broad and familiar, had worked close to mine on the railing, until our fingers were almost touching. I drew my arm to my side and said, "I do have one talent."

"Then do it. Show me, Annabelle."

I reached for the sash of my dressing gown. Stefan's astonished eyes slid downward.

The bow untied easily. I let the gown slip from my shoulders and bent down to grasp the hem of my nightgown.

"Annabelle—"

I knotted the nightgown between my legs and turned to brace my hands on the railing. "Watch," I said, and I hoisted myself upward to balance the balls of my feet on the slim metal rod while the moonlight washed my skin.

"My God," Stefan said, reaching for my legs, but I was already launching myself into the free air, tucking myself into a single perfect roll, uncurling myself just in time to slice into the water beneath a silent splash.

9.

"You are quite right," called Stefan, when my head bobbed at last above the surface. "That is an immense talent."

"I was club champion four years running." The water slid against my limbs, sleek and delicious.

He pointed to the side of the ship. "The ladder is over there, Mademoiselle."

"So it is."

But I didn't swim toward the ladder. I turned around and kicked my strong legs and stroked my strong arms, toward the shore of the Île Sainte-Marguerite, waiting quietly in the moonlight.

10.

I lay in the rough sand without moving, soaking up the faint warmth of yesterday's sun into my bones. I thought I had never felt so magnificent, so utterly exhausted and filled with the intense pleasurable relief that follows exhaustion. The water dried slowly on my legs and arms; my nightgown stiffened against my back. I inhaled the green briny scent of the beach, the trace of metal, the hint of eucalyptus from the island forest, and I thought, Someone should bottle this, it's too good to be true.

I didn't count the passing of minutes. I had no idea how much time had passed before I heard the rhythmic splash of oars in the water behind me.

"There you are, Mademoiselle," said Stefan. "I had some trouble to find you in the darkness."

I sat up. "You haven't rowed all the way over here!"

"Of course. What else am I to do, when Annabelle dives off my ship and swims away into the night?"

I rose to my unsteady feet and took the rope from his hand. "Let me do that."

"I assure you, I can manage."

"If your wound opens—"

"Don't be stupid." He pulled on the rope and the boat slid

up the sand. I took a few steps away and sat down again. My legs were still a little wobbly, my skin still cool after the long submersion in the sea. Stefan reached into the boat and drew out the silver bucket and a pair of glasses.

"You've brought champagne?"

"What's this? Did you think I would forget the refreshment?" He sank into the gravelly sand next to me and braced the bottle between his hands. His thumbs worked expertly at the cork until it slid out with a whisper of a pop.

"You are quite mad."

"No, only a little. A little mad, especially when I saw Annabelle's body lying there like a ghost in the moonlight, without moving." He handed me a foaming glass. "And then I thought, No, my Annabelle would never swim so far through the water and then give up when she had reached the shore. But here." He set down his own glass in the sand and shrugged his dinner jacket from his arms. "You must take this."

"I'm not that cold, really. Nearly dry."

"And how would I answer to God if Annabelle caught a chill while I still wore my jacket?" He placed it over my shoulders, picked up his glass, and clinked it against mine. "Now drink. Champagne should always be drunk ice-cold on a beach at dawn."

"Is it dawn already?"

"We are close enough."

I bent my head and sipped the champagne, and it was perfect, just as Stefan said, falling like snow into my belly. Next to me, Stefan tilted back his head and drank thirstily, and the beach was so still and flawless that I thought I could feel his throat move, his eyelids close in bliss.

"That woman," I said. "The blond woman, the one who came to visit you. Is she your mistress?"

"Yes," he said simply, readily, as if there couldn't possibly exist any prevarication between us.

"She's very beautiful."

"That is the way of it, I'm afraid. Only the rich deserve the fair."

I laughed. "I thought it was the brave. Only the brave deserve the fair."

"A silly romantic notion. When have you ever seen a beautiful woman with a poor man? An ugly man perhaps, or a timid one, or a stupid one, or even an unpleasant one. But never a poor one."

"Do you love her?"

"Only so much as is absolutely necessary."

I swallowed the rest of my champagne and set the glass in the sand between us. My vision swam. "I don't quite know what you mean."

"No," he said. "Of course you don't."

He lay back in the sand, and after a moment I lay back, too, a few inches away, listening to the sound of his breath. The beach was coarse, not like the sand on my father's beach; the little rocks poked into my back. Stefan's jacket brushed my jaw, enclosing me in an intimate atmosphere of tobacco and shaving soap. The moon had slipped below the horizon, and we were lit only by the stars, just as we had been on the first night as we rushed through the water toward the safety of Stefan's yacht. I had known almost nothing about him then, and ten days later, having lived next to him, having spent hours at his side, having talked at endless length about an endless variety of subjects, I didn't know much more.

"I love your library," I said. "You have so many lovely books."

"Yes, it is the family library, collected over many generations."

"Your *family* library? Don't you think that's risky? Keeping it all on a ship?"

"No more risky than keeping it in our house in Germany, in times like this. When a Jew is no longer even really a citizen."

I lifted my head. "You're a Jew?"

"Yes. You didn't know that?"

"I never thought about it." I laid my head back down and studied the stars. Stefan's fingers brushed my hand, and I brushed them back, and a complex and breathless moment later we were holding hands, studying the stars together.

"Tell me, Annabelle," he said. "Why have you never asked me how I came to be shot in the leg, one fine summer night on the peaceful coast of France?"

"I thought you'd tell me when you trusted me. I didn't want to ask and have you tell me it was none of my business."

"Of course it is your business. I will tell you now. The men who shot me, they were agents of the Gestapo. You know what this is?"

"Yes, I think so. A sort of secret police, isn't it? The Nazi police."

"Yes. They rather resent me, you see, because instead of waiting quietly for the next law to be passed, the next column to be kicked out from under me, I am seeking to defend the country that I love, the real Germany, the one for which my father lost his eye and his jaw twenty years ago."

"I see."

"I will not bore you with the details of what I was doing that night. But you are in no danger from the French authorities. I want you to know that, that I have not made you some sort of fugitive. But it was necessary, you see, that the man who shot me didn't know what became of me, or who had helped me to safety."

"My brother."

"Yes, de Créouville and his friends. And you." He lifted my hand and brought it to his lips, which were warm and soft and damp with champagne.

My heart was jumping from my chest. I felt my ribs strain, trying to contain it. I opened my mouth to say something, and my tongue was so dry I could hardly shape the words.

"I'm glad," I said, "I am *proud* of my brother, that he was helping you."

"Yes, he is a good man."

"I suppose"—I swallowed—"I suppose you'll go on doing these things, whatever they are. You will go on putting yourself in this danger."

He didn't speak. We lay there in darkness, shoulders touching, hips touching, hand wound around hand. I might have drifted to sleep for a moment, because I opened my eyes to find that the stars had disappeared, and the sky had turned a shade of violet so deep it was almost charcoal. Next to me, Stefan lay so still I thought he must be asleep. I didn't move. I was afraid to wake him.

I thought, I will remember this always, the smell of him, cigarettes and champagne and salt warmth; the strength of his hand around mine, the rhythm of his breath, the rough texture of sand beneath my head.

"It's almost dawn," he said softly.

"I thought you were asleep."

"I was."

The water slapped against the sand. A perimeter of color grew around the horizon, and Stefan sat up, still holding my hand. "The sun will be up soon," he said. "We can't see it yet, because of the cliffs to the east. In Venice, it is fully light."

"I haven't been to Venice."

"It is beautiful, a kind of dreamy beauty, like a painting of someone's memory. Except it smells like the devil, sometimes." He nodded at the faint violet outline of the Fort Royal, just visible above the trees. "I have been staring at that building through my porthole, every day. Thinking about the men who were imprisoned there."

"Yes, I noticed that book, when I brought it from the library. The Dumas, the one about the Man in the Iron Mask."

"Except it wasn't really an iron mask. It was velvet black, according to those who saw him. Voltaire was the one who turned it into iron, for dramatic purposes, or so one supposes."

"Have you ever been inside?"

"No." He paused and smiled. "Would you like to go now?"

"What, now? But it isn't open yet."

"Even better. We will have the place to ourselves." He swung to his feet, a little awkwardly, and pulled me up with him. "A good thing, since you are only wearing a nightgown and my dinner jacket."

"What about your leg?" I said breathlessly.

He shrugged. "Don't worry about my leg anymore, Nurse. You are off duty, remember?"

11.

We walked slowly, because of my bare feet and Stefan's leg, and because the world around us seemed so sacred and primeval, like

Eden, filling with pale new light, fragrant with pine and eucalyptus. There was a long straight *allée* leading directly to the fort, and we saw nobody else the entire way. "There are fisherman in the village," Stefan said. "They are probably setting out in their boats. And there will be a lot of tourists later in the morning and the afternoon."

"I'd rather wake up early and spend time with the fishermen. I'd rather see the place as it really is, as it used to be lived."

"Yes, the tourists are a nuisance. Have you been to Pompeii?"

"No. I've never been to Italy at all."

"We must go there someday. You would like it very much. It is as if you have walked into an ordinary old village, except you begin to walk down the street and you see how ancient it is. There are shards of old pottery littering the ground. You can pick one up and take it with you."

"Don't they mind?"

"They only really care about the frescoes. The frescoes are astonishing, though they are not for the faint of heart."

"Are they violent?" I asked, thinking of the gladiators and the casual Roman lust for blood.

"No, they are profoundly erotic."

A bird sang at us from within a tree somewhere, a melancholy whistle. The low crunch of our footsteps echoed from the woods.

"There are also casts," Stefan said. "They found these hollows in the ash, the hardened ash, and so they had the good idea to pour plaster of Paris into these hollows, and when it dried and they chipped away the molds, there remained these exact perfect casts of the people who had died, who had been buried alive in the ash. You can see the terror in their faces. And *that*, my Annabelle, is when you realize that this thing was real, that it actually happened, this unthinkable thing. Each cast was a living person, two thousand years ago. These casts, they are proof. They are photographs of a precise moment, the moment of expiration. They are like the resurrection of the dead."

"How awful."

"It's awful and beautiful at once. The worst was the dog, however. I could bear the sight of the people, but the dog made me weep."

"You don't mind the people dying, but you mind the animals?"

"Because the people knew what was happening to them. They knew Vesuvius was erupting, that the town was doomed. They couldn't escape, but at least they knew. The dog, he had no idea. He must have thought he was being punished."

"The people thought they were being punished, too. That the gods were punishing them."

"Yes, but we humans are all full of sin, aren't we? We know our mortal failings. We know our own culpability. This poor dog never knew what he had done wrong. Here we are."

A wall appeared to our right, behind the trees. I looked up, and the dawn had broken free at last, gilding the peaks of the fort, which had somehow, in the course of our conversation, grown into a forbidding size and complexity. Ahead, the trees cleared to reveal a paved terrace.

"Can we go in?" I asked.

"We can try."

The sun had not quite scaled the rooftops yet, and the terrace was in full shade. We walked up the path until an entrance came into view, interrupting the rough stone of the fort walls: a wide archway beneath a modest turret. There was no door, no impediment of any kind. A patch of white sun beckoned on the other side.

"Are there any soldiers about, do you think?"

"No, the garrison was disbanded some years ago, I believe. It is now a—I don't know if there is some particular term in English—a *monument historique*. I suppose it belongs to the people of France."

"Then it's mine, because I am a person of France, after all," I said, and I walked under the archway and up the stairs to the patch of light that squeezed between the corners of two buildings.

"But you are not simply a person of France, are you?" said Stefan, coming up behind me. "You are a princess of France."

"That doesn't mean anything anymore. We're a republic. We shouldn't even have titles at all. Anyway, I'm half American. It's impossible to be a princess and speak like a Yankee."

"It suits you, however. Especially now, when the sun is touching your hair."

I stopped walking and turned to Stefan, who stopped, too, and returned my gaze. He was almost a foot taller than I was, and the sun had already found his hair and eyes and most of his face, and while he could sometimes look almost plain, because his bones were arranged so simply, in the full light of morning sunshine he was beautiful.

"Don't look at me like that," he said.

"Like what?"

"Like you want me to kiss you."

"But I do want you to kiss me."

Stefan shook his head. "How can you be like this? No one in the world is like you."

"I was going to say the same about you."

He lifted his hand and touched the ends of my hair, and such was the extraordinary sensitivity of my nerves that I felt the stir of each individual root. "I don't know how I am going to bear this, Annabelle," he whispered. "How am I going to survive any more?"

I didn't say anything. I didn't want to disturb the delicate balance, one way or another. I took a step back, so I was standing against the barracks wall, which was already warm with sunshine, and Stefan followed me and raised his other hand to burrow into my hair, around the curve of my skull. His gaze dropped to my lips.

"*Alles ist seinen Preis wert,*" he said, and he lowered his face and kissed me.

I held myself still as his lips touched mine, lightly at first and then deeper, until he had opened me gently to taste the skin of my mouth. I didn't know you could do that, I didn't know you could kiss on the inside. I thought it was all on the surface. He tasted like he smelled, of champagne and cigarettes, only richer and wetter, alive, and I lifted my hands, which had been pressed against the barracks wall, and curled them around his waist, because I might never have the chance to do that again, to hold Stefan's warm waist under my palms while his mouth caressed mine. He cradled the back of my head with one hand and the side of my face with the other, and he ended the kiss in a series of nibbles that trailed off somewhere on my cheekbone, and pressed his forehead against mine. I relaxed against the barracks wall and took his weight. A bird chattered from the ridgepole.

"All right," he said. "Okay. Still alive."

"I'm sorry. I don't really know how to kiss."

"Don't ever learn."

I laughed softly and held him close against my thin nightgown. The new sun burned the side of my face. I said, "I suppose your mistress wouldn't be happy to see us now."

Stefan lifted his head from mine. "As it happens, I do not give a damn what this woman thinks at the moment, and neither should you. But come. The groundskeepers will be coming soon, and then the tourists. It will be a great scandal if we are seen."

"I don't care."

"But I do. I will not have Annabelle de Créouville caught here in her nightgown with her lover, for all the world to stare." He gave my hair a final stroke and picked up my hand. "Can you walk all the way back in your bare feet, do you think?"

"Must we? I wanted to see the rest of the fort."

"We will come back someday, if you like."

His voice was warm in my chest. I wanted him to kiss me again, but instead I followed him around the corner of the barracks to the stairs. *Your poor feet,* he said, looking down, and I said, *Your poor leg,* and he kissed my hand and said, *The lame leading the lame.*

I said, *I thought it was the blind, the blind leading the lame,* and he said, *I am not blind at all. Are you?*

No, I told him. *Not blind at all.*

There were two weather-faced men smoking on the terrace when we passed under the arch. They looked up at us and nearly dropped their cigarettes.

"*Bonjour, mes amis,*" said Stefan cheerfully, and he bent down and lifted me into his arms and carried me the rest of the way, to hell with the wounded leg.

12.

An hour later, we were standing inside the *Isolde*'s tender, a sleek little boat with a racehorse engine, motoring across the sea to my father's villa on the other side of the Cap d'Antibes. The wind whipped Stefan's hair as he sat at the wheel, and the sun lit his skin. Against the side of the boat, the waves beat a forward rhythm, and the breeze came thick and briny.

We hardly spoke. How could you speak, after a morning like that? And yet it was only seven o'clock. The whole day still lay ahead. We rounded the point, and the Villa Vanilla came into view, white against the morning glare. Stefan brought us in expertly to the boathouse, closing the throttle so we wouldn't make too much noise.

"I will walk you up the cliff," he said. "I do not trust that path."

"But I've climbed it hundreds of times. I walked down it in the dark, the night we met."

"This I do not wish to think about."

The house was silent when we reached the top. No one would be up for hours. There was a single guilty champagne bottle sitting on the garden wall, overlooked by the servants. Stefan picked it up as we passed and then looked over at the driveway, which was just visible from the side as we approached the terrace. "My God," he said, stopping in his tracks. "Whose car is that?"

I followed his gaze and saw Herr von Kleist's swooping black Mercedes, oily-fast in the sun. "Oh, that's the general, Baron von Kleist. I'm surprised he's still here. He didn't seem to be enjoying himself."

"Von Kleist," he said.

"Do you know him?"

"A little."

We resumed walking, and when we had climbed the steps and stood by the terrace door Stefan handed me the empty champagne bottle and the small brown valise that contained my few clothes. "You see? You may tell your brother I have returned you properly dressed, with your virtue intact. I believe I deserve a knighthood, at least. The Chevalier Silverman."

"What about me? I was the one who nursed you back to health, from the brink of death."

"But you are already a princess, Mademoiselle. What further honor can be given to you?"

All at once, I was out of words. I was empty of the ability to flirt with him. I parted my lips dumbly and stood there, next to the door, staring at Stefan's chin.

His voice fell to a very low pitch, discernible only by dogs and lovers. "Listen to me, Annabelle. I will tell you something, the absolute truth. I have never in my life felt such terror as I did when I saw you lying on that beach this morning in your white nightgown, surrounded by the rocks and that damned treacherous Pointe du Dragon."

"Don't be stupid," I whispered.

"I *am* stupid. I am stupid for you. I am filled with folly. But stop. I see I am alarming you. I will go back to my ship now. It is best for us both, don't you think?" He kissed my hand. I hadn't even realized he was holding it. He kissed it again and turned away.

"Wait, Stefan," I said, but he was already hurrying down the stones of the terrace, and the sound of his footsteps was so faint, I didn't even notice when it faded into the morning silence.

13.

I passed through the dining room on the way to the stairs, and instead of finding it empty, I saw Herr von Kleist sitting quietly in a chair, eating his breakfast. He looked up at me without the slightest sign of surprise.

"Good morning, Mademoiselle de Créouville," he said, pushing back his chair and unfolding his body to an enormous height.

"Good morning, Herr von Kleist." I was blushing furiously. The champagne bottle hung scandalously from one hand, the valise from the other. "I didn't expect anyone up so early."

"I am always up at this hour. May I call for some breakfast for you?"

"No, thank you. I think I'll take a tray in my room."

"We have missed you these past ten days."

"I've been staying with a friend."

"So I was told." He remained standing politely, holding his napkin in one hand, a man of the old manners. The kitchen maid walked in, heavy-eyed, holding a coffeepot, and stopped at the sight of me.

"*Bonjour*, Marie-Louise," I said.

"*Bonjour*, Mademoiselle," she whispered.

I looked back at Herr von Kleist, whose eyes were exceptionally blue in the light that flooded from the eastern windows, whose hair glinted gold like a nimbus. He was gazing at me without expression, although I had the impression of great grief hanging from his shoulders. I shifted my feet.

"Please return to your breakfast," I said, and I walked across the corner of the dining room and broke into a run, racing up the stairs to my room, hoping I would reach my window in time to see the *Isolde*'s tender cross the sea before me.

But it did not.

1.

Annabelle waits for her to finish, like a woman who's done this before: waited patiently for someone else to finish vomiting. When Pepper lifts her head, she hands her a crisp white handkerchief, glowing in the moon.

"Thank you," says Pepper.

"All better? Can we move on?"

"Yes."

The engine launches them back down the road. Pepper leans her head back and allows the draft to cool her face. Annabelle bends forward and switches on the radio. "That was too late for morning sickness," she observes.

"I don't get morning sickness."

"Lucky duck. Nerves, then?"

"I don't get nerves, either." She pauses. "Not without reason."

The static resolves into music. The Beatles. "Yesterday." So far away. Annabelle pauses, hand on the dial, and then lets it be. She sits back against the leather and says, "Are you saying the bastard's been threatening you?"

"He's been trying to find me, and I've been making myself scarce, that's all."

"Why? He *is* the father, after all."

"Because I know what he wants." Pepper examines her fingernails. She thinks, You're an idiot, Pepper Schuyler, you're going to spill it, aren't you? You're just going to lose it right here. Her throat still burns. She says, "I didn't even tell him. He found out, I don't know how. He called me up at the hotel and yelled at me. Why couldn't I get it taken care of, he wanted to know."

"What a gentleman."

Pepper gives up on her fingernails and looks out the side. They're passing close to the ocean right now, that grand old Atlantic, toiling away faithfully under the moon. "He was very good at the chase, I'll say that. I always swore I'd never sleep with a married man. I know what everyone says about me, lock up your husbands, but the truth is I just flirt. Like a sport, like some women play bridge. And silly me, I thought he knew that. I thought we weren't taking it past first base, until we did, one night. Big victory, big glasses of champagne, big beautiful hotel suite, and before you know it, the all-star hits himself a home run right out of the park, a grand goddamned salami. Oopsydaisy, as my sister Vivian would say."

Annabelle drives silently. She keeps one hand on the wheel and one elbow propped on the doorframe beside her. Pepper steals a glance. Her head is tilted slightly to one side, showing off her long neck. The skin is still taut, still iridescent in the moonlight. What bargain did she make with the devil for skin like that? Whatever it is, Pepper would happily take that bargain.

What was the point of an eternal soul, anyway? It just meant you spent eternity in fleecy boredom, strumming your harp. Pepper would rather have twenty good years on earth, flaunting her iridescent skin, and then oblivion.

"What are you thinking?" asks Pepper.

Annabelle raises her head and laughs, making the car swerve slightly. "Do you really want to know?"

"It beats the Beatles."

"I was thinking about when I fell in love, actually. How grateful I am for that. We were in the South of France, in the middle of August, and I was nineteen and just crazy about him. We were right by the sea. I thought I was in heaven."

"What was his name?"

She pauses. "Stefan."

The radio plays between them, the instrumentals, a low and mournful string. Someone believes in yesterday. Pepper stares at her thumbs in her lap and thinks about the night she lost her virginity. There was no sunshine, no Mediterranean, no mysterious Stefan. There was a friend of her mother's, after a party. She had flirted with him, because flirting gave you such a rush of delicious power. Such confidence in this newfound seventeen-year-old beauty of yours, that a man twenty years older hung on your every banal word, your every swooping eyelash. That he would tell you how you'd grown, how you were the most beautiful girl he'd ever seen. That he would lead you dangerously into a shady corner of the terrace, overlooking Central Park, and feed you a forbidden martini or two and kiss you—you'd been kissed before, you could handle this—and then do something to your dress and your underpants, and a few blurry moments later you weren't handling this at all, you were bang smack on your back on the lounge chair with no way to get up, and maybe it was a good thing he'd fed you those martinis, maybe it was a good thing you couldn't remember exactly how it happened.

The song changes, some new band that Pepper doesn't recognize. She reaches forward and shuts off the radio.

2.

They reach Cocoa Beach at half past one o'clock in the morning. A bank of clouds has rolled in, obscuring the moon, and Pepper can't see a thing beyond the headlights. She's too tired to care, anyway.

"Here we are," Annabelle says cheerfully. "The housekeeper is in bed, but the cottage should be ready."

"You do this kind of thing often?"

"No. I just had a hunch I'd have company."

Pepper stumbles out of the car and follows Annabelle across a driveway and up a pair of stone steps. A little house by the beach, she said, but this is more like a villa, plain and rough-walled, like something you might find in Spain or Italy, somewhere old and hot. The smell of eucalyptus hangs in the air.

Annabelle holds open the door. "I expect you're tired. I couldn't keep my eyes open when I was pregnant. I'll save the tour for tomorrow and take you straight to bed."

"I've heard that one before."

Annabelle laughs. "I expect you have, you naughty girl."

Pepper is just awake enough to appreciate the lack of censure in Annabelle's voice. Well, she is European, isn't she? She has that welcome dollop of joie-de-whatever, that je ne sais no evil.

She's not one to judge. Maybe that's why Pepper spilled her guts back there, in the middle of the road, like a cadaver under dissection. Or maybe it was the moon, or the goddamned ocean, or the baby and the hormones and the nicotine starvation. Whatever it was, Pepper hopes to God she won't regret all this over breakfast.

"We bought the place in 1941," Annabelle was saying, as they passed through the darkened rooms. "It was built in the twenties, during the big land rush. We got it for a song. It was in total disrepair, not even properly finished, but the bones were good, and there was plenty of room for the children, and it was all by itself, no nosy neighbors. There was something rather authentic about it, which is a difficult thing to find in Florida."

"I'll say."

"I mean, except me, of course!" Annabelle's midnight exuberance is almost certifiable. Pepper wants to throttle her. Of course, six months ago, Pepper could midnight with the best of them. Six months ago, midnight was just the beginning. That was how she got into this mess, wasn't it? Too much goddamned midnight, and now here she was, stumbling through an old house in the middle of Florida, knocked up and knocked out.

A latch clicks, a door swooshes open, and now they're in a courtyard, full of fresh air and lemon trees. Annabelle turns to the wall and switches on a light. Pepper squints.

"Just over here, honey," says Annabelle.

Pepper follows. "I don't mean to be pushy, but does this guest cottage of yours happen to have a working lavatory?"

Annabelle claps a hand to her cheek. "Oh, my goodness!

What an idiot I am! It's been so long since I had babies. Come along. My dear, you should have said something. I didn't realize you were so polite."

"I'm not, I assure you. I just didn't happen to spot any flowerpots along the way."

The grass is short and damp. They've moved beyond the circle of light from the house. Pepper sees a rectangular shadow ahead and hopes to God it's the cottage, and nobody's waiting inside. Peace and quiet, that's all she needs. Peace and quiet and a toilet.

A step ahead, Annabelle opens the door and steps aside for Pepper to enter first. The smell of soap and fresh linen rushes around her.

"Home sweet home. The bathroom's on the right."

3.

When Pepper emerges from the bathroom ten minutes later, Annabelle is standing by the window, looking into the night. From the side, her face looks a little more fragile than Pepper remembers, and she thinks that maybe Annabelle is right, that she isn't really beautiful. The nose is too long. The chin too sharp. The head itself is out of proportion, too large on her skinny long neck, like a Tootsie Pop.

Then she turns, and Pepper forgets her faults.

"All set?"

"Yes. Thanks for the nightgown and toothpaste. I'm beginning to think you had this all planned out."

"Maybe I did." Annabelle smiles. "Does that make you nervous?"

Pepper yawns. "Nothing's going to make me nervous right now."

"All right. Sleep in as long as you like. I'll have coffee and breakfast waiting in the main house, whenever you're up. Is there anything you need?"

"No, thanks." Pepper hesitates. Gratitude isn't her natural attitude, but then you didn't spend your life dangling elegantly from the pages of the Social Register without learning how to keep your legs crossed and your hostess well buttered. "Thanks awfully for your hospitality," she adds, all Fifth Avenue drawl, emphasis on the *awful.*

"Oh, not at all. I'm happy I could help."

Pepper's radar ears detect a note of wistfulness. She sinks on the bed, bracing her arms on either side of her heavy belly, and says, "Helped me? Kidnapped is more like it."

"Miss Pepper Schuyler," Annabelle says, shaking her head, "why on this great good earth are you so suspicious? What have they done to you?"

"A better question, Mrs. Annabelle Dommerich, is why you care."

An exasperated line appears between Annabelle's eyebrows. She marches to the bed, drops down next to Pepper, and snatches her hand. Her hand! As if Annabelle is the mother bear and Pepper is Goldilocks or something. "Now, look here," she actually says, just like a mother bear, "you are *safe* here, do you hear me? Nobody's going to call you or make demands on you or— God knows, whatever it is you're afraid of."

"I'm not afraid—"

"You're just going to sit here and grow your baby and think about what you want to do with yourself, is that clear? You're going to relax, for God's sake."

"Hide, you mean."

"Yes, hide. If that's what you want to call it. There's a doctor in town, if you need to keep up with any appointments. The housekeeper can drive you. You can telephone your parents and your sisters. You can telephone that horse's ass who put you in this condition, and tell him he can go to the devil."

Pepper cracks out a whiplash of laughter. "Go to the devil! That's a good one. I can just picture him, hanging up the phone and trotting off obediently into the fire and brimstone, just because Pepper Schuyler told him to. Do you have any idea who his friends are? Do you have any idea who owes him a favor or two?"

"He's no match for *you*. Trust me. You hold the cards, darling. You hold the ace. Don't let those bastards convince you otherwise."

Pepper stares at the mama-bear hand covering her own. The nails are short and well trimmed, the skin smooth and ribbed gently with veins the color of the ocean. Annabelle doesn't use lacquer.

"You still haven't answered my question," Pepper says. "Why do you care?"

Annabelle sighs and heads for the door. She pauses with her hand right there on the knob. Dramatic effect. Who knew she had it in her?

"All right, Pepper. Why do I care? I care because I stood in your shoes twenty-nine years ago, and God knows I could have used a little decent advice. Someone to keep me from making so many goddamned mistakes."

ANNABELLE

Antibes • 1935

1

A week passed. Charles had left with his friends before I returned; I was now wise enough to suspect why. Herr von Kleist packed up his few trunks and roared away in his beautiful Mercedes Roadster later that afternoon. My father—as always—rose late, retired late, and reserved nearly all of his time for his remaining guests. I had little to do except wander the garden and the beaches, to practice my cello for hours, to walk sometimes into the village, to examine the contents of my memory for signposts to my future.

On the seventh day of my isolation, I woke up under the settled conviction that I would move to Paris, to Montparnasse, and teach the cello while I found a master under whom to study. It seemed a natural place for me. I was both French and American, and I had read about how the streets and cafés around the boulevard du Montparnasse rattled with Americans seeking art and life and meaning and cheap accommodation. If a certain handsome young German Jew were then to turn up on my stoop one day, perhaps requiring immediate medical assistance, why, I would take him in with cheerful surprise. I would find a way to weave him into the hectic fabric of my happiness.

I was not going to wait any longer for my life to start. I was going to start my life on my own.

I repeated this to myself—a very nice tidy maxim, suitable for cross-stitch into a tapestry, a decorative pillow perhaps—as I walked down the stairs on my way to the breakfast room, where I expected the usual hours of peace until the rest of the household woke up. Instead, it was chaos. The hall was full of expensive leather trunks and portmanteaus, the rugs were being rolled up, the servants were running about as if an army were on the march. In the middle of it all stood my father, dressed immaculately in a pale linen suit, speaking on the telephone in rapid French, the cord wound around him and stretched to its limit.

"Papa?" I said. "What's going on?"

He held up one finger, said a few more urgent words, and set the receiver in its cradle with an exhausted sigh. He closed his eyes, collecting his thoughts, and then stepped to the hall table and set down the telephone. "*Mignonne,*" he said in French, opening his arms, "it is eight o'clock already. You are not ready?"

I took his hands and kissed his cheeks. He smelled of oranges, the particular scent of his shaving soap, which he purchased exclusively from a tiny apothecary in the Troisième, on the rue Charles-François-Dupuis. "Ready for what, Papa?"

"You did not see my message last night?" His eyes were heavy and bruised.

"What message? Papa, what's wrong?"

"I slipped it under your door. Perhaps you were already asleep." He released my hands and pulled out a cigarette case from his jacket pocket. His fingers fumbled with the clasp. "It is a bit of a change of plans. We are leaving this morning, returning to Paris."

"But we were to stay another week!"

"I'm afraid there is some business to which I must attend." He managed to fit a cigarette between his lips. I took the slim gold lighter from his fingers and lit the end for him. I concentrated on the movements of my fingers, this ordinary activity, to keep the panic from rising in my chest.

"But what about our guests?" I said.

"I have left messages. They will understand, don't you think?" He pulled the cigarette away and kissed my cheek. "Now run upstairs, *ma chérie*, and pack your things. Come, now. It is for the best. One should always leave the party before the bitter end, isn't it so?"

"Yes," I said numbly, "of course," and I turned and ran up the steps, two at a time, and burst without breath into my room, where I stayed only long enough to snatch the pair of slim black binoculars from my desk and bolt down the hall in the opposite direction, to the back stairs.

It was now the third week of August, and the sea washed restlessly against the rocks and beaches below as I stumbled along the clifftops, sucking air into my stricken lungs. I inhaled the warm scent of the dying summer, the weeks that would not return. I thought, I don't care, I don't care if we leave now and return to Paris, I have my own plans, I will live in Montparnasse, I will be sophisticated and insouciant, and he can find me or not find me, he can love me or not love me, I don't care, I don't care.

I skidded to a stop at the familiar rock, the rock where I had sat every day and watched the traffic in the giant mammary curves of the bay, in the delicate cleavage of which perched the village of Cannes. From here, you could see the boats zagging lazily, the ferries looping back and forth to the îsles Lérins, to Sainte-Marguerite, where the fort nestled into the cliffs. I climbed to the top of the boulder and lifted the binoculars to my eyes and thought, I don't care, I don't care, please God, please God, I don't care.

From this angle, to the east of the islands, it was impossible to see where the *Isolde* lay moored—if she still lay moored at all—behind the Pointe du Dragon. I had tried—no, I hadn't *tried*, of course not, I had only dragged my gaze about as a matter of idle curiosity, but there was no glimpse of the beautiful black-and-white ship, longer and sleeker than all the others moored there in the gentle channel between the two islands. I had taken her continued presence there as an article of faith. I had watched the boats ply the water, the stylish motorboats and the ferries and the serviceable tenders, and refused to think about the honey-haired woman who had come to see Stefan that first morning, and whether she was making another trip. Whether an unglamorous nineteen-year-old virgin was easily forgotten in the face of those kohl-lined eyes, that slender and practiced figure.

My legs wobbled, and the vision through the binoculars skidded crazily about. I planted my feet more firmly, each one in a separate hollow, and set my shoulders. The sea steadied before me, blue and ancient under the cloudless sky, and as I stared to the southeast, counting the tiny white waves, as if in obedience to a miraculous summons, I saw a long yacht come into view, around the edge of the point, black on the bottom and gleaming white in a rim about the top of the hull, steaming eastward toward Nice or Monaco, perhaps, or even farther south toward Italy.

The Cinque Ports were supposed to be beautiful at this time of year, and Portofino.

My heart grew and grew, splitting my chest apart, lodging somewhere in my throat so I couldn't breathe.

"She is a beautiful ship, don't you think?" said a voice behind me.

I closed my eyes and allowed my arms to fall, with the binoculars, onto my thighs. I thought, I must breathe now, and I forced my throat to open. "Yes, very beautiful."

"But you know, ships are so transient and so sterile. Nothing grows in them. So I have been thinking to myself, I must really find myself a villa of some kind, somewhere in the sunshine where I can raise olives and wine and children, with the assistance of perhaps a housekeeper to keep things tidy and make a nice hot breakfast in the morning, and a gardener to tend the flowers."

My chest was moving in little spasms now, taking in shallow bursts of air. I said, or rather sobbed, "And what—will you do—in the winter?"

"Ah, a good question. Perhaps an apartment in Paris? One can follow the sun, of course, but I have always thought that it is best to know some winter, too, so that the summer, when it arrives, is the more gratefully received."

I turned to face him. A tear ran down from each of my eyes and dripped along my jaw. Stefan stood with his hands in his pockets, right next to the rock, staring up at me gravely. His hair had grown a little, a tiny fraction of an inch, perhaps. I leaned down and put my hands on his shoulders.

"How strange," I whispered. "I have just been thinking the same thing."

He reached up and hooked me by the waist and swung me down from the top of the rock.

"Hush, now," he said, between kisses. "Annabelle, it is all right, I am here. *Liebling*, stop, you are frantic, you must stop and think."

"I don't want to think. I don't want to stop." I kissed his lips and jaw and neck, I kissed him everywhere I could, wetting us both with my tears. "I have been stopping all my life. I want to live."

"Ah, Annabelle. And I would have said you were the most *alive* girl I've ever met."

"That's you. You have brought me to life."

Stefan paused in his kisses, holding my face to the sunlight, as if I were a new species brought in for classification and he had no idea where to begin, my nose or my hair or my teeth. "Tell me what you want, Annabelle," he said.

"But you know what I want."

He took my hand and led me up the slope, where a cluster of olive trees formed an irregular circle of privacy. He urged me carefully down and I put my arms around his neck and dragged him into the grass with me. "I thought you had gone off with her," I said, unbuttoning his shirt.

"What? Gone off with whom?"

"The honey-haired woman, the one you used to make love to."

He drew back and stared at me. "My God. How stupid. What do I want with her?"

"I don't know. What you had before."

"What I had before." He lowered his head into the grass, next to mine. His body lay across me, warm and heavy, supported by his elbows. "You are the death of me," he said softly. "I have no right to you."

"You have every right. I'm giving you the right."

He turned his mouth to my ear. "Don't say that. Tell me to stop, tell me to take you home."

"No. That's not why you came for me, to take me home."

He lifted his head again, and his eyes were heavy and full of smoke. "No. God forgive me. That is not why I came for you."

I touched his cheek with my thumb and began to unbutton my blouse, and he put his fingers on mine and said, "No, let me. Let me do it."

He uncovered my breasts and kissed me, and his hands were gentle on my skin. "So new and pure," he said. "I don't think I can bear it."

I spread out my arms in the warm grass.

"God will curse me for this," he said.

"No, he won't."

He kissed me again and lifted my skirt to my waist. I hadn't worn stockings or a girdle. He worked my underpants down my legs and leaned over my belly to touch me with his gentle fingers, in such an unexpected and unbearably tender way that my legs shook and my lungs starved, and at last I made a little cry and grabbed his waist, because I couldn't imagine what else to hold on to. His shirt was unbuttoned and came away in my hands. "Tell me to stop, Annabelle," he said.

"Please don't stop. I'll die if you stop."

He muttered something in German and fumbled with his trousers and lowered himself over me, so that his forearms touched my shoulders and he arched above my ribs. I felt his legs settle between mine, pushing me apart while the grass prickled my spine. I loved his breath, the tobacco smell of him.

"Put your arms around me, Annabelle," he said, and I pressed my palms against the back of his sunburned neck. He reached down with one hand and bent my knee upward, and I thought, My God, what have I done? He said, with his hand still on my raised knee, *Are you sure, Annabelle, are you sure you want this?* and I nodded my head once, because even when you looked down from the heights to measure the distance to the surface, and the terror turned your limbs to water, you knew you had to dive, you had no choice except to jump. And as I nodded, I lifted my other knee because I thought I'd be damned if I didn't jump in with both feet. Stefan's eyes went opaque. He sank his belly down to mine and said my name as he pushed into me, just my name—twice, a cry that was more like a groan, *Annabelle, Annabelle*—but I, Annabelle, had no air in my lungs to say anything at all, no way of telling him what I felt, the splitting apart, the roar of panic smothered by the gargantuan joy of possession.

He lay buried and still, breathing hard, and I thought, so dizzy I was almost sick, So that's it, it's over, we've made love, but then he moved again and I cried out, and he stopped and kissed me and said my name again, stroking my hair. *Open your eyes*, he said, but I couldn't. He moved again, kissing me as he went, and the sickness undulated into something else, a collusion between us, his skin on my hands, the roughness of his breath. I opened my eyes and thought, My God, this is it, now we are making love.

2.

We lay submerged for ages, while the morning went on without us. I had no will to move, no idea what movement was. At some point I opened my eyes and found the slow crump of my heartbeat against Stefan's ribs. He was beautifully heavy, pinning us to the earth, and in my bemusement I thought he had fallen asleep. The tiny green leaves rustled above us, as if nothing had happened, nothing had changed at all. I watched them move, watched the patient blue sky beyond them, the wisps of dark hair near my eyes. Stefan's neck was smooth and damp beneath my fingers. Between my legs, I was shocked and stretched and aching, and I did not want it to stop, I wanted this abundance to continue forever.

When he spoke, the softness of his voice stunned me.

"*Gott im Himmel.* Annabelle. I did not expect that."

"It was unexpected and beautiful."

"Everything about you has been unexpected and beautiful." He pushed back my hair, which had come loose across my face. "Look at you. What a brute I am."

"I didn't give you a choice."

"A man has always the choice. Did I hurt you?"

"No, no."

"Yes, I did. I hurt you. I tried to be gentle, but I have never done that before, been with an innocent."

"Never? Really?"

"Never. And I can't seem to regret it. A cad as well as a brute." He kissed my lips, rose up on his hands, and lifted himself carefully away. He gazed back at me and his face was deep with remorse. I sat up and laid my bold palms against his cheeks. "Don't look at me like that."

"Like what?"

"Like you want to take it all back."

"No, never. It's done now. We're in God's hands."

"Listen to you. A moment ago you were offering me a villa by the sea and a shameless apartment in Paris."

"Because I did not think you would be so foolish as to accept. I thought you would slap me as I deserved and stalk back to your father's house."

"But I'm unexpected."

"Unexpected and beautiful." He pulled my hands from his face and kissed each one, and he drew me into his chest and settled us in the grass. I lay bare and marveling in the curve of his body, thinking, My God, we are lovers now, we have actually made love together.

The silence stretched out lazily. I said, "I've shocked you, haven't I?"

He laughed. "You have shocked and delighted me beyond words. But I must think a little. I must think what is to be done now."

"You mentioned a villa."

"Yes, I did. But this villa is something of a dream, and there is a reality to be considered first." He shifted me on his chest and reached for his jacket, and this time he drew out his cigarettes and lit one briskly with his gold lighter. "Do you know what I have been thinking about, this past week?"

"I know I've spent the past week wishing that I did."

"I have been thinking how I have arranged my life in a certain way, according to certain principles, and a rather arrogant belief that this was what God intended of me, and he would therefore overlook any little sins I might commit. And I have been wondering whether perhaps God has intended something entirely different, or if he has merely decided he should punish me after all."

"Is this one of those little sins?"

"Yes, I suppose it is, according to the covenant. But I don't regret it, I will never regret this moment. I am only pondering the path now before us." He lay there, smoking quietly with one hand and holding me to his chest with the other. "You are a great complication, you know," he said solemnly, after a moment.

"Am I?"

"A tremendous complication. So I suppose, before I ponder this matter any longer, I should humble myself to ask you what *you* want. What path you imagine for us. Since I find myself bound to you, by the pint of your blood that communicates in my veins, and now by honor, so therefore I am your servant on earth."

This time, it was my turn to laugh. "I love your chivalry. You talk like a man from a hundred years ago."

"Hmm. Yes. And what is your plan for this ancient servant you have brought under your command?"

"Well. I like the sound of this villa of yours, with the olives and the grapes." I paused, because I had left something out, and I wanted to see if he would supply the word for me. But he said nothing, and I went on: "And then there's that talk about Paris, and by a strange coincidence, I was just thinking this morning that an apartment in Montparnasse might be the very thing for me."

"Montparnasse! Annabelle in Montparnasse?"

"Yes. Why not? It's crammed with Americans and art. It's the most interesting place in the world right now. I could live in some grubby little room above a café and teach the cello to the daughters of the bourgeoisie."

"You realize that in Montparnasse, you will be expected to take a new lover every night, as a matter of course?"

"Ah, but I'm unexpected, remember? I think I'll be happy with just the one."

"I see. I suppose, so long as this lover is me, I cannot object."

"Yes, this lover would be you." I rolled over and propped my chin on my hands, atop his chest, between the white sides of his unbuttoned shirt. Stefan stubbed out his cigarette in the grass and cupped his hands around the backs of my bare shoulders. I felt suddenly daring and desirable, like somebody's mistress. I said, "What do you think of my path, Herr Silverman? Would you like to travel it with me?"

He kissed me. The smoke was returning to his eyes. He kissed me again, a little harder. "This is your path. This is what you want of me."

"Only if you want it, too."

He studied me, kissed me, and then studied me again, as if the kiss might have made a difference. "All right, then. All right, Mademoiselle de Créouville. I will see what I can arrange. I will take care of everything for us. But come. The tide will be turning soon. I must be off." He reached for my blouse and helped me into it.

"The tide?"

"Yes, the tide. I have left the tender at the Hôtel du Cap."

"But where are you going?"

He was standing up, fastening his trousers, buttoning his shirt. "To my ship, of course. She is off to her winter mooring in Monte Carlo, which I must oversee. You will stay with your father for a few more days, and then I will return and take you—"

My hands froze on my buttons.

"What is it?" he asked.

"My father. My God, I forgot all about it."

"Forgot about what? Why are you laughing?"

"I can't stay here with my father. He's leaving this morning for Paris. That's why I ran out here, to see if I could find you somehow, because he's already packed, we're to leave right away. Poor Papa, he's probably mad with impatience by now."

"Ah, yes. So it is true. I heard a rumor that a certain impoverished prince was experiencing some new difficulties in his poverty, which is why I woke up this morning and thought perhaps it was time to act. Well, then. It seems God, in his wisdom, has arranged things in a very satisfactory manner. You will come with me, of course. We cannot have you going off to Paris with your father and forgetting me altogether."

"I don't think there's much chance of my forgetting you."

He kissed my hand. "Then come. We will telephone your father from the hotel."

"What on earth am I going to tell him?"

"The truth, of course. That you're not yet ready to leave the seaside, and will spend the last few days of summer with your very dear friend, with whom you were staying before."

"And then?"

He picked up his jacket, slung it over his shoulder, and leaned down to place a soft kiss on my lips. "And then we will see what comes next."

3.

When we caught up with the *Isolde* in Monte Carlo, she was already moored in the harbor, surrounded by a few dozen yachts of similar proportion, but without her elegance. Stefan pulled me to the tender's wheel. "Wait here just a moment," he said. "I have a few instructions for the crew."

I kept the tender close, no easy feat in the constant chop of the busy harbor. The sun beat on my head; I hadn't worn a hat. I looked up the familiar sides of the ship and remembered how I had arrived with Stefan at this exact spot in the middle of the night three weeks ago, on the brink of adventure, and now here I was again and the adventure had grown into dazzling dimensions, an infinity of adventure.

I looked at my hands: one on the wheel, one on the throttle. There was still a soft ache between my legs. My skin felt as if it had been rubbed all over by a very fine grade of sandpaper. An hour ago, I had been lying on the grass with Stefan, and now I was running away with him, we were lovers running away together.

True to his word, Stefan climbed back down the ladder a few minutes later and jumped nimbly into the boat. I smiled up at him and he took my shoulders and said, "My God, you're here. It wasn't a dream."

I laughed, because I'd been thinking the same thing. "No, of course not."

There was a hum of energy surrounding him, crackling the air. I wanted to fling my arms about his neck and kiss him, but instead I stepped back from the wheel so he could grab it. He took the wheel in one hand and the throttle in the other. "Let's go, *Liebling*," he said.

"Where are we going?" I shouted, over the engine and the salt breeze.

"I have a friend who keeps a place here, just outside of town. He lets me use it when the ship is in port for repairs and so on. It's very nice, though the staff is all gone. I hope these nuns of yours have taught you to cook in addition to applying tourniquets."

"I guess I can boil an egg or two, in a pinch."

"Good. There is plenty of wine and a bakery in the fishing village, a kilometer away. I will bring us our daily bread, how does that sound?"

I leaned into his ear and said, "I don't have any things with me."

"Ah, don't worry. Did I not say I would take care of everything for us?" He brought his arm around my shoulder, drawing me close as we edged westward out of the harbor, toward Stefan's little place, just outside of town.

4.

The house was small and beautiful, a miniature villa tucked into the cliffs, made of crumbling yellow bricks and crumbling red tile on the roof. There was a tiny dock and boathouse and a stairway cut into the rocks, leading up to the house.

Inside, the house smelled like the sea and the eucalyptus that grew near the windows for shade. "First of all, I must draw you a bath," said Stefan. "I am a terrible blackguard for taking you on a forced march like this, instead of making sure you are comfortable."

"I'm perfectly comfortable," I said, and he laughed.

"You are such an eager little liar, Annabelle, *Liebling*. Come. Let us see if the old boiler is working."

Stefan got the boiler working, and in half an hour the taps ran hot. He showed me the rooms, the kitchen and the living room, and the beautiful terrace overlooking the sea, planted with lemons. The bedroom upstairs had a balcony that opened out into the lemon branches, so that the scent of lemons mingled with the brine and the eucalyptus. Stefan stood behind me and stretched out his hand. "See there, to the east? You can just find the *Isolde*, if you look hard."

I peered past his pointing finger. "Oh, yes! I see her."

"I have always loved coming here. It is the most peaceful place I know, and yet Monte Carlo is a half hour's walk away. I come here to be alone and think."

"Then I'm interrupting your solitude."

"No, you are improving it beyond measure. I have never wanted to bring another human being here until now." He kissed my temple. "Let's get you in your bath."

He made the strangest chambermaid I'd ever known, moving about the marble bathroom with his cigarette stuck at the corner of his mouth, sniffing a bottle of bath oil while the faucet poured forth with hot water. He added a few drops to the tub and replaced the lid. "That will do, I believe," he said, and turned to me. His hair curled with the steam. He smiled, the kind of too-wide smile that made me think he was nervous. "I will walk into the village and get us a little lunch while you are soaking, Mademoiselle. But there is no hurry. Is there anything else I can do for you? How are you feeling?"

I thought, I love you.

He frowned. "Annabelle?"

I took the cigarette from his fingers and crushed it into the tray on the windowsill. "I'm very well, Stefan, thank you. I guess losing your virginity isn't a mortal illness after all, whatever those old nuns used to tell us. Now, will you help me with this dress?"

5.

When Stefan returned, an hour or so later, he found me standing on the balcony, wrapped in a dressing gown that was several sizes too large. I held up my flopping arms. "The best I could do. But at least I'm all freshened up."

He dropped the net bag on the floor. There was a soft thump of a bottle hitting wood. "Oh, God," he said.

"Is something wrong?"

"No."

I pushed my loose hair over my ear. The sun flooded Stefan's face, turning his eyes to caramel, touching the tiny bristles of his beard. He looked stricken and beautiful. I nodded at the bag on the floor. "Did you find lunch?"

He stepped toward me and laid his hand along my cheek. "I don't remember," he said.

6.

"So, then, Mademoiselle. You enjoy this sort of activity," said Stefan.

"Shouldn't I?"

We were sitting together on a chair on the balcony, perfectly still. I was on Stefan's lap, wrapped in a single white sheet and glowing like a forge. The sea glittered before us, crossed by lazy boats. I smelled the lemon and the eucalyptus and thought, I will always remember this, the scent of lemon will always remind me of this moment.

"Not every woman does," he said, and then added hastily, "or so I am told."

"Well, I do. I enjoy it very much indeed."

He kissed my hair. "For this, I am most profoundly glad."

"But you know," I said, after a moment, "I think I like this even more. The afterward."

"This?"

"Yes. Sitting together like this, still humming. Close your eyes." I passed my hand over his eyelids. "Do you feel it?"

"Hmm. Yes. I see what you mean."

"It's as if I'm inside your skin, and you're inside mine at the same time. Like we can say things to each other, without speaking."

"And what am I saying to you now, *Liebling*?"

I listened carefully to his heartbeat. "That you have fallen in love with me. That you love the way my skin smells, and the way my belly feels under your hand."

"Ah, very good. But you didn't mention the rest. How I love your hair and your soft, round breasts and your enormous brown eyes, and your crooked toes and your legs, and the hollows of your arms, and your wide American mouth, and the way you look at me when I am inside you."

"How do I look at you?"

"As if I could do anything. As if I am invincible."

"But you are. You *are* invincible." I stretched out my leg and wiggled the foot. "Are my toes really crooked?"

"Yes, they are beautifully crooked. I want to kiss every one of them."

I laughed. "You see what I mean? This is the best part of all."

"No, love. You are the best part of all. Because this has never been the best part for me, until you were in it."

"Why? What did you do before?"

He yawned. "Left, if I could. Now don't talk anymore. Close your eyes and listen to my heart instead."

I closed my eyes and counted the beats of his heart. When I reached infinity, the faint drone of an engine interrupted the quiet. I lifted my head and saw a motorboat breaking away from the harbor traffic, in a straight line toward us. "Someone's coming," I said.

Stefan opened his eyes and lifted his head from the chair. "Ah. I believe that will be my coxswain, bringing your cello."

"What cello?"

"The cello I found for you this past week, from a very reputable dealer in Monte Carlo who assures me it is an Amati. I am hoping you will try it out and tell me I have not been taken for a fool."

7.

I played for nearly an hour, while the tears swam from my eyes: The first Bach cello suite, which I knew from memory, restless and hopeful, each note emerging from inside the miraculous wood like the revelation of a mystery. And then Chopin, because there are certain things that only Chopin knows how to say.

When at last I laid the beautiful curves back in their case and wiped the strings clean, I kissed Stefan on the lips and told him he was not a fool.

8.

Later that afternoon, we climbed back down the cliff to walk on the stone beach. Stefan held my hand as we scrambled over a stand of slippery rocks, exposed by the tide. "About our villa," I said. "Can it be by the sea?"

"Wherever you like."

"I want it to be just like this. I want to look out in the morning and see the water, and think about the Romans and the Etruscans crossing the harbors, and Hannibal with his elephants, and Dido waiting for Aeneas. And Napoleon's ships sneaking across to Alexandria, and Nelson coming after him."

Stefan's eyes narrowed into the sun. His skin was darker now, a smooth golden tan, as if he'd spent the past week entirely outdoors. Doing what? I wondered. He said, "I love that, too. How ancient it is. How we are all mere specks in time, perched on the shore, watching each other pass in turn."

He was holding the last end of a cigarette in his other hand. I pried it loose and tossed it on the rocks and put my arms around his neck. I kissed him and he kissed me back until we fell on the rocks together, laughing, and he put my hands away. "No, we must stop," he said. "It's too soon. I am not such a brute as that. It is tempting fate, making love so much."

"I can't stop. I have to touch you, to remind myself that it's real."

He held me against him while the sun grew heavy across the water. A seagull cried furiously nearby, the only movement in the world, except for the quiet beat of Stefan's heart against my back. I loved his smell, his warm arms secure around me. I thought I had nothing to fear now.

"Yes," he said at last. "I know what you mean."

9.

After a dinner of cold chicken and bread and cheese, I played the Boccherini in B-flat major, one of my favorites, in the lemon-scented courtyard, until the sky was black and full of stars, and Stefan drew the cello from my hands. His face was so tender it hurt my throat. "Time for sleep, Annabelle. You have had a long day, haven't you?" he said, and I told him I wasn't ready to sleep yet, and he carried me to bed anyway, where we made love for the third time. Stefan thought we shouldn't, not just because of tempting fate but because he was afraid of hurting me. I said it hurt only a little, just at the beginning, and I didn't mind that because of what came after.

He was worried and careful and thoroughly aroused. I loved that: how I could make him want me, against his own premonitions, even against his own conscience. I loved the skillful way he moved inside me, the way he turned me on my stomach and asked how I liked this, if it gave me more pleasure or less, more relief or less from the tender abrasion. I never imagined you could mate like that, like beasts, feverish and deep, and I cried out that yes, yes, I liked it very much.

When we finished, there was nothing left on the bed but the

two of us, panting softly against each other. *I have been very selfish today, Mademoiselle,* Stefan whispered, and I wanted to tell him that it was the opposite, that he had given me everything, but I was too tired even to move my lips.

10.

The strangest part, stranger even than having made love to begin with, was sleeping next to him. He was hot and large by my side, his arm heavy over my ribs. I didn't know if he was sleeping or keeping watch. I kept waking up, though I was exhausted, just to make sure he was still there, that he hadn't left, that his smell—smoke and after-dinner cognac and a kind of warm, sweet sweatiness—still surrounded me.

Once, it didn't. I sat up and saw his shadow against the bedroom window. I called his name and he came back to the bed, and I told him I was afraid he'd gone away.

No, he said, never that.

Then what were you doing? I asked.

I have been thinking about the two of us, that's all. Now go to sleep.

Only if you sleep too.

I will, *Liebling.* I will now.

11.

I first heard about Peggy Guggenheim from one of the other girls at Saint Cecilia's. Until then, I hadn't quite understood what my father had done that was so awful. I thought my mother was to blame somehow, that she had been hard and unforgiving over some simple human crime, and she should have been kinder to him.

But one night, while we were saying our prayers, Camille Montmorency had leaned over to me and whispered that *Peggy Guggenheim a sucé la bite de ton père*. I was only thirteen, and I had never heard of such a thing, either in English or in French (in which, like most things, the concept was rendered more elegantly). I denied it fiercely, of course, but the seed was planted. So that summer, at the Villa Vanilla, I asked my brother about it. He had looked at me speculatively and said he guessed I was old enough to know by now. He explained what had happened, how mother had returned home early with a headache from some party, and found the two of them locked in what the French (again, more elegantly) call *le soixante-neuf*, right there in the ancient marital bed of the de Créouvilles. Upon investigation, it seemed they had been carrying on an affair for some time, and in fact Papa had been carrying on such affairs with multiple women over a great deal of time, and did not see why he should desist from such innocent pleasures, simply because his so-Puritan wife disapproved of them.

From that instant, my sympathies had switched sides. I couldn't hate my Papa, of course, who was always kind in those few moments he could spare for me. But this Peggy Guggenheim. How I hated her. I read about her in the newspapers, and the more I read the more I hated her. She would sleep with anybody, she had no morals at all. No man was safe from her talons.

For a long time, I lived in despair. I thought there was no escape from being either a Peggy Guggenheim or a victim of such women, unless you didn't marry at all, unless you never allowed yourself to fall in love. Like most adolescent obsessions, this had faded over time, but I'd never quite lost the dread entirely. It had hovered like a ghost in the back of my heart, sometimes howling and rattling its chains, and sometimes quiet. On the first night I slept in Stefan's bed, an image woke me with a jolt in the hour before dawn: Stefan standing half dressed before a window, like a man I had glimpsed once at the Villa Vanilla, holding the head of a glossy-haired woman who knelt between his legs.

"What's the matter?" said Stefan, waking, too.

The dream was so vivid, I thought it had actually occurred. My heart was pounding; my stomach felt as if it had been turned the wrong way. "How do I know you're not going to sleep with Peggy Guggenheim?" I demanded.

Stefan was still half asleep, and understandably confused. He propped himself up on his elbows. "Peggy Guggenheim? Why the devil would I want to sleep with her? She is as old as my mother."

"With anyone. How do I know you're not going to sleep with someone else?"

He stared at me with his morning eyes. His hair spilled recklessly into his forehead. He was not ignorant; he must have known the scandal of my parents' marriage. "You don't," he said gently.

Stefan's face looked exactly as it had in my dream, except his eyes were open now, instead of closed in rapture. I rolled over into the pillow, away from him, and he laid his palm on the small of my back.

"You don't know that, Annabelle. You simply have to trust me."

"How do I trust you?" I whispered.

"Do you want me to make a promise to you? I will, if you want, but everyone can make a promise."

"No. I don't want you to promise me."

His hand was warm and still on my back. "So I will tell you this, Annabelle. I am not one of your Christian saints, but I am a fair man. It seems to me that since I am the first man you have ever had in your bed, it is only justice that you are the last woman I will have in mine."

I stared at the dark wall and reflected.

"I don't know. That sounds an awful lot like a promise."

"No, it is not. A promise is like the law, it can be broken. Not without consequence, but it can be broken. This is more like your American constitution. It is the terms by which I have allowed myself to form this union with you."

I turned over and found his face close to mine, too close and too shadowed to make him out. "But why? Why me?"

He shrugged. "Because you are Annabelle. I can either be the man who deserves the love of Annabelle de Créouville, for whose happiness this fidelity is essential, or I will have to do without her. And since it seems I cannot do without you . . . well . . ." He shrugged again. "So there it is."

"Well," I said, when I could speak, "you seem to have given this some thought."

"Yes. Now stop looking at me in this manner, or I will be forced to make love to you again, and you will not be able to walk."

I slid my arms around his neck. "But why would I need to walk anywhere?"

12.

We stayed at the little villa by the sea for three days and four nights. The skies were blue and hot, the evenings full of stars. We didn't see another soul, except when we went into town for food, and we shed our modesty and our clothes in the luminous August air and bound ourselves together, sometimes only talking and sometimes making love, sometimes silent and sometimes clamorous, sometimes slow and gentle and sometimes feverish, sometimes in bed and sometimes on the balcony or in the courtyard or the bath.

And once—because after all we were young, and this was the ancient sun-drenched coast of Europe—on the beach after dark, in the company of a bottle of ice-cold champagne and a thick blanket to soften the ground.

The sun had been exceptionally hot that day, and by evening the temperature in the house was almost unbearable. After a late dinner, we had swum in the sea to cool off and dragged ourselves onto the blanket, still dripping. The moon hadn't risen yet, and I could hardly see Stefan's body against mine. His skin tasted like salt. He lifted himself on his elbows and eased slowly inside me, and as he did, he said something in German, under his breath.

"What does that mean?"

"Nothing, love."

I wrapped my legs around him and said that wasn't fair, we couldn't keep our thoughts from each other after all we had done.

He went still inside me. The rocks rubbed my back through the blanket. Stefan touched my hair with his fingers and moved again, a slow rhythm. "I will tell you if it comes true, Annabelle, but not before."

"A wish?"

"Yes, Annabelle. Now let us put you on top of me instead, so we do not injure your beautiful back on these damned rocks."

He rolled over and positioned me above him. I came first, in a cry that ricocheted gently from the cliffs, until Stefan gripped my hips and followed me. Afterward, we slept on the beach until the air began to cool, and Stefan carried me up the path to the house, and into a bed that had never felt so soft.

13.

On the morning of the fourth day, I woke to find Stefan already awake and dressed, smoking on the balcony while the sun crept up from behind Italy.

"You're up early," I said.

"Yes." He nodded to the harbor. "The ship is ready, as you see."

I lifted my hand to my brow. I couldn't see anything; the glare of the rising sun found my eyeballs at a crucifying angle. "What a pity. Can't we stay a little longer?"

"No, my love. We cannot. We have already ignored the world too long."

His voice was stern and melancholy. I came around in front of him and knelt between his outstretched legs. The new pink sunshine coated his face. I laid my hands on his thighs and said, "So do we leave for Paris now? Or do we search for our villa with the olive groves and the vineyards?"

He took the cigarette from his mouth and stubbed it out in the ashtray on the floor. "Ah, yes. This path we will travel together."

"Yes. Our path. Or have you changed your mind?"

I was naked between his legs, and the breeze touched my skin, cool with the early sea. Stefan's eyes were wholly absorbed in me. He touched the tiny bumps on my arms. "I have not changed my mind, Annabelle. You know that. But listen to me. This thing you want, this path, it is a complication for me. It is a path I did not imagine until now, and there are some family affairs I must arrange. On my own, love, back home in Germany. Do you understand?"

"Of course."

He leaned forward, until his face was inches away from mine. "No, don't look at me like that. I am *happy* to do this. I am so happy, I will make these arrangements of mine with the utmost haste, so I can return to you, and we can plant our olives and our vineyards before the winter sets in. But in the meantime, you must stay here a little longer, Annabelle, just until I can arrange for—"

"Stay here without you?"

"Yes." He hesitated. "Just for a short while. Just until I can return to you."

"But I can't stay here, all alone. I'll have to go to Paris, to my father—"

"No! No, not to your father. Listen to me. This is why I have been thinking, on my ship last week and late at night when you are asleep. I have an idea. Do this for me, Annabelle. You know that right near your father's villa is the Hôtel du Cap."

"Of course I know it."

"If I take a room there for you, if I leave you some money, can you stay there quietly until I can return for you?"

His hands were curled around my arms, and his eyes had lost their smoke and grown sharp and intent, like a general planning a campaign. I hardly recognized him. I said, a little bewildered, "But how long will that be?"

He hesitated. "I don't know. As soon as I can, is that fair? And I will write to you faithfully, whenever possible, though you must not try to reply. We will find you a quiet room, and in a week or two when the summer is over this circus will be tranquil, the crowds will have left. Say you will do it, Annabelle, you will wait there for me."

Wait for Stefan, while he went off without me. To Germany, to his friends and old mistresses, the life he had without me. I felt the old panic rise up in my chest.

"But—I don't know, I haven't thought —what will my brother say?" I said helplessly.

"Don't tell him. God, don't tell him about us, not until I return and I can come to him properly. Can you promise me?" He took my face in his hands and kissed me so passionately, I couldn't breathe. "Promise me. You will wait quietly, you will tell no one about us. I must make things safe for you first, Annabelle, safe for us both, and then we will have no more secrets from the world. We will be together before God and man."

I wanted to protest. But how could you say *no* to words like that? When you are so young, and he is so urgent. When the blood thrills down your fresh new limbs at the idea of waiting in a room at the Hôtel du Cap, overlooking the autumn sea, for your lover to return to your arms.

I was so young, and we had just made love. My heart was turned over, my body remade. In three days and four nights, I had come to think that everything was possible, that you could live by love alone. I had come to think that my mother had made a terrible mistake, that she had chosen a title over love, decadence over purity, but I in my extravagant wisdom had chosen so much better than she had. I had chosen Stefan, and things would be different for me.

So I kissed him and said *Yes, yes,* and he helped me dress, and I helped him pack up the house. We climbed back down the cliff to where his motorboat bobbed by the little jetty, waiting to whisk us away to paradise. To the Hôtel du Cap.

14.

We drove without speaking around the curves of the Antibes road, straight to the hotel, where Stefan with careless arrogance arranged a room under the name of Mr. and Mrs. Silverman. The clerk didn't raise a single eyebrow. My cheeks were bright with shame. I scribbled out a note and addressed the envelope to my father in Paris. Stefan tipped the clerk generously.

"There, you see?" he said, tossing his hat on the chair, when we had arrived in the room and dispatched the bellhop, who had led us to our room and pretended to carry our nonexistent luggage, with a ten-franc note. "Nothing could be easier."

I turned around in a slow circle. "You said something about a discreet room?"

"This? This is nothing. Besides, if we had asked for a cheap room, the clerk would have thought it suspicious."

I glanced down at my dusty and rumpled skirt, my bare legs. "I'm not exactly dressed like a lady, am I?"

Stefan lit a cigarette. "You are perfect. A perfectly respectable woman who has been out walking all morning. If you were a prostitute, you would be wearing stockings and a silk dress."

"And how would you know that?"

He smiled and shrugged. "Common knowledge."

I came to stand against the French door to the balcony, as far away as I could from the open entryway to the bedroom. The walls and furniture were dressed abundantly in blue toile. Our house by the sea was so simple, I had almost forgotten what decoration was like. My cheeks were still pink; I felt the heat simmering just under my skin. Across the room, Stefan leaned against a too-delicate chair and watched me.

"So, my *Liebling*," he said. "Why don't you take a nice bath, and I will order us a room-service lunch to make up for all the humble meals I offered you in Monte Carlo."

"I loved those meals. I loved eating them with you."

"This is very kind. But there is something to be said for fine cuisine, too, don't you think?"

"Very well," I said. "But no mushrooms."

He smiled and picked up the curving receiver of the telephone. "No mushrooms."

15.

When I emerged from the bath, a table had materialized in the middle of the room, covered with white linen and silver domes. Stefan stood by the open French door, smoking and watching the sea crash into the cliffs beyond. He had poured himself a drink, which sat half empty on the console near his elbow, next to an ashtray already half full of stubs. His hands were crammed in his pockets. Without looking at me, he removed the cigarette from his mouth and asked me how I enjoyed my bath. I said very much, and it was true. The miracle of water.

"Good." He placed his fist on the doorframe, and his knuckles were white. He asked me how I was feeling.

I thought, I love you.

He turned his head. His eyebrows were worried. "Annabelle?"

"I'm feeling famished, Stefan, after that thing you did to me this morning, when we were supposed to be packing."

Stefan picked up his drink and finished it off. He looked into the glass, as if he could somehow conjure more. "Are you, now?" he said.

"*Famished.*"

"Then I suppose it is fortunate I ordered such an immense quantity of food."

Under the silver domes, there was roasted chicken and delicate new potatoes, haricots verts and a fragrant red Burgundy. We ate without saying much. Afterward we had chocolates and coffee, and Stefan sat back in his chair and smoked a cigarette while I tucked my feet up under the robe and sipped from a delicate demitasse cup. The coffee was hot and strong and expensive. "When do you leave?" I asked.

"I ought to have left already."

"But that would hardly have been polite."

"No." He let out a paper-thin stream of smoke and smiled vaguely at me. He had taken off his jacket and his tie; the day was growing warm, and even the sea breeze from the balcony couldn't budge the heat from the noontime sun, which streamed directly through the south-facing window. I spotted a bowl of gardenias sitting on the console next to the doors, the source of the perfume.

"I'm going to miss you," I said.

"Yes." He stubbed out the cigarette and rose. I watched him walk to the balcony doors and open them to the widest possible extent. The breeze moved his white shirt. I set down my cup and went to him.

"What's wrong?" I whispered, touching his back.

He raised his arm and pointed. "Look. You can see Sainte-Marguerite from here. There is the fort where I kissed you."

"Stefan, for God's sake. Tell me."

He sighed deeply. "You are ruthless, Mademoiselle. You are like the damned bloodhound on the scent sometimes."

"Yes, when I have to."

His hand, which was braced on the doorframe, dropped away and slipped into his pocket. "I have been pondering my own selfishness, I suppose."

"You weren't being selfish. I was. I threw myself at you, I wanted whatever you had to give me."

"No, I mean my whole life. I have been very thoughtless, without even realizing it. I have simply taken pleasure and tried, on occasion, to return it. And now there is you, Mademoiselle."

"A complication."

"Yes, a complication. But something else. I have been trying to think of the English word. A reckoning? I am forced to consider my own sins, for the first time in my life, and it is a sober task."

"I don't know why making love to me should make you consider your sins."

He touched my cheek. "Because you are an innocent, Annabelle, and for all my crimes I had never yet corrupted the innocent."

"You didn't corrupt me. That was the opposite of corruption. Those were the most beautiful days of my life."

Stefan let out a sigh and turned away to light another cigarette. "Can there be any more proof than *that*?" he murmured, and he walked through the French doors to the balcony and leaned his elbows on the railing. I followed him. He plied the cigarette between his fingers and said quietly, "I have had the feeling, since we drove away from the house, that I was leaving behind my own happiness. That when I made love to you there this morning, it was the last time I ever would."

The sun lit the curling tips of Stefan's hair. I laid my elbow on the railing and faced his gaunt profile. "Oh, so is that what's brought on all this moping? A premonition?"

He turned. "You are a silly blithe American gentile, Annabelle de Créouville, with no respect at all for the perversity of the universe."

"Because the universe is not perverse. The universe is beautiful. Look at us here, the two of us, finding each other among billions."

"Yes," he said, "that's what is so perverse."

"I don't understand."

He smoked quietly for a moment, staring into the trees below us. "Do you want to know how I imagined my life ten years ago, Annabelle? This is how my life was supposed to go. I go to university, I join my father's firm, I manage our businesses without, I hope, disgracing myself. I enlarge the family fortune. I find a nice lovely Jewish girl, as a good Jewish son is supposed to do, and we settle down together and grow old and everybody is happy, me and my family and my nice Jewish wife, and whatever else God chooses to bless us with."

"And now there is me," I whispered.

"Now there is you."

"I don't want to upset your family."

He looked up. "My family, Annabelle? My *family?*"

"Because I'm not a Jew."

Without warning, Stefan whirled around and slammed his fist against the paved wall behind us. I heard the sick sound of his flesh connecting with the pale stone. He said, into the wall, "No, Annabelle. You are not a Jew."

From the gravel path below came the sound of female laughter, as bright and unexpected as sleigh bells in the hot afternoon. A hundred yards away, the Mediterranean glittered and heaved, speckled with shipping, yachts and fishing boats and ferries and tenders, all of them absorbing the last hours of summer in perfect contentment and lazily unaware of the perverse universe contained atop this small hotel balcony. I picked up Stefan's hand and kissed the torn and bleeding knuckles, one by one. I said, "Stay with me here, then. Stay a few days, away from everything else, your family and obligations and these stupid rules we're supposed to follow."

"I have already done that, as long as I could. I cannot just pretend it isn't there, Annabelle. I cannot just hide with you forever. I have to find some way for us to live."

"It doesn't matter how we live, as long as we're together."

He shook his head. "You are so *young*, Annabelle. What am I going to do with you?

"You're going to come inside and take me to bed. You're going to let me show you how wonderful the universe can be."

Stefan studied my mouth. His face remained still, while his eyes filled with smoke. The laughter grew louder and then ended abruptly, as a door closed below us. He took his hand from mine, folded his arms, and looked at me gravely. "You do not understand a word I have said, Mademoiselle. Nothing could be worse than such audacity. The universe would then be ten times against us."

I untied the sash of my robe, right there on the open balcony while the woman laughed below us, and it occurred to me that we had done this before: me parting a dressing gown, Stefan gazing at me with astonished rapacity, as I prepared to commit an act of unexpected daring.

"On the other hand, the universe might just be forced to surrender and join us," I said, and I opened up the robe.

16.

You see? You were wrong, after all. No thunderbolts from above. We survived.

Speak for yourself, Mademoiselle.

So you're not worried about the universe anymore?

Liebling, if you think I am capable of any rational thought at this moment, then I fear you have still much more to learn about this business of making love.

(I laid my head against his bare shoulder.)

You know, I'm not asking you to leave your family. I would never do that.

Of course you would not, Mademoiselle. Which is why these delicate matters are left to me.

17.

I wanted to go walking that afternoon, but Stefan insisted we stay in our room. He would leave in the morning, he said, and he didn't want to share me with another living creature. He didn't want to have to nod and smile at other guests when he could be filling his eyes with me.

I slipped from his arms and took out my beautiful new cello from its case. I tuned each string and played the entirety of the first Bach cello suite in G major—prelude, allemande, courante—while Stefan lay on his back in the bed behind me and smoked in silence. When I finished, he asked me to play something else, and I did. For an hour I played for him, until he got up to pour himself another drink and came up behind me to kiss my neck. I put down my bow in mid-measure. No, he said. Don't stop. I want you to play everything you have ever played for me, one more time.

That will take a while, I said.

We have all night.

18.

The afternoon fled, and I had to stop before my fingers bled. Stefan made me put on a dressing gown and ordered dinner. What about the restaurant? I asked, and he said no, we would have dinner here on the balcony, just the two of us, while the sun sank and the pungent Mediterranean colors faded to indigo.

When the table was cleared away, I told Stefan we had to go outside now, because the rooms were so full of smoke that I couldn't breathe. All right, he said, I suppose it's dark enough.

We walked along the gardens and cliffs without saying much. The air was cooler now and gentle and smelled of newly caught fish. I took the breeze deep into my lungs. Stefan held my hand. When we came to the Eden-Roc, he led me down the stairs to the little stone beach and put his arms around me as we looked out to sea.

"What do you think of Capri?" he said.

"I don't know. I've never been there."

"It is beautiful. We will have the sea and our privacy. We can raise our olives and our children. I will have my agent look into some villas there."

A wave washed up, higher than the rest, and wet my toes.

"What about the wine?" I whispered.

"I am not certain if the soil is suitable for vineyards. I will investigate this for us. But if we cannot make wine?"

I covered his hands with mine, around my waist.

"Then I suppose we'll have to be content with what we have."

19.

We returned to our room smelling of the sea. The smoke had left through the open windows and the balcony doors, and I made Stefan promise not to light any more cigarettes. We undressed and got into bed, me on the left and Stefan on the right, the way we had arranged it from the first night. Let's just sleep, Stefan said, facing me in the darkness. I want to see if I can resist you.

You can't resist me, I said, and I was right. You will wake up tomorrow and you won't be able to walk, Stefan said sadly afterward, cradling me against him, and I told him I was at the Hôtel du Cap, I didn't need to lift a finger if I didn't want to. The windows were all open, and the room was cool and new. We lay quietly entangled, inhaling the gardenias, inhaling the salty marine scent of each other, and I thought, This is the last time, I will wake up tomorrow and he'll be gone. And I won't be able to walk.

20.

Once, during the night, I sat up and saw Stefan's shadow against the bedroom window. I called his name and he came back to the bed, and I told him I was afraid he'd gone already.

"No," he said, "not yet. In a few hours, before the sun comes up. Go back to sleep, Annabelle, *Liebling*."

"What were you doing?"

He took me back against his chest, in the way we had been lying before. "I put some money in the desk drawer for you. There is also the name of my banker in Paris, who will help you if you need anything else while I am gone."

"What else would I need? You won't be gone that long, will you?"

"I mean in case there is an emergency, or you perhaps need to tell me something."

In my innocence, I couldn't imagine what I would need to tell him, other than everything. I lay there quietly, matching my breathing to his, paying attention to each respiration so I would remember them all.

Stefan said, "Also, I have been thinking a little, about this constitution that governs our union."

"You wish to add an amendment or two? An escape clause?"

"No. I have been thinking that perhaps *constitution* is the wrong word. It is maybe more like a covenant."

"Stefan," I said in French, "I think I'm falling in love with you."

He lifted my hair and kissed me in the tender sliver of skin above my ear. "*Oui, Mademoiselle de Créouville. C'est la même chose avec moi.*"

21.

When I woke up, the sun was just rising, and Stefan was gone.

I rolled onto my stomach and went back to sleep, with his pillow pressed across my breast.

PEPPER

Cocoa Beach • 1966

1.

The shower in Annabelle Dommerich's guest cottage runs hot as blazes, the way Pepper likes it. She closes her eyes while the water burns down her back, turning her skin red, raising blisters almost. Like a disinfectant.

The baby stirs. Pepper looks down at her belly, the curious round ball of it, and pushes her finger against a protruding wet lump. The lump shifts and pushes back, and Pepper, transfixed, says the only thing that comes to mind.

Hello.

How crazy, being pregnant. You said to yourself casually, "I'm pregnant," like you might say you were bored or sunburned, and in the beginning that's what it was, a theoretical condition, manifest in inconvenient little symptoms that had no obvious link to the biological reality, the peculiar fact that a new and separate human being was growing inside the center of you. You didn't notice the human being until much later, and you still couldn't quite picture it in your head, a baby. A real one. A tiny fat red little person.

I'm sorry about all this, Pepper adds. (Not aloud, for God's sake.)

But that's the trouble. Sorry isn't enough, is it? You could never be sorry enough.

2.

Because she hadn't set out to sleep with another woman's husband, had she? She had her scruples, believe it or not. Everyone always said, *It's Pepper Schuyler, lock up your husbands,* but it wasn't true. This was the first husband she'd ever slept with.

She'd taken the job after Vivian got married, because a girl had to do something with her life; she couldn't just sit around waiting for her own Dr. Charming to show up, and anyway Pepper wasn't really interested in marrying Dr. Charming. Too much fun to be had, too many adventures to record in the precious few years of excitement your youth and beauty—they did run together, youth and beauty, didn't they?—allowed you. New York was getting old, and she looked down the New Jersey Turnpike toward Washington and said *I'll have that.* Of course, Dad wouldn't even consider law school—*I've wasted enough money educating daughters*—so she made a few phone calls, called in a few favors, and what do you know, the new junior senator from New York needed a Girl Friday.

So that part was all on the up and up. Pepper needed a job in Washington, Pepper found the best job going for a sparky young woman with an English degree, grades not to be ashamed of, manner polished, face and figure top-drawer. She never imagined she would fall in love.

She's always scorned that phrase, *falling in love*. It implies a certain lack of conviction, a lily-livered helplessness that Pepper despises. How could you just *fall* in love? You stepped into love willingly, didn't you, and if it wasn't convenient, you found someone else to step into: *Voilà*. So maybe that was why it happened. Her guard was down. The hours were long, the quarters close, the job intense, the man himself so . . . well. Let's pick an example. One night, working late, everyone else gone, the old story. He offered her a ride home. She accepted. The convertible, the warm breeze, the Lincoln Memorial passing in a noble floodlit blur. They got to talking. His thick hair rustled, his eyes gleamed. She thought, alive and sleepy at the same time, What would it be like to kiss him? And then he did. Kiss her. Pulled over on the deserted street next to the Potomac and kissed her, and he tasted of the bottle of Scotch they'd been sharing, and cigarettes, and warm human mouth. She had wrapped her hand around the nape of his neck and kissed him back, an act of instinct, because at two o'clock in the morning after a long day's Washington work you clean forgot about a wife you'd never met, tending a litter of unknown children. He pulled away, looking adorably confused. *I'm sorry, I didn't mean that. The Scotch, I guess.* And Pepper patted her hair and agreed that it must have been the Scotch, and they didn't say another word, and that was when it started. That was when she fell in love with him, tumbled right off the branch and never hit bottom, and maybe she should have quit there. Yes, that was her mistake, that she didn't quit right there. Because once she started falling, the sex was inevitable, one way or another. Yes, she had gone home and scrubbed herself all over, thought,

What have I done? And then, I will never, ever do that again. But when a man liked sex as much as he did, and a woman was as beautiful and besotted as Pepper, they had better get the hell away from each other, or one day at least one of them will have too much to drink, will be working too hard and feeling sorry for herself and let her guard down. One day they will end up drunk in a hotel bed somewhere, making love three times in one night, and at least one of them will come to repent it.

And that's exactly what happened.

3.

So there it is, the ticking face of her gold Cartier watch, and it says *Eleven o'clock, you lazy bitch,* and it can't be wrong, can it? Pepper pushes open the French door to the main house and calls out *Hello?* like a question, because the only two sounds are the fountain tinkling in the courtyard and the relentless songbirds in the lemon trees, who seem to have taken a wrong turn looking for Sleeping Beauty.

In the dining room, calls out Annabelle.

Pepper might well ask *Where's the dining room?* but instead she follows her nose to the coffee and the bacon, and her nose—another valuable Schuyler inheritance—doesn't lead her astray. The dining room has high ceilings and a pair of French doors open to the sunshine and the songbirds, and, more important, a heavy wooden sideboard loaded with breakfast in chafing dishes. Annabelle sets down her newspaper and waves to the chair opposite, which is set with cutlery and an empty coffee cup. The pot stands to the right.

"Good morning," says Annabelle. "Please help yourself."

Pepper is already snatching a plate and sinking a silver serving spoon into an impossibly creamy batch of scrambled eggs. Bacon. Link sausage. Porridge (ignored). Pitchers of orange and tomato juice. Pepper picks the tomato, even though she's in Florida. "Clara will bring your toast," says Annabelle.

Pepper sits and pours the coffee. "Thank you."

"You're welcome. Feeling better?"

"Divine. Do you always have a spread like this at breakfast?"

Annabelle laughs. "Poor Clara. I told her I had a guest, and she's so used to a houseful, she doesn't know how to do it differently. Luckily, I'm a good eater."

"How many is a houseful?"

"Oh, my goodness. Including the older ones and their spouses and kids?" Annabelle ticks on her fingers, frowns, and ticks again.

"You're a grandmother?"

"Oh, yes. Several times over."

The coffee is hot and dark as oil. Pepper adds a pinch of sugar but no cream. "You don't look it."

"I was a young bride."

"Where are all these teeming hordes now?"

"My youngest are in college. The older ones settled in New York, the Washington suburbs. But everyone meets here at Christmas and in the spring. The din is atrocious."

"You make it sound so alluring."

Annabelle folds up her newspaper and finishes her coffee. Pepper gazes at the slim blue pack of cigarettes resting at her one o'clock position, next to the saucer, a blue-and-white pattern: Wedgwood, maybe. As a young debutante, Pepper never paid much attention to china; that was her older sister Tiny's expertise.

Tiny's one of those girls who picked out her wedding pattern when she was eight years old.

Annabelle stands up and hands her the newspaper across the table. Her eyes are as warm and sympathetic as chocolate. "You might want to take a look at the headlines," she says. "Something about one of your sisters."

4.

Pepper considers calling her mother first. She taps her fingernails against the telephone receiver, *click click click,* and stares out the mullioned window to the deserted beach across the road.

Mums doesn't know about the baby. That's why Pepper buried herself at Tiny's house in Cape Cod at the beginning of summer, because she couldn't face Mums and Daddy. She couldn't even face Vivian. Strange that she should go running to Tiny in her time of trouble, to perfect Tiny, who never set a well-turned toe in the wrong place. Maybe she knew all along that Tiny had a juicy little secret of her own. Maybe she sensed the unhappiness churning behind Tiny's immaculate shell, as opposed to the happiness that beams right out of Vivian's eye sockets these days. Maybe she knew Tiny would prove a better companion in misery, during the slow, hot summer in Cape Cod.

Or maybe Annabelle was right. Maybe she was just trying to punish herself.

When Pepper was thirteen or fourteen, out in East Hampton for the summer, she wore her first bikini. She'd bought it in town with her careful hoard of spending money, and the following day, a Wednesday, she made her debut on the beach atop a colorful beach blanket, stretching her golden limbs toward the sun. No umbrella. A pair of older boys had wandered over within five minutes, the neighbor boys, sixteen and eighteen. *If it isn't little Pepper, all grown up,* the eighteen-year-old said, toeing a friendly sprinkle of sand onto her bare abdomen. They had played a little volleyball, they had splashed in the surf. Billy (the older one) had put his hands around her naked waist and tossed her into a wave or two. Later, when she walked away to change, he had followed her and kissed her behind the weathered gray boards of the bathhouse, and while he was kissing her he slipped his hand inside the wet triangle covering her right breast and rubbed her nipple. *I have to go now,* she said, breaking away, and she had run up the steps and into the house before he could catch her—she could sprint, Pepper, when she had to—and there was Mums on the back porch, reading a newspaper, drinking something clear with a slice of lime and plenty of ice. Pepper never forgot the look on her mother's face when she burst up the final step, panting, a little blurry. The sad shake of her head. *You're like me, aren't you?* she said. *You just can't help yourself.* And Pepper said, *Don't be a square, we were just having fun,* and Mums said, *Sure, fun for him,* and Pepper said, *You don't understand anything,* just exactly like every teenager since the beginning of time.

Mums hadn't gotten mad. Mums kept her cool. She just laughed and finished her drink and said, *Well, for God's sake, whatever you do, don't let them get you pregnant.* Those exact words. Pepper recalls them like yesterday's breakfast.

Click click click.

Pepper lifts the receiver and dials up her sister Vivian in Gramercy Park.

"PEPPER! MY GOD! WHERE ARE YOU?"

"I'm in Florida, love, keeping up my suntan. How's things?"

"MY GOD! HAVEN'T YOU HEARD?"

"What, that Tiny's getting a divorce? Old news."

"YOU KNEW ABOUT IT ALREADY?"

"Of course I knew about it." Pepper examines her fingernails. "I was on the Cape all summer, wasn't I? I had a ringside seat."

"AND YOU DIDN'T SAY ANYTHING?"

"For God's sake, stop shouting like that. It was a private little matter, wasn't it, and anyway, it's not the kind of thing you can talk about over the telephone, in-laws lurking in every corner. Especially when your sister writes the nosiest gossip column in New York."

"It is *not* a gossip column." With dignity. "It's a witty and elegant disquisition of social customs in our magnificent little town. And it's the most-read page in the entire *Metropolitan* magazine."

"I rest my case," says Pepper.

The line goes quiet.

"Vivian?"

"I'm here."

Pepper winds the cord around her fingers. "Have you talked to Tiny about it?"

"No, as a matter of fact. She's nowhere to be found. Mums got a letter from her yesterday. She's not saying what's in it. Poor Mums, she had her heart set on Tiny being First Lady. Now she's stuck with a divorcée and a doctor's wife. Her dreams crumbled in the dust. I guess it's all up to you now, Pepper, sweetheart. Any promising young senators up your sleeve?"

"Actually, I'm pregnant," says Pepper.

Again with the silent receiver.

"Vivian?"

"Say that again, Pepper. I'm not sure I heard you properly."

"I'm pregnant."

"That's what I thought."

"Don't fall all over yourself with congratulations."

Vivian draws in a long breath that crackles against Pepper's ear. "Well, well. My God. Knocked up, the middle child. You're sure?"

Pepper looks down at her stomach. "Pretty sure."

"Does Mums know?"

"Of course not."

"When are you due?"

"February."

"FEBRUARY! But that's—that's—"

"Soon. I know."

"Holy moley. How the hell did you hide it from Tiny?"

"I didn't. She knows. That's why she let me stay on the Cape into the autumn. Fixing up that old car of hers."

Vivian snorts. "Oh, *now* I get it. I should have smelled a rat, Pepper Schuyler rattling around in a greasy old garage for months on end. And I thought there must be a man involved."

"Oh, there was. A delicious one. Regretfully, he wasn't mine. He was Tiny's."

"TINY!"

"Indeedy. The ex-Mrs. Hardcastle. Not so virtuous as one might think."

There is a groan, as of stones being laid atop an already heavy burden. "Stop. You're hurting my ears. I'm going to have to sit down."

"Sit down? You, Vivian?"

"Well, I'm in a delicate condition, too, if you'll recall. By my legitimate husband, I feel compelled to add."

"That's a first."

"No sass from you, young lady. I was respectably married for *several* months before Junior arrived."

"Do you want a medal for that?"

A creak of springs sounds faintly in the distance. Pepper props herself on the edge of the sofa table and waits for Vivian's familiar voice to reappear in her ear. The knot in her belly is beginning to unwind, under the tug of Vivian's familiar banter. Why didn't she call up Vivian before? They were born only eleven disgraceful months apart, after all, and it might as well be none. The snappy, happy Schuyler girls, tearing apart Manhattan and putting it back together again. Two and a half years ago, when Vivian moved into her own apartment after college, a dismal grubby fifth-floor walkup (it's always the fifth floor of a five-floor walkup, isn't it?), they had gone out to six different nightclubs before dawn, had smoked and drank and laughed and kissed all kinds of unsuitable men. And then they had gone back to Vivian's grubby apartment, holding each other up as they mounted the vomit-scented stairs, and collapsed together on Vivian's bed. Not another man in sight, at the end of the night: just two sisters, holding each other up.

"So. How are the hemorrhoids?" Vivian asks.

"Speak for yourself."

"You're feeling good, then?"

"Tip-top. I never tossed a single cookie."

"Ah, the luck of the wicked," says Vivian. "Have you been seeing a doctor?"

"I guess that depends on what you mean by *seeing*."

"Not in the biblical sense."

"Then yes. At reasonably regular intervals. Everything seems to be shipshape." The telephone cord crosses Pepper's belly in elongated squiggles. It's the same dress as last night, the blue tunic that matches her eyes. Pepper watches the fabric move, the cord shift. Baby's restless. "Any more questions?" she adds, though of course there is one last question, the obvious question, the biggie, the question even Vivian is almost too tactful to ask.

"So. Who's the father?" asks Vivian.

"No one you know," says Pepper.

"Not at present, maybe, but I can guarantee he's going to know me shortly." Vivian's tone is that of a cumulonimbus, towering on the horizon.

Pepper's already shaking her head, almost as if her sister can see her. "Down, Vivian."

"If this little man-swine thinks he can get my sister in trouble and walk away scot-free—"

"I don't want to have anything to do with him, do you hear me? Not a single goddamned thing." The words hurt her throat; she actually places her hand against the cords of her neck as she says them. The last word, *thing*, is just a whisper, stripped of conviction. Pepper shuts her eyes and squeezes her throat, squeezes hard, until her windpipe lies flat against the hard muscle. If she can't breathe, she can't speak, can she? She can't tell Vivian about the telephone call and the notes, the messages to the hotel, Captain Seersucker, the men outside who might be tourists and might not.

"That bad, is it?" Vivian says.

"Yeah."

"So come home."

Pepper shakes her head. "Can't."

"Why not?"

"Because I like the weather down here, that's why."

"At least tell me where you are."

Pepper hesitates. "Cocoa Beach."

Vivian sighs again, and for some reason Pepper thinks of her father, who was also there that day when she was fourteen, the day she wore her first bikini and found out what the older kids got up to during the summer, and who looked up from his newspaper when she ran in from the porch, clutching Mums's words to her half-naked bosom. He was sitting in the chair next to the window, and he looked as if he'd swallowed a peach pit. *Had a good time?* he asked, in such a way that Pepper knew he'd seen every little thing from his perch up there above the beach, where he liked to spend his summer days watching the pretty girls go by. She said *Go to hell,* like every other teenager since after the war, while inside her head she thought, *My God, you old drunk, why don't you go out and tell Billy he can't just cop a feel like that, I mean, go out and thrash the sonofabitch for grabbing your fourteen-year-old daughter's tits behind the bathhouse.* Care, for God's sake.

But he hadn't, had he? He hadn't heard what was pounding inside her head. He turned to the ashtray and made busy with the cigarette, and somewhere in the middle of all that stubbing he said, *Put something on, will you, before you start a riot.*

Pepper was on her own, he meant. In these matters, Pepper would have to take care of Pepper.

Vivian speaks carefully into her ear. "You're sure you're all right, honey?"

Oh, Vivian. You with the nice doctor husband and the nice

little cherub, the pretty sun-filled apartment in Gramercy and the glamorous job writing about glamorous people. Vivian, whose pregnant belly is perfectly legitimate, created in mutual love with her nice doctor husband. No more reckless nights out for Vivian, no more commiseration between Vivian and Pepper. How could you commiserate with someone who had no misery to share with you?

"I'm sure," says Pepper, and before either of them can say anything else, she hangs up the receiver in its handsome ivory cradle, and for a long while afterward that rattle is the last sound in the room.

5.

But you can't keep Pepper cooped up indoors all day. Sooner or later she finds her way to the beach across the road, where the weather is mild and the surf gentle. The tide reaches a few feet below the line of seaweed that serves as a high-water mark, and after a quarter-hour of walking, Pepper decides it's on its way out.

The comely young doctor in Chatham said that a long, brisk walk every morning was good for the baby and good for her. So Pepper walks briskly, a mile or so up the beach, and the sun is so warm she sits down on the deserted sand and stretches her toes toward the ocean. No curious eyes on her belly, no men grabbing her arm in a stairwell and telling her they had something important to discuss. No messages. No urgent notes. *Pepper, I don't know what kind of game you're playing, but we have to come to some kind of agreement here. A man in my position . . .*

A man in his position. A man in his position could do whatever the hell he wanted, couldn't he? He could call on any resources he needed to track her down.

Three hundred thousand dollars was supposed to buy her safety. But where could she go that he couldn't find her? Her family, maybe. Her family would protect her, if they had to. The Schuylers might snipe among themselves, but they banded together effectively against outside attack. That was how they'd survived, while other families rose and fell around them: they stuck together. They held the line.

Except that this was no ordinary attack. And *attack* in any case meant casualties, and who knew what kind of casualties might be inflicted on innocent bystanders, as a result of Pepper having accidentally fallen in love and broken a commandment or two?

Pepper sits up. The sand falls away from her hair. She stares at the plumb horizon and thinks, My God, I made love to this man, we shared a hotel bed. We shared drinks and cigarettes and sex, we shared our bodies, the rummage of our souls.

And now this. Wondering whether her family is even safe. Whether her family would be safer if she goes to them, or safer if she does not. A doozy of a decision for Pepper to make, at a time like this.

6.

As Pepper crosses the road and starts along the circular drive toward the house, a pair of dogs lopes out to greet her. Weimaraners. She allows herself to be sniffed and inspected, and apparently she passes muster, because the dogs fall back to her heels and escort her inside like a visiting dignitary.

The rooms are still and sepulchral. Pepper was too distracted to pay much attention earlier—maybe she's still too distracted, but the long walk and the long ocean have settled her nerves just enough to make room for curiosity—and now she recognizes the quiet elegance of the house, the villa-like proportions, the simple furnishings. Annabelle Dommerich has taste. Pepper tosses her hat on the dining room table and wanders into the living room, from which she placed her telephone call to Vivian a few hours ago.

"Annabelle?" she calls out. "Mrs. Dommerich?"

One of the dogs nudges her hand. Dogs are marvelous, aren't they? No matter what your sins, if a dog can stand you, there must be some hope left for your soul. Pepper takes in the square proportions, the blue-and-white décor—Greece, she thinks, or some other lovely spot perched on the Adriatic, washed by a pale, hot sun—and she thinks, I could just about like this place.

The dog nudges her hand again, and Pepper, turning away from a large abstract painting, realizes that no one answered her call. The air is overgrown with silence. She casts a final glance along the four walls, the neat furniture, and as she fondles the dog's ears and prepares to leave, she thinks, That's strange, something's missing from this charming blue-and-white room overlooking the ocean, home in certain seasons to a large and fruitful family. Something no happy home ever lacks, something even the Schuylers display in silvery abundance, crowding every possible surface.

There aren't any photographs.

7.

Pepper crosses the hall, calling Annabelle's name. She sticks her head inside the next room, which seems to be a music room of some kind: there is a handsome ebony piano next to the window, and a straight-backed chair placed before a wooden music stand. A cello case is propped against the wall.

Pepper prepares to withdraw her head, but something on the opposite wall catches her eye. She steps closer and sees a large black-and-white photograph—yes, a photograph at last—depicting a dainty dark-haired woman on a stage somewhere, holding a cello between her knees. Her face is rapturously crinkled, a kind of ecstasy of concentration, and her arms have been caught in the very act of creation. She's wearing a dress that might be any color from black to scarlet, but you didn't really notice the dress, did you? You noticed that rapturous face, those poised and graceful arms, the curving cello between her legs.

Annabelle Dommerich, in the act of ecstatic creation.

Annabelle Dommerich. Wasn't there something familiar about that name, after all?

Pepper begins to breathe again, and that's when she notices that she had, in fact, stopped. Breathing, that is. That her chest had frozen a little, at the sight of that photograph. How old is that black-and-white image? How long ago did Annabelle Dommerich play the cello on a stage like that? Impossible to tell by the dress or even the hairstyle. Annabelle is so perfectly ageless.

So. Annabelle Dommerich's got a history of her own—not an everyday, trials-and-tribulations history, births and deaths and whatever else, but the kind of breathless and brilliant history that gives Vivian her *Metropolitan* magazine fodder. Fame and fortune and forbidden passion. But more than that. A rare black Mercedes, fleeing into the German night and then disappearing into a shed on Cape Cod.

A cello.

Pepper runs her curious finger along the curve of the top of the cello case, which is old and leathery and somewhat battered, not the kind of case you'd expect from a world-class musician. On the other hand, why not? Pepper doesn't do symphonies, at least not since the entire junior class at Nightingale-Bamford went to a matinee at Carnegie Hall, a compulsory exercise. It was the end of autumn, and a famous pianist was performing, but Pepper had spent the first half of the concert in the ladies' room with Edie Brooks-Huntington, whose boyfriend had just jilted her. Edie was a weepy kind of girl, went through a box of tissues at least, so Pepper took her seat only after the intermission, and even then, for the first ten minutes, her brain was occupied with plots for revenge against the Faithless Michael, until at last the music stole over her, note by note, and she realized that the piano was in some mysterious way expressing the exact same emotion. That the piano lamented, too; the piano wanted revenge.

Pepper never returned to Carnegie Hall. But she hadn't forgotten that moment of companionship with the grand piano. When, several years later, she was passing by Daddy's study and heard that same piece of music floating through the doorway, she had actually paused in the hallway outside and pressed her quiet hand against her ribs, until the last note bled away and the needle scratched to the end of the record, and Daddy had risen from his chair, lifted the arm, and changed the record to something else, a violin concerto, never knowing that Pepper stood there in the hallway, hidden by the door, sharing the music with him.

Pepper looks back at the photograph—one single photograph in the whole entire pad, and this would be it—and calls out softly, maybe not even meaning to be heard.

Annabelle?

8.

When she reaches the dining room, the French doors stand open to the courtyard, channeling a tide of ripe lemon and spicy eucalyptus. Pepper opens her throat and breathes it in. "Annabelle?" she calls again.

The dogs start off down the opposite corridor. Pepper follows them. Beautiful, athletic things. Their coats are a healthy silver-taupe, their tails undocked and wagging briskly. The hindquarters disappear around a corner, and for the first time Pepper hears a human voice, fondly scolding the dogs, *Oh, you wicked things, there you are, stay down now.* But it's not Annabelle Dommerich; it's the woman who brought in Pepper's toast and refilled her coffee.

"Oh, hello, Clara," Pepper says. "I don't suppose you know where I might find my hostess?"

Clara says, "I was just coming to find you, Miss Schuyler. Mrs. Dommerich left an hour ago."

"Left? Where to? Errands?"

"Oh, no. Gone off on one of her trips again." Clara offers an apologetic smile and sticks a hand into her apron pocket. She pulls out a sheet of thick ecru writing paper, folded in half. "She told me to tell you she was sorry not to say good-bye in person."

Pepper takes the paper. The dogs have run on ahead, to the kitchen, probably. The note weighs heavily between her fingers, and for some reason she doesn't want to open it here, in front of Clara. Just in case. "Good-bye? That sounds rather dramatic. Did she say when she'd be back?"

"No, ma'am. She usually doesn't. But she did say you're to make yourself right at home while she's gone."

ANNABELLE

Antibes • 1935

After a day or two, I could walk again. I was ready to see the world, the good earth I would shortly inherit with Stefan, or at least that little corner of it occupied by the Hôtel du Cap. My trunks appeared, and a note from Papa: *Enjoy yourself, mignonne, and remember my home is always open to you. Kisses, Papa.* I fingered the paper and thought, What a strange thing for a father to write. But then, what else could I have expected?

In the desk drawer, I found an envelope containing ten thousand francs and a scrap of notepaper bearing a name and a Paris address I didn't recognize. I put them both away. I didn't want to look at them; I didn't want to think about what they represented. I put on my sandals and my hat and slipped down the stairs and along the graveled drive to the Eden-Roc pavilion overlooking the bay.

The hotel beach was small and rocky and not much used—most guests preferred the saltwater pool nestled into the basalt—and I had no company when I stripped away my dress and arched across the gathering waves into the sea. I swam for an hour, until my limbs were limp, until my head was heavy, and then I crawled shivering to the shore and lay there on the stones while the last of the August sun warmed my back.

When Stefan comes back, I thought, we'll lie here together, except the air will be much cooler. We'll put on our robes and curl up together in the shelter of the cliff, and Stefan will bring out a bottle of champagne, and we will laugh about that night on the tiny beach on Sainte-Marguerite, and how we kissed for the first time in the fort while the sun rose over the rooftops.

My skin dried, and then my swimming costume. I stopped shivering. I realized the emptiness in my belly wasn't loneliness but hunger, and I put on my dress and climbed the stairs to the tearoom. I ordered coffee and a small plate of sandwiches. As I waited, I heard a laugh like sleigh bells from the table behind me, and there was something so familiar about the noise and the throat from which it came that I feigned interest in the architecture around me and glanced over my shoulder.

Isn't it funny, the way we know when someone's watching? At the exact instant my eyes found the laughing woman's face, her eyes slid directly to mine, and though she was wearing a beautiful curved hat and an afternoon dress, I recognized her lips and her eyes and the shape of her chin before I turned back to my white tablecloth and my view across the bay, while my breath tripped up in my chest.

Stefan's mistress. She was wearing less kohl, and her lipstick this afternoon was fresh and berry-red, but you couldn't mistake a face like that. The waiter arrived with my coffee and sandwiches, and I drank the coffee without thinking and scalded my tongue.

She hadn't recognized me. Surely she hadn't recognized me.

"I beg your pardon," said a drawling English voice behind

me, "but you're the nurse from the yacht, aren't you? You're Stefan's nurse."

I set down the cup and looked up into her face, which was less beautiful and more riveting than I remembered. She had languorous green eyes: that was the trick. The rest didn't matter, when you had eyes like that, but the rest of her was still marvelous. Her hair was honey-dark and glossy beneath the crown of her hat, and she wore the kind of dress that film stars wore, the kind of dress that actually anticipated what everybody would be wearing next year, without really trying. It was navy blue and absolutely snug around a carved miniature waist, and the color made her berry mouth pop out from that silky tanned face.

I rolled my own unvarnished lips together and nodded. "You have an excellent memory."

"Yes, rather. So do you. You recognized me straightaway, didn't you? How is he?"

"All better."

"Of course he is. He's such a feral thing. Do you mind if I join you?"

"If you like."

She turned her head to the table where she'd been sitting. "Peter, darling. I'm going to be a few minutes. Do run up to the room and fetch my bathing costume, there's a good chap."

Her companion, a middle-aged man in a white jacket, looked us both over and stubbed out his cigarette. "I thought we weren't swimming today," he said petulantly.

"I've changed my mind. Run along, now, and for heaven's sake stop sulking."

Peter rose from the table. He had thinning blond hair and a very slight belly interrupting a frame that was otherwise lean.

"Your servant, ma'am." He sighed, and picked up his hat and left the room.

Stefan's mistress turned back to me and smiled. "He's a good sort of egg, really, but awfully dull. Do you mind if I sit?"

"Please." I gestured.

"My name is Alice. Lady Alice Penhallow." She sat down and held out a slender hand, weighed down with rings.

I hesitated for an instant and then took her hand. Her grip was soft and uninterested. "Annabelle de Créouville."

At that, her eyebrows lifted. "Gracious me. Are you really? We all thought you were just a rumor, the prince's cloistered daughter. Well, that's trumped me, for certain. I don't suppose I stand a chance now."

"Haven't you moved on already?"

"Peter? He's lovely, at least when he's not sulking, but really just an expedient. I won't say I've been hanging about for any particular reason, but perhaps I have. I suppose you've slept with him, however."

I flinched.

"Yes, of course you have. He's irresistible that way, isn't he?" She plucked a sandwich from my plate and nibbled at the end. "And so fearsomely rich, like all good Jews. I don't blame you a second. I rather thought I was in trouble, when I first saw you on the yacht. And then he didn't invite me back. Did he mention me at all?"

"Not very much, I'm afraid."

"No, of course not. He's always observed a certain code of courtesy, even when he's juggling us about like ninepins. I've never heard him say a cross word about any woman." She swallowed and nibbled again, like a glamorous rabbit. "Even his wife."

You never do see it coming, do you? A shock like that. I suppose that's why it's a shock. Like an automobile collision, like the time I was eight years old and my nanny was taking me to a children's party, not far from this very spot. We were late, and she was driving fast. There had been a calamitous afternoon thunderstorm, and I suppose my nanny was too young and inexperienced to know that if you were driving fast enough, your automobile (however heavy) would skim like a seaplane across the surface of a good-sized puddle. I sat in the back, watching the landscape go by, thinking about one of the older girls who would be at the party and how she liked to pull my braids and call me the Princess of Crybabies, the Princess of Crayfish (she was American, too, the daughter of one of the rich expatriates who flooded this particular stretch of coast in the twenties), when I heard a sharp noise and I was flying, and then there came a horrific smash of metal and I thought, Someone's had an accident, and the very next instant my head hit the front seat and I realized it was us. I don't know how I survived. I had cuts and bruises and a broken finger; the nanny spent the next two months in the hospital with her leg in traction, contemplating the folly of speeding through the rain on your way to a children's party. Her head was never quite the same.

Even when he's juggling us about like ninepins, said Lady Alice, nibbling my sandwich, and I was flying through the air.

Even his wife, she said, and I heard a crash and thought, Someone's had an accident, and I realized it was me.

"His wife," I said, after a pause. "Of course."

But Lady Alice was an old hand. "What, didn't you know he was married?"

"I . . . He never mentioned . . ."

"Oh, you poor darling." She set down her sandwich, and she

really did look concerned. Up close, she was younger than I imagined. The sleek glow of her skin was genuine, not manufactured, and the bosom beneath her swinging neckline had that springy quality you couldn't bring back, once it was lost. "Now I really *am* upset with him. That's the sort of secret a man shouldn't keep to himself. Though perhaps he assumed you already knew. I thought everyone knew."

I hardly heard her. I certainly didn't comprehend her, not until later. The room was falling in pieces around me. My stomach was sick, rejecting the alien morsels of sandwich and coffee. I put my hand to my mouth.

Lady Alice reached across the table and touched my forearm. "Does it matter so much to you?"

I couldn't speak. *Wife.* The word turned in my brain. My mother had been a wife, until another woman slept with her husband. A very bad woman, a woman I hated, who was now me.

"Where is he now?" she asked gently.

"Germany," I said. I was too stunned to say anything but the truth, and Lady Alice was so improbably sympathetic, as if we had somehow found ourselves fighting on the same side in a long and muddy war. "He went back to Germany two days ago to . . . he said . . . to settle some affairs. He was going to come back for me."

Some family affairs, he had said. Some arrangements, which I was not to mention to anyone. I was not to mention anything about us to anyone, and especially not to his good friend Charles.

Lady Alice was replying, in a soothing voice, "Of course he was. You mustn't doubt that. I'm quite sure he cares for you very much. You're the kind of girl he *would* care for, now that I think about it. You're nothing like his usual sort. I'm sure he'll come back for you. He always keeps his word." She snapped her fingers.

"Perhaps he was going to see her, to tell her he had found someone serious this time . . ."

"She knows?"

Lady Alice laughed. "She's the greatest fool alive if she doesn't."

A small black fly had found its way to the edge of my plate. The hairlike legs climbed in the direction of the sandwiches, delicately uncertain, hardly daring to hope. I didn't have the heart to brush it away. I listened to the gentle clink of china around me, the patter of conversation, and thought, I am the greatest fool alive.

"My dear girl," said Lady Alice, "are you quite all right? You look as if you might be sick."

I said that I was all right, thank you.

She continued. "When he comes back, you mustn't let him off the hook. You've got to ask him very specific questions. I know it's terribly romantic to have a love affair—it's your first, isn't it? I was the same way—but they're like worms, you know, they'll try to find a way to wiggle off, any way they can. What has he told you about himself?"

What, indeed? "Not a great deal," I said, and I realized how true it was. We had talked for hours, we had spent long days together, and in my newfound wisdom I thought I knew him. I knew the shape of his face and the color of his eyes. I knew that his skin tanned easily. I knew that he was handsome in pajamas and dinner jackets and especially nothing at all, except when he was in a grim mood; I knew that he was about six feet tall and quite lean, that he was made of neat, well-packed muscle, though he wasn't bulky by nature. I knew that he could sail, that he preferred tennis to golf; that he had gone to boarding school in England and university in Berlin, though I didn't know which ones he attended and I couldn't have said what he studied. I knew that he disliked excessive displays of emotion, though he felt deeply. I knew that he preferred martinis before dinner and brandy after it, that he tolerated whisky only if it was served neat at room temperature. I knew he smoked strong Turkish cigarettes that he had delivered from a tobacconist in Paris. I knew that he spoke German, English, and French with great fluency, that he had a smattering of Spanish and Italian, that he read Virgil in the original Latin. I knew that he had a high tolerance for pain and a low tolerance for nonsense. I knew that he liked women. I knew that women liked him. I knew the way his face grew heavy when he wanted me, the way his eyes filled with smoke. I knew the way his body shuddered when he achieved his *petite mort*. I knew the way he sank upon me afterward, the sensation of his weight, the distribution of his limbs. I knew the smell of his skin.

But I didn't know his father's name. I didn't know the town where he lived. I didn't know what business his family was in, shipping or textiles or banking. I didn't know what, exactly, he was doing the night he fell bleeding into my life; I didn't know if his parents were alive, or if he had any siblings, or if he had any close friends other than my brother. I didn't know his age. I knew exactly where he existed in my heart; I had no idea where he existed in the universe.

I didn't know he had a wife.

"The truth is, they're all beasts," Lady Alice was saying. "Every man alive, even dear old Peter, would happily get his leg up on another woman if he could, and if he thought he could get away with it. You mustn't let it destroy you, darling. Enjoy him, by all means. Fall in love with him, if you like. I suppose you already have. But for heaven's sake, enjoy him with your eyes open."

I looked up. "Do they have children together?"

She frowned thoughtfully. "I think there's a son. He doesn't say a word about him, however. I've always thought he isn't fond of children; you know how careful he is."

"Careful?"

"Yes, always." She paused and leaned forward. Her beautiful green eyes turned round under the pencil-thin lines of her eyebrows. "My dear girl. You don't know what I'm talking about, do you?"

"Of course I know."

"No, you don't. Oh, the rat. The dirty little rat. I say, he really *had* better come up to scratch, or he'll hear from me about it. You're how old?"

"Nearly twenty."

"Nineteen. The horror. It doesn't bear thinking about. Well, we'll cross our fingers, won't we? Peter! There you are. I'm afraid there's been another change of plans."

I swiped my thumbs at the corners of my stunned eyes and looked up at Peter's weary face. He was holding a straw basket in one hand and a bottle in the other.

"Another one?" he said.

Lady Alice took the bottle from Peter's limp hand and examined the label. "Yes. Poor Annabelle here has had a dreadful shock. This will do for a start. Would you mind fetching us a pair of glasses? There's a dear chap."

Peter slunk obediently off to the bar. Lady Alice returned her attention to me. Her smile was bright and large and white-toothed, almost American.

"Don't worry about a single little thing, my dear. Alice knows exactly what to do."

Second Movement

"Paris is always a good idea."

AUDREY HEPBURN

ANNABELLE

Paris • 1935

1.

I hadn't planned on marrying anyone, let alone the Baron von Kleist. I didn't want to sleep with anyone, ever again, though Lady Alice said it was like falling off a horse: you should climb back on right away, or you would develop a complex. Lady Alice was big on complexes. She was devoted to modern psychoanalysis. She had explained everything to me on the night train to Paris: I had gone to bed with Stefan because my father was a philanderer, and my mother was dead, and my brother paid no attention to me. I had all sorts of unresolved desires that I had gathered up and transferred onto Stefan's person, like the decorations on a Christmas tree. All quite natural, she had said breezily, and nothing to be ashamed of. There were worse ways to lose your virginity. One day, she would tell me how she lost hers, but not yet. The story was not for the young at heart.

By then we were already bosom friends. I had told her my history over that first bottle of wine, and I don't remember what I said over the second. We had left for Paris that night, without even composing the customary note of vicious explanation. I wanted the break to be quick and clean; I wanted to flummox Stefan as thoroughly as he had flummoxed me. I wanted to leave no sign that our connection had even taken place, except for the precious Amati cello and the ten thousand francs, both of which I had left behind in the room Stefan had paid for in advance— *two months' accommodation, Madame Silverman. Are you* quite *sure you wish to depart so soon?* asked the astonished clerk—along with the scribbled name and the address in Paris.

I hadn't wanted the temptation. I hadn't wanted a single thread to dangle near my hand, asking to be pulled.

At dawn, the wagon-lit from Nice had deposited us like so much refuse into the greasy morning stink of the Gare de Lyon, and we shared a taxi to the rue de Berri and the shabbily grand apartment of my astonished father. It was the last day of August, and Paris was rubbing its eyes and waking up to the rising autumn. And that is how I came to become intimate with Johann von Kleist.

2.

It wasn't Carnegie Hall, or the Paris Opéra. But the music room in my father's apartment was large and beautiful, and the end of it contained only me; in the rest of the space crammed my father's friends, cheek by jowl with Lady Alice's companions in debauchery. An atmosphere of hushed reverence coated the furniture. The lights were hot on my skin. At the front of the threadbare orchestra, the conductor's baton angled in the air, and the conductor's eyes found mine.

In that instant of anticipation—as my mind skimmed across the bars of music ahead, encompassing thousands of notes into a single three-dimensional model, a living thing built of sound—I almost forgot Stefan.

3.

We held a party afterward in the drawing room. The long balcony doors were thrown open to the syrupy air of early October. Papa brought out champagne and Lady Alice brought out her friends. "You were smashing!" she shouted in my ear, and she handed me a glass of champagne and stood on a chair. She was wearing a ravishing violet dress, a glittering V neckline that ended just above her navel. Nobody but Lady Alice could have pulled it off so elegantly. She raised her glass and her voice. "*Bonsoir, mesdames et messieurs!*" she called out, and everybody hushed, because it was Lady Alice.

"Thank you all for joining us tonight, to celebrate the musical debut of my precious talented friend, Annabelle de Créouville." She held out her hand to me and hauled me up on the neighboring chair. There was a roar. I wore black, because I was a Serious Musician, and my neckline was actually that: a line halfway up my neck, separating black from porcelain white. But the material was a lovely lithe satin that clung to my breasts and waist and hips, all the way down to a magnificent fishtail below, wide enough to accommodate a cello between my knees—like a tiny beautiful black mermaid, Lady Alice said, except for the scales—and I knew I was just as *ravissement* as she was. She went on, enjoying herself thoroughly: "I plucked this flower from the dry soil of the Mediterranean a month ago, ladies and gentlemen, and just look how the darling thing has bloomed. Drink your champagne, love." (I drank.) "And I hope *all* of you drink loads of champagne and get terribly drunk, so the real fun can begin." Another roar. "Now enjoy yourselves, darlings, and remember to thank Annabelle's father for all the marvelous bubbles."

She jumped down and I jumped after her, and someone took me by the neck and kissed my cheek. I pulled away, laughing, and set my empty champagne glass on the table. A full one was placed in my hand. Charles came up and embraced me and told me I was wonderful. He had brought several friends with him, and they all lined up and explained how moved they had been by my performance. One of them was American, extremely tall, wearing the kind of canine open grin that was all over the States and so rare over here, though his eyes were serious and European. He was holding a glass of champagne in one hand and a newly lit cigarette in the other. He transferred the champagne skillfully into the grip of his cigarette fingers and held out his hand.

"That was wonderful, Mademoiselle de Créouville," he said, in an endearing American accent that made me want to fall on his chest.

"It's Annabelle," I said, taking his hand.

"I especially enjoyed the Dvořák. My mother used to play that one on her old Victrola when I was a kid. Really took me back, and it's a lovely piece of music to begin with. I won't exactly *admit* you brought a tear to my eye, but that doesn't mean you didn't." He winked.

"Well, thank you very much, Mr. . . . ?" I lifted the last word inquisitively.

"Greenwald," he said. "Nick Greenwald."

"Mr. Greenwald. Thank you for coming, and especially for your very extravagant praise."

"It's Nick, and I don't think I was being extravagant at all." He leaned forward. His eyes had softened a bit, and though I couldn't see their color beneath Papa's aging chandeliers, I liked their shape, and the trustworthy way the skin crinkled around them when he smiled, which he was doing now. "Actually, we've met already. I guess you don't remember. In a certain boathouse, at the beginning of August? I lost my dinner jacket that night."

The champagne caught in my throat. He waited patiently while I coughed. When I raised my head again, he was still smiling. "I'm a little insulted you didn't recognize me, actually," he said, "but I guess you had plenty of distraction."

"Yes."

"I hear you stitched the old man right up, though, and sent him happily on his way."

"I wasn't the one who stitched him up."

He shrugged a pair of wide American shoulders. "Close enough. Did he ever tell you anything about what happened that night?"

"No, as a matter of fact. He didn't tell me much at all."

"I see." He swirled the champagne in his glass, as if he wanted to say something else and didn't know how.

My throat hurt. I needed to take Nick Greenwald by the arm and ask him a thousand questions: how he knew Stefan, and what Stefan was doing now, and did he know Stefan's wife, and what was she like? Had Stefan returned to the Hôtel du Cap to find me, and what had he done when I wasn't there? But I had spent the last several weeks ignoring those questions when they scored along my brain, on the street and in the café and in my bed at night, and I wasn't going to start reopening the wound now, when it had finally begun to knit.

"Well," I said, tilting my glass toward him, "all's well that ends well."

Nick Greenwald touched his glass to mine, but his face wasn't in it. He bent his head a little closer to me, and his lower eyelids squinted upward in concentration. "Yes. All's well that ends well, right?"

"As far as I know. The last I heard, Stefan Silverman was heading back to his wife and son in Germany."

"Daughter," said Nick.

I smiled. "Daughter. I must have misheard. But I haven't heard from him since. Your information is much better than mine."

"Actually, I haven't heard from him since the end of August."

"Well, then. He must be very happy indeed," I said.

Nick lifted his cigarette thoughtfully. "So you haven't heard anything at all?"

"No. Should I have?"

Maybe I said it too eagerly, because Nick Greenwald removed the cigarette from his lips and leaned so close, I could smell the champagne on his breath. "Because I got a note from him, just before he left, that there was a girl who might need help. And I had a hunch just now, watching you play . . ." He trailed off expectantly, and I thought, *It's him, my God, the friend in Paris.*

I knit my other hand around my glass, so it wouldn't shake. "I have no idea what you're talking about. I don't need any help."

"Listen, I'm not going to tell your brother, if that's what—"

A hand fell on my shoulder, and I turned gratefully into the glowing face of my papa—*C'était magnifique, ma chérie, magnifique!*—and by the time I turned around Nick Greenwald was gone.

Thank God.

So I pushed Nick and Stefan out of my mind, and we laughed and drank and smoked for hours and hours, until Paris drained the last guest away just before dawn, and I fell asleep on a cherry Empire sofa with one hand resting on my cello case, still wearing my marvelous black dress, like a dark mermaid beached on a red shore.

4.

I had a lesson the next morning in Neuilly, not a long walk, but impossible while carrying a cello. I rang up Charles and asked if he would mind driving me there in his car, a wretched Renault from the previous decade. His voice on the other end was not pleased.

"Charles," I said, "when you dragged me from my nice comfortable garden wall to the boathouse last August, did I hesitate for even a second? Or did I scramble down the cliff path in my slippers and sacrifice ten days of my life to the service of your friend?"

"That's not the same thing." He paused. "What time is the lesson?"

"Eleven o'clock. But the traffic will be immense. You'd better come now, dressed or not."

5.

"Is everything all right?" Charles said, as we spun around the Étoile, dodging a lumbrous delivery truck in a display of expert metropolitan reflexes.

"Everything's wonderful."

"Because you seem different."

"In what way?"

"I don't know. I was thinking about it last night, while you were sawing away up there in your black dress. I wouldn't have recognized you."

"Thank you."

He changed gears noisily and swerved down the avenue de la Grande Armée, toward Neuilly. A flower seller looked up from his daffodils and tulips and thrust his hand into the air. "And then on the telephone this morning. I hung up the phone and thought, You know, I'll bet she'd never do that now."

"Do what?"

"Drop everything and run down the cliff and spend half of August nursing a gunshot wound, without asking any questions."

"Yes, I've learned to ask questions now," I said.

The buildings slid by, cafés and shopfronts, Paris in the reckless enthusiasm of springtime. The sidewalk tables were already out, and the patrons smoked languorously and drank small cups of coffee. Charles had the top down, so I could smell the unmistakable city air: the bread ovens, the cigarettes, the sultry stench of automobile exhaust. I could hear the accordion lilt of a street musician, somewhere nearby. I had always loved Paris, the little I knew of it, and I loved it even more now. I loved the hustle-bustle, the knowledge that I played a small but essential note in this glorious symphony.

"But you're quieter, too," said Charles.

"Am I? I don't think so."

"That's why I asked if something was wrong. I can't put my finger on it. There used to be this light inside you, this spark of life, and it's gone out. Even last night, when you were laughing, you didn't seem happy. And you're pale."

"I've always been pale."

He sighed. "All right. If you don't want to talk about it."

We stopped in midstream, waiting for the traffic ahead to clear. My cello sat on the seat between us, its black rounded end sticking up like a third head. I placed my hand around the edge, near the metal fastening, and as I did I heard my own voice echo back from an Antibes cliff: *That's you. You have brought me to life.*

The car jerked forward, and I pushed the thought away.

6.

The lesson lasted an hour, and I emerged into the open air to find a steady spring rain soaking the pavement, and not a taxi in sight. I trudged to the Métro. By one o'clock in the afternoon I was thrusting open the door to the apartment on the rue de Berri, bellowing for lunch.

Alice had just arisen. "But what about breakfast?" she asked innocently, lighting a cigarette. She was dressed in an emerald-green kaftan and managed to look expensive, even creased with sleep.

"Breakfast is long past. But you can have eggs and coffee if you like. What are these?"

"Flowers for you, *ma petite*. Lovely, aren't they?"

"For me?" I dropped my cello case against one of the chairs and stared at the vase on the round center table, which overflowed with close-packed blooms, all of them conspicuously out of season. I realized I had smelled the stargazer lilies all the way from the entrance hall.

"Rather a humbling moment for your obedient servant." Lady Alice joined me at the table, bringing an air of reverence with her. "One's used to having worshipful flowers all to oneself."

"What's this?" asked my father, from the doorway. He looked even more exhausted than Alice, though he was already washed and dressed, his dark hair damp against his neck.

"Flowers for your daughter," said Alice.

He walked across the room to join us and placed a kiss on Alice's shoulder, where the kaftan had slipped down. (What, this shocks you? I assure you, it took them all of two weeks.) "From whom?" he asked.

"Not Charles," I said.

"No, Charles hasn't two francs to rub together," Alice said confidently. "But I took the liberty of opening the card myself." She plucked it from the table and handed it to me. "Some German chap."

"German!"

"Don't be silly, darling. A nobleman, with terribly elegant handwriting. See for yourself."

I opened the card.

WITH GREAT ESTEEM ON THE OCCASION OF YOUR MUSICAL DEBUT

Across the top, the name *Johann von Kleist* was engraved in discreet black letters.

"*Mon Dieu,*" said my father. "What a very great surprise. I didn't know the fellow had it in him."

7.

In the beginning, Lady Alice had loved the idea of Paris. *We'll make you into a goddess,* she had said on the train. *We'll be the queens of Montparnasse.* She could use a change herself, something more interesting than luxury. She was tired of sleeping with rich men; she would try poor artists now, and see if that saved her soul.

As I said, that resolution lasted all of two weeks, not that my father was all that rich anymore. But he wasn't poor in the ordinary sense of the word, and the apartment was grand and littered with treasures, and the two of them actually seemed to be in love. Like to like, I supposed. Alice now wafted an air of delicate self-satisfaction like the most precious French perfume, and naturally her attention turned to my own affairs.

"Of course you should see him," she said to me, over lunch. "That's what would complete things for you—your rehabilitation, I mean. A love affair."

"I don't want to have a love affair."

"Of course you do. They're great fun, for one thing, and for another, I think you need it. I was talking to an analyst the other day, and he said that you need to go to bed with someone else soon, before you develop a sexual complex."

"You and your complexes."

"They're not *my* complexes, darling. They're yours."

"I suppose your analyst proposed himself to do the honors."

She tipped her cigarette into the ashtray. "He did, in fact. But that doesn't mean he's not right."

"You do realize it's all nonsense, this psychoanalysis business. This modern obsession with sex."

"No, it's true. The sexual instinct is perfectly natural, it's our life force, and when we suppress it the way you do—"

"Herr von Kleist is twice my age," I said.

"Generally speaking, when it comes to lovers, the older the better," said Lady Alice. "I daresay you haven't looked at him properly. I did, at the concert. He was sitting at the back, looking aloof and powerful. That's what age does to a man, the lucky chaps."

I thought of what Charles had said, on the pathway down to the boathouse. "Also, he's probably a Nazi."

She blinked. "But why should that matter? You're just going to bed with him; it isn't as if you're discussing politics and the Rhineland. I slept with a committed Communist once, the son of a filthy-rich banker. It was quite nice. We saw each other for a month or two, and he gave me the loveliest presents. I heard he later tried to bomb the Bourse."

The waiter arrived with lunch. We were sitting in the café around the corner, a sidewalk table that Lady Alice had obtained for us with a single silky gaze from her green eyes. She liked sitting outdoors, being on display. She would fold one gamine leg over the other and drape her hand with its cigarette around the curve of her knee; the other hand would caress a cup of coffee or a cocktail of some sort, depending on the hour (or not). Her honey hair would glint in the old autumn sunshine. Cafés were expensive, and cash was never all that plentiful in my father's household, but somehow Alice always scraped together enough francs for a coffee and a sandwich at the Maginot.

"Besides," she said, when the waiter had left, "that's part of the old frisson, isn't it? Knowing you really shouldn't sleep with him, and then you do." She winked at me over the crust of her sandwich.

Well, I couldn't argue with that, could I? I thought about the horrifying inevitability with which I'd fallen into bed with Stefan. Yes, he was forbidden and dangerous. He was older and German and Jewish; he had just been mysteriously shot in the leg. What man could have been more perfectly unsuitable for me?

So maybe Alice and her analyst were right, and I had a deep psychological appetite for unsuitable men. That was it, that was all it was. I hadn't been in love at all, I was simply acting out a kind of script, like an actress playing herself. And now the play was over, and everyone had left the stage and gone home.

Well, not quite everyone. Nick Greenwald. Stefan had sent a note to Nick Greenwald before he left France, asking him to look after this girl he'd fucked over the summer, in case she was pregnant.

I lifted my knife and fork to the omelet before me. "It's just a vase of flowers," I said. "There's no address. He was just being kind. He's a friend of my father's."

"*Kindness* is a dozen tulips, not a bouquet worth a thousand francs."

"A thousand francs! How do you know that?"

"Because I'm an expert, my dear. I can look at a thing and know its worth in a second. It's my particular talent. And what they say about love and money, that high-minded philosophy, it's rubbish. You can always tell how much a man values you by the presents he gives you."

"Heartwarming."

"Isn't it?" She put down her sandwich and lit another cigarette. "So I can assure you, Annabelle, darling," she said, smiling, blowing smoke into the sidewalk, "we haven't heard the last from this baron of yours."

Of course, she was right. The afternoon post brought a letter, addressed to me, on snowy thick stock, begging Mademoiselle de Créouville for the honor of accepting Fraulein Frieda von Kleist, age eleven, to her list of students.

8.

Eight days later, a few minutes before eleven o'clock in the morning, I arrived at the von Kleists' apartment, a magnificent fifteen-room residence occupying three floors of a monumental Haussmann building on the avenue Marceau, for Fraulein von Kleist's first lesson on the cello.

Alice drove me there in Charles's battered Renault. He had departed Paris abruptly a few days earlier, leaving behind the usual brief note, without any clue regarding his destination. But he had written a postscript, entirely atypical: *Cheer up, Sprout,* which was his childhood nickname for me.

"I can't tell you how thrilled I am," said Alice. "This is exactly what you need."

"Yes, another fifty francs a week."

"You should hold out for a hundred. I'm sure he'll pay whatever you ask."

The car rolled to a stop at the curb. I looked up at the monumental entrance and remembered that last scene at the Villa Vanilla, the look of terrible grief in von Kleist's blue eyes, and the feeling that he had lived many decades longer than I had. There was something frightening about that, the knowledge of his experience and his misfortune. As if misfortune were somehow contagious, like a disease.

Alice watched me pull my cello through the door. "Shall I pick you up afterward?"

I rested the cello on the pavement and closed the door. "No, thank you. I'll take a taxi."

I was ushered into the entrance hall promptly by a house-keeper in a neat black-and-white uniform, who called me *votre altesse* and asked me if I needed refreshment. I declined politely and sat down in a chair next to an empty Second Empire fireplace while my pulse knocked in my throat.

I am here to teach music, I thought. That is all.

The clock chimed, the door opened promptly, and a servant announced that Fraulein von Kleist was ready for her lesson.

She was a lovely girl. She had her father's icy coloring, except that on her the effect was bright and ethereal rather than arctic. She actually rose to her feet and curtsied when I entered, and her face was full of reverence. "Mademoiselle de Créouville," she said, in perfect French, "I am so gratified that you have agreed to take me on. When I listened to you play at His Highness's apartment last week—"

"Were you there?" I asked, surprised.

"Oh, yes! It was wonderful. My father had spoken so highly of your talent, and I have always wanted to learn the cello. I adore the voice, don't you? Oh, of course you do! How silly of me. But really, it's so rich and melancholy and delicious. Papa told me you were giving a concert, and I begged him to let me go." She spoke sunnily, not at all like a girl who had lost her mother; in fact, her entire body—she was quite tall and slender, so that she looked older than eleven—radiated sunshine, from her pale blond hair to her luminous young skin. She'd said the word *melancholy* with the kind of relish only a girl of her age and innocence could muster.

"I'm very flattered," I said.

"Of course, he hurried me away when the concert was over. He said the party afterward was just for the grown-ups." Frieda might have let her eyes roll a fraction of an inch, and I nearly laughed because she reminded me of myself, and here I was, not twenty years old, feeling ancient by comparison.

"Your father is very wise. Is this your instrument?"

She turned to the cello, which was propped against a sturdy armchair, bow resting gently on the cushion. "Yes. Is it acceptable?"

"It looks very fine."

"Papa's very serious about music. He said there was no point in getting an inferior instrument."

I ran my fingers along the strings. "I understand you play the piano?"

"Yes, and the harp."

"So you can read music already, and have some musical theory."

"Yes, Mademoiselle. I could read music almost before I could read books."

She was so eager and happy. I smiled at her and settled on the piano bench next to the armchair.

"Very good, Fraulein," I said. "Now sit down, pick up your bow like so, and we will begin with the A string."

9.

The lesson was an hour, and when the elegant ormolu clock on the mantel read five minutes to eleven, the door of the music room opened and Herr von Kleist walked inside, wearing a plain military jacket of field gray and a pair of riding breeches.

I looked up from the music, but he motioned for us to continue and sat down on the sofa by the window, one leg crossed over the other. He was wearing leather riding boots the color of cognac, polished to an oily gleam. He sat absolutely still against the blue damask, while the sunlight fell on his pale hair and his daughter concentrated ferociously on her bowing. At one minute to twelve, he rose to his feet.

"Very good, Mademoiselle de Créouville. I appreciate your patience, teaching a novice."

"Not at all. I wish all my students were so eager to learn."

He turned to his daughter. "Frieda, my dear. Thank Mademoiselle for her time and trouble."

"Thank you, Mademoiselle!" She rose to her feet, bow in hand.

"You're welcome, Fraulein. You are an excellent student."

I showed her how to loosen her bow and put away the instrument in its case. When she finished, von Kleist told her to go upstairs to Fraulein Schmidt for her lunch, and as soon as the door closed behind her, he turned back to me with an expression I might almost have called sheepish.

"She is my youngest," he said, "so I indulge us both with a governess, instead of sending her away to school."

"She's a lovely girl. Whatever you're doing, it seems to be the right thing."

"Thank you, Mademoiselle. Luncheon is now being served. Would you care to stay?"

I had been expecting something from him—an invitation to meet later and more discreetly, or perhaps a note of some kind—but not this, abrupt and formal and respectable. My fingers froze on the fastening of the cello case. "I don't wish to impose," I said.

"Nonsense. I have already made the arrangements with my housekeeper. Frieda will eat upstairs with Fraulein Schmidt."

I could have refused. I thought, If I am going to refuse him, if I'm not going to go through with this, I should do it now. But as I straightened from the cello, and my mouth, panicked and guilty, opened to make the excuses, I caught a glimpse of von Kleist's stiff face, and the vulnerability of his eyes, and I felt a surge of perverse power.

The clock chimed noon. I smiled. "In that case, I should be delighted."

10.

Von Kleist's silent housekeeper ushered us into a small but elegant dining room—the family dining room, he assured me—which was already set intimately for two. The spring sun burst through the pair of large windows, overlooking what must be the garden below, or perhaps a courtyard. I glimpsed the nearby buildings, the multitude of windows and balconies, and felt the unbearable visibility of the city. A bowl of delicate new white roses nestled in the middle of the silver and crystal, and a bottle of champagne in a bucket next to one of the chairs. Von Kleist held out the other one for me.

Lady Alice had dressed me in sky-blue silk that morning, because it suited my eyes, she said. My dark hair and my large brown eyes, my round little French figure and my large red American smile. *He can't resist you in a dress like that,* she said, and I told her I wasn't sure if I wanted him to resist me or not, and she laughed and said, *You'll make up your mind after he pours the champagne,* and as von Kleist eased the cork softly out of the bottle—the familiar pop made me flinch—and drizzled it into my glass, I wondered how she had known. The champagne was Laurent-Perrier, and the worn label suggested something vintage. I remembered what Lady Alice had said over lunch, about the value of a man's presents. Or perhaps he simply liked vintage champagne.

Von Kleist filled his own glass and said, "I hope you are comfortable, Mademoiselle."

"Quite comfortable. This is a lovely room."

"Thank you. I have leased the apartment for some time, since I first came to Paris." He sat down and lifted his glass. The sunlight entered his eyes. "I am very glad to see you are well, Mademoiselle."

I touched my glass to his. "It's Annabelle. And I'm glad to see you're well, too."

When we had finished lunch, the sun had tipped over the

roof and the room had turned blue and almost dusky. Herr von Kleist asked if I would like to see the other principal chambers of the apartment and I said I would. He stood and helped me from my chair, and his hand was dry and large in contrast to mine. When I stood, dizzy with champagne, he seemed enormous.

"How tall are you, really?" I asked.

"A hundred and ninety-six centimeters."

"It's very intimidating."

"Is it? I hope not."

"Yes, it is. You have almost thirty-two centimeters over me. More than a foot." I didn't know why I was saying these things. I had had too much champagne. I stared at the buttons of von Kleist's uniform, holding the field gray forcibly closed over his warlike chest, and I thought it was impossible that someone so big could covet someone so little.

"But why should that frighten you?" he said. "It is the natural duty of the large to protect the small."

I had to tilt back my head to see his face, which was shadowed and quizzical in the absence of the sun. "I'd like to see the library first," I said.

11.

We made a circuit, and ended in the library again, where the housekeeper had laid out coffee. It was now two o'clock. "I'm afraid I've kept you from your work," I said.

"Not at all. What do you think of the place?" He accepted a cup and saucer. Men poured wine, women poured coffee and tea. There was something in there, an important reflection, but I was still a little too dull from the champagne to capture it.

"It's magnificent and beautiful and terribly orderly," I said.

He laughed for the first time, and it was richer than I imagined. "You were perhaps expecting chaos from me?"

"No." I laughed, too. "But it's very different from my father's apartment. Of course, they'd cleaned it all up for the concert, but you must have noticed the dilapidation."

He shrugged politely. "I like the peace, you see. If there is disorder, it is hard for the spirit to be peaceful."

I nodded to the silver-framed photographs clustered on the round table by my side. "Is that your wife?"

"Yes."

I set down my cup and lifted one of them, of a blond woman who held a giggling flaxen-haired child in her arms. They were outdoors, in a field of some kind, with a tree in the background to the left. The woman was smiling hugely. "She looks happy. And quite young."

"She was. She was seventeen when we married. We knew each other as children. When I returned home from the front on convalescent leave, I discovered she had grown rather abruptly into a young lady, as girls do. I fell in love with her at once. By the end of summer we were engaged, and the wedding took place in October, before I left for the front again. I had just turned twenty."

"Then you had many happy years together."

"Yes. We were very happy. She is holding our second child in that photograph. Marthe. She was four then; she is now fourteen and at school."

"And the others?"

He was sitting in the armchair, several feet away. The coffee cup rested in his lap, and a single index finger curled around the handle. He looked not at the photograph, but at me. "Frederick, our oldest. He is fifteen. Then after Marthe came Klaus, who will be thirteen next month. And Frieda." He paused. "My wife's name was Frieda. We had not yet christened the baby when she died."

"I'm very sorry."

"Yes," he said. "So was I. At the time, I thought I had accepted her death as God's will, but looking back, I see how bitter I was, and how melancholy."

"Of course you were. You loved her very much."

His gaze shifted at last to the photograph. "It is impossible to describe how much."

The room was protected from the sunlight, as libraries are, and the glow that came from the half-shaded windows fell softly on his face. I had thought last summer that thirty-eight was a vast age, but as I looked at him now I thought thirty-eight was terribly young.

I rose from my seat and went to the corner of the sofa, next to the chair in which he was sitting. His knee nearly touched my dress. It was massive and thick next to mine, the knee of a giant. I couldn't quite comprehend his size; it was so out of scale to what I was used to. He was still wearing his boots and riding breeches. He had apologized earlier for not changing. I laid my hand on his knee, and the patella alone was so huge, my palm couldn't quite cover it.

"You must have been very lonely," I said.

He didn't move, but his eyes met mine, quite steady. "No. It is impossible to be lonely when there are children about."

"Is that why Frieda still has her governess?"

He removed the cup and saucer from his lap and set them down on the rug next to the chair, which seemed to me a reckless act of disorder. "You are very perceptive, Mademoiselle," he said.

"Please, it's Annabelle. And it doesn't take much perception to see that you're lonely."

"If I am to call you Annabelle, then you must call me Johann."

I smiled. "I can't. It's far too casual a name to be flinging about in front of that uniform."

"We are at an impasse, then, Mademoiselle."

"So it would seem."

He lifted my hand from his knee and kissed the ends of my fingers. "My intentions are not dishonorable, you know."

"I didn't think they were."

"Yes, you did, or you would not have taken so long to reply to my note."

I smiled. "All right. I did."

"Then why did you accept my offer?"

His expression was grave and impermeable before me, as if he had staked his all on my reply. His hand still enclosed my fingers. "I suppose I was grateful for the flowers," I said. "And I need the work."

"If you are short of money, Mademoiselle—"

"No, no. I have exactly what I need. I will gladly accept payment for today's lesson, however."

"Of course. But I am afraid I have forgotten to ask the fee."

"A hundred francs an hour. I hope you can afford it."

He studied me without speaking. His thumb moved slightly, sliding against the knuckle of my index finger. I thought, Here it is, this is the moment. Time to make good. But my limbs were like molasses, too thick to move. I imagined him kissing me, pushing me back on the sofa, pulling up my dress. I imagined his bristling hair under my fingers, his weight on my limbs, and the bristling hair turned dark and curling, and the body moving on mine belonged to Stefan.

I said boldly, seeking out his gaze, "Lady Alice thinks you want me to be your mistress."

"Lady Alice should know that I don't keep mistresses."

"And I don't allow myself to be kept." I lifted his hand and drew the warm fingers against the side of my breast, atop the sky-blue silk that Lady Alice had chosen for me. His bones were heavy and stiff. "But I don't want to be lonely, either."

"Annabelle," he said, without moving his hand, "this is not necessary."

"I think it is."

He looked utterly unmoved. But my thumb, pressed against his wrist, detected a bounding radial pulse, and his pupils were like drops of oil inside his pale irises. I thought, when his lips parted, that he would lean forward and kiss me, but instead he said gently, "Why, Annabelle? So that you can become a mosquito, like the others?"

"A mosquito?"

"Don't you remember what you said to me on your garden wall, last summer? You could study the bugs without becoming a mosquito."

I couldn't breathe. Before I even realized that my eyes had blurred, a tear dropped onto von Kleist's hand, sliding between the knuckles, and then another. And I had never cried once since August; I had prided myself that I hadn't shed a single tear.

His hand moved from my breast to my chin, and his thumb wiped my cheek. "You don't need to be a mosquito for me, Annabelle. I would rather prefer that you were not."

"I'm sorry. I've made a fool of myself, haven't I?"

"No." He drew out a handkerchief from his pocket and put it in my hand. "Annabelle, if you want me to make love to you, I will make love to you. I don't think I can resist you if you ask me. But let it not be because you are wishing I was another man."

"No." I folded the handkerchief and gave it back to him. "You are far better than that."

"No, keep it. A souvenir of this first meeting." He sat back in his chair and lowered his hand to retrieve his coffee cup, while I wrestled with my composure. "Do you ride, Mademoiselle?"

"I used to, before we moved back to America."

"I ride every morning in the Bois de Boulogne. Perhaps you will allow me to mount you there, from time to time." He finished the coffee in a final gulp, rose to his feet, and held out his hand to me. "But come. You must go now, Annabelle. I will drive you home myself."

12.

When I burst through the doorway of my father's apartment half an hour later, my hair was full of wind and sunshine and my arms were full of cello. I dropped the instrument in its place next to the sofa and looked about for Lady Alice.

She wasn't there, but the afternoon post lay on the table, a few notes only. One of them was postmarked in Paris and addressed to me. I opened it and read that Nick Greenwald had something important to communicate to me about a mutual friend, and would I meet him at my earliest convenience?

I tore the notecard into small pieces and threw it in the wastebasket.

13.

Two days later, I went riding in the Bois de Boulogne with Johann von Kleist.

We met at six o'clock outside my apartment, where Johann was waiting in his rumbling black Mercedes roadster. My eyes were hooded and sleepy, my hair bound back in a clumsy chignon. I had unearthed a set of my mother's old riding clothes in a back closet of the apartment, but Mummy had been tall and they were too large. Yesterday in the market, I had found a pair of secondhand boots that nearly fit.

"I will take those to my valet afterward," said Johann, as we drove through the chill morning air, "and he will polish them properly for you."

Already my nerves were coming alive. Maybe it was the vibration of that enormous engine, the energy in the car's swooping curves. I glanced at Johann, who sat rigidly in his seat, polished bright, as if he'd been up for hours. He wore his officer's cap over his blond hair, and his eyes were fixed on the half-dark streets ahead. I had no idea how he packed those legs under the dash. He was so tall, he looked over the rim of the windshield rather than through it.

We were met at the avenue Foch by Johann's groom, who

held two gleaming horses by the reins, one a large bay and the other a smaller chestnut mare with a wide and irregular white blaze down the length of her head. Around the rim of the trees ahead, the sky was a pale and expectant blue. The entire city of Paris lay between us and the sunrise. The groom stepped aside and Johann helped me mount. "Just like old times," I said, gathering up the reins.

"Like the bicycle, isn't it?" said Johann, and when I looked down I saw that the sunrise was touching the top of his cap, and he was smiling.

He was right about bicycles. My muscles remembered how to ride, though my legs didn't appreciate the activity. We entered through the empty Porte Dauphine and angled left to the lakes, and Johann asked me how I felt and if I thought I should like to go faster. I said I would. When I nudged her, the chestnut moved willingly into a gentle trot, and I found the rhythm at once, the slight and steady up-down that still lingered in my bones, like a waltz I had danced long ago. Around us, the grass and trees were wet with dew, and a yellow-pink haze floated in the air. "It's easier than I thought," I said to Johann. "And the park is beautiful at this hour."

"Yes," he said, looking at me.

He wasn't smiling, but his face was softer. He rode like a centaur, like he had come into the world on top of a horse. In the primeval mist, he might have been a thousand years old, dressed in leather and blue paint, riding across the steppes with an army of barbarians, except that he was manifestly not a barbarian. You could not imagine Johann von Kleist without his pressed uniform and his polished boots.

We went off the gravel path and into a meadow, damp and

fragrant with new grass, and as the ground opened up I realized how perfectly alone we were, how obviously he was courting me. He didn't want to have an affair; he wanted more from me, and the possibility was too huge, the length and breadth of the opportunity too impossible to imagine. For an instant, I pictured myself a baroness at twenty, with a rich estate in Prussia and four stepchildren, with an apartment in Paris and a fine upstanding husband who would keep me in silks and jewels and never, ever stray.

"You love riding, don't you?" I said stupidly, because I had to say something.

"Yes."

I thought of his expression a moment ago. I said in French, "You seem different somehow. A little softer, perhaps?"

He chuckled, a relaxed sound. "Maybe so. It is the rhythm, I believe, and maybe the freedom, too. And the horse, naturally. The horse has none of the vices of humanity." He reached down and patted the bay's neck.

"I see what you mean. You can be yourself with a horse, can't you? You don't have to pretend anything, like with people." I had switched back to English.

"Yes, exactly. And then one dismounts and goes home and to work, and puts the mask back on. So it goes."

"I suppose you wear a very stern mask at work. I shudder to think about it," I said. "What does a military attaché do, exactly?"

"Nothing very interesting, I'm afraid. A great deal of paperwork."

"But you must meet loads of important people."

"Annabelle," he said, "unless you want me to put on my very stern mask again, we must change the subject."

"I'm sorry. I didn't mean to pry."

"It is not you who should be sorry," he said.

"That's a cryptic thing to say."

He nudged the bay faster. "Come along. Let us see how well you sit a canter."

14.

At the lower lake we dismounted and watched the last of the mist float off the water. The horses stretched their necks to the grass and I sat on a rock, while Johann braced his booted foot next to me and took out a cigarette case. "I didn't know you smoked," I said.

"On occasion."

"Is that even possible?"

"If one is disciplined." He leaned down and offered me the open case. I shook my head. He took one, a long white brand with which I was not familiar. He lit himself up with a gleaming silver lighter and smoked silently, watching the water. A bird cried softly from the trees. I felt his boot near my leg, the unending heat of his body.

I broke the silence first. "Where did you learn to speak English so well?"

"In England. My father died of peritonitis when I was six. My mother married an Englishman a few years later, and I lived at home with them until I was old enough for boarding school."

"But what happened during the war?"

He put his hand in his pocket, fingering something there. His lighter, I thought. "I fought for Germany, of course. I was wounded twice but somehow escaped being killed. A miracle, I think. My stepfather was not so lucky. He was killed on the third day of the Somme."

"How horrible for your mother."

"She died not long after. I'm afraid I never saw her again, once the war began." He lifted the cigarette, which was nearly finished, and inhaled slowly. "They had two children. My sister Margaret, who is nine years younger, and my brother Benedict, who was born a month after my stepfather died." He dropped the cigarette in the grass and crushed it under his heel. "In another hour the lake will be full of boats. Would you like to go boating someday?"

"Yes, but not here. It's too public."

He took my hand to lift me to my feet. "I agree."

15.

We finished where we started, near the Porte Dauphine, now crowded with people and morning light. The groom was waiting next to the black Mercedes. He jumped to attention when he saw us, like a marionette.

"I will drive you home, of course," said Johann.

"Only if it won't make you late for your work."

"Do not concern yourself with that."

"The lateness or the work?"

"Either one."

It took much longer to drive home, because of the traffic. Paris was in full flow. The streets stank of fish and garbage and exhaust. "I would stop for breakfast," said Johann, "but I'm afraid I do have an appointment."

We wound our way down the crowded avenues and narrow streets to my father's apartment, in a massive silence met by the roaring undertone of the engine. Johann looked up dubiously to the building. "I hope it is safe, at least. Not so licentious as that damned villa last summer."

"Oh, very safe. Not all that warm in winter, but safe."

He dropped his gaze to my face and frowned. "I don't like this for you, Annabelle."

"Do you have a better suggestion?"

"Not at present." He climbed out of the car and walked around to my side, next to the sidewalk, where he opened the door and grasped my hand to draw me out of the low-slung seat. He straightened my hat and tucked a piece of loosened hair behind my ear. "You are windblown and beautiful, Mademoiselle," he said, kissing my hand. "I will come for you again on Saturday morning."

16.

I lay for an hour afterward in a warm bath, staring at the ceiling and wondering what to do with him. Whether I wanted him for myself, or just to banish the memory of Stefan. Whether it was possible to inoculate yourself against future heartbreak. Whether one man could keep you safe from wanting another.

PEPPER

Cocoa Beach • 1966

1.

On the ninth day after Annabelle's departure, Pepper takes the Ford Thunderbird out of the garage and drives herself into town.

Well, maybe "day" isn't quite the right word for it, when you consider that the sun has already fallen and the sky is purple-black. Back home in New York City, there will be a hard frost overnight, and the last tenacious leaf will shiver to the ground. But here in Florida, the daytime temperature touched eighty degrees, and Pepper wandered up and down the beach in a too-short sundress borrowed from Annabelle's closet (she has decided not to trust the Breakers with her current address) while the dogs chased each other in large circles across the empty sand, until the shadows lengthened and the horizon turned pink, and Pepper thought, I've got to get out of here, I've got to do something.

Itchy feet. They've gotten Pepper into trouble before, and they'll do it again. Tonight she's painted them both a fresh, crisp red at the tips and slipped them back into her sandals, and the one on the right is pressed against the accelerator, the faster the better. A tiny toe beats a tattoo into the wall of her abdomen, as if in sympathy, or maybe protest. Or else warning?

Well, too late for that.

Now her hair flutters in the draft, her lipstick is warm and sticky-red on her lips. She glances in the rearview mirror, and her skin glows back at her, reckless and pregnant. She's not out to find a man, of course not. She just needs to know that she's still beautiful. That her face, which has gotten her into so much trouble before, is yet capable of more.

2.

As usual, the trick is finding the right spot. There's always a spot, and Pepper has a nose for them. She parks the car and reaches for her pocketbook on the empty passenger seat. She checks her lipstick in the mirror and slings her cardigan over her shoulders.

Inside, the air is polished and classy and not too old. Pepper pauses in the doorway, just long enough for someone to catch sight of her, and then it passes in a familiar ripple through the room. Awareness. The electric pause, the drinks set down, the sidelong stares. There is the usual narrowed hostility from one of the women, the quick look away from the man who pretends he doesn't give a damn, the shy glance into the whisky from the one who thinks he doesn't stand a chance, the bold stare of the one who's confident he does. The same old chain reaction, the same old Pepper.

The thing about Pepper is, she hasn't actually slept with that many men, if you line them up end to end. There was the father of her baby, of course. Oopsy-daisy. There was a supremely eligible young man in New York, before she left, a friend of her cousin Nick Greenwald: a lawyer who wanted to marry her, a man she probably should have married if she knew what was good for her. Before that, a photographer who enchanted her, who was her lover for a year and a half, who called her his muse and took thousands of pictures of her; a man whom she actually thought she might marry, until he moved to Paris one afternoon with a seventeen-year-old fashion model, a change of heart she discovered two weeks later from a mutual friend. An older man, one summer on Long Island, on the sly. A boy in college who worshipped her. The man on the terrace, who sent her bouquet after bouquet, note after note, begging her to see him again, until even her parents took notice and registered disapproval.

But mostly, Pepper loves to flirt. She loves the joy of the hunt, though she stops short of the kill. Like any Thoroughbred, she was born to run. That's what matters, after all: the knowledge that you were the fleetest animal in the pack, and who cares if you get to stand in the winner's circle with the flashbulbs popping and the garland looped around your neck? All you need, all you really feed on, is the knowledge that you're the most desirable woman in the room.

Until it doesn't matter anymore.

Because she's not the same old Pepper, is she? Because at this very second, her right hand, obeying a primeval impulse, lies across the apex of her belly. She couldn't have stopped it if she tried, if she actually held it down with her left hand. She, the predatory Pepper, is now on the defensive. She's got something worth protecting.

She can't win. She can't go back. Somewhere around the fourth or fifth month of pregnancy, she crossed an invisible line, a Rubicon of biology, and became a mother. She doesn't belong here anymore. She may never belong here anymore.

The reflection breaks over her like one of the more vigorous waves washing up on the beach this afternoon—the surf was brisk, the weather was on the move—and for an instant she hesitates, there in the doorway with all eyes on her.

The instant passes and so does Pepper, right back into the Thunderbird, right back to the old house by the sea, though she maybe makes a wrong turn or two along the way.

3.

By the time Pepper undresses and crawls into bed, her limbs are done for the night. Her brain, on the other hand, doesn't know when to quit.

The room is peacefully dark, not a drop of light. She lies on her side, gazing at the space where the opposite wall should stand—if she could see it—and forces her eyes shut, except that they keep pinging open again, like a child's pop-up toy, indefatigable. The baby kicks around in sympathy.

After half an hour or so, she sits up and turns on the light. What's happening to her, that her body is so weary and her brain can't stop jumping? She wants to sleep. She wants to finish something first, and she doesn't know what it is.

Pepper used to sleep naked. It's a sensual thing, a freedom thing, but since coming to Annabelle's house, since jumping awake at every little whisper in the night, wondering if they've tracked her down already, she's taken to wearing underwear and a long shirt. She still resents them for it. She swings her legs over the side of the bed and reaches for the linen robe draped across the nearby chair. She slings her arms inside and belts the sash high, above her bump. She leaves the slippers behind and makes her way softly across the midnight courtyard to the main house, which is unlocked, and pauses in the doorway, because she doesn't know what she's doing here.

In the absence of purpose, she wanders to the kitchen and pours herself a drink of water from the tap. The house is so silent, she wants to scream.

She stares through the kitchen window into the black courtyard. This silence, my God, this void. This itchy absence of sound. She would talk to anybody right now, just to get rid of the quiet. But mostly, she thinks, gazing at the corner of the courtyard where the lemon trees grow side by side with the bougainvillea, she wants to talk to Annabelle. Gentle, frank Annabelle, who disappeared nine days ago.

She sets the empty glass in the sink and turns off the light. There is no Annabelle; even her dogs sleep elsewhere, in Clara's quarters, down a corridor somewhere. She wanders back into the hall, bumping into corners, feeling her way along until her fingers strike air where the study should be. A pretty room; Pepper's seen it from the outside. Though the furniture is sturdy and wholesome, and the colors richly neutral, Pepper has the feeling that this was Annabelle's office and not her husband's.

She steps inside and flips on the light.

The switch illuminates not an overhead fixture but the lamp on the desk, an old-fashioned number that looks like a retrofit from the days of kerosene. The rest of the desk is mostly empty.

A telephone sits at the corner. Pepper's heard it ring once or twice. It seems to have its own line; the one in the living room doesn't ring in tandem. At the top of the desk is a small clock. Pepper walks around the corner and reads it. Half past one.

If she picked up that telephone right now, at half past one in the morning, and she called her mother and said *I'm pregnant, Mums, I want to come home*, what would her mother say in return?

She pulls out the chair and sinks down to stare at the telephone.

She could call Vivian again. She *should* call Vivian again.

She should call her mother.

She puts out her hand and rests it on the smooth bakelite curve of the receiver, just centimeters away from the round dial, the little black numbers and letters. *Hello, Mums, you'll never guess. Pepper's in trouble. Big, big trouble. Maybe even a little bit scared. Maybe, for once in her life, not quite sure what to do next.*

The hand falls away.

Also, at the top of the desk, there is a pair of handsome pens in a small marble stand. Right next to the clock, right next to half past one in the morning.

Pepper doesn't write letters. She writes the occasional thank-you note, when she has to, but the humility and patience of letter writing don't exactly flow like milk and honey in her veins. She'd rather talk to you in person, face-to-face, so she can put all her talents to use.

But maybe this is one of those things you wrote down on paper, instead of telling them live and unrehearsed. Pepper takes one of the pens out of its holder and fingers the tip. Dear Mums and Dadums, It's the craziest thing. Dear Mums and Dadums,

I'll bet you're surprised to see a letter from me, your own daughter. Dear Mums and Dadums, I think it's time I told you something.

Yes, that was it.

Pepper leans down and rummages through the desk drawers until she finds a box of stationery, thick and expensive and anonymous, no monogram or heading of any kind. She selects a few sheets and squares them on the blotter. She picks up the pen and writes the date and *Dear Mums and Dadums,* and that's when she hears the front door opening and closing, so softly you'd have to be paranoid to notice it.

4.

For an instant, Pepper freezes. She grips her pen and thinks, It's Annabelle, of course it's Annabelle, but that doesn't stop her heart from smashing against the wall of her chest. Doesn't stop the adrenaline from hurtling through her veins.

The lamp.

Pepper pushes back the chair and launches herself to the switch on the wall. She turns off the light and flattens herself in the lee of the half-open door.

The house has gone still again. No footsteps, not the slightest sound. But there should be footsteps, shouldn't there? If someone's just entered the house. Annabelle's heels should be clattering happily along the flagstones of the entry. She should be rattling her car keys, setting down her suitcase, tossing her pocketbook on the table, going through the mail. But there's nothing, a distinct void of noise, as pregnant as Pepper's belly. She puts a hand on top, just to be sure, and tries to stop breathing.

And then. A voice. Deep but soft, a male voice that wants to be heard by one person alone.

"Who's there?"

If she could, Pepper would dissolve into the wall, become one with the paint and the plaster. Wouldn't that just fix everything? Pepper Schuyler, dazzling socialite, shimmering Girl Friday, now a wall in a seaside Florida villa.

The baby turns around and slugs her in the kidneys.

Pepper releases a tiny gasp, just a tiny one, but it's enough.

"Who's there?" This time, it's a demand.

Precious little light filters through the window and the half-open door. Pepper looks around slowly, keeping her cool, trying to remember what lay where. From the hallway outside comes the sound of footsteps, heavy, muffled by the rug.

The bookshelf along the wall. Pepper reaches out her arm and fingers her way along the top, something, anything. A metal shape finds her palm, too small, but that's all there is. She can feel the footsteps now, vibrating the floorboards beneath her slippers. The object is slender but heavy, a small statue of some kind. Pepper slips back behind the door, just as it begins to move, just as a hand appears around the edge.

She swings.

But the hand, the damned hand actually knows she's coming. Before she can snap her elbow forward, the fingers enclose her wrist, stopping the arc of the blow, and the next thing she knows, she's tucked in a headlock against a too-solid chest, the metal object drops on her right foot, and as she opens her mouth to scream, the voice from the hallway growls in her ear.

"What the hell have you done with my mother?"

ANNABELLE

Paris • 1935

1.

At first, I refused to believe that I was pregnant. It didn't seem possible; August was like another lifetime, an Annabelle who no longer existed. The antiseptic language of reproduction—*The average emission of the human male contains some three to four hundred million individual gametes*—had nothing to do with the breathless and beautiful act of intercourse with Stefan, the long heat-soaked hours in his arms.

I ignored the signs staunchly, inventing every possible excuse, until I could not. Until Alice caught me vomiting in the bathroom at the end of October and brought me a worn white washcloth from the linen cupboard, which she ran under the faucet and handed to me with a sigh of resignation. "I suppose it was inevitable, the two of you so young and virile," she said. "Really, he ought to have known better. I'll ask around for a doctor. You will have to get it taken care of at once, of course, before poor von Kleist suspects anything."

I straightened. "What do you mean?"

"My dear, he's not going to want to have an affair with a pregnant woman. He's certainly not going to want to wait around until the child's born. And unless you've slept with him already, he won't possibly believe it's his."

"No." I sank down on the stool and put my face in my hands. The washcloth was cool and damp against my cheek. "I haven't slept with him."

I hadn't even kissed him. I arrived every Tuesday morning for Frieda's lesson, and had lunch with Johann afterward, though we took no more tours of the apartment and he hurried back to the embassy after driving me home in the black Mercedes.

On Thursdays and Saturdays we went riding in the park. Johann called for me promptly at six, and I was back in my father's apartment by nine-thirty, soaking my worn muscles in a hot bath. The pattern had become so regular, I arranged my week around it. Twice a week, on Tuesdays and Fridays, a large bouquet of flowers arrived from a fine Parisian florist. The blooms varied, but they were always fragrant and expensive. Alice and I would sit around the table and admire them as we drank our morning coffee. "I do hope he's getting his money's worth, then," Alice said, a week ago, and when I told her that he wasn't, not even a sou, she laughed. "Trust you to find the only man in Paris who doesn't make his mistress earn her keep," she said, shaking her head, and I didn't bother to argue that he wasn't keeping me at all. He sent flowers and gave me lunch and paid me a hundred francs a week for Frieda's lesson: that was all.

On the other hand, he demanded nothing of me except my conversation, and not very much of that. It wasn't that we didn't talk; he was just economical with words and ideas. We spent most of our time in a kind of easy and understanding silence, a relief after the frenetic energy of Alice.

"Well, then," she said. "I'll see what I can do. You'll burn in hell, of course, but then won't we all?"

2.

A month before my mother died, we had an enormous row. I was eleven and old enough to know things. There had been a father–daughter tea at my school, and of course I had no father to go with me, and so I went with my uncle, the husband of my mother's sister, and sat awkwardly with him, drinking watery tea and eating stale cake, while the other girls laughed and talked with their genuine fathers, basking in their warm baths of paternal adoration. I came home and threw my hat against the wall in the parlor that smelled of lemon polish and damp wool. "It's *your* fault, *you* left him! Why did you leave my father? You were cruel to him so he found another woman."

She had slipped her index finger in her book and closed the pages over it. Her face had gone a little pale. "You mustn't speak about things you don't understand, Annabelle."

"I understand more than you think. You drove him to someone else, and then you left him, and now I don't have a father. I could be in France, I could be a princess, and instead I'm stuck *here*!" I pointed to the faded wallpaper, the shabby furniture, the tired knickknacks on the shelves, the battered radiator that banged in the corner. "And it's your fault!"

"You'll understand when you're older. It's not that simple."

"When I'm grown up, I'm going to be a *good* wife. I'm going to lavish my husband with love so he'll never go to another woman. I'm going to make sure my children have a father."

She replied in a quiet monotone that—at the time, so young—I had wrongly imagined was emotionless. "Darling, sometimes it doesn't matter how good you are, and how much you love your husband. There are some men who need more than that, who will never be happy with just one woman. I did what I thought was right for you."

I had stamped my foot on the threadbare rug and told her she was wrong, that it was her fault. I would never do such an awful thing to my children. I would make sure they had a father who loved them.

Oh, Annabelle, she said.

I hate you, I shouted.

Then I had run up the stairs to my room and shut the door and put my head under the pillow, so I wouldn't hear her crying.

3.

The day after Alice discovered me in the bathroom, I went to the doctor, though not the one she recommended. I had no intention of seeing Alice's doctor. I had seen the women in the convent hospital who had tried to get rid of their babies. Some of them had died. Others had been so ravaged inside that it was a wonder they had lived. We had treated them, of course, but the nuns had told us afterward that these were the wages of sin, that God might forgive a woman for some things, but not for this. Stefan's child was my punishment for having loved Stefan without repenting, for having shared sexual passion with a married man.

I went instead to my father's doctor, a man named Périgault who looked nearly sixty and had gentle hands. He told me what I already knew, that I was going to have a baby at the end of May.

"Very well," I said. "What do you recommend?"

Dr. Périgault drummed his fingers against the edge of the desk. His eyebrows made a ragged line along the top of his spectacles. "I recommend you find a husband, Mademoiselle de Créouville, with preference to the man who is the father of your baby."

I stared at his gray hair, at the bushiness of his brows above the round wire frames of his eyeglasses, and I wondered if he had known my mother at all.

"What very helpful advice, Doctor," I said. "But I'm afraid that isn't possible. The man is already married."

4.

Lady Alice was waiting outside in Charles's old Renault. When she saw me, she dropped her cigarette on the pavement and reached across the seat to open the door. "Well? All sorted out?" she said.

"I'm pregnant, if that's what you mean."

"And didn't the good doctor give you lots of lovely advice?"

I turned my head to the blur of striped awnings and said, after a moment, "I swore, when I was a child, that I would never raise my children without a father. I would never do what my mother did."

"Darling, everyone's doing it these days. Well, not everybody.

But it's not like thirty years ago, when your life would be ruined. Actually, it might make you a divine novelty, if you play your hand properly."

"I don't want to be a divine novelty."

"What do you want, then? To be some stupid respectable housewife in the *banlieues*, tending her flowers and her fat old husband?"

"It doesn't have to be so extreme."

"Yes, it does. Nobody stays in love forever, and then you're just stuck together out of habit and inertia and bloody sniveling children. If you simply go on having passionate affairs, you never have to give it up. It's like being in love constantly, for ever and ever, only with different people."

"Until you're old and nobody wants to sleep with you."

She laughed and leaned her elbow on the doorframe. A delivery van reared up before us, and she wound around it, grinding what was left of the gears. "That will never happen to me," she said. "I'll kill myself before I get old."

"What a rosy picture you've painted for me. I can't wait to get started."

"All I'm saying is that you're looking at this all wrong. There's no law that says you have to get married. So you're convinced you have a propensity to sleep with philanders, because of your mother and father and all that. I'm sure my analyst would agree with you there. But don't weep about it. Every girl wants to, if she admits it. If she would let herself. They're heaps more fun, for one thing."

"But then they leave you, or they sleep with someone else."

"What's the matter with that? You simply find yourself a new one. They're not rare, I assure you."

"Because it hurts," I said. "It hurts like the devil."

The signal changed again, and we charged forward. I clutched the side of the door until my knuckles turned white.

Lady Alice glanced at my face and nearly drove the Renault into a lamppost. She straightened the wheels and set the brake, oblivious to the horns sounding around us. "Why, you poor thing. Is it that bad?"

"Yes, by God. It *is* that bad. It is for me. It's horrible."

She reached for my shoulders and drew me down into her scented lap, there by the curb, next to a shabby bar tabac and a florist putting out the last hardy blooms of the season. My tears stained her silk dress in large patches, but she never said a word about it, then or since.

5.

The next day was Saturday, and Johann picked me up as usual at six o'clock. By now, it was still quite dark at that hour, and chilly enough that I wore a thick scarf over my riding coat. The wind froze my cheeks. I stared silently ahead as the street unfolded in the glare of Johann's headlamps, and I thought, I'll have to tell him today. I can't go on pretending.

I would tell him when we stopped for his cigarette at the lower lake, and that would be that. This was the last time we would drive together like this, through the Paris dawn in his beautiful oil-black Mercedes, to the horses waiting at the Porte Dauphine.

We stopped at our usual spot, near the lower lake. The sky was just beginning to lighten. Johann lit his usual cigarette and said, "Is something wrong, my dear? You are quiet this morning."

"I'm always quiet." I watched him suck on the cigarette for a moment. His lips were thin, and when he smoked, they seemed to disappear altogether. I wondered what it would have been like if I had kissed him, if I had asked him to make love to me. I found myself regretting that I hadn't. I turned my head, until he existed only in the corner of my eye, and said, "I'm going to have a baby."

He didn't reply at first. I don't think he even moved. He stared at the lapping water and flicked some ash into the grass, and after a moment he said, "I see."

"It happened at the end of August, when everyone had left. I was lonely and innocent. A very stupid little affair. I never saw him afterward."

He said, "Do you *want* to see this man again?"

"No. Never." On the lake before me, a pair of swans glided free from the mist, white against the black shore. "I found out he was married."

"I see," he said again. He finished the cigarette and turned to me. His face was pale and stern. "You are in no condition to finish our usual ride, I think. Let us return to the car."

We rode miserably back to the Porte Dauphine. Johann kept his mighty bay to a walk, a half length ahead of me, and I watched his upright back, the reddened plane of his jaw, and wondered if I would see them again. The trees thinned and the darkness lifted, revealing a heavy layer of autumn cloud that obscured the chimney pots of the emerging buildings. The air was damp and cold and smelled of smoke. When we reached the groom, Johann jumped off his horse and helped me dismount.

We had driven several minutes before I realized we were heading in the wrong direction. "I thought you were taking me home," I said.

"I thought we might go to my apartment instead, where we can have breakfast and discuss what is to be done."

"There is nothing to be done. I'm having a baby in the spring. I suppose my father won't turn me out; it's not as if he has any ground to stand on."

Johann said nothing. The smell of exhaust, the movement of traffic was turning me a little sick. We arrived at the avenue Marceau, and Johann helped me out of the car and up the stairs to the louvered double doors on the second floor. We went to the study, and Johann asked the housekeeper for breakfast to be brought on a tray. He led me to the sofa and made me sit; he sat down next to me and picked up my hand and asked how I was feeling.

Numb, I thought.

"Well enough," I said.

"You must take good care of yourself," he said. "It is an important business, having a baby. There is a new life to be considered."

"Yes." I said the word without really meaning it, because I still hadn't translated this state of being—pregnancy—with a living baby. The one didn't seem to have anything to do with the other. I couldn't conceive that there was a human being growing inside me: my child, Stefan's child.

Johann patted my hand. "Good, good."

"You're being very kind," I said, looking down at our linked hands. "I don't deserve your kindness. The father—"

"Shhtt," he said sharply. "You are not to speak this black-guard's name. You are not even to think it. From now on, as far as I am concerned, as far as you and the world are concerned, I am the father of this child."

My head snapped up. "*You?*"

"Yes, Annabelle." He kissed my hand. "You are, I think, in need of a friend, a devoted friend. A husband."

"Husband?" I said stupidly.

"Forgive me. I am not elegant with words, as some men are. I am not skilled at wooing. But I have wished for some time to marry you, Mademoiselle de Créouville, and I think perhaps the earlier this service is performed, the more convenient it will be."

His words reached me from a distance. When I tried to breathe, the air was too thin. I said, in a voice so faint it couldn't possibly have been mine, "You can't be serious. I'm carrying another man's child."

He shook his head. "If we marry, Annabelle, the child is mine. He will have my name, he will have a home and a father and four doting brothers and sisters. God willing, we will give him more of them, in time."

"But your own children. A stepmother. They will hate me."

"On the contrary, Frieda will be delighted. She adores you. She has in fact been hinting to me, and not too delicately. The others, I suspect, have long wanted me to find someone to cheer me a little."

"You are mad," I whispered.

"No, I am not mad. I have never been so clear in my objective. I am in love with you. I have been consumed with you since I first saw you in your father's home, playing your cello for a roomful of people who were not worthy to hear you."

"Johann, stop," I said desperately.

"I realize I am not a handsome man, nor a charming man, but you will find me a faithful and devoted husband, my

Annabelle"—he kissed my hand again—"if you will allow me that honor. You are weeping."

"I don't deserve this. I don't deserve your kindness."

"It is not kindness, Annabelle. I am taking gross advantage of your situation to win the hand of a woman to whom I could not otherwise aspire. Now relieve my anxiety and tell me you will marry me."

He didn't look anxious. His large face had taken on color, and his eyes were bright, but his expression had hardly changed at all. My pulse clicked in my ears, my head rang. Marry him. Marry Johann. Safe, stern, faithful Johann, who had no hidden wife, no mistress. Johann, who loved me so much, he would take my shameful baby, too. I stared at his pale bright eyes, washed free of color, and I knew I would never catch Johann in bed with Peggy Guggenheim. I would never walk into a party and count a dozen other women he had slept with. Imagine that, a lifetime of secure love, a houseful of children and loyalty. Between myself and the cautionary tale of my mother's life, I would have Johann standing in protection, a reliable giant.

I had spent the last few weeks half expecting him to propose, half preparing to reject him, half preparing to accept him, and now that the opportunity had arrived, at the exact moment I had thought it lost forever, I didn't know how to reply. I stammered a helpless cliché: "I don't know what to say."

"You must say yes. You must. You have no choice. I am determined, Annabelle."

"Then yes," I said recklessly, and a wave of shock passed across my stomach. Marry Johann. I pulled my hand from his grasp and reached up to snatch his face between my palms, so I wouldn't be afraid of what I had just done. Who could be afraid, when Johann von Kleist stood between you and the world? "Yes, Johann. I'll marry you."

I crashed my lips into his, and the violence of his response made me gasp into his mouth. He seized my shoulders and stood, lifting me with him, holding me against his chest while he kissed me. The blood roared so loudly in my ears, I didn't hear the knock on the door, but Johann did. He set me back on the floor and took up my hand, and he told the surprised housekeeper to congratulate him, because Mademoiselle de Créouville had just agreed to become his wife.

6.

We were married the following Saturday, first at the German embassy by the ambassador and then at the Mairie de Paris, where our papers were properly stamped and the marriage made official. My reeling father attended, and a delighted Lady Alice, and all four of Johann's children, along with his sister, who had traveled from Berlin. Charles had still not returned, and nobody knew where to find him.

Afterward, we all had dinner at the Ritz, where Johann and I were to spend the night before leaving on our wedding trip to Rome. I sat between the two oldest children, Frederick and Marthe, who were perfectly friendly, if perhaps stiff. I couldn't blame them. Had their father given them any hint that he was thinking of marrying? Or had they just received telegrams at school, and the necessary train tickets to Paris? Frederick liked to play sports and ride like his father; Marthe was fond of tennis and books. They had been to Florence last summer with their father to see the art and enjoyed it very much, but their favorite part was when they woke up at dawn and drove to Siena for the Palio. One of the jockeys had fallen off, not fifteen feet away from where they were standing, and had nearly been killed. Frederick described this scene with vigor, using the salt and pepper to illustrate the various positions. I stared at his moving hands and thought, My stepson.

My father drank a great deal to overcome his shock. He gave a splendid toast and remarked on the absent Charles: *He will now think more carefully before leaving town without a forwarding address, eh?* Everyone laughed. Johann also rose and gave a brief toast, thanking everyone for attending on such short notice, but at his age one had lost the patience for a long engagement. He thanked me, his new wife, for the favor of marrying him, and he promised to make my happiness the study of his life.

We had a small but elegant white cake. Johann's half-English sister Margaret took pictures of us cutting it. When everyone finished, she shepherded the children to taxis, though not before lining them up to kiss their father and their new mother good-bye. The scent of sugar hung behind them. My father and Alice left shortly after that.

7.

As a surprise, Johann had booked the legendary Imperial Suite for our wedding night. It was only seven o'clock, but the November sky had already been dark for hours, so the evening felt much later.

We hadn't kissed since the moment of our engagement. There

was too much planning to be done, too many logistics to be sorted out. We had not had five minutes for romance, and Johann was, after all, an orderly man, who wanted to wait until our union was properly sanctioned. Now the plans had been executed, the logistics completed. We were man and wife, and there was nothing to do but to be married.

At the door to the suite, Johann bent down and lifted me into his arms to carry me across the threshold. I gasped at the opulence of the rooms. There was a bucket of champagne on the table in the drawing room, next to an enormous vase of fresh red roses, just opening and deeply fragrant. Johann opened the bottle and poured out two glasses. We drank to each other. Johann set down his glass and lit a cigarette with quick, nervous fingers. I had never seen him nervous. The understanding of his anxiety calmed my own jumping pulse, my panicked blood. I took his hand and asked him to show me the other rooms.

We saw the dining salon, the marble bathroom, the guest bedroom. We arrived at the splendid master bedroom, gilded, hung with silk damask, where the imperial bed confronted us, as wide as the ocean. I began to shake again, because it was done, there was no turning back: I was now irrevocably the wife of Johann von Kleist, and in a moment he was going to start kissing me, he was going to start making love to me. That was his right as my husband. A man who wasn't Stefan was now my husband. A man who wasn't Stefan was going to make love to me, consummating our marriage, and without the least warning a cry of grief ripped the interior of my lungs, like a cat clawing for escape: a cry of what in French we call *agonie*, because it was November and August was gone forever.

I must put August out of my mind, as if it didn't exist.

Johann took my champagne glass from my hand (it was only half finished) and set it on the bedside table next to his. He put out his cigarette in a small gold tray shaped like a seashell. He removed his splendid dress uniform jacket and hung it carefully in the wardrobe, and then he drew me into his enormous arms and kissed me, without uttering a word, and I thought, It's better this way, it's better that we don't say anything at all.

8.

It seemed almost silly, afterward, to fall asleep in bed together at the absurdly early hour of eight-thirty in the evening, though it would have been equally silly to rise. It was our wedding night, after all.

Johann climbed out of bed to fetch his cigarettes. When he returned, the mattress bowed to his weight, and I rolled helplessly into his side. He smoked for a while, without speaking, and finished his champagne. I fell asleep to the sound of his breathing and woke at eight to find my husband fully bathed and dressed, having already ordered breakfast, which was laid out neatly around a vase of fragrant gardenias on a table next to the bed: the start of our married life.

PEPPER

Cocoa Beach • 1966

1.

Pepper screams. Not because of the headlock, but because a current of pain has just thundered up her foot like an approaching freight train, and then slammed into her brain in a cataclysmic explosion, like you see in the movies.

Without warning, the arms drop away, and Pepper staggers face-first onto the oriental rug.

"Jesus!" the man says. "You're pregnant!"

The lamp flashes back on. Pepper rises on her elbow and clutches the top of her foot, encased in its slipper. Already a bubble of numbness is forming around the pain, an ominous sign. "Holy *fuck*," she whispers.

"Who the hell *are* you?"

"You just broke my foot."

"I didn't break your foot!" He crouches down next to her and lifts her hand away. "Oh. Jesus. Ouch."

"I'll say." An unfamiliar pricking sensation surrounds Pepper's eyeballs, like she might—please, God, no!—actually cry.

"Can you wiggle your toes?"

Pepper tries. "No."

"Damn it. I guess it's the ER. What the hell did you do?"

"What did *I* do? *You* were the one who grabbed me in a headlock, sonny."

"*You* were the one lurking behind the door in my mother's study, about to clobber me! *In the dark!*"

"I thought you were a burglar!"

"Me? For all I know, *you're* the burglar."

"Oh, you've got a nerve. Do I look like a burglar to you?"

Pepper lifts her head, tosses back her hair, and gives him a gander, just to make her point. And . . . well. Not quite what she expected, is he? Big young man, broad shoulders, dark hair, strong face, cranky eyebrows. Annabelle's son? Not that she cares. Not that it matters whether she cares, because in that instant of connection, right before her eyes, the cranky expression transforms to astonishment.

"Jesus. Pepper *Schuyler?*"

She frowns, or rather deepens her frown. "I'm sorry. Do I know you?"

His hand falls away from her foot. He looks at her face, blinking a little, as if to clear his eyeballs of her image and replace it with one he likes better. "I guess not," he says. "All right. You sit here, I'll get some ice."

"I'm not just going to *sit* here and wait for *ice*."

Annabelle's son rises to his feet and stares down at her. "Well, Miss Schuyler. I don't mean to be rude, but I'd say you don't really have a choice."

2.

"So how exactly did you hurt that foot?" asks Annabelle's son, as they drive to the hospital through the dark Florida night in the same Ford Thunderbird Pepper drove earlier that evening. Except that Annabelle's son has put the top back up, and her hair is quiet about her face.

"Because you stepped on it, you big ox."

"No, I didn't."

Pepper sighs. "It was the thing I was about to hit you with."

"What thing was that?"

"I don't know. It was dark. Some sort of statue on the bookshelf. I dropped it when you grabbed me."

He starts to laugh. "You were going to hit me with Mama's *Grammy?*"

"Her what?"

"Her Grammy Award. A music award. She's a cellist. You know, plays the cello." He motions with one hand, a fair bowstroke.

"I *know* she plays the cello. Obviously." Pepper speaks with dignity, and tries to ignore the rich quality of his laughter, which would be far more attractive if she weren't holding a bag of ice to her throbbing foot, thanks to his existence on this earth. She adds: "We're friends."

"God, I hope so, or I'll have to have you arrested for trespassing."

"Oh, wouldn't that be rich. Considering she practically kidnapped me and dragged me to her lair."

"Oh, really? Sounds like Mama, all right."

That laugh again. Pepper looks out the window, though there's nothing to see, just black shapes sliding past, houses and palm trees and telephone poles crawling with vines. There's always something a little overgrown about Florida, isn't there? As if the landscape is just waiting for its chance to take over again.

"Sure, go ahead and laugh," she says. "You're not the one with a broken foot, being held against your will."

"Nice try, but I'm not buying it. No one holds Pepper Schuyler against her will."

She turns her head and narrows her eyes at his dark profile. "You seem to know a lot about me, for a man I don't know from Adam."

"I work for a law firm in Washington. I've seen you around."

"Oh, another lawyer. I should have known."

"You've got a problem with lawyers?"

"No. I just seem to attract them, that's all."

He shrugs. "Flies to the honeypot. So how did Mama kidnap you?"

"I sold her a car."

"A car? What kind of car?"

"Didn't she tell you?"

There is a little silence. He checks the rearview mirror, slows the car, makes a left turn across an empty street, into an even emptier street. He drives competently, she'll give him that: fast and easy, clutch and gears in perfect synchronization. His hands are large and firm on the steering wheel, a detail Pepper admits reluctantly, because she's in no mood to find any man attractive, let alone this one, who just broke her foot.

"No," he says at last. "Why? Should she?"

"It's a mighty nice automobile, that's all. Cost her a fortune. Where's this hospital of yours, anyway? North Carolina?"

A nice easy chuckle. "No. Coming right up. How are you feeling?"

"Like a pregnant woman with a broken foot."

"I'm glad to hear it."

"Oh, a masochist, too. It figures."

A flurry of lights appears before them on the right-hand side of the road. He brakes carefully, and Pepper has the feeling he's grinning, the bastard.

"I'm not a masochist. I just figure you must be all right, if you can still snap like a turtle."

3.

"I suppose I should ask your name," Pepper says, as he's carrying her to a wheelchair inside a pair of thick arms. Her nose bobs along next to his neck, which smells absurdly of soap, sweet and clean. Soap! Who still smells like soap at two o'clock in the morning? Annabelle's son, apparently. She tilts her nose away.

"Oh, Mr. Dommerich will do."

"Not for what I have in mind."

"You're a tough customer, Miss Schuyler." He deposits her in the wheelchair and swings around to grasp the handles. "It's Florian."

"Florian?"

"Dare I hope it rings a bell?"

"It's not Tom, Dick, or Harry, anyway."

"Well, I guess you'll remember me now, at least. The ox with the oddball name who broke your foot." He pushes her confidently down an antiseptic white corridor. A nurse looks up from the station as they pass.

"Mr. Dommerich!"

"Well, hello, Nurse Smith. Long time no see. Late shift tonight?"

"Lucky me." She glances down at Pepper, and her mouth turns downward. She points her sharp finger to the right. "Labor and delivery is that way."

Florian laughs that laugh again. "Nope, not yet, Smitty. Just a broken foot. We're headed to the ER."

He must have flashed her a hell of a smile as he said it, because she brightens like a Christmas tree, right before she flushes like a beet.

"Oh! Of course! The ER is straight ahead," she sort of stammers, and Pepper rolls her eyeballs.

"I know. But thank you, Smitty. I'm just flattered you recognized me." He puts the faintest emphasis on the word *you*.

"Of course. I—I didn't realize you were married, Mr. Dommerich."

"Full of surprises," he says, over his shoulder.

Pepper says, once the nurse is behind them: "On familiar terms, I see."

"My dad was in and out of here for a while before he died. I got to know the joint pretty well. Here we are."

"Oh, God, I'm sorry. Of course. I wasn't thinking."

"What, an *apology*? Christ, what's next? You'll be thanking me, and I'll expire from shock." He addresses the orderly at the admittance desk. "Good morning. Not too busy, I hope?"

The orderly points to the door. "Labor and delivery, not ER. Don't they tell you anything?"

"No baby tonight, actually. Broken foot, if I know my meta-tarsals, and it's a doozy. The right one. How's the wait?"

The orderly looks down at Pepper's foot and frowns. He pulls out a clipboard from a stack, sticks in a sheet of paper, and hands it to Florian. Pepper makes a move to snatch it away, but Florian shoos her expertly. "You sit tight with the ice bag, all right? I'll take care of this."

"Are you the husband?" says the orderly.

Pepper opens her mouth to say no.

"Looks like it," says Florian.

The orderly laughs. "Name?"

"Florian Dommerich."

"I mean your wife's name."

"Oh. Pepper."

A frown. "Her real name, Mr. Dommerich."

There is an awful little silence. Pepper is still sitting in her state of shock; the casual word *wife* seems to have glued her jaw shut.

"Darling," says Florian, "what *is* your real name? I've forgotten."

Nobody knows Pepper's real name, if she can help it. She stares mutinously at the orderly, whose blue ballpoint pen stands poised over the paperwork on his desk.

"She's kind of funny about it," Florian says. "Wouldn't tell me until right before the ceremony, and even then she made me whisper the word, so only God could hear me. Just one of her adorable little foibles."

She was going to kiss him. She was going to murder him.

"I don't have all night, Mrs. Dommerich," says the orderly.

Florian coughs. "You can't just write down Mrs. Florian Dommerich? We are one flesh, after all. Joined at the hip."

"Is *your* foot broken, Mr. Dommerich?"

"Well, no."

The orderly points his pen at Pepper. "So I'll be needing *her* name, okay? And condiments don't cut it, not in the ER, not on my watch."

"With all due respect——"

"Prunella," says Pepper. "Okay? It's Prunella. Family name."

The orderly's eyebrows rise. Behind her back, Florian's chest makes a grave little shudder that travels through his arms to vibrate the wheelchair. He lifts one hand and snaps his fingers.

"Ah! That's it. How could I forget?" he says. "Prunella."

4.

On the way back to the villa, Pepper asks him why he did it.

"Did what?"

"Pretend you were my husband, back there."

"Oh, you know. Makes the paperwork easier, doesn't it? No awkward questions."

His tone is light. His tone is mostly always light, as if nothing is too serious for him to handle, everything's a joke; that taking a stranger, a heavily pregnant woman, to the emergency room in the middle of the night and pretending she's your wife is . . . well, just one of life's little adventures. He's rolled up his shirt-sleeves, and his forearms are sturdy, his hands strong as they hold the wheel. He is altogether dependable.

"Well, it ends now, okay?" she says. "No husbandly privileges when we get back."

"Perish the thought." Florian reaches for the radio dial and fiddles with it. Static, mostly, and then a thin stream of lonely trumpet pierces the noise. "I also figured you might need a break."

"A break, do I?"

"You know, holed up like this, no one around to rub your feet and buy you jars of pickles. Mama's got a nose for folks in trouble. I thought maybe you didn't need any more of it. Trouble, I mean."

There are all kinds of heroes, Annabelle said, on the ride up to Cocoa Beach, and as Pepper stares at the gray landscape a week and a half later, through an entirely different windshield, she hears those words again. Almost like the woman's sitting right there, like a chaperone—yes, right there delicately on the bench seat between the two of them, Florian and Pepper—and whispering in Pepper's ear.

"I can handle trouble, all right. People say it's my middle name. My first name, too, if you think about it."

"Oh. Prunella, you mean?"

"Don't get sassy."

"I'll get sassy if I feel like it, Miss Trouble. It's the least I can do for you, get you snapping again. Back in fighting-turtle form."

"What the hell does that mean?"

Florian slows the car and turns, and Pepper realizes they're already back at the house, that the dark space washing away to her right is the ocean, and the line of pink above is the breaking dawn.

"It means I like you how I saw you in Washington, Pepper Schuyler, even if you wouldn't give me the time of day. I like you conquering the world, not sitting back and letting it conquer you."

Pepper looks through the bug-spattered glass at the approaching garage and bursts into tears.

5.

She hates the crutches, and the crutches hate her. Florian knows better than to offer help. He just opens the doors wide as she comes to them, and smiles from the corner of his mouth as she swears.

"Need anything else?" he says, when she swings herself through the doorway of the guest cottage and tosses the crutches on the floor.

"Trust me, you've done enough."

"All right, then. Keep the handkerchief. Take your pills. Sleep as long as you like. I'll tell Clara to keep the coffee warm."

He starts to close the door, and Pepper says *Wait*.

Florian pauses with his large hand on the doorknob, eyebrows expectantly high.

"Thanks," she says.

He places his hand to his chest and staggers backward, shutting the door as he goes.

ANNABELLE

Paris • 1936

1.

By the time I saw Nick Greenwald again, in the first week of March, the baby had grown quite large, and I had to dress carefully to disguise the size of my belly. I was glad I did. Nick took off his hat and reached for my hand, and his eyes ran up and down me as if to assess me for slaughter.

"Good morning, Frau von Kleist," Nick said formally. "Thanks for agreeing to meet me here."

"It's Annabelle, and I can't stay long. I have an appointment in half an hour."

The appointment was manufactured, but my reluctance was not. I had told Johann in the morning, before he left for the embassy—since January, he had been working day and often night, something to do with treaty obligations—that I was going shopping for baby things today, and I hadn't lied. The evidence sat on the floor next to my chair: a small assortment of wrapped packages, and many more to be delivered to the apartment later in the afternoon. But I knew without asking that my husband wouldn't be pleased at my meeting another man alone—he trusted me without reserve, he said again and again, but he did not trust other men around me—and so I hadn't asked. I had only agreed to meet with Nick because I was afraid of the consequences if I didn't: Nick showing up at the apartment, or, worse yet, Stefan himself.

For months now, I hadn't let the thought of Stefan intrude on my happiness. I had forced him away with an iron discipline. I was happy, I told myself: I felt fit and healthy as my pregnancy progressed; I had had a luxurious honeymoon, a husband who worshipped me daily, a beautiful Paris apartment, an affectionate stepdaughter. After a month in Italy, motoring about in Johann's magnificent Mercedes, we had traveled straight to Westphalia for Christmas, where Johann had introduced me to the staff of his estate as the new baroness, and the children had arrived home to celebrate the season. We had all gotten along well, though Frieda was the only one who sought me out, to play the cello together and to take walks on the bitter winter grounds. "You must give them time, of course," said Johann. "They will learn to love you as I do."

"Not *quite* as you do, I hope," I had replied, because my new husband had spent those weeks in Italy like a penitent who has finally emerged from a long and grueling fast, far more interested in the feast he had married than the art and monuments surrounding us. But that was what a honeymoon was for, wasn't it? To seal man and wife together, before they faced the world again. When you made constant love to someone, you drove out everything and everyone else, until you almost forgot there *was* a world outside your union, full of messiness and complication and old lovers. All that physical intimacy made you feel as if you really *were* in love, you really *were* married forever.

Just that morning, I had opened my eyes to Johann's farewell kiss, and I had thought how handsome he was, how I couldn't imagine another face bending down to mine in the morning. And, of course, he wasn't handsome, not objectively. But at that moment, while the baby kicked softly in my belly, and the sheets smelled warmly of Johann, I loved his face too much to think him otherwise.

So as I stared down Nick Greenwald's lanky form across the grubby café table, I stiffened my chest against him and thought that he deserved that little lie about the appointment.

"I'll be brief, then," said Nick, lighting a cigarette and signaling the waiter. His face was grim and his eyes, when they looked at me, were hard and resentful. "I just have a few questions for you, on behalf of a mutual friend."

"I don't believe I owe you any answers."

He raised his eyebrows. The waiter arrived, and Nick ordered coffee. He took a long drag of his cigarette, and when the waiter had passed out of earshot, he blew out the smoke and said, "I suppose you've heard he's out of prison now."

"*What?* Who?"

"Stefan."

I couldn't breathe. The baby kicked against the wall of my stomach, and I put my hand on my side. "He's in prison?" I whispered.

"You didn't know?"

"No. I never heard a word from him, not since August."

Nick sat back in his chair, and a little of the resentment left his eyes, which, in the watery March sunshine that percolated through the window next to us, proved to be a charming shade of hazel. "I don't understand. Your brother never told you?"

"I haven't seen Charles since he left town in November. He doesn't approve of my marriage."

"It was a shock."

"It shouldn't have been. My husband is a good man. He's loyal and faithful, and I love him." I pushed hard on the word *faithful*, and my hand moved in a slow circle on my side, around the baby's protruding foot.

Nick's gaze dropped to my hand and back again. "So I see."

"If you have any questions," I said, "I wish you would ask them."

"Why did you meet with me, if you're so in love with your husband?"

"Not because I felt I owed you any explanation."

"Really? None at all? Not to *me*, I mean. I'm only here because Stefan asked me to see you."

My palms were damp. I flattened them against my dress. "Did he?"

"Yes. He rang me up a week ago, from Frankfurt. They're not letting him out of the country, you know. They're following him everywhere."

"I don't understand. Who's following him? Why was he in prison?"

His voice lowered. "The Gestapo, for God's sake. Don't tell me you don't know."

"I know a little. Not very much. Is he all right?" My throat shook a little.

"Well, he was arrested as soon as he set foot in Germany, the twenty-ninth of August. He was put in the new camp at Dachau, near Munich. Have you heard of it?"

"No."

"It took us months to figure out where he was, and then your brother went off to try to get him released. That was November. They finally let him out in February, banged up but alive, and your brother got him settled and came home to Paris, and that's when he found out, as you know, that you were married to von Kleist and expecting a baby already. And meanwhile Stefan was going crazy over there, he wanted to jump the border and find you, and when I told him the news over the telephone I thought he was going to shoot himself. He said there had to be some mistake. I said there wasn't." Nick crushed out his cigarette in the ashtray, just as the waiter arrived with his coffee. He added a teaspoon of sugar and took a careful sip. I couldn't speak. I watched his lips. He put down the cup and said, "He seemed to think the baby might be his."

"It isn't," I said instantly. "I started meeting Johann as soon as I came to Paris. I was furious and I wanted to forget, and Johann—"

"Furious?" said Nick. "Furious with Stefan?"

"Yes, because he hadn't told me he was married. And I had always sworn I would never go to bed with a married man, I would never do that to another woman, because of my mother. It killed my mother."

Nick was staring at me, astonished. His hand lay still on his cup; his back was rigid against the chair. "Are you kidding me?" he said. "*That's* why you left?"

"Yes. And I happen to think it was a damned good reason. I wouldn't ever knowingly betray another woman. So I married Johann, and yes, we're having a baby together, and I am certain, *certain*, that I've done the right thing this time, and I'll be damned if I let you convince me otherwise." I sat back, breathless, cradling the round ball of my belly, the fetus who was beating an irregular rhythm against my abdomen, unused to all this turmoil.

"All right," Nick said. "Keep your voice down."

I picked up my glass of water and drank it dry. Nick lit another cigarette and turned back his head to watch the smoke ebb upward into the stained ceiling. His fingers played with the sugar spoon, turning it this way and that in the cradle of his hand.

"I have to admire your principles," he said. "Most girls would carry on the affair anyway. But not Annabelle. She doesn't sit around feeling sorry for herself. She doesn't confront him and make a big stink. She just runs right off and marries the first man who asks her, a nice boring old German general who won't ever break her heart."

"He's not boring. He is the best man I know. And I make him happy. Every day, every morning I wake up and I know I've done the right thing."

Across the room, the waiter eyed us, arms crossed, resentful that we were taking up one of his best tables at the window with a glass of water and a cup of coffee. The baby was pressing against a nerve, making my right toes go numb. I shifted in my seat and opened my mouth to close the conversation.

"I don't know if I should tell you this or not," Nick said.

"Tell me what?"

He set down the sugar spoon and ran his thumb around the rim of the cup. "Can I ask you a question? Who told you he was married?"

"Lady Alice Penhallow. His old mistress. I met her at the Hôtel du Cap, after Stefan left."

"Ah. Good old Lady Alice. And she didn't tell you that his

wife had actually left him by then, had taken their daughter last March and gone off with some lover of hers, some neighbor, a childhood friend, as I understand it? That Stefan had gone home to give her the divorce she wanted, so that he could marry you, and that was when they caught him, crossing the border into Germany?"

The air left the room. The swallowed water rose up in my throat. I gripped the edge of the table, but it didn't help. "Excuse me," I said to Nick Greenwald, and I rushed to the dirty staff toilet in the back, where I heaved up the water and what remained of my breakfast, and then I heaved up nothing at all, just dry yellow bile and nothing else.

2.

Lady Alice wasn't at home, but my father was, still nursing his head from the night before. "Is something wrong, *mignonne?*" he asked, removing the ice pack from his head, and I said there was nothing wrong, I just had a question I needed to ask her.

He fell back on the sofa and closed his eyes. He assured me he would have her telephone me when she returned.

I went back downstairs to the waiting taxi. Nick Greenwald had offered to drive me home, but I refused. Actually, he had been quite kind. "It's a damned thing," he said, "an awful damned thing," and I remembered my brother told me that Nick had had some sort of love affair, back home in the States, that had gone badly. It was hard to imagine any girl breaking Nick Greenwald's heart, but Charles said Nick had been a wreck when they first met, drinking all night, taking women home from parties and discarding them afterward. There had been some legendary house party at a Loire chateau. Charles refused to disclose the details, and I had pieced together a few rumors that I thought could not possibly have been true. But that was the trouble about rumor, wasn't it? You never knew what to believe. You never knew for certain if a man was a hero or a villain or an ordinary human being.

But Charles had also said that Nick had returned from the house party a changed man: had sworn off drink (mostly) and women, and had singlehandedly rescued his family firm from the brink of bankruptcy. Again, that information might or might not have been true; all I knew was that Nick Greenwald couldn't have been kinder as he found me a taxi outside the café and helped me inside with all my packages, which I would have forgotten if Nick hadn't noticed them. He had rested his elbows on the edge of the door and gazed at me with compassion.

"It's a damned thing," he said again.

"Yes."

"What the hell do I say to Stefan?"

I gripped his arm. "Please don't tell him anything at all. Don't say anything to anyone."

"Hell," said Nick Greenwald. He lifted himself away from the taxi door and we pulled away from the curb, and the sight of his face, bruised and tender, stayed with me the rest of the afternoon, until Johann came home.

3.

During our wedding trip, Johann and I had spent a week on the Amalfi Coast, driving from village to village, and one evening, over dinner, Johann announced that he wanted to visit Pompeii the next day. I told him I wasn't interested, and he agreed we should go to Positano instead, but as I lay in bed that night, locked inside the coil of Johann's sleeping body, I thought about his disappointed face and his deep interest in military history and Roman civic organization, and when I woke up the next morning I told him that I had changed my mind, and if he wanted to visit Pompeii we should go.

It was the middle of November, and there were very few visitors. We pulled off the dusty road at nine o'clock and Johann pointed out the window and said, "There it is." I followed his finger and saw a cluster of crumbling yellow buildings, looking exactly like every other decrepit Italian village, except for an absence of the familiar red-orange roof tiles, and I thought, My God, it's just like Stefan said.

We wandered for a few hours among the buildings and monuments, the perfect amphitheater and the paved streets. At one point I bent down and picked up a shard of ochre-colored pottery and said, "Look at this. Let's take it back with us," and Johann said no, we should leave it here where it fell, like a soldier in battle. He pointed out the expert grading of the streets, the drainage, the orderly layout of the buildings. We walked for some time, and after consulting a map Johann suggested we visit the Antiquarium, where many of the frescoes and the artifacts were displayed, along with some plaster casts of the victims. I said no, I didn't want to see that at all, and Johann frowned in disappointment and looked back down at the map.

All right, I said. *Let's go.*

The museum was crammed with shelves and displays, a superabundance of antique detritus. I walked past great glass cases in which mothers clutched their children, and merchants clutched their bags of treasure, and I averted my eyes. Johann made his way more slowly, studying the angles of death, the quality of the plaster. We turned a corner, and there before us was a case containing a dog on its back, contorted in agony, bearing a thick collar around its sternum. I put my fist to my mouth and turned away, sobbing, and Johann said, *Annabelle, what's wrong?* and I said, *It's true, the poor dog, look at his face, the poor thing, he never knew.*

Johann patted my back and said, "Ah, don't fret so, Annabelle. It's just a plaster cast, not a real dog. Nothing to cry over." After a moment, he took my hand and we moved on to inspect a collection of gold bracelets in the shape of coiled snakes.

The pottery shard had traveled quietly that day in the pocket of my skirt, and I kept it now in the bottom of my drawer, beneath my underwear, where Johann would never dream of looking.

4.

I rose from the floor of the nursery, where I was inspecting fabric samples. I had brought the phonograph into the room, and the room was full of Puccini. "You're home early," I said to my husband.

Johann walked to the phonograph and lifted the needle away. The music stopped in mid-phrase, with a tiny scratch. He caught my hands and helped me up just as I found my feet. "Yes, it was rather a trying day, and I decided that there was no point in being such an important man if I could not leave my work to others and join my bride when she is expecting our baby."

"Not for another ten weeks."

He bent down and kissed me. "It cannot be soon enough for me. Are these for the nursery?"

"Yes. The curtains. What do you think?"

"Make sure they are good and thick. A well-darkened room is necessary for good napping."

I looked again at the samples. "Oh, of course. I didn't think of that."

"That's why it's useful to marry a man who has had children already. You see what a clever girl you are?"

I sank back to my knees on the rug and picked up two swatches, one in each hand, and I hated them both. "Yes, a very clever girl."

Johann crouched next to me. "Annabelle. Look at me."

I looked up.

"You have been crying, haven't you? Are you well?"

"I'm quite well, it's just these stupid swatches the draper gives me. None of them are right, and it will still take weeks to have them made, and the baby will be here soon, and I don't know what to do—"

He drew me against his woolen chest. "Shh. Calm down. It is nothing, Annabelle. It doesn't matter, the color of the curtains. The baby will not even notice, I promise you."

The wool scratched my forehead. I heard Nick's voice: *I thought he was going to shoot himself.*

The parting began again in my ribs. I took Johann's lapels in my fists and forced Nick's voice away. I forced away the image of Stefan on the telephone, fresh from the prison where they had sent him after he crossed the border into Germany on the twenty-ninth of August, listening to Nick Greenwald explain that Annabelle de Créouville was not waiting faithfully for him in Paris, but instead had married a Prussian baron and was pregnant with his child. I pictured Stefan's shocked dark eyes, his gaunt face.

"Annabelle," Johann said gently. "You are distressed."

I looked up and thought, It's not his fault, it's my fault. What had Stefan said? *We are in God's hands now.* I remembered feeling a warm glow when he said those words, because in my innocence I thought they meant that God had brought us together, that we were intended for each other, and God would solve all our difficulties and bring us together.

But, as usual, I had misunderstood. It seemed God had not intended me for Stefan, after all. He had intended me for Johann von Kleist, who had lost so much in his thirty-eight years, and needed a fresh young wife to comfort him.

The thing was done.

There was a brief knock, and the nursery door burst open. It was Frieda, telling me that Lady Alice was on the telephone for me.

5.

"Darling, I had no idea," Lady Alice said. "It's not the sort of gossip that spreads easily. If she'd been somebody important, of course, I might have heard about it."

I glanced out the tiny round window into the courtyard. Johann hated the telephone, and we had only one in the apartment, relegated to a closet off the library. I wondered if she was telling the truth, and whether it mattered.

"Anyway," she went on blithely, "the fact remains, he never told you about her, or the daughter. That's not fair play, is it?"

"No."

"So it makes no difference, really."

"Yes, it does. If I'd known she'd left him, I might have waited for an explanation, at least." I spoke in a hushed whisper.

"But he still would have been caught at the border and thrown in prison, wouldn't he? So there's no telling how everything might have worked out. And think of poor Johann. Aren't the two of you just appallingly happy these days?"

"Yes, we're very happy."

"So there's no use thinking about it, is there? What's done is done. You're far better off with your lovely loyal old hound of a Prussian, the one you're married to. Put the whole matter out of your head. I assure you, Stefan will have no trouble finding another pretty young thing to lick his wounds for him. And whatever else needs licking."

She made perfect sense. Stefan would surely be back to his old ways in no time, and I had faithful Johann and the baby, who needed me. There was only Nick Greenwald's voice at the back of my head—*I thought he was going to shoot himself,* and sometimes *He seemed to think the baby might be his*—and Nick's voice was easily silenced, if I concentrated hard enough, if I drowned it out with other things.

"All right," I said. "I suppose so, when you put it that way. I was just feeling low, and a little guilty."

She laughed right into the receiver, crackling the hairs of my ears. "Oh, for heaven's sake, darling, don't do *that*. Life is far too short to look back."

6.

That night, Johann made respectable married love to me in our bed, turning me on my side and entering me from behind so the baby would not be crushed between us, a position we had adopted a month or two ago.

When we had both caught our breath, he cupped his hand around my heavy womb and said, "Annabelle, I will be very busy in the next few days. I may have to go away."

"Where to?"

"Perhaps to Berlin. Perhaps to a few other places." He paused. "There is nothing to worry about."

"Should I be worried?"

"I have just told you, there is nothing. But if I send word that you are to join me somewhere, to leave Paris at once, you will do so, won't you?"

"Why, Johann? What's going on?"

"You know I cannot say."

My heart thudded in its empty cavity. I thought, What if we go to Germany? Stefan is in Germany. I said, "You can't even hint? Don't you trust me?"

"It isn't a matter of trust, *meine Frau*. It is a matter of honor. But you will do as I ask, won't you? You will come to me at once, if I send for you?"

The baby stirred under his hand. I laid my fingers over his and said, "Can you feel him?"

"Yes, of course. The tiny foot, right there. But you have not answered my question, Annabelle, *Liebling*."

"Yes, Johann," I said, staring at the wall. "Of course I will come to you."

He let out a sigh onto the top of my head. "Good. Because there is one thing I cannot bear, and that is the absence of my Annabelle. And of our little child, it is unthinkable."

"You should never worry about that. I'm yours now."

"Yes, I know that. I know your noble heart. It is what I prize most in you." He kissed me tenderly. "I have always loved this part, when my wife is round and beautiful, and we lie here in our bed and wonder what our child will be like when he is born."

"Yes." The tears fell silently into the pillow. "I love this, too."

7.

At dawn the next morning, nineteen German infantry battalions entered the Rhineland, on the eastern border between France and Germany, in violation of some treaty, I forget which, made in the previous decade, which had guaranteed its permanent demilitarization.

I learned all this from the housekeeper, because Johann had already left the apartment. For the next several days, I did not see my husband, who worked and slept at the German embassy, waiting for the French response. He later told me that if the French had mobilized, if the French had offered even a hint of military opposition, they would have had to retire at once, the defeat would have been total.

But the French did not mobilize, and Johann returned home nine days later, after a further trip back to Berlin for debriefing, heavy-eyed and triumphant.

When we were alone in our bedroom, he sank to his knees

before me and lifted my dress to kiss my swollen skin. "Now our child will be born into a safe, strong Fatherland," he said, "with nothing more to fear."

8.

I went into labor twelve weeks later, on the ninth of June—*first babies are always late,* said Dr. Périgault, shaking his head as if the babies were somehow willfully to blame—and gave birth early the next morning to a boy, eight pounds thirteen ounces, bearing a shock of black hair and a pair of lungs like an army sergeant.

"He has his mother's coloring," said the nurse, handing the army sergeant to his father for the first time, later that afternoon.

"Thank God for that," Johann replied. He looked into the baby's squashed red face with the same rare rapture as he had regarded me on our wedding night, and touched his cheek with a most delicate finger. The squalls faded into gasps, and then silence.

The nurse smiled beatifically. "Have you decided on a name?"

"Yes," I said, exhausted and entranced, from the nest of white pillows on my hospital bed. (His wife, Frieda, had hemorrhaged to death at home before the doctor could arrive, and Johann refused to take any chances with me.) I watched Johann straighten the swaddling into a more expert tuck. The baby looked tiny and safe and quiet in his enormous arms, and the breath fell from my lungs.

I turned my face to the nurse. "His name is Florian, for his grandfather."

Intermezzo

"June suns, you cannot store them
To warm the winter's cold"

A. E. HOUSMAN

1.

It was three days before Christmas, and the girls and I had motored into Berlin to shop, leaving Florian at home with his father and brothers.

We traveled not in Johann's black Mercedes, which we left in Paris, but in the massive Daimler Johann kept here in Germany, driven by a chauffeur in a field-gray uniform. The trip took two and a half hours along a highway of rich new asphalt, and Frieda did most of the talking.

"He has a new tooth coming in, the one on the right side," she said. "Did you see it?"

"I didn't need to *see* it. I've felt it the past few days," I said, and I laughed to cover the ripping sound in my chest, because I hated leaving my son even for an hour, let alone for an entire day of shopping in Berlin. *The Baroness von Kleist, she is such a devoted mother,* they said in Paris, bewildered, where mothers of a certain class happily handed off the baby to the nursemaid after a friendly morning cuddle, but the truth was far more elemental than that, a chemical intensity of emotion that had begun its slow combustion about the third or fourth day after Florian's birth, in some tranquil hour before dawn, when he was suckling at my breast and his eyes wandered up to mine in such a perfect representation of Stefan that I felt the universe move in my marrow, as if I had fastened all my ideas of the infinite upon a single black eyelash. The sensation might possibly be described in music or in mathematical equations or in geometric designs, but not in words.

Johann had been the one to suggest, two nights ago, that I leave Florian at home and go into Berlin for the day. We had converted a box room adjacent to our bedroom into a small nursery, and I was there in my dressing gown, nursing Florian inside a pink haze of bliss. I had looked up, bewildered, and said, "Go into Berlin? But what about the baby?"

"He will be looked after well. The housekeeper knows what to do. He has a father who adores him, and brothers who tolerate him without too much complaint."

"But his milk!"

"We have some bottles. And he is eating now." He knelt down next to the chair and touched my hand. "Annabelle, *Liebling*, you are a wonderful and devoted mother, but you must learn to leave him a little, too. He is six months old. The doctor says you should not even be nursing him still, or he will get a complex."

"That's nonsense. You and Lady Alice and your complexes. I know my son far better than old Périgault. Look at him, he's perfectly healthy."

"It is not a question of physical health. It is his attachment to you. We do not want our fine strapping son to become a mama's boy, do we?"

Yes, we do, I thought passionately. I gazed down at Florian's working mouth, his inquisitive dark eyes, and my arms ached around him.

Johann went on. "The two of you, you are like a closed link, and nobody else comes inside. But we all need you, *meine Frau*. Our girls need you, and our boys. And you know how desperately *I* need you, your poor lonely husband."

He had chosen his tactics well, like the general he was, and he knew I couldn't resist an appeal like that. So here I sat in the monumental Daimler, rushing into the center of Berlin, heart bleeding out into the seats, discussing Florian's new tooth with my stepdaughters.

"Does it hurt?" Marthe asked practically. "The tooth, I mean, when you feed him."

"Not really. He's very good."

Frieda said, "He is. He is the most darling baby. I can't wait until you have another."

I laughed again. We were just turning the corner of Leipziger Platz, and the crowds thickened at once, a mass of woolen coats and hats, the steady buzz of humanity. "One baby at a time, sweetheart. Look, we're almost there. Where shall we start?"

"Wertheim, of course!" Frieda said.

Marthe frowned and looked out the window.

Berlin's largest department store was predictably packed, from its ground floor overflowing with hats and scarves and haber-dashery to its monumental staircases like the channels of an ant farm. We shouldered through the entrance into a warm draft of perfume-scented air. Frieda exclaimed with joy at every display. Though she lived in Paris, in the heart of the fashionable district, we hardly ever went shopping. I was too occupied with Florian, and Johann disliked the idea of letting her roam free among the shops and streets. *It is nothing but material excess,* he said, *nothing but decadence.*

Marthe seemed to share her father's opinion. She trailed behind us with her arms folded across the chest of her red woolen coat. She was a beautiful girl, almost a young lady, who (like Frieda) wore her spun-gold hair in a thick braid around her head like a crown, a few shades richer than her father's. Her large blue eyes were set in a perfect oval face that Johann said was an exact replica of her mother's, down to the picturesque freckles on her nose. Her school reports were uniformly excellent; Johann was immensely proud of her. Of the two sisters, she was the more reserved, although she had a lovely singing voice and often joined me in the evenings, after dinner, when Johann encouraged his wife and children to come together and play Christmas hymns. Just now, however, her pink mouth was turned down at the corners and tight in the middle, not festive at all.

I fell back and took her arm. "Is something the matter, darling?"

She pulled the arm away. "No, Mother."

Frieda picked out a cashmere scarf for her father and leather gloves for the older boys. We went upstairs to the children's department, where she found a pretty blue woolen hat for Florian. She paid for everything herself from a carefully husbanded allowance, and watched with a radiant face as the little packages were wrapped in paper.

Marthe's arms were still folded. She tapped her toe against the floorboards and stared somewhere above us, to the tops of the polished shelves.

A woman passed by, pushing a baby in a perambulator. The

baby was about Florian's age, maybe a month or two younger, propped up against his white bedding—it was a boy, wrapped in a pale blue knitted sweater and matching cap—and his curious eyes caught mine. I put my hand against the counter to support myself and thought, Johann is right, it's healthy to be away for a bit, but I didn't feel healthy at all. My breasts hurt, my nipples smarted. I felt the milk leak eagerly into my brassiere and was glad for my thick coat, my tweed jacket beneath it, the practical cotton shirt from which such stains could easily be washed.

The packages were wrapped and bound in string for a delighted Frieda. We edged our way through the hot crowd to the stairs. "Are you all right, Mother?" asked Frieda, slipping her hand into mine, and I said of course I was all right, I just needed a bit of air; it was so warm in here with all the people.

We started down the stairs. Marthe trailed a step or two behind. Ahead of us in the crowd was a man wearing a navy blue hat above a neat navy blue suit; a line of dark curling hair showed below the brim of the hat, against a strong white neck.

There was something so familiar about that neck, that hair. The carriage of his head.

No, it's impossible, I thought. Of course it was impossible. Germany was a very large country, and Stefan was supposed to be in Frankfurt; he was in Frankfurt when he spoke to Nick Greenwald.

But I could not look away from that dark hair. I thought I could discern every strand. I stretched my neck in an effort to catch the man's profile, the line of his jaw, the shape of his nose. My heartbeat thudded in my neck and fingertips. The hat disappeared for an instant, and I sidled past a pair of women, pulling Frieda along with me, wheeling around the corner for the next flight. "Wait, Mother!" Frieda said, and I stumbled downward, running my eyes feverishly over the mass of identical hats seething before me.

"Mother!" called Marthe from behind, and at the same second her voice reached my ears, I caught sight once more of the familiar neck, the familiar dark hair, and I darted down, feet flying, fingertips thudding, like a woman holding a single ticket in a sweepstakes, who knows the odds are impossibly against her, who didn't until this moment realize that she wanted so badly to win, who knows in her heart that she *can't* win. But she still thinks, as the number is drawn among millions, that it will be hers.

I let go of Frieda's hand to take the man's navy wool elbow, and I shouted, *Stefan!*

I realized, as I turned, that the man was at least two inches too short. My cheeks already burned by the time I saw the shape of his nose (too large) and the line of his jaw (too narrow).

"*Es tut mir leid, es muss ein Irrtum sein,*" he said. There must be some mistake. The girls assembled at my elbows. Frieda had dropped her packages on the stairs. The man helped her pick them up, while the other shoppers flowed around us, grumbling, like a river parting around an unwelcome obstruction.

Marthe turned to me, still frowning. "Who is Stefan?" she said.

2.

We had lunch in a small restaurant nearby: tea and sandwiches and hot cabbage soup. I wasn't very hungry. "Mother, it is so hot in here. Why don't you take off your coat?" asked Frieda, and I opened the top two buttons and said I would be fine. My hands were still clumsy as I operated my spoon. I set my teacup carefully in its saucer so it wouldn't shake.

We talked very little. I paid the bill and walked out the door behind the girls, and as I turned to close the door behind us I noticed a sign in the window I hadn't seen on the way in:

JUDEN NICHT WILKOMMEN

3.

We visited a few more shops and found the chauffeur parked on the corner of Wilhelmstrasse, as we had arranged, at three o'clock. The light was already starting to fade. Marthe was still quiet as we started off through the streets of Berlin. She kept her arms folded across her chest and looked out the window, at the passing buildings, while Frieda exclaimed about all the goods in the shops.

"And that hat for Florian," she said, turning to me. "Won't he look just sweet wearing that hat?"

I opened my mouth to say, Yes, of course, we would take a photograph of him wearing it on Christmas morning.

Marthe's head turned. "It's un-German," she said.

"What's that?"

"The *Warenhausen*, they're un-German. We should not have gone there, to Wertheim."

"Un-German?" I said, astonished. "How could Wertheim possibly be any *more* German?"

"They are owned by the Jews, these department stores. Good German businesses suffer because of them." Her mouth compressed in a belligerent line.

"But that's nonsense. Who told you this?"

"It's not nonsense. We have been learning it all at school. The *Warenhausen* are like great leeches set on the cities. They sell cheap goods, and all the money goes to make the Jews richer. Wertheim is the worst of all."

Frieda was quiet, her lips parted in a small round hole of astonishment. I stared at Marthe's profile, stern and blond. Through the window, I saw a few flakes of snow shooting behind her, like distant meteors.

I said quietly, "Have you talked to your father about this?"

"He feels the same way."

"I find it difficult to believe that the man I married is a bigot," I said, "and I am disappointed beyond words to find this true of my daughter."

She turned to the window and muttered something in German. I couldn't quite pick out the words—I was still learning the language—but Frieda gasped and looked at me. I took her hand and shook my head.

Frieda leaned toward Marthe and whispered in her ear. Marthe went on staring at the shooting snowflakes, the bleak brown winter suburbs, and didn't reply.

I leaned my head back against the cloth seat. Under my skin, in the cavity around my heart, I could still feel the splinters of shock from my flight down the stairs. If I closed my eyes, I could still see that line of dark hair against a white neck, and it really did belong to Stefan, even though it hadn't; I thought I could feel him move in my head and lay a soothing hand on my splintering skin. I thought, *What should I say, Stefan? What do I say to her? What do I do?*

And he said back, *You know what to do, Annabelle.*

Frieda's body was warm and lithe next to mine, new and untried. I drew her against me and put my arm around her shoulders. "It was lovely shopping with you today, girls, but I confess I can't wait to be back in our nice warm house with your father and the boys."

4.

Before we even entered the house, I could hear Florian's cries. "He wouldn't take the bottle," Johann said, haggard, almost tossing the baby into my arms.

"Thank God," I muttered, because I was ready to burst. I collapsed into the chair and ripped open my blouse. He nursed furiously for half an hour before falling unconscious against my skin, trailing a thin line of contented milk from the corner of his mouth, and I kissed the top of his dark head and promised him I wouldn't go away like that again.

"Perhaps we should consider weaning him," said Johann. He stood at the window, watching the lines of snow cross the glass and disappear into the black night.

I moved Florian carefully to my shoulder. "Not yet."

"But soon, perhaps," said Johann, so softly that I looked up in surprise. His face was dark against the window, and golden with lamplight on the other side. One pale eye regarded us. He let the curtain fall back and said, "I would like to have more children."

"Of course we'll have more children. But he's still a baby, and there's plenty of time."

"I will be forty years old next month."

I smiled. "But I'm only just twenty-one. Anyway, you've got plenty of children to occupy you for now. How many does one man need, really?"

"I miss you."

"Johann, I'm right here. I sleep next to you every night."

"We have not made love since he was born."

"I didn't realize you wanted to." Florian burped against my shirt. I picked up a cloth, dabbed my shoulder, and brought him back into the cradle of my arms. His eyes were closed, and the sight of his cheeks brought the splinters back to my skin.

"Of course I want to make love to you, Annabelle. I am only a man, after all. But it is for you to decide when you're ready to have another baby."

Again I looked up in surprise. "But we don't have to make a baby. There are many ways to prevent conception."

He frowned. "What do you know of these?"

"Lady Alice."

He brought his fist against the window, making it rattle through the curtain, and pushed himself away to cross the room. "A man does not wear a sheath with his wife, Annabelle. They are for whores and mistresses."

"Nonsense," I said crisply.

He muttered something to the carpet.

"I'm simply not ready for another baby, Johann. I want to wait until Florian is at least a year old before we try again."

"A year!"

"Johann, please. It's not unreasonable, is it? We can still make love, if you want."

"If *I* want? Don't you want to make love with me?"

I looked back down at Florian's sleeping face. "Of course I do. But we must take precautions, that's all."

He came toward us in two giant strides and knelt next to the chair. "Annabelle, I need you. Look at my two hands. They are aching to touch you again, the way we used to. Don't you ache for me?"

I looked at him helplessly. "Of course I do."

"No, you do not. Of course you do not." He closed his eyes. "But you are so good and loyal, Annabelle. That, I could not do without. I could not live without your loyalty. You don't understand, I think, how much I need you."

"Then touch me, Johann. Kiss me."

"I cannot. I cannot stop if I do."

"I'll put the baby to bed."

He rose and looked down at us both. "No. I don't wish to disturb you."

He walked to the door, and I called after him. "Johann, there's something I need to speak to you about."

He stopped with his hand on the door handle and said, over his shoulder, "So do I, with you. But it is time for dinner, *Liebling*. It can wait."

5.

At Johann's house in Westphalia, which his family had owned since the seventeenth century, we dined at a magnificent walnut table in a paneled room, attended by two servants, and we dressed in formal clothes. The wine was always German. After the main course was cleared away and the table stripped for dessert, Johann dabbed his mouth with his napkin and rose to his feet.

I sat at the other end of the table, with the girls on my right and the boys to my left. I drank the last of my wine and set down the glass. Everyone had turned to Johann, who stood there like a colossus, making even the table seem small. He looked around the room, across the tops of our heads, and I had the feeling he was hesitating.

"Johann, what's the matter?" I said.

"I have a bit of an announcement." He pressed his fingertips into the edge of the table. "I have been asked to assist the government with a project of great importance in Berlin, which will shortly require us to move to the capital for a certain period."

"Move to Berlin?" I said stupidly.

"Yes, my love. We will live in Berlin, much closer to the children and their schools, which, among other things, will enable us to raise Florian in his own country with a proper understanding of his home and his native language."

"I don't understand," I said.

Frederick spoke up, saying something enthusiastic in German, and Johann stopped him.

"Speak in English, Frederick, so your mother can understand us."

"I'm sorry," Frederick said, glancing at me with his startling pale eyes, exactly the same shade as his father's. "It is wonderful news, that's all. We will be more like a family again."

"That is my hope," Johann said, smiling benignly across the

table, as if he had not just laid the perfect ambush and executed it without mercy. "Don't you agree, my love?"

My face was hot. Johann's image blurred in front of me. I laid my napkin on the table and rose.

"Excuse me," I said. "I believe I'll go check on the baby."

6.

I had fallen in love with the Kleist family estate at the moment Johann had driven me up the road in his black Mercedes Roadster. The top was up, because it was December, so I couldn't see the house itself until we had come around the last bend in the graveled drive, and then it appeared, yellow-walled, in perfect proportion, too sober to be called baroque and too exuberant to be classical. In the center grew a small blue dome, decorated with elegant stone scrollwork. The shrubbery outside was covered in sacking against the bitter frost.

"Oh, it's lovely!" I had exclaimed, peering forward through the windshield. "Why didn't you tell me it was so lovely?"

"Would you have married me sooner if I had?"

I had turned and kissed his cheek. "I don't think it would have been possible for me to marry you sooner."

He had taken me on a long and thorough tour—*You are the baroness now, my love, it is all yours*—which had taken most of the afternoon and evening. I had felt disoriented in the profusion of rooms and furniture and artwork, the reek of beeswax and old plaster, and held on firmly to Johann's elbow, wondering how on earth I could possibly be expected to manage all this.

The next day, while the younger ones were outside playing in a new fall of snow, and Johann had settled himself in his office to scale a mountain of neglected paperwork, I had begun to explore the house on my own. The eastern wing was my favorite. At the other end of the library was a pair of intimate rooms, connected by a door that could be left open or shut, where I could read quietly by myself, or practice the cello. The decoration was simpler, as if the old castoff furniture had traveled here to die in peace. Johann told me that his wife, Frieda, had spent much of her time there, too, and I had often wondered how much we were alike, and whether we would have liked each other.

After Johann's grand announcement at dinner, I didn't return to the dining room, nor to the music room, where we usually spent the last of the evening. Johann found me around ten o'clock in the smaller of the two rooms, playing Schubert while the snow blew horizontally outside the window and the gusts of wind made the chimney whistle.

"It was just a surprise, that's all," I said, without looking up from the music. "You should have told me."

"There wasn't time."

"Of course there was time. But you wanted to tell me in front of the children, so I couldn't contradict you." I rested the cello against my knee and looked up.

"But why would you want to contradict me?" He appeared genuinely bewildered. "It's a great honor, this post. A tremendous advance for my career."

"Paris is my home."

"Annabelle, we are a family. You are German now."

I rose from the chair passionately. "I am not German! I won't be German. Do you know what your daughter said today, when we were leaving Berlin? She said that we shouldn't shop at

Wertheim, because it's owned by a Jew. She said the department stores are like leeches, sucking Germany dry."

He blinked his eyes. "What's this?"

"It's true. That's what they're teaching her at school. And all over Berlin there are signs in the shops and restaurants, about Jews not being welcome. I don't know much German, but I understood that. It's disgusting, the bigotry. I won't live in a city like that. I won't allow my son to be poisoned like that." I knelt and laid the cello in its case and picked up a cloth to wipe the resin from the strings.

Johann stood silently in the center of the room. His hands were closed against his sides, flexing slightly. "He is *our* son," he said quietly.

"Go ahead," I said. "Go ahead and denounce it."

"Annabelle."

"Please denounce it, Johann. You can love Germany and still denounce this. If you *do* love Germany, you will."

"Of course it is distasteful," he said.

"Distasteful? Is that all?"

"What do you want me to say, Annabelle? Of course I do not share this opinion."

"But you won't do anything about it, will you? You'll go on supporting these horrible men who stir up people's lowest instincts just for their own gain. You'll allow them to poison your own children instead of standing up for what's right."

"That's not fair, Annabelle. This . . . this thing, it is just a kind of sickness, a malady of spirit. It will pass. It will fade away, when times are better. It always does."

"But in the meantime, people will suffer. It isn't *right*, Johann. I won't live here. I won't do it."

"You speak as if Germany is the only place where this happens, the only place where Jews are not welcome. Look at France, the Dreyfus affair. Look at the pogroms in Russia. Even in New York and London, Jews are not received in the clubs or the drawing rooms. It is simply how things are." Johann's face was turning red, right up to the roots of his hair, so that his pale blue eyes looked like chips of ice perched in a tomato aspic.

I tilted up my chin to face his passion. "Don't be disingenuous, Johann. You know what's going on here."

"I am not. I admit it's wrong. But this is not such a great matter as you say. It is just a yearning for racial separation, which is a primeval human instinct, and therefore difficult to control. We see it in all countries. I do not advocate it. I have nothing against the Jews. But I understand why these passions are stirred, and I understand there is nothing to be done. It must simply run its course."

"Run its course? Are you mad?" I stabbed my finger at his chest. "You're a powerful man, an army general, a baron! You can do something! But you won't, will you? You're too scared of that stupid man. You're scared they will call you a Jew lover, or say you're un-German. You're—"

"You know *nothing* about this, Annabelle. *Nothing.* Don't speak of things of which you are ignorant."

"Oh, of course. How stupid of me. My job is to lie on my back and spread my legs and make more babies, and to raise your children and adorn your house, not to have opinions and especially not to discuss them. I don't know why I bother with this old thing anymore." I kicked the cello case. "It's not as if you're going to let me out of the house with it, God forbid."

Johann's face was aglow, his shoulders rigid. He turned and grasped the edge of the mantel with his right hand, so forcefully

I thought it might splinter. The clock ticked endlessly next to his chest. "Forgive me," he said at last. "I have made you unhappy."

"I am not unhappy. But I don't want to move to Berlin."

"It is only temporary. Six months, or perhaps a year."

"I can't do it."

He picked up the poker and nudged a charred log into place. "You have become a champion of some cause, it seems."

"I'm a champion of humanity. And it's inhuman, what I saw in Berlin. What your own daughter said to me."

He went on poking needlessly at the simmering fire. He was still dressed in his dinner jacket, sharp and black against the pale blue walls and the creamy mantel. Sometimes I forgot how big he was, until his size rushed against me—like now, when I measured him and realized he took up half the wall. I wondered how we looked together, to an outsider: my delicate bones against his blunt ones. When I was wearing high evening shoes, the top of my head came to his collar. I must look like a child next to him.

"I wonder," he said, in the same soft voice, "whether it is really Berlin you object to."

"What else would it be?"

He set the poker in the stand and turned to me with his bleak face. The blood had drained away from his skin, as if he had gained conscious control of his unruly circulation. Another gust hit the chimney, and the wind whistled down the column at a furious pitch. The sound made me shiver.

"I don't know," he said. "Perhaps you would like to tell me, Annabelle."

"There's nothing to tell. I don't understand."

"Marthe tells me you met a man named Stefan at the department store today."

I crossed my arms. "I saw someone on the stairs, in the crowd. I thought I recognized him, but I was wrong. It wasn't him. Very silly."

"Did you want it to be this man? This Stefan?"

"Of course not! He just looked familiar, that's all. Is that what you're so mournful about this evening?"

Johann stepped away from the mantel and took my left hand in a sandwich between his. "I want to make you happy, Annabelle. I want to be a husband to you."

"You *are* my husband, Johann. I don't understand."

"I mean the husband you *want*. The husband in your heart."

There was something so melancholy in his voice, as if his own heart lay in two pieces on the floor between us. I leaned forward and touched his cheek. "You are, Johann. Of course you are. You're a wonderful husband, the most wonderful father to Florian."

"But you cannot follow me."

"I can't go against my own conscience. If you really loved me, you wouldn't want me to."

He sighed and released my hand. "Is it really your own conscience? Or is this only an excuse?"

"Johann, wait. You're turning everything upside down, you're making it sound as if—"

"I must go to bed now, *meine Frau*. I will be very busy over the next few weeks." He turned and walked to the door. "I hope you will change your mind."

"Johann, stop."

But he didn't turn back. His body swallowed the door like a blotch of deep black ink.

Third Movement

"Where there is marriage without love, there will be love without marriage."

BENJAMIN FRANKLIN

ANNABELLE

Paris • 1937

1.

When I woke up on that hot July morning, seven months later, I had not the slightest intention of betraying my husband by the end of the evening.

I had expected the usual day, the usual routine of caring for Florian and managing our small household, perhaps a walk to the park if it wasn't too sultry, a visit to the nearby shops when Florian took his nap, reading and music in the evening. There was almost always a letter from Johann in the morning post, to which I replied by afternoon; sometimes Lady Alice would stop by to visit and gossip. In a few weeks, we would pack for a month in Westphalia, until the younger children went back to school and Frederick left for university. An entire month, in which to mend together the tattered ends of my marriage.

You see? I still held out hope.

At the end of the Christmas holidays, I had returned to Paris while Johann remained in Berlin. We had explained to our families that Johann's post was only temporary, so we hadn't wanted to upset our routine, or give up the Paris apartment, which was so desirable. Johann had arrived with me to help me with the luggage, and he had left by ten o'clock on the wagon-lit to Berlin, without staying a single night. He wrote faithfully every day, a single page describing his activities and the weather, ending each letter in a copperplate *Yours always, Johann,* and I replied faithfully to every one.

In April he had come to Paris for a few days on business. I had met him in the morning at the Gare de Lyon in the Mercedes, and he had driven us back to the apartment and taken Florian in his arms and exclaimed over how well he had grown, what a fine boy he was. His stony face had softened with love. The two of them had spent the rest of the morning on the floor of the nursery, trying out one toy after another, while the delicate spring sunshine lit the windows.

I had tried to make my husband welcome. I had kissed him and taken his arm, I had planned dinner and the theater to show him how wonderful things could be, safe in Paris with his son and his young French wife. I thought if we could just go to bed again, the way we had before Florian was born, we could find our way back. I would feel once more like Johann's wife. I would absorb myself once again in the duties and pleasures of matrimony, and I would no longer see Stefan's face in a department store crowd, or on the train, or in the park eating ice cream on a bench. Lady Alice had helped me pick out a gown for the evening. When we arrived back home, I asked him to help me with the zipper.

He had gazed at me sadly for a moment, as if to say, *Poor Annabelle, trying that old trick.* He had walked around to my back and drawn down the zipper. Then he had excused himself and gone to the bathroom to brush his teeth.

And out of nowhere came the prayer: *Thank God.*

I suppressed it at once, of course. But the prayer couldn't be un-prayed. God had heard me and knew that for that instant, I had been grateful my husband didn't want me, after all.

On the way to the Gare de l'Est a few days later, I said, "Your back doesn't have to be so straight, Johann. You might try to understand." He had occupied himself with the manic Paris traffic and hadn't replied. Florian sat on my lap, playing with the buttons of my blouse. We pulled to the curb across from the terminus and Johann had got out of the car with his valise. I slid to the driver's seat, put my hands on the wheel, and looked up expectantly for his farewell.

Johann had gazed back down at me with his ice-chip eyes. "Frieda misses you. When she is home from school on the weekend, she hopes every time she will see you there."

I said I missed her, too.

For a moment, he seemed to soften, and he touched my hair and said we would have time this summer to be a family again. He kissed Florian's cheek, and then he turned away and picked up his valise and crossed the street. Florian stretched out his arms and started to cry.

When I came back home to the vast and empty apartment, I put Florian down for his nap and wandered back to my own room to spread myself out on the bed I shared with Johann. I stared at the canopy overhead, which was not quite so monumental as the one at Schloss Kleist. It was a happy yellow silk instead of a twilight-blue velvet, and it made me think of the sun. It made me think, for a moment, what would happen if I did not go to Westphalia in August.

If, instead, I put Florian in the Mercedes with me and

drove down to the little sun-drenched villa by the sea in Monte Carlo.

2.

"It's a great shame, of course," said Lady Alice philosophically, that hot July morning, "but I suppose he's served his purpose."

"What purpose is that?"

"Why, saved you from infamy, of course. That *is* what you wanted, isn't it?"

"No. I wanted a father for my child. I wanted a partner to share my life with."

"Then I suppose the great shame is you forgot he was German."

"I don't care that he's German," I said. "But I can't live there. Not now."

She rolled her eyes and reached for the teapot. She was still living with my father, which was something of a miracle, and even more miraculously, they were quite happy together. Papa's face glowed when she came into the room. She hardly ever went out at night, at least on her own, and she had even taken to wearing dresses that displayed no more than an inch or two of her breasts. "I don't know," she said. "I think they've managed to order things rather well, haven't they? You should have seen Berlin five years ago. Absolutely ramshackle. Of course, it's heaps more fun that way, but one's got to be sensible and think about the economy from time to time."

"I don't think you've thought about the economy in your life, Alice, and what's all this about being sensible?"

She set down the teapot and the strainer and sank her spoon into the sugar. "The thing is, I'm going to have a baby."

"What?"

"Isn't it charming? A bit of an accident, I'll admit, but your father can't contain his delight now that it's done. You'd think he had impregnated an entire nunnery."

"My God."

"I think you're supposed to congratulate me, darling."

I rose at once and kissed her cheek, and told her she could go through Florian's things and have whatever she wanted. *But what about your own babies?* she asked, and I said there wasn't much prospect of that at the moment, and she said, *Nonsense, you have all August ahead of you, and how could Johann possibly resist?* If that was what I wanted, of course. To have a nice conventional marriage and a belly fat with my husband's child.

At that moment, Florian wandered by—he had just begun to walk—and paused at my knee, looking up at me with his most hopeful expression, and I lifted him into my lap and buried my face in his sweet-smelling hair.

3.

When Lady Alice left, I found my hat and gloves and brought out Florian's perambulator from the corner of the entryway. "I'm taking the baby for a walk," I told the housekeeper, and just as I maneuvered the wheels into place and reached for my son, my brother Charles strolled through the door, whistling a jazz song.

I nearly dropped the baby.

"Charles!" I screamed.

"Well, hello, sister dear." He kissed my cheek as if we'd last seen each other a week ago. "Is this the little tyke? My God, he looks like you."

That was what everyone said, that he looked like me, because he had my darker coloring instead of Johann's. But that was the thing about coloring; it was the superficial detail that everyone noticed. If you looked more closely, you saw that Florian really had Stefan's coloring, and Stefan's eyes, and most certainly Stefan's chin and jaw.

But people saw what they expected to see.

Florian looked into Charles's face and burst into tears.

"Now, now, darling," I said. "This is your uncle Charlie."

"Jesus Christ," said Uncle Charlie. "I guess I am."

4.

We struck off toward the Jardin des Tuileries, Florian's favorite excursion. "I don't suppose this means you've forgiven me," I said.

"Forgiven you for what? Marrying that old Nazi?"

"He isn't a Nazi."

"Beg to differ. By Christ, it's hot. Do you want to get an ice cream?"

"He isn't a Nazi. He's a member of the party, of course—he has to be. It doesn't mean he shares their beliefs. Here, you take him," I said, offering the handlebar to Charles.

"What do I do?"

"You push it, Charles. It's not that hard."

Charles dropped his cigarette on the pavement and took up

the handlebar. "Nice little machine," he said. "Well sprung. Little guy seems to like it, at any rate."

"I wish you would tell me why you're here. It's making me nervous you're going to tell me some awful news, that you've got cancer or liver cirrhosis."

"No, it's not that. Actually, it's Nick."

"Nick! Nick Greenwald? He's got cancer?"

"Calm down. No, he's not sick. He's going back to New York. His father went toes-up a month ago, and he's got to take charge of the home office."

"I see."

We paused to cross the Place de la Concorde, a complex maneuver that absorbed our attention until we reached the high black railing around the Tuileries and the warm green scent of the trees. I heard the tinkling of the carousel above the blaring of traffic behind me. Florian, who knew what was coming, gripped the edge of his perambulator and tried to climb out.

"Anyway," said Charles, looking unspeakably out of place as he pushed the baby carriage along in his threadbare suit and boater hat, "there's a party tonight, a farewell bash kind of thing, and Nick asked me to bring you along to say good-bye."

"Why does he want me to come with you?"

"I don't know," Charles said innocently. "Maybe he just wanted to give us a chance to break the ice and get to know each other again."

My brother stared straight ahead, squinting, sturdy and handsome, as he pushed Florian's carriage along the fence, toward the entrance along the rue de Rivoli. His cheeks were a little pink from the sun, or maybe it wasn't the sun.

I put my hand on his and made him stop. He looked down

at the pavement below the shining chrome handlebar. I put my hands on his waist and turned him toward me, and I put my head against his chest.

"I've missed you," I whispered.

His arms came around me.

"I missed you, too, little Sprout," he said, into my hair.

5.

So that was how I came to stand before Stefan Silverman on a July night in 1937 at the bar of the Hotel Ritz in Paris, married and restless, like a housecat left alone for the weekend, who has already eaten all the food in her dish.

PEPPER

Cocoa Beach • 1966

1.

Maybe it's the painkillers. When Pepper wakes up, she has to blink several times at the wall to remember her own name, and several more times to recall where she is and why. The room is full of sunshine. Her stomach moans with hunger. She hasn't slept so deeply since she was a child.

She sits up, and her foot explodes with pain.

Oh, God. The study, the letter, the front door, Florian, *OUCH*, hospital.

Florian.

Florian Dommerich. Annabelle's son.

Pepper sinks back on the pillow. A few feet away, the cheerful yellow curtain represses a brilliant sunlit afternoon, just bursting to get through the window glass and fall on her naked skin. Her crutches lean against the nearby wall, in a pool of discarded nightgown. Pregnant, on the lam, and now this. A broken foot that's taken up a nice neat throb of pain, in rhythm with her heartbeat.

Florian Dommerich. She remembers the name. She now remembers that at some point, at some Washington party, she was introduced to a man with the unusual name of Florian. But she doesn't remember that specific moment of introduction, not even if she screws her eyes shut and digs deep. She doesn't remember looking up into a handsome face, or admiring a pair of sturdy forearms as she shook a large and dependable hand. Because it was already too late, wasn't it? She was already besotted with another man. Life was like that, wasn't it? You got on the wrong train and missed your stop, and then you couldn't go back. By the time you retraced your steps, the right train had already left, gone, departed, the train not taken.

It's a depressing thought, and should keep a woman in bed for the rest of the day. But that's not Pepper, is it? Pepper shakes out her hair and thinks, Well, who needs trains, anyway? Noisy big smelly things, never on time, breaking down in all the wrong places. Better off without them.

She swings her feet to the floor and reaches for the bottle of pills on the bedside table, the ones the hospital pharmacy dispensed to her before she left. The label on the side says MRS. PRUNELLA E. DOMMERICH, and she'll be damned if she tells you what the *E* stands for.

2.

The table in the dining room is laid for one, and breakfast is still laid out on the sideboard in a series of patient silver chafing dishes. Pepper sets the crutches against the wall and helps herself. Clara wanders in with a pot of coffee, gratefully received, and after the first scorching gulp Pepper sets down her cup and asks Clara if Mr. Dommerich is around.

He's taken the dogs for a walk on the beach, Clara tells her, and from the shining look on Clara's face, she envies the dogs.

"Has he, now?" says Pepper. She eats two helpings of eggs and six slices of crisp bacon, washed down with coffee. The sun spills against her back through the French doors, warm and cheerful. A shame she can't see the beach from here, but the dining room lies against the courtyard, probably to catch the sunset. (Strawberry preserves on the toast, don't you think? The toast is always tip-top, the butter melted just so, the rich flavor complementing the sweetness of the preserves.) Oh, but don't misunderstand! Not because of Florian walking the dogs. Heavens, no! That's incidental. She just wants to watch the *beach*, the flat and infinite ocean, to remind her how unimportant she is, just another speck of pregnant sand under the sun. Pepper wipes her mouth on the napkin, drains the last of the coffee, and rises.

Clara's back in the kitchen. Pepper calls out a *Thank you* anyway, because the Schuylers have their faults but they always thank the staff, whether or not they mean it. She rises, grabs her crutches, and heads for the door.

3.

The dogs find her first. Dogs love Pepper and she loves them back, because dogs never let you down. Their idolatry never dims. Toby inspects her crutches while Oliver inspects her crotch. She fondles a silky head and tells him how wicked he is, and he agrees, tongue lolling.

A whistle. The dogs swivel their ears, toss her a pair of identical apologetic glances—*Duty calls, ma'am!*—and race back up the beach.

Pepper removes the crutches from her armpits and drops them on the sand. The tide's low, exposing irregular lines of refuse that reek familiarly of rot and brine. She lowers herself into a warm hollow. When she was little, she would walk along the beach in summer with her father and sisters, and they would look for sea glass. Tiny liked the clear ones most (diamonds are a girl's best friend, don't you know), but Pepper and Vivian fought over the colorful ones, the ones that still retained bumpy traces of lettering, hinting at a past life as a bottle of tonic or a jar of preserves. Eventually they worked out an amicable split: Vivian kept the blue glass, and Pepper the greens and browns. The shards still sit in a large glass container in her old bedroom in East Hampton, unless Mums threw it out. But then Mums doesn't throw things out, does she? So it's probably still there, sitting on the window ledge, catching the sun.

A wet nose finds Pepper's hand, and she closes her eyes and smiles.

"I'm pretty sure the nice doctor said you were to rest that foot as much as possible."

She lifts her heavy right foot, bound snugly in plaster of paris. "I'm resting it right here, aren't I?"

Florian sits down next to her, smelling like the sea. Toby climbs between his knees and licks his chin with a long, thick tongue, which Florian just manages to keep away from his lips. "Slept well?" he says.

"I did indeed. Those were lovely pills. You should break my bones more often."

"Well, you're looking better."

"What does that mean?"

He holds up his hands, palms out. "Nothing. Just, you know, a little haggard last night."

"Haggard?"

"And then your hair." Waggles his forefinger next to his ear.

"Well. My God. It's a wonder you didn't just call an ambulance and save yourself all that trouble."

Snaps his fingers. "Damn it! Why didn't I think of that? Could've slept like a baby instead."

"Don't lay that at *my* door. You slept when you got back."

Toby lopes off with Oliver, a game of tag, and Florian settles back in a hollow and puts his hands behind his head. His feet are bare and bony, his dungarees rolled a few inches above his ankles, wet at the edges and dusted with sand. "Not really," he says.

"Oh." She wiggles her toes. "Sorry."

"There you go again with the apologies."

"Crazy, huh? Must be the dope they gave me."

"Or the baby. I hear they do things to your minds."

He brings the subject up so naturally, Pepper forgets to be awkward. She puts her hand on her stomach and says, "Tell me about it."

No reply. The water rushes in and out, stirring a crusted patch of seaweed left behind at the last tide. The dogs cross before them. Pepper stares at Florian's toes, the healthy and unbroken bones of his feet, attached to a pair of strong ankles. She wonders what the rest of him looks like, under those damp and wrinkled dungarees and that sky-blue shirt that's rolled up to each elbow. If she looks out of the bottom corner of her eye, she can just make out the shape of a well-hewn thigh. She pictures that clean square-cut face, that dark curling hair, those chocolate-brown eyes, and God, just kill her now. It's been so long since she's kissed a man, *so long* since she's held a man in her arms, that she actually—while staring at his toes and calculating the difference in height between big toe and second toe, because wasn't that supposed to signify something?—yes, she actually contemplates what it would be like to have sex with him. What it would be like to kiss Florian. Be naked with Florian. Whom she just met yesterday.

The baby makes an inquisitive movement under her hand.

Oh, yes. The baby. The baby! Thanks ever so much, baby dear, for reminding Pepper that she might as well give this fantasy free rein, go all the way, indulge herself to the limit of her imagination, because that's all it is. Fantasy. The sex-starved fantasy of a pregnant woman, who is alluring only in memory. The formerly alluring Miss Pepper Schuyler.

"Can I ask you a personal question?" Florian says.

"That depends on whether you want it answered."

"Why are you having this baby, all by yourself?"

Pepper struggles to her feet, and in a flash Florian is up beside her, steadying her elbow.

"All right," he says. "Too personal."

"I'll tell you what. I'll answer yours if you'll answer mine."

"Fine. Sock it to me."

"What are they saying in Washington?"

"About you?"

"Yes, you big lug. About me. About where I am and why I left."

He shrugs. "Just that you're another Fifth Avenue deb, can't handle a real job. Had a fight with your boss and split."

"For real?"

"What do you mean, *for real*? I don't lie, Pepper."

"No, of course you don't."

"Honest to God. You shocked the bejesus out of me last night, and not just that you turned up in my mother's study. Of all the girls in the world."

She exhales slowly. There's some meaning in that last sentence, but she's too relieved by his news to give the words the attention they deserve. Florian bends down and hands her the crutches, fitting them under each arm, just like the orderly last night.

"You really shouldn't be walking around like this. You should be slumped in a chair with your foot up on a stool."

Pepper turns her head and looks at him straight. "Get real, Dommerich. Me sitting on a chair all day?"

He laughs, just as the dogs come up behind him and knock him in the knees, sending him staggering nearly into her arms, except that her arms are caught in the crutches. At the last instant, he whirls himself safely around the edge of her. "All right, all right. Here you go, boys." He picks up a stick and catapults it down the empty beach, and they stand there together, watching the eager hindquarters pump away, the sand fly like dust beneath the paws. Toby reaches the stick first, and Oliver disputes it with him. Florian turns as if to say something, and stops with the words still in his mouth.

"What is it?" Pepper pushes her hair behind her ear.

"Damn it all, you really are beautiful, you know that? I'm sorry. I know you couldn't care less at the moment, but God almighty. When the sun's on you like that."

"You should have seen me before." She whistles.

"I did see you before, remember? And I thought you were

beautiful then. But Jesus." He shakes his head and steps forward to meet the incoming dogs.

"I'm a mess," she calls after him. "You can't even see my cheekbones. Or my waist."

He hurls the stick. "My dad always said Mama looked best when she was pregnant. He said it was the greatest sight in the world."

"Yeah, well, it was *his* baby, wasn't it? His wife and his baby."

Pepper turns and plunges her crutches into the sand, heading back to the house. Seconds later, Florian catches up with her. "Hey. Hold on."

"Look, I don't need your pity, all right? And I certainly don't need you taking advantage of the situation."

"Taking advantage? Of *you*?"

"I think I know when a man's trying his luck."

"Wait a second." He takes her arm and pivots to face her, just as they reach the edge of the empty road separating the villa from the beach. "You honestly think I would make some kind of move on my mother's houseguest? My mother's *pregnant* houseguest?"

"That's what it sounded like from my end."

"Trust me, I've got no reason to make a move on you."

"Then what was all that about? *Oh, Pepper, you're so beautiful, even when your belly's all the way out to Kansas.*"

He shrugs. "Statement of truth, and a fact you're already plenty well aware of. I also happen to think you're a bossy hoyden who thinks a little too much of her sex appeal and likes to sail way too close to the wind. *And* your toes are crooked."

"My toes aren't crooked."

"They are the hell crooked."

Pepper looks both ways and crosses the street. Behind her, Florian whistles for the dogs. When she hears the scratch of toenails on asphalt, she says, over her shoulder, "Because I wanted it."

"Wanted what?"

"Wanted the baby. That's why I'm having it."

4.

A half hour later, Pepper sits in the blue-and-white armchair in the living room overlooking the ocean, flipping without much interest through a year-old copy of *Vogue* magazine. Her foot reposes on a matching blue-and-white ottoman, and her face, when she looks up to find Florian and a pair of root beers, should have warned him away.

Not Florian. He holds out a root beer, still frosty, cap removed. "Peace offering."

"I didn't realize we were at war."

"You sounded pretty warlike out there."

"That's just me." She takes the bottle. She hasn't drunk root beer since she was a kid, and she's surprised to find that it still tastes exactly like it used to.

Florian settles himself in the matching chair and balances the root beer in his cupped palms. "I have a few questions."

"Some men never learn."

"Not personal ones, this time. At least, not that personal. I was wondering about Mama, actually. When she split. What she said before she left."

"Why's that?"

"Because I haven't heard from her in two weeks, and she usually telephones about something or other every couple of days."

Pepper shrugs. "Your guess is as good as mine. We're not exactly lifelong friends. She bought the car from me, took me to dinner, dragged me to her lair, and left the next afternoon. She never said why."

"Didn't leave a note?"

"She left a note, but it just said that something had come up, and she'd be back in a few days."

"How long ago was that?"

Pepper swallows back her root beer. "Nine, maybe ten days ago."

"And you weren't worried?"

"Well, no. Should I have been?"

"This is normal behavior in your book? Inviting a stranger to stay in your house and then disappearing for a week and a half?"

"Oh, I've seen odder, believe me."

"You didn't wonder where she'd gone?"

"Not really. I was just grateful for the hot breakfasts."

The dubious eyebrows.

"All right, I wondered a little," Pepper concedes. "But she's a big girl, wouldn't you agree? She can go where she likes. Clara said she goes on trips like this sometimes. Anyway, it would have seemed rude just to call a cab and catch a flight home, without saying good-bye."

"For what it's worth, I'm glad you didn't."

"Thank you," she says acidly.

He smiles, almost as if he means it. "No, really. I'm just

surprised you stayed on so long, that's all. Don't you have family to hurry back to?"

"No more than most people."

"Because of the holiday, I mean."

"What holiday?"

"Pepper," he says, looking at her seriously, "Thanksgiving is in three days."

Pepper chokes on her root beer. "What?"

"It's Monday. Thanksgiving is Thursday. That's why I'm here, because Mama's supposed to join us at my brother's house for turkey and pumpkin pie, and no one's heard from her in two weeks."

"Thanksgiving." Pepper dabs the corner of her mouth with her forefinger. Jesus, what's happening to her? She can't even keep track of the calendar. "How about that."

Florian's frowning at her, and the crease in his forehead mesmerizes her momentarily, so that when he asks her if everything's all right, she answers with all honesty: "Yes. Perfectly."

"So then why aren't you off on a jet plane, Miss Trouble, heading home for turkey with your folks?"

"We aren't the cuddliest family, rumor has it."

"They don't know about the baby, do they?"

"Of course they know." She finishes the root beer and sets it down on the lamp table. "Two of them do, anyway. My sisters."

"But not your parents."

"You know," she says, steepling her fingers together and leaning forward, "I think the larger problem here is Annabelle. Let's talk about her. Where the devil might she have gone to?"

He sighs and rubs the adorable furrows in his forehead. "You name it. Ever since Dad died, she's gone off on these little trips, a few days here or there, not letting anyone know where she is. Then she pops back up as if nothing happened. It's just that it's been a couple of weeks now, and Thanksgiving's coming up, and we're all kind of waiting for her to let us know she's still alive."

"Don't you ever ask her where she's been? Since you're such a cute and loving family."

"She just says she's doing research."

"For what?"

"I don't know. Genealogy or something. We were just happy she found something to keep her occupied. She stopped playing her cello when Dad was diagnosed, just stopped cold turkey."

"Really? That doesn't sound good."

Florian rose from the chair and set down his bottle with a crash next to Pepper's. "Oh, thanks."

"Oh, relax. I'm sure she's fine." Pepper pauses delicately. "You know, there's another explanation, though you probably don't want to hear it."

"What's that?"

"Maybe your mother has a gentleman friend."

From the shocked expression on Florian's face, she can tell he's never considered this possibility. "What, *Mama?*"

"She's a very attractive woman."

He stares at Pepper as if she's just renounced her American citizenship and run off to join a Soviet collective. "You don't understand. She would *never.*"

"Oh, yes, she would."

"Dad and Mama . . . they were like . . . I can't explain . . . they had this connection. They never even argued. Dad was German, did you know that? They fled the Nazis together, back in 1938. They raised us all together. We had to change our names, because the Gestapo was after us. Dad and Mama, they were everything to each other."

"I'm sure that's true. But—well, I don't mean to shock you, but a woman has her needs. If you know what I mean."

He snaps back: "Look, Pepper. Not every woman is like *you*. If you know what I mean."

The words are so crisp and cruel, so unlike Florian, that Pepper has to pick through them all, one by one, to assemble their meaning. She returns his stare, and when he drops his gaze to the floor, she knows she heard him right.

"I'm sorry. I didn't mean that."

"Yes, you did." Pepper swings her feet to the rug and reaches for her crutches. "No hard feelings. I mean, I can't exactly argue with you, can I?"

"What does that mean?"

She puts the crutches under her arms. "I like sex. Actually, I love sex. I think sex is fucking terrific, excuse the pun, when it's done right. If that makes me different from the girls you know, well, I am most profoundly sorry for them all. You, too, I guess. Excuse me."

She hops past his stiffened figure—she's getting a little more agile with the crutches, by now—and into the hallway, thinking she'll head to her room, maybe even pack her few things and call a taxi for God knows where, but the sharp ring of the doorbell stops her halfway.

Mama! shouts Florian, from the living room.

She turns, just in time to see Florian shoot around the corner and reach for the doorknob.

But it's not Annabelle Dommerich on the other side. It's a very, very pretty girl with golden curls and blue eyes and a polka-dot dress (yes, actual real live polka dots, white on yellow), who flings her arms around Florian's neck and kisses his cheek like she could eat it right up. "You're back!" she says, when she's done, and then she notices the astonished pregnant woman in the hallway behind him.

It speaks volumes for her confidence that not a single trace of jealousy crosses that very, very pretty face. She blushes a little—she's a nice girl, after all, and she's just been caught throwing herself on a man's chest—and ducks around Florian's stunned shoulder to hold out her hand, the exact way a good debutante should.

"Hi! I'm so sorry, I didn't see you there!"

"Obviously."

"I'm Susan Willoughby. A friend of the family. Are you staying with Mrs. Dommerich?"

Pepper props one crutch against the wall and shakes Susan's outstretched hand. "Why, yes, Miss Willoughby," she says. "Yes, I am."

ANNABELLE

Paris • 1937

1.

Stefan held out his hand to me. "Good evening, Frau von Kleist. This is a tremendous surprise."

"Yes, a great shock." I put my hand in his palm.

He brought the gloved fingertips courteously to his lips. "You're looking exceptionally well. I think marriage suits you."

"Now, now," Charles said. "Nick and I have agreed that we're not holding the Nazi against her any longer."

"He's not a Nazi." I took my hand back, but the faint pressure of those lips remained on the beds of my fingernails.

Stefan straightened, and the light from one of the chandeliers caught his face. He looked the same, only horribly different, because there were a few lines now at the corners of his eyes and mouth, and a scar ran neatly along his left temple and underneath the cover of his hair.

"My God," I whispered.

Stefan looked a little quizzical, and then touched the scar with his finger. "Ah, of course. A souvenir, as the French say.

One should never try to escape from prison without an accurate map of the premises."

Charles said, "Are you all right, Annabelle?"

"Just a bit dizzy. It's terribly hot, don't you think?"

Stefan set his drink on a nearby table and wrapped his hand around my elbow. "I will take Frau von Kleist for some air."

"No! I'm fine."

"Actually, you're awfully pale," Charles said, frowning. "Go with Stefan. I'll fetch a glass of water."

"There is no need," Stefan said. "I will find water."

2.

I followed him numbly. There didn't seem to be a choice; I didn't seem able to choose another path except to follow Stefan's smooth black back down the length of the bar, where he stopped and made an inquiry from one of the bartenders, which ended in a glass being pressed into his hand.

I had thought in the beginning that he was drunk, but his steps were steady as he led me out of the bar to the busy corridor, and down the corridor to a small plain door, which he opened to usher me inside. It was a private sitting room of some kind, empty except for the usual elegant furniture. Stefan urged me into a chair and went to open the window. I stared at the glass of water in my hand.

"There, now," he said, turning toward me, leaning against the window. "Is that better?"

"Yes."

"I didn't mean to surprise you like that."

I sipped the water. "Did you know I would be here?"

"I thought it was possible."

I thought, This is Stefan standing before me. Stefan, real and whole, the same bone and muscle, the same brain and voice and hair I had loved, the arms that had held me, the mouth I had kissed and the ribs I had counted, one by one. It was not possible that he was here, Stefan, *Stefan*, a few yards away, Stefan, who had fathered a child with me. Florian's father. Now a stranger.

I looked into the glass. "How long have you been in Paris? I thought you were in Germany. Nick said you couldn't leave the country, it was part of the terms of your release."

"Hmm. It appears I am a fugitive, then."

I snapped up. "Are you?"

"Yes." He shrugged. "Really, it makes little difference, one way or the other. They cannot actually arrest me without consulting the French authorities first, and the French authorities are not particularly inclined to cooperate with requests from the German ones."

I couldn't meet his gaze. My eyes stopped somewhere around his neck, which was deeply tanned next to the glowing starched white of his collar. I wanted to say how sorry I was. I wanted to say how much I had suffered, knowing he had suffered, and that it was my fault, because he had been arrested coming back into Germany for my sake. I wanted to say how I had tried to avoid ever seeing him again, and how I had been sick with wanting to see him again. I wanted to say what a mistake I had made, running off like that: how I had thought marrying Johann was the right thing, the noble thing, and now maybe it wasn't, that you couldn't just make yourself love someone when your heart had lodged somewhere else, you couldn't pretend something was love when it was not.

I wanted to tell him we had a son.

Or did he know that already?

I curled my fingers around the hard glass, in the shape of a prayer.

"Annabelle," he said gently, "don't be frightened."

"I'm not frightened."

"You look like death. Very beautiful, but deathly. Come, now. It isn't that bad, surely? I am not so fearsome as that."

"I'm not afraid of *you*," I said.

"Then why will you not look at me?"

This was the trouble with Stefan: I couldn't lie to him. How could I lie to Stefan? How could I say things to him that weren't true? It was like lying to yourself. There was no point.

"Because I'm ashamed. I made you suffer."

"But you have suffered, too, haven't you?"

"Yes."

"And you have suffered because I didn't tell you the truth, I didn't tell you about Wilhelmine, because I was bloody terrified that you would run away from me and never come back. So I have been the author of my own suffering. It is no more than I deserve, for being a faithless husband and a false lover. And if you don't look at me this moment, Annabelle, I will not forgive myself."

I looked at him.

His face was calm and golden in the lamplight. He was so beautifully proportioned, leaning there against the window, his hands braced on the wooden sill. I had forgotten that about him, the perfect arrangement of his limbs.

"Tell me about her," I said. "Tell me everything."

He sighed. "We are no longer married. She is married to her lover, a man named Matthias, who was her lover at university and—what is the word—jilt? There was a stupid argument of some kind, and he jilted her. That is why she agreed to marry me, because she was angry at him. And I married her because our families were close, and it was the wish of my parents."

"Did you love her?"

"Yes, as one loves a dear friend. A very careless love. I had other interests, political interests, and I was often gone, and I thought nothing of seeking other company when I was gone."

"Company like me."

"Not like you."

I set down the glass of water and rose from the chair. "And your daughter?"

"Else. She lives with her mother. She is three years old and beautiful and astonishing. She breaks my heart when I think of her, because I believe I have failed her most of all." He paused. "She is very fond of Matthias. I saw her a month ago, before I left Frankfurt, and I was almost a stranger to her. Wilma is pregnant again, she will have the baby in September, and Else is over the moon to have a baby sister. She will not consider that it might be a boy."

"I'm sorry."

"It's no more than I deserve. I was away. I was trying to rescue the fucking world from itself. I fell in love with another woman. I allowed my wife to fall in love with another man." He patted the sides of his chest, as if hunting for his cigarettes in a pocket, and then he found my eyes and stopped. His hands fell back to the windowsill behind him. "I will do everything I can for my daughter," he said. "I will open my veins for her if she needs it, but I have lost her for myself."

"Oh, Stefan—"

"But you. Tell me about your son."

There was no particular emphasis on the words. His expression didn't change, except to brighten a little, the way it does when you turn the conversation from something melancholy to something new.

I said, "His name is Florian. I don't think I could have lived without him."

"Yes." He hesitated. "I would like to meet him one day, unless you think it is improper."

"Why do you want to meet him?"

"Because he is yours, of course."

I stood there looking at him, because I couldn't think of anything to say. Not one word to say to him, to Stefan.

"Annabelle?" he said.

"I can't believe this. I can't believe we're talking like this."

Stefan turned away and braced his knuckles on the windowsill. The street outside was dark, except for the passing flashes of the headlights, the dull sodium glow of a nearby lamp gilding the top of his hair. "This is what I meant, Annabelle."

"The perverse universe."

"Yes."

"You seem to have accepted it without any trouble. I thought you would be drunk and angry, if I saw you again. I thought you would hate the sight of me."

"I *am* drunk and angry, Annabelle. I am so angry I cannot breathe, sometimes. I am so consumed I cannot sleep. But I am not angry at *you*. I do not hate the sight of you." He paused and said something I couldn't hear.

"What did you say?"

He turned his head to the side. "I said, there is not one moment I have not wished you well. But maybe that is not quite the truth. There was the moment Greenwald told me the news. There are the moments I think of you with your husband."

"Don't, please."

"Don't think of you? Or don't speak of it?"

"Both."

"Does he treat you well?"

"Oh, yes. Yes, he is very kind. He loves me very much."

"He would be an even greater blackguard than I am if he did not."

I looked down at my dress, the embroidered mauve silk that slunk down my limbs and ended a fraction of an inch above the oriental rug. Alice and I had gone to one of the ateliers together, and she had made me order this one, which she said suited my figure and my coloring perfectly. I had telephoned Johann in remorse that afternoon and told him the price, expecting him to tell me to cancel the order. But he had said, gruff and astonished and full of static, "But of course you must buy this gown. You must be dressed suitably." I had told him that it was a very decadent dress, and he said that the Baroness von Kleist was expected to wear gowns according to her station, there was nothing decadent about that. This was in March, a few weeks before his visit in April. The dress was delivered a month later.

I touched the tiny leaf of a trailing vine, embroidered delicately in pale green and silver, and said, "He's in Berlin just now. He's been there since Christmas."

"Yes, I had heard."

"Is that why you're here in Paris?"

The air in the room was warm and thick, so much that though my arms were bare, I felt the prickles of perspiration in the small of my back. Stefan leaned in to the enormous panes of the window. The gathered draperies touched his black shoulder.

"Annabelle," he said softly, gazing through the glass, "I did not come here to take you away from your family. I think I have done enough ruin to marriages already."

"But you wanted to see me."

"Yes. I needed to see you again. I needed to see that you were safe, that you were well."

"I *am* safe and well. It isn't the same, of course. Not the same as with you."

"Annabelle, I know that."

"How do you know?"

He turned, so that his shoulder held up the windowpane, and his hand played with the swoop of the silk curtains. The light from the streetlamp outlined his profile. "Because my Annabelle is not capable of loving another man in the same way she loved me. Certainly not within the space of a few months."

I sank back into the chair and buried my face in my hands.

"Shh. Don't, love."

"*Why* did you come? It was so much easier when you were a beast. When I hated you. I nearly forgot you, did you know that? I nearly pushed you out of my memory. And now I can't, I can't force you out, you're always there. Why couldn't you be a beast?"

"I am a beast."

"You should have told me in the beginning."

"I know that!"

"We were so close! All those hours and days together, those beautiful days. I slept next to you. I was inside your skin, remember? How could you hold me like that and not tell me you had a child, a *daughter*!"

"Because I was scared to death, Annabelle. I thought, She will run away; she won't understand. She will think I am like her father. And maybe I was, maybe you were right, maybe I *am* just a fucking beast and never deserved you."

"If you'd only told me she left you!"

"I didn't dare. I was so besotted, do you not understand that? Do you not comprehend that I was out of my mind for you? I loved you so much, I couldn't think or breathe or hear. I was stupid, stupid with love. I thought, If I can just keep her from knowing until the divorce is arranged. I thought, If we can just—" He turned away from the window and yanked a cigarette case from his inside pocket. "I'm sorry, I know you hate these."

"I don't hate them."

"The last day, at the hotel . . ." He lit himself up and paced along the opposite wall.

"Because you wouldn't stop. The rooms were full of smoke."

"I'm sorry." He stopped in front of an enormous portrait of a young lady, dressed in white, and gazed up at her. "I'm sorry I didn't tell you."

"You didn't trust me."

"No, I suppose I didn't. I couldn't imagine that you would still want me."

I looked down at my hands, which were damp with my tears. But I wasn't crying now. My eyes were dry. "Don't be stupid.

There was nothing I wouldn't have forgiven you for, if you'd asked me. When did I ever deny you anything you asked for?"

He made a noise like an animal and kicked the thick wooden baseboard beneath the painting. The thump was catastrophic, like someone had fallen through a table.

I heard Nick Greenwald's voice: *It's a damned thing.* I wondered if Stefan's shoe had actually splintered the wood.

Stefan said, "The perverse universe, you see. Didn't I tell you? And now we are here in this room, and my hand that holds this cigarette is shaking, because I want to touch you so much, and I cannot."

"But why not?" I said, and the door banged open.

"There you are," Charles said. "What the hell was that noise?"

3.

The motor wouldn't start, so Charles went to find one of the Ritz chauffeurs to help. I stood outside on the rue Cambon, inhaling the heavy night air, the dirty, warm smell of Paris. The sky was clear, but there was too much light from the city to see the stars. I thought of the August sky above the *Isolde*, and how Stefan and I would sit in our deck chairs and count the stars together, and Stefan would drink his martinis and smoke his cigarettes and the smoke would drift like a ghost in the space between us, like another person. When he finished the first drink, some member of the crew would bring him a second, but that was all. *You don't appreciate the third,* he said, when I asked him why. *It's better to stop at two.* Later, at our little house, the stars weren't quite so plentiful because of nearby Monte Carlo. There were no martinis in the courtyard or the garden, just a shared bottle of wine and the smell of lemon and eucalyptus, and Stefan's cigarettes, one by one, until I asked him to stop.

Then I will need something else to do with my mouth, he said, and I gave it to him. I always gave him what he wanted.

I wrinkled my nose, because I could smell someone's cigarette now, but it didn't belong to Stefan, whose cigarettes were a special Turkish variety and bore a particular odor that made my blood jump. I turned my head and saw a man leaning against the wall, in the shadow between two streetlamps. His body was long and lean, and I realized it was Nick Greenwald.

He had disappeared shortly after dinner, and the beautiful dark-haired woman, too. I realized it only now. When I hadn't been observing Stefan from the corner of my eye, I had been picking out Stefan's voice at the other end of the long table. I had been tracing his movements with some primeval part of my brain that detected such things without seeing them. I had been wholly absorbed in this man who was not my husband. I hadn't noticed Nick Greenwald at all, once the necessary toasts had been made.

I called out to him now and asked if he needed a lift home. A silly question. Nick was as rich as Croesus, Charles had once said, or at least Croesus's banker cousin. He was never in need of anything.

No, thanks, he called back.

I walked toward him and put my hand on his arm. "Is everything all right?" I asked.

"No," he said. He lifted his arm, causing my hand to fall away, and put his cigarette to his mouth. "I just did a stupid thing, that's all."

"Is there anything I can do to help?"

He turned his head, as if he just noticed me there, and straightened from the wall. "Yes, there's something you can do," he said, and he took me by the ears and bent his head down and kissed me.

His lips were soft and tasted strongly of Scotch whisky, and I was too surprised to do anything but hold on and kiss him back. It lasted only a few seconds, five or six at most, though it seemed like forever, the way time warps in funny ways when you're in shock.

Then he lifted his head and said he was sorry.

"What was that for?" I gasped.

He dropped the cigarette on the pavement and crushed it under his shoe. "I just didn't want her to be the last girl I kissed, that's all. Good night, Annabelle. Take care of my old buddy Stefan, will you?"

I wanted to tell him that Stefan wasn't mine to take care of, but Nick Greenwald was already striding down the sidewalk to the corner, where a long, dark automobile reclined by the curb.

I cupped my hands around my mouth. "Good luck in New York!"

He waved his hand and opened the door of the car. The engine started without a hitch, and Nick Greenwald roared away down the rue Cambon.

4.

The old Renault was hopeless, and we took a taxi home. It was now two o'clock in the morning and I had been awake since the previous dawn. I leaned my head against the window, but my eyes wouldn't close.

Charles eyeballed me from across the seat. "So, Sprout. Slap me if I'm out of line. Is there something going on with you and Stefan?"

I raised my head. "How could there be? He's been in prison."

"Well, I thought I noticed what old Papa would call a frisson in there."

"You're imagining things. I'm married, remember?"

He laughed from the bottom of his chest. "All right, all right. Whatever you like. Look, did he get around to talking about anything special?"

"Stefan? No, nothing in particular."

"Thought he wouldn't. And now I guess I know why."

"Oh? And what's *that* supposed to mean?"

Charles crossed one leg atop the other and wrapped one hand around his ankle. With the other hand, he reached inside his jacket pocket and produced a pack of cigarettes. He shook it open and held it out to me. I declined.

"Tell me, Sprout," he said, lighting his cigarette, "what do you know about this husband of yours?"

I was still a little reckless from the wine at dinner, from the half hour in the salon with Stefan, from Nick Greenwald's unexpected kiss. What a goddamned night, I thought, and now this. There was a distant rumble of thunder through the sultry air.

I folded my arms. "Johann? He's a devoted father and husband, an expert in military history, and an unimaginative but enthusiastic lover with an organ the size of Gibraltar."

"Christ, Annabelle!"

"You asked what I know about him."

"That's not what I meant."

"Then *tell* me what you mean, for God's sake! I am so *sick* of all your innuendos, all of you, talking in your codes."

"Innuendoes?"

I waved my hand. "All of you. Your secret club."

Charles sucked on his cigarette, glanced at the driver, and rolled down the window an inch or two. He said, in a low voice, "Here's the thing. We toss around this term *Nazi,* you and I, but there are Nazis and there are Nazis."

"Tell me something I don't know."

"Well, I don't know what you don't know. That's the point. I don't know how much you know about your husband and what, exactly, he's doing in that new position he's got in Berlin."

"He's part of the Oberkommand."

"Yes, but do you know what he does?"

Another crash, louder this time, and a wave of rain crackled suddenly against the window. The taxi had stopped; the driver was swearing under his breath.

"Not exactly, no. Whatever they do in the general staff. He doesn't talk about his work."

"No, of course not." He tipped the end of the cigarette over the window's edge, releasing the ash. "We'll be printing textbooks one day about them, the Nazis, how to consolidate power. A few years ago they were the joke of Europe, and now look. Anyway, the old Prussian aristocrats hate them, have always hated them, but they've had to join the party or be shut out."

"Like Johann, you mean?"

"Well, that's the thing, you know. These Germans, they put loyalty to *Deutschland über alles,* especially after what happened in the war and after it; I mean, you can't blame them for closing ranks after Versailles. So these Junker barons, who should be leading Germany out of this madness, they just sit on their hands and say *ja, ja,* and now Hitler's a goddamned emperor, he can do what he wants. And it's nearly impossible to say who's really behind him, or who's just afraid of him, or who's just keeping his mouth shut and hoping it all blows over. Do you know what I mean, Annabelle?" He blew an expert stream of smoke through the crack in the window and turned to stare at me. His face was lined and serious in the gloomy gray light, not at all the jaunty tennis-playing Charles I carried in my head, and I thought of the scene in the boathouse, and the blood, and the urgency, and I realized I didn't know my brother at all.

The rain drove hard against the window. The taxi lurched forward and stopped again, and the driver released a torrent of vulgar French.

"Are you asking me to spy on my husband?" I asked softly.

"That's an ugly word."

"It's an ugly thing to do."

"Well, you're the one who keeps insisting he's on the right side. That he's not a real Nazi. And if you're right, and he's not, well—" The taxi moved again, and he braced himself against the seat ahead, nearly dropping the cigarette.

"Well?" I said.

"Maybe you could help us out."

"You? You and Stefan?"

"And a few others. A band of brothers, you might say. Trying to find a way in, trying to stop this thing at the highest level. Do you know what I mean?"

I didn't say anything. The audacity of it.

"Come on, Sprout." Charles nudged me. "What do you think?"

The rain picked up speed against the window. I thought about Florian, asleep in his crib upstairs, his cheeks flushed and a little damp. I knew exactly how he looked when he slept, exactly how he felt, his puppy-sweet smell. I knew every intimate detail about my son.

"And whose idea was this?" I asked. "Stefan's?"

A slight hesitation. "Mine. Stefan was supposed to ask you about it tonight."

I looked out the window and recognized the Café Maginot, where I sometimes still met Alice for lunch, when I could get away. The apartment on avenue Marceau was just around the corner. "I'm not going to spy on my husband for you. I'll talk to him, if you like, the next time he's in Paris, but I'm not going to spy on him."

Charles straightened against the seat. "That's all we ask," he said eagerly. "Sound him out. Find out how he feels, *really* feels, not just the patriotic backwash they spit up to strangers. Groom him, if you can. Let me know what he says about everything, anything, the Jews and Nuremberg and Hitler and Weimar and the Treaty of fucking Versailles."

"It's a long way from privately objecting to the Nuremberg laws to betraying your country," I said, full of acid.

Charles dropped the stub of his cigarette out the window. "Don't worry," he said, smiling at the corner of his full mouth. "If he bites, we'll take it from there."

"And if he doesn't?"

"Then you'd better the hell divorce the lousy Nazi bastard, or I'll never speak to you again." The taxi stopped. Charles reached forward to pay the driver. "I'm kidding you, Sprout. But think about it, will you?"

I sat back and let him pay, let him walk me swiftly across the sidewalk to the shelter of the building entrance, without once telling him that I already had. I already had thought about it.

5.

I went to see Stefan the next day. I had a hunch, based on his intimate familiarity with the Ritz, that he was staying there himself. I was right. I arrived in the lobby at half past noon, while Florian was taking his nap, and Stefan popped out of the elevator on his way to lunch at twelve forty-five.

I rose from the bench. "Hello, Stefan."

At least I had the satisfaction of shocking him. "I was just going to find you," he said, taking off his hat, and his face was pale beneath his tan.

"Then I've saved you the trouble, haven't I? I have a question for you. It won't take long. Is there somewhere we can be private?"

He cast an eye around the teeming lobby. "There's my room."

"I can't think of a better place. You're not in the Imperial Suite, are you?"

"God, no."

"What a pity."

In fact, the room was a standard box on the fourth floor, overlooking the Place Vendôme. The window was cracked open, but the air was still stuffy. I tossed my hat and my white cotton gloves on the writing desk. "You wanted me to spy on my husband?" I said. "That's why you came to Paris?"

He stood edgily by the door. "That was the excuse, yes."

"You *do* know how a wife gets information from her husband, don't you? You *do* know how marital intimacy is achieved?"

"Yes."

I threw my pocketbook across the room. It hit the wall with a bang, sending lipstick and compact and loose change flying in all directions.

"Annabelle—"

"To hell with you all!"

"Annabelle, calm down—"

"Don't tell me to calm down. I'm tired of being calm. I'm tired of keeping every last little lousy thought inside. I'm tired of being moved about like a pawn on a chessboard—"

He closed his hands around my upper arms and forced me to sit on the bed. "Listen to me. Just listen to me for *one moment,* Annabelle."

"I said yes." I looked up at him mutinously. "I told Charles I would do it."

His hands were warm and rigid on my arms, and his face was so close I could count the flecks of color around his black pupils. If I could have dropped my gaze to his mouth, I imagined his teeth would be bared.

"That is your choice, of course," he said, and he released my arms and straightened.

"You don't care?"

"I don't have the right to care, do I?"

"So you just went along with the idea. Oh, yes, excellent, let us turn Annabelle into a whore with her own husband—"

"Stop this," he said. "Just stop it. It wasn't my idea, all right? I certainly did not want you to agree to it. But I went along with this plan, because it gave me an excuse to see you, Annabelle, to leave fucking Frankfurt and get you in a room and talk to you and just—my God—just to *see* you. That's all. I wanted to see you, just once." He turned away and went to the window, which he forced open another foot, and leaned down to take in the air.

"That's why you left Frankfurt?"

"Yes."

"But you might have been arrested again."

"What the hell do I care about that? Anyway, it is much easier to avoid these chaps if you know they're looking for you."

I rested my palms on either side of my legs and stared at my knees. My dress had ridden up a few inches, and my stockings were bare to the sunlight that crept past Stefan's body into the room. I turned around his words: "To see me, just once."

"Yes."

A horn sounded from an angry motorcar on the street below, and the sound was so distant it might have belonged to another universe.

I realized I should not have come here. Nothing could have been more foolish than this. Poor Johann, I thought, and then, I should leave.

I should leave now.

I lifted my face and saw my own reflection in the mirror above the desk: fair skin, wide American mouth, dark hair curling in the heat, dark eyes large with alarm. My red lips moved. "Well, what do you think?"

"About what?

"Do you think I could help? That Johann would help you?"

He stared quietly down at the street below. The brim of his hat curled up against the windowpane.

"I don't know," he said at last. "You could answer that better than I could, I suppose."

There was a ceiling fan above the bed, stroking the hot air in long sweeps. It wasn't much, but at least it was circulation. It was movement. I concentrated on the stirring at the back of my neck and said, "He almost never talks to me about politics, though. It's two separate compartments in his mind: family and politics. I got him to talk about it once, last Christmas, and it ended rather badly."

Stefan lifted his head from the window. "Did he hurt you?"

"No. God, no. He would never do that." I smoothed out the creases in my dress. "I think it's fair to say he believes in Germany rather than Hitler. But I don't think he sees them in opposition. He thinks the worst aspects of Nazism will simply go away when times are a little better."

"He's wrong."

"Well, I'm willing to ask him, if there's the smallest chance."

Stefan straightened and folded his arms against his white shirt. "I thought you were angry about our little plan."

"I don't mind talking to Johann, if it helps you. I just didn't want you to want me to do it."

"Did I ask you to do this, last night? Did I say one word about it?"

"No."

"No, I didn't, because it makes me sick to think of you with him, plying him for information. I don't want to give you a single reason to go back to Germany and to be his wife."

"Well, I *am* his wife."

"I know you are."

"And there must be some reason I'm his wife, instead of yours. It must have some purpose. So maybe this is it. This is why I'm married to Johann."

"Ah, yes. Your continuing belief in a logical universe, despite all indication to the contrary."

"Is it so wrong, to have faith?"

He stared at me for a moment, head tilted to the right, and then he walked across the room to the chair before the desk and sank into the seat. "All right, then. Let us suppose you were designed by God to lure the general to the just cause. What then? Let us suppose he takes your bait, and we formulate a plan to overturn Herr Hitler and his odious ideas. Let us suppose it is successful, and Germany is saved, maybe Europe itself is saved, hurrah. We are all heroes, we are all grateful to Herr von Kleist and his loyal wife, who helped him to see the justice of our cause." He laid his arm on the desk and rubbed one finger against the polished wood, back and forth. His eyes held mine, narrowed and hard. "What then, my dear Frau von Kleist? Do you leave him in the lurch?"

"I—I don't know."

"Or perhaps we have already run off together, you and I. Perhaps you have left your husband and son—"

"I would never leave Florian."

"Then perhaps you have torn the boy away from his father and brought him with you to live with me, a stranger. Is that all part of this faith of yours?"

"You're being cruel."

"The *thing* is cruel, Annabelle. The whole damned thing." He reached into his jacket for his cigarettes and placed one in his mouth. "Have you heard of the fucking Nuremberg laws?"

"Yes, I—I have. It's horrible. Something to do with property and registration and—"

"I will explain. First of all, this legislation means that I am not a citizen of Germany any longer, because I am a Jew." He paused to light the cigarette. "It means also that—I speak hypothetically, of course—should you happen to divorce your honorable husband for my sake, I cannot marry you, because a Jew cannot marry a gentile, it is against the law. And I cannot say *Aha!*, I will simply marry you here in Paris and then take you home to Germany, because the marriage is null and void the instant we cross the border."

"Since we are speaking hypothetically," I said, "I will then observe that marriage isn't necessary to me. I'm long past caring about a piece of paper."

"Ah! Well, that is what is so elegant about these laws, Annabelle, because it turns out it doesn't matter if we are man and wife, we are still breaking the law, since in Germany a Jew cannot fuck a gentile. Did you know that? He cannot fuck a gentile, he cannot make a mongrel *Mischling* baby with her. They will send him to the camps if he dares to try. Do you know about these camps, Annabelle?"

I thought of Florian and his sweet dark hair curling on his temple, his red mouth and soft tongue, and I wrapped my hands around my knees so they wouldn't shake. Stefan's face was bright with passion, a few yards away. I said softly, "Then I suppose—again, hypothetically—we would simply live elsewhere."

"Brilliant! Yes. The perfect solution to our hypothetical dilemma. Except that my daughter remains in Germany, to say nothing of my parents and siblings, which is a little problem for me, you understand. The people I love, our business. Our damned

money, of which there is so much. Shoes, you know." He laughed
bitterly. "The irony, eh? My family sells the Nazis the very boots
with which they seek to kick us."

"Can't you convince them to emigrate?"

He laughed again and reached for the ashtray in the corner
of the desk. "Oh, yes. I can see the conversation now: *Mother,
Father, listen to me. I have in mind to marry again, a dazzling
woman, you'll adore her, except for a few small matters. She is a
gentile, and the divorced wife of a fucking Nazi general, so unless
you are prepared to leave Germany, which you have told me again
and again you will never do, why, you will never see us again.*"

I whispered, "Surely not."

"And there is my daughter. My daughter, Annabelle. How
do I say to my Else, *Good-bye, my dear little love, I have fallen
in love, and unless your mother and stepfather kindly agree to
emigrate for our sake, I cannot see you again?* I cannot do it,
Annabelle. I will damn myself forever if I do. No. I am already
damned. I am damned to hell for loving you, who are married
to another man. And if I say, well then, to hell with right and
wrong, I will break God's law and take this woman I love to
my bed, married or not, then I am breaking also the law of
the Nazis." He brought his fist down on the desk and pointed
to the bed with his other hand, the one holding the cigarette.
He was almost shouting now. "*This* is the perversity of the
universe. Do you understand now, Annabelle? Do you understand this perversity? It is so perverse that my own family is
in perfect harmony with the damned Nazis on this point. So
at last I have fallen in love, in the manner of the great roman-
tics, but if I want to marry this woman, if I want to take this
woman I love back to my own country and fuck her, I am

breaking the law, Annabelle. I am breaking the *fucking law* in my own home!"

"But they can't do that! I'm a French citizen, I'm an American, too, and they can't tell me I can love one man and not another."

Stefan tossed the cigarette in the ashtray and leaned down on his elbows to bury his hands in his hair. "Don't you see, Annabelle? That is exactly the point. That is exactly what they are trying to do."

"Then let's not let them win," I said passionately. "Right now, let's beat them, let's love each other."

"I thought we were speaking hypothetically."

"Don't be stupid, Stefan."

He sighed, rose from the chair, and picked up my pocketbook from the floor. One by one, he added the contents: lipstick, compact, ticket stubs, coins. "They already *have* won, my love. It is already done. I am not going to ask you to divorce your husband. We are not going to fuck like a pair of fugitives, not in this room now, not in Paris or Berlin or any damned place." He snapped the pocketbook shut and reached for my hat and gloves. "I am going to drive you back to your apartment now."

I stood numbly. The breeze from the window moved my dress against my legs. I held out my hands for my hat and gloves and pocketbook, and Stefan gave them to me, white-faced. Our fingers nearly touched, but not quite.

"My God, you are beautiful, though," he said softly. "The shape of your eyes. That skin. I thought my memory must have been mistaken."

When I first realized I was going to have a baby, before Johann had proposed, while I was sick with pregnancy and with the thought of what I had done with Stefan, I had spent many hours staring up at the ceiling above my bed, reconfiguring the scenes of our meeting in such a way that I could have resisted him. I could have prevented this entire disaster. I decided he wasn't really all that handsome, and his charisma was just a mirage, an image of an oasis in a desert, easily ignored. That sense of connection with him, those hours of discovery, had been proven a lie: I hadn't really known him at all.

But I had been a fool, hadn't I? Standing here before Stefan's bed, two years later, a wholly different Annabelle, a wife and mother, accepting my hat from his hands without quite touching his fingers, I returned Stefan's gaze with equal wonder. I realized that no one could be so breathtaking, no one could be so familiar and so perfectly connected to me. His bones were like my bones. The shape of my eyes was like the shape of his.

How can we bear this? I asked.

(He took the hat from my hands and placed it gently on my head.)

Because we have to. Because you will know my heart is somewhere in the world, beating for you.

(I secured my hat and wiggled my fingers into my gloves. I asked if I would see him again.)

No, he said. It was for the best if we didn't.

6.

Eight days later, we lay side by side on Stefan's bed on the fourth floor of the Paris Ritz. The wooden fan rotated slowly above us. The heat had intensified, an almost unbearable compression of July air, ninety-nine parts automobile exhaust and one part oxygen.

"We should drive away somewhere," I said.

"Where? The heat is general across Europe, I believe."

"Anywhere. We could go to Versailles, or to Antibes. Your friend's house in Monte Carlo."

"I'm afraid he is living there himself, at present."

"What about your yacht?"

Stefan blew out a long cloud of smoke. "She is anchored in Capri. I am thinking of selling her."

I sat up, shocked. "You can't sell her!"

"Why not? There is not much point anymore. How can I sail in her again, when your darling shade haunts every last corner? Lie down, now. You are blocking the air from the fan."

I sank back into my hollow in the bedspread. I was damp with perspiration, and so was Stefan: all sheen and languor, not because we had made love three times in the past hour—we had not—but because today was the twenty-fourth of July, and all Paris was gripped with heat, and we lay together on a bed, fully clothed, down to our shoes.

That was our rule, you see. We could not possibly be having an affair if our shoes remained snug on our feet, if our clothes remained intact, if we did not touch each other's skin except by accident or necessity, such as the handing over of the gloves and the hat, or the pouring of a drink, or the lighting of a cigarette, which I sometimes liked to do for him, simply because I envied the cigarette.

"It is still a matter of sin, however," Stefan had said, the second day we had met like this. "We are indulging in the most elemental intimacy, and there is also the necessity for self-abuse, without which I could not possibly lie here next to you every day with any pretense of tranquility."

I'd told him that this wasn't strictly necessary, that there were plenty of women downstairs who would be happy to perform on him whatever form of abuse he required, and he hadn't answered except to snort and reach for his drink on the bedside table. I had spent the following twenty-three hours wondering what particular meaning was contained in that snort, until Stefan opened the door to my knock the next day and took my hat and gloves, and it wasn't that I had forgotten the question: I simply ceased to care about the answer.

I came back the next day, and the next. I developed an affectionate relationship with the plasterwork of the ceiling above the bed. I imagined how we must look from above, and how the gilded borders formed a kind of picture frame around the two of us, Annabelle and Stefan, lying on our backs in the center of the bed, elegantly dressed, not quite touching. I knew each repeat, each fold and flaw, each nick in the paint and the gilding as I knew my own skin. I followed the familiar creamy progress of a scroll and said, "What are we doing here?"

"I haven't the slightest idea," said Stefan. "This is an unpre cedented exercise for me."

"I don't think it's a sin. How can it be a sin? It's so pure, existing like this with you."

"My dear, it is worse than a sin. We could commit the physical act of adultery, and we would not, in the middle of it, be so perfectly attached as we are like this."

"Then why don't we make love? Since it's the lesser of two evils."

"Because the one would not negate the other. Because if we made love, it would not make this existing together any more innocent."

The shadows of the fan blades chased themselves fruitlessly around the ceiling. They had lengthened by at least two centimeters since I had arrived. The minutes bled out, one by one, and soon there would be nothing left. I would rise from the bed and take my gloves and my hat, and I would walk out into the shimmering sidewalk as if I had not left all my blood inside.

"Then let's at least hold hands," I said.

"We should not under any circumstances hold hands, Annabelle."

My fingers touched his, and our damp hands curled together on the bedspread.

7.

My father adored Florian, and the affection was mutual. I would watch them play together on the floor next to the sofa, spreading toys and books all over the august inlaid floors of the apartment, and feel a strange combination of bemusement and betrayal.

"You weren't like this with me or Charles," I said, the day after I had held Stefan's hand on the fourth-floor bedspread of the Paris Ritz.

"Wasn't I?"

"No. You were off amusing yourself most of the time."

"I am amusing myself now," he said, demonstrating a proper rhythm on the samba drums, and I looked at Alice, who reclined on the sofa with a magazine. She smiled beatifically and shrugged her bare shoulders.

We went into lunch a half hour later, and no amount of squealing and messiness could interrupt Papa's enchantment with his grandson. "Thank God he does not have his father's coloring," Papa said, "as if someone had poured a measure of bleach over his head."

Alice suppressed a giggle.

"I happen to like Johann's coloring," I said.

"Oh, of course. It suits him perfectly, doesn't it? Like a great Teutonic iceberg."

"Papa!" said Florian, and he threw his bread on the floor.

I bent over to retrieve the bread. "He can understand more than you think, you know."

"Yes, of course. He is the cleverest boy, aren't you, *chouchou*?" Papa made a face, and Florian squealed.

I gazed at the two of them over the rim of my wineglass. "I suppose you might as well get used to this, since you're starting over again with one of your own."

"Oh! We're getting married, by the way," said Alice. "Next month, at the Hôtel du Cap. I should very much like you to be matron of honor, if your family can spare you."

I stopped the wine on my lips. "Married?"

"Yes, of course," said Papa. "I am not such an old blackguard as that."

I set down the glass and wiped my fingers on my napkin. I thought, Poor Mummy. "Oh, I can imagine your asking. But I can't imagine a clever girl like Alice accepting you."

"I hadn't much choice, I suppose. But I believe I know how to manage him."

"You manage me extremely well," Papa said, and they exchanged a look of such happiness that I lost my breath.

Why, they're in love, I thought, and the panic rose up from my chest to choke me. Alice wasn't supposed to be happy like this; she was supposed to be restless and eternally dissatisfied, and I was supposed to be the wise matron who had chosen her partner well, who dispensed wise advice about the care and management of husbands, and the joys to be discovered in a wholesome family life.

Florian jettisoned another piece of bread. His caramel eyes grew round and wet. "Want Papa," he said, between heaving sobs, and he stretched out his arms to me.

I lifted him from his chair and held him against my chest, and his little heartbeat pattered against mine, his little fist curled around mine. "Presumably you'll do a far better job of managing him than Mama did," I said.

"But that was my fault, *mignonne*," said Papa.

"Oh, you're admitting it, are you? That's a step in the right direction."

"I am older and wiser, that's all," said Papa. "Is it not possible for an old dog to learn his new tricks? I have determined that sexual congress is perhaps not so essential to happiness, after all."

"But bloody important, nonetheless," said Alice.

"Better late than never, I suppose," I said.

Alice lit a cigarette. "But can you come? To the wedding, I mean. Will you be irrevocably in Germany, or does he let you out on good behavior, from time to time?"

"I'm sure he won't mind if I slip down for a few days."

I began to ask Alice about the arrangements, dress and flowers and guests, and Papa excused himself. I stroked Florian's damp hair. The storm had passed, and his breath tickled the hollow of my throat, steady and gentle. Alice watched the door, and when it had closed behind my father's neat gray-suited back, she turned to me and asked me what was all this about my having an affair.

My hand went still on Florian's hair. "I'm not having an affair."

"Then it's all perfectly innocent, your meeting a man every day at the Ritz?"

I whispered, "Where did you hear that?"

"The usual birdie. You haven't even bothered to disguise yourself, I'm told. Such an amateur." She reached for Florian and settled him on her lap to play with her necklace. "It's Stefan, isn't it?"

I hesitated. Was there any point in lying to her? "Yes, it's Stefan, but it's not what you think."

"My dear, you don't think I disapprove, do you? Enjoy yourself, by all means. When the cat's away and all that. I'm hardly the girl to judge." She held Florian's fingertips and let him rise to his feet on her lap. He laughed and grabbed her cheeks, and her arms went around him as if she were born for it, born to cuddle a baby on her lap. "Just watch yourself, lovest. I suspect this particular cat doesn't like his little mouse to play."

8.

Can I ask you something?

Whatever you like, Annabelle.

What did you say to me, that time we made love on the beach?

(Stefan smoked his cigarette and sipped back the rest of his brandy.)

Don't say you don't remember.

Yes, I remember. I remember it well. I was praying to God that we would make a baby together in that moment, so that you would have no choice but to become mine, and vice versa.

(Around and around went the blades of the fan.)

I suppose it was a selfish thing to pray for, after all. You were not even twenty. But I could not help myself. I wanted some sign that I was not deluded, that God in his mercy had actually meant me for you.

(Around and around, making long swishing sounds like the ocean.)

Is something the matter, Annabelle?

No, Stefan. Nothing's wrong. But I think it's probably time for me to go home now.

9.

When I returned home, Florian hadn't yet woken up from his nap. He slept on his stomach, wearing only a shirt and napkin, damp and a little flushed by the heat. I stood by his crib and touched his dark hair. His fist made a twitch, a flexing of his small perfect fingers, and I remembered how I had watched Stefan sleep one afternoon in Monte Carlo, naked on the bed, in the exact center of a beam of white sunlight. The utter peace of him. I remembered thinking how beautiful he was, and how lucky I was that I would spend my entire life watching him like this, as he slept off the bliss of lovemaking inside a patch of sun.

10.

I turned on my side to face Stefan's gaunt profile. "What if I don't go to Germany next month? What if we take Florian in the car with us and drive to Antibes for my father's wedding?"

Stefan's hands were folded beneath his head. He stared up at the rotating shadows on the ceiling. "You are not to ask me these things, Annabelle. You are to say to me, *Stefan, this is what I want,* and I will do it. God forgive me. I will find a way to give you what you want."

11.

"I can't do it," I said to Charles. "I can't spy on Johann for you. It's not honest."

We were walking along the Seine with Florian, poking into the bookstalls and perspiring. Charles stopped and turned to me. A book lay open in his hands. Proust.

"But it's not spying," he said. "Not really."

"That's not why it's dishonest. It's dishonest because I'll have to pretend everything is normal. That I'm still in love with him, if I ever really was."

Charles looked shocked, standing there holding his open Proust. Florian darted around the corner of the bookstall, and I launched myself after him, losing my hat to the hot wind. He giggled and made me chase him, and when I caught him at last, I blew a raspberry into his tender throat and told him how much Mama loved him, how beautiful he was, how miraculously like his father.

"Papa!" he exclaimed, and he threw his arms around my neck.

12.

It was the twenty-ninth of July, and Stefan and I faced each other atop his bed on the fourth floor of the Paris Ritz. Our shoes were off—it was too hot, I said, and it was silly to think that shoes made any difference—and I was tracing my finger down the scar on the side of Stefan's face.

"I think I'm ready to tell you something," I said.

He put his finger across my mouth.

"Let's not talk," he said. "It is too hot to speak."

13.

When I arrived home at the avenue Marceau an hour and a half later, I put my key into the lock and realized at once that something was different. A current of energy ran from lock to key to hand, as if someone had wired the door for electricity while I was out visiting Stefan at the Ritz.

I turned the handle and opened the door, and there was a great peal of laughter from the drawing room, yes, a great peal of laughter from a delighted Florian, and an answering roar from deep in an enormous chest.

14.

The day my mother's appendix burst, we were on Cape Cod, staying with her sister and my multitude of cousins. Mummy had complained of a sour stomach the night before, and my aunt, always intensely practical, always a little jealous of Mummy's French title and perhaps a little smug that the expensive French marriage had ended exactly as she had predicted on their wedding day, told Mummy she had always been too soft, and to take an Alka-Seltzer and go to bed.

The next morning, I awoke to a strange quiet in the house, as if every floorboard had lost its will to live. I looked across the still air to Charles's bed, which lay empty and unmade, the sheets flung back in haste.

I sat up, and the door cracked open. It was my cousin Franklin, golden-skinned and blue-eyed and white-toothed, a perfect American teenager. He was off to Harvard in the fall, and eventually he was supposed to be president. Charles hated him. He took cheap shots at football, Charles said.

"Awake?" asked Franklin.

"Why is the house so quiet?"

He told me that the house was so quiet because everyone was at the hospital, and everyone was at the hospital because my mother had been taken there in the night, and now she was dead.

Dead, I said.

Dead, said Franklin. I'm sorry.

I said it was a stupid joke, and Franklin said he was sorry but it wasn't a joke. It was appendicitis. They had tried to operate, but it was too late.

I sank back in my pillow and drew the blanket over my head. I said four Hail Marys, and when I finished the last one I knew it was true, that Mummy was gone, that I would always hate Franklin Hardcastle for saying he was sorry when he really wasn't.

Later, when the shock had worn off, I wondered how the floorboards had known. How the house had known something was wrong before I had.

15.

In the drawing room, Florian was riding on top of Johann's back as if my husband were a horse in the Bois de Boulogne. Johann saw me first. He lifted his large head in mid-whinny and his face shed its delight.

"Johann," I whispered. "I thought you were in Germany."

He reached behind his back and grasped Florian's kicking legs, and he maneuvered the two of them until he was standing before me with Florian in his arms, clinging for dear life. His eyes were a clear and somber blue.

"My wife," he said, "my darling wife, I had to come. I have missed you so much."

I opened my mouth to reply, but the door from the hallway banged open and a ball of blondness hurtled into my arms. "Mother!" exclaimed Frieda, and I burst into tears instead.

16.

Johann asked me if I had eaten, and I said I had. He gave Florian to Frieda and said she must play with her brother while Papa talked with Mother. He had given me his handkerchief, and I was still cleaning myself up while he took my hand and led me into the bedroom and closed the door. He picked up my other hand and fell to his knees and kissed my fingers. "*Mein Liebling*, my treasure. My wife. Annabelle. I am so sorry."

I thought, This can't be happening. I'm supposed to meet Stefan in an hour, I'm supposed to pack two suitcases—one for me and one for Florian—and meet Stefan on the eastern side of the Place Vendôme at four-thirty precisely, where he will be waiting in a hired automobile to drive us south to Antibes.

I tugged my husband upward. "Johann, please. Get up. Don't say that."

He moved his hands to the small of my back and pressed his mouth into my stomach. "Ah, your smell," he said. "My God. I am holding you finally. I have been so sick, Annabelle, and I have been wrong. My son, I have missed him so much."

"He's missed you, too," I whispered. My hands went to his hair, because what else could I do? The short blond bristles were soft on my palms.

"On my knees, Annabelle, I ask you to forgive me. Forgive your old husband, who became too stiff and proud and forgot what it is like to be twenty-one."

"There's nothing to forgive, Johann. Please. Get up."

He rose and pressed me to his chest. "It was Frieda. She said to me, *Father, you are moping, I have never seen you so unhappy. You must do something.* And she said, *Annabelle is not like Mama, you cannot make her something she is not.* And I realized she was right. I have been an old fool with his young wife."

"Stop, Johann. You're not old, you're not a fool, it's just—"

"Annabelle, please."

I pushed him away. "Johann, I can't. I have to think."

He picked up my hand and kissed it. "Listen to me. Listen to this one fact at least. I have told the Oberkommando in Berlin that I am resigning my post there and returning to Paris, in my old role if they will have me, and as a private citizen if they will not. I have withdrawn the children from their schools. This September, the boys will start at Charterhouse, my old school in England, and the girls will move here to Paris with us. She is so delighted, she would not stop talking on the train."

"But your career. They will ruin you. They'll say you're disloyal."

"I do not give a damn what they say."

"Oh, Johann."

He kissed my hand again. "If that is what you want, Annabelle. If I am not too late to win back your esteem."

I stared at my hand inside his, at the size of Johann's fingers. I felt as if someone had attached a tube to my chest and drained away my vital fluids.

"I cannot live any longer like this," said Johann. "I cannot live without my wife and my little son. I cannot go back to that. I will do whatever you want."

Through the door came the sound of Frieda's laughter, and the scurry of Florian's feet on the sleek parquet floors that smelled of beeswax.

Johann said, "We need you, Annabelle."

In my head, I said four Hail Marys, and when I finished the last one I knew he was telling the truth.

I slipped my hand from his. "I'm so hot and dusty, Johann. I need to take a bath."

17.

The cars buzzed along the middle of the Place Vendôme and around its corners, but not one of them came to a stop along the eastern side. I checked my watch at four twenty-eight, and again at four twenty-nine, and very resolutely waited until four thirty-two before checking again. The sun burned the crown of my hat. My hands grew damp inside my white cotton gloves.

At four thirty-nine I crossed to the western side of the Place Vendôme and approached the front desk of the Hotel Ritz. I inquired whether Stefan Silverman had passed through the lobby, and the clerk, who must have recognized me, said that Monsieur Silverman had checked out of his room two hours ago.

Thank you, I said. Was there any message for me?

No, there was not.

If he returns, will you please give him this note?

(I handed the clerk a sealed envelope.)

Of course, Madame, said the clerk. Would there be any reply?

No, I said, I didn't need any reply, and I walked out of the Paris Ritz and returned to the apartment on the avenue Marceau.

18.

"Have you had a good walk?" Johann said, rising from his desk. The chair scraped painfully against the floor. His face was pale and vulnerable in the faint afternoon sunlight.

"Yes, thank you." I hid my trembling hands in the folds of my skirt.

The clock ticked behind me on the mantel. Johann gazed at

my hair, eyes puckered fearfully, lips parted as if he wanted to ask me a question.

He is so tall, I thought, so large and formidable. He commands an army. And he cannot ask me a question.

"I will go and see the cook about dinner," I said, and I turned and left the room.

19.

After dinner, I played the cello with Frieda, and when I went to the nursery to put Florian to bed, I found him curled up on the floor with Johann, who was reading him a story.

"Time for bed," I said.

My husband hoisted a sleepy Florian onto his massive knee. "There we are, son. Your mama commands us to go to bed, and we must always obey Mama."

Johann carried him to his crib and laid him in the sheets. It's too hot for blankets, I said, and Johann leaned down and kissed Florian's forehead. He brushed back the dark curls and said Papa's darling boy had grown, he was a little man now. Florian's eyelids sagged at the familiar timbre of Johann's voice.

I turned off the light.

20.

In the beginning, when I had returned to Paris after Christmas, I had kept to my own side of the bed and left Johann's side empty, the way the wives of some soldiers still laid a place at the table for the missing husband. After the disastrous April visit, however, I began to creep over the invisible line that separated his space and mine, inch by inch, until I lay sprawled every night in the center of the bed, like a defiant starfish.

Now it was July, and my husband had returned to our home and asked for my forgiveness. He had fallen to his knees and reminded me that I was, after all, his wife. He had brought his young daughter who needed a mother, his big arms in which my son fit so securely.

I slipped off my dressing gown and drew back the counterpane and raged at the white sheets. *It's a damned thing,* Nick Greenwald said, shaking his head. The bathroom door opened behind me.

"Annabelle," said Johann.

I closed my eyes.

21.

I waited while he fit a sheath awkwardly on himself. When he entered me, I held back the gasp in my throat and lay still beneath him. I will not feel this, I thought, but friction is friction and flesh is flesh, and my body was young and starved of love. We rocked together silently for long minutes, until my reluctant heels found the backs of his legs.

What he did next astounded me. He rolled onto his back and brought me with him, so that I wobbled above his mountainous chest and sank down hard. He put his thick hands on my hips and ordered me in German to use him hard—I don't think he knew the words in English—and as I rose and obediently fell he said more German words, admiring my waist and breasts and my snug little *Muschi*, lifting his hips to meet mine, and I thought in despair, closing my eyes, I'm sorry, Stefan, I'm so sorry, I can't help it, I am going to come.

Then I lay flat on the damp white mountain of Johann's sternum and stared at the wall, while his hand traced the cavity of my spine. It is done, he said, we are man and wife again.

PEPPER

Cocoa Beach • *1966*

1.

Susan is creasing her very, very pretty forehead. "You're saying nobody's heard from her since last week?"

"Seems so," says Florian. "Pepper's the last one to speak to her."

Pepper spreads her hands. "She didn't say where she was going, I'm afraid, and I never had the chance to ask her."

"Oh, dear." Susan gazes up at Florian's face. "And she's been acting so oddly since—well."

"Since Dad died."

"She seemed all right to me," says Pepper. "She spoke of him fondly, of course, but she wasn't exactly grief-stricken. On the other hand, she had just dropped three hundred large on an old car, so—"

Florian turns to her. "What did you say?"

"The car. The car I sold her."

"Three hundred *thousand dollars*?"

Pepper looks back and forth between the two of them. They're sitting at the dining room table, Florian and Susan on one side and Pepper on the other, a pitcher of lemonade and an exquisite Meissen plate between them, piled high with macaroons. The sun has just begun to tilt through the French doors, and it forms a halo over Susan's golden hair. "You didn't know?"

"What kind of car costs three hundred thousand dollars?" Susan says breathlessly. Her eyes are large and far too blue for Pepper's taste.

"A Mercedes. A 1936 Special Roadster. Only a few of them were ever built."

Florian chokes. "A *what* Mercedes?"

"A very special Mercedes," says Pepper. "In fact, the exact same one in which your mother fled Germany back in 1938. It turned up in my sister-in-law's shed on Cape Cod, and I spent the summer restoring it."

Under Florian's astounded gaze, she reaches for the pitcher of lemonade and refills her glass. The lemon slices bump lazily against the spout. No one has touched the macaroons. Pepper lifts one up and sniffs it. "Almond?" she says.

"Coconut. Clara's secret recipe. Did you just say it was the same car she and Dad drove out of Germany? The exact one?"

Susan's eyes are like a pair of awed wet cornflowers. "And you restored it? All by yourself?"

"I had a little help," Pepper says modestly.

"But how did it end up in a shed on the Cape?"

Pepper gestures with her cookie. "Now, that, you see, is the mystery. Maybe that's what your mother is trying to find out. My God, these are the macaroons they serve in heaven."

Florian leans forward. "How do you know it's the same car?"

"Because she told me."

"How did she know?"

"I think she'd recognize her own car, don't you? And trust me, this isn't the kind of car you'd mistake for another one. Every part is engineered and hand-fitted and caressed into place. It's the most beautiful thing you've ever seen."

Susan smiles at Florian's cheek. "It's so romantic, don't you think?"

Pepper and Florian turn to her in tandem. "Romantic?"

Jinx, Pepper thinks.

"Why, that she'd spend all that money to buy back the car that carried her and her husband to their new life." She aims the cornflowers at Florian, flutter flutter. "It's beautiful, really."

He bolts to his feet.

"I don't care if it's beautiful or not. My mother's driven off in a three-hundred-thousand-dollar car without telling anyone where she's gone, and I'd like to find her before the coroner does!"

Susan's alarmed. "The coroner!"

"That's a little dramatic, don't you think?" says Pepper.

Florian brings his knuckles to rest on the table. "You want to see dramatic? This is my *mother* we're talking about!"

"That's true, the poor dear, but as the dead German said, what doesn't kill a girl makes her stronger. She's around somewhere, alive and kicking. Trust me."

"*Somewhere* is a damned big word, Schuyler. Considering we don't even know where to start looking."

"Cape Cod?"

"She did *not* drive to Cape Cod. Not in November."

"How do you know?"

"Trust me, all right? She can't stand the cold. She lives for sunshine."

"You see? We've narrowed it down already. Somewhere sunny in November, check."

"She had to have told you something. She had to have left *some* kind of clue."

"Well, she didn't. I'll show you the note. I've seen telegrams more verbose."

"Did she take a lot of luggage?"

"I'm afraid I didn't count, since I wasn't even there when she left. Any more questions?"

Florian sinks back in his chair and runs a hand through his hair. His eyes are puckered with worry, poor thing. What kind of mother is Annabelle Dommerich, to inspire such illogical concern for her welfare? Because motherhood doesn't always end so well for the Schuylers. Motherhood usually goes splash head-first into a vodka tonic, with lime. He says grimly, "We'll just have to start calling hotels, I guess."

"That will take ages."

"I know." He swears softly. "Anyone got any better ideas?"

Pepper taps her chin and examines another macaroon. Her fourth, if she allows it entrance, but then she's never tasted macaroons like melted coconuts, and what if she never has the chance again? Florian picks up his glass and stares keenly through the trickles at a refracted courtyard full of lemon trees. Behind him, the brass carriage clock on the mantel lets out a pair of delicate chimes.

Susan clears her very pretty throat. "I'm sorry, this is going to sound really dumb. But have you thought of searching her study?"

Florian is shocked. *Shocked.* "You mean ransack her private papers?"

"I'm sorry. I know. Dumb idea."

Pepper sets down the macaroon and reaches for her crutches. "Jesus Christ, Susikins. I'm starting to like you after all."

2.

Susan bends flexibly to the rug, flashing a dangerous length of golden thigh. "What's Mrs. Dommerich's Grammy doing on the floor?"

"Breaking my foot."

Susan picks up the statuette and arranges it on the shelf with reverent hands, while Florian eases himself into Annabelle's desk chair and sets eight fingers along the edge of the polished wood, ever so gingerly. He frowns and lifts up a piece of paper. "What's this?"

"Nothing." Pepper snatches it away. "I already told you, I was writing a letter."

"On my mother's stationery?"

"Oh, please. It's not personalized."

"So you *were* writing home, after all. Commendable."

"You're not supposed to read people's personal correspondence."

"I beg your pardon." He offers a smile that comes off like a scowl. "Isn't that exactly what we're doing now?"

Susan turns from the shelf, sets her hands on her dainty hips, and beams. "Don't you just love this room? If I had a study of my own, I'd want it to look *just like this*."

"Imagine that," murmurs Pepper. She settles herself on the edge of the desk, an inch or two away from Florian's leftmost pinkie finger, and admires the plentiful curve of his shoulder. He looks a little too large for the chair, a little out of place in the room, which is distinctly feminine without being an inch pink. Something about the creaminess of the paintwork and the attractive arrangement of the furniture. Or maybe it's the cheerful yellow paisley armchair in the corner, an article no man would ever allow in his private study. "I was just thinking," she says softly.

"And?" Florian is lifting up the blotter a fraction, opening up the drawers a crack, wearing an expression that suggests he's changing diapers instead.

"About that morning. Afternoon, really. I slept in a wee bit. I had breakfast in the dining room, and Annabelle was there, and there wasn't any talk about going away. In fact, I distinctly recall her suggesting we go into town later and shop."

"Shop?" Florian's head pops up, like Sherlock sniffing a clue. "Shop for what?"

"It doesn't matter what. Clothes for me, clothes for the baby. Who cares. My point is that no earlier than half past noon on the date of her so-called disappearance, she was planning on hanging around. And then she left. So what caused her to leave?"

"A telephone call?" suggests Susan.

Florian snaps his fingers. "Or the mail."

"She did say she was going to catch up on the post while I went for a walk."

Florian looks down at the tidy desk. "No mail here."

Pepper shimmies off the desk and hops to the door. "Clara!" she calls out, into the pristine hallway, and a moment later the housekeeper arrives at a canter.

"What is it, Miss Schuyler? You need your pills? You need more macaroons?"

"No. I mean yes! *Yes, please,* to more macaroons. But can you also tell me where you stash Mrs. Dommerich's mail, when she's away?"

3.

For the record, Pepper's not the slightest bit concerned about the health and safety of Mrs. Annabelle Dommerich. The woman is no shrinking cornflower. Besides, if the Nazis couldn't thwart her, nobody could, right? But Pepper has inherited—along with her tip-tilted dark blue eyes and her penchant for choosing the wrong man—the Schuyler nose for dirt, and her talented proboscis began twitching madly right about the moment handsome Florian uttered the magic words.

Ever since Dad died.

Now, what could *that* possibly signify, except that Annabelle's hiding something under her ladylike fingertips? Something like . . . let Pepper ponder for a moment . . . *dirt.*

Not that it's any of her business. But when did Pepper ever mind her own business? Your own business is so unfruitful, so tedious, so lacking in neat solutions and satisfactory conclusions. But the beeswax of others! It gives you a charge, doesn't it, a burst of not-too-commendable energy to plow right past your own tribulations and frolic about in the muck of someone else's. For a change.

"The trouble with your mother," Pepper says, head bent over an open manila folder, "among other things, is that she's so damned organized. Really, who pays the bills and files everything away just hours after getting home from abroad?"

"She hates loose ends." Florian doesn't look up. He's sitting in the desk chair, flipping through a file folder that rests on his lap, looking as if he'd rather poke through a garbage can.

"Or she's hiding something."

Susan says, a bit throaty, "This feels so naughty, looking through her papers."

"Oh, admit it, you're enjoying the thrill. Not that there's anything thrilling to discover, unless you're turned on to know she paid five dollars a week to have the flowers watered." Pepper tosses the folder aside and bends back over the file drawer. "Dommerich. You're awfully quiet over there. Tell me more about this genealogy research of hers."

"I don't know. She was pretty vague."

"You don't say."

"She would clip things from newspapers and magazines. There was someone she had in Washington, looking up records and archives."

"Do you happen to know his name?"

"Nope."

Pepper flips past the files, which are organized alphabetically, until she comes to a tab marked in thick black letters: HARRIS.

"Was it Harris?" she asks. "The man in Washington?"

"No idea."

She pulls the file free and flips it open. A fan of typewritten letters spreads out before her, some attached to newspaper clippings with small silver paper clips. *Dear Mrs. Dommerich,* one began, dated March of 1965, *The possible lead in San Diego appears not to be significant after all. (Please see the attached report for details.) I have now begun research into the candidate in*

Oklahoma [there is an angry blue margin note: *Not Oklahoma! Coast!!*] *and will shortly provide an update . . .*

Genealogy, my aunt Julie, thinks Pepper.

There is a ceiling fan overhead, twirling the air in lazy circles. The draft ruffles the thin corners of the letters—cheap typing paper, the kind they used in small and ramshackle offices—and in the lull of conversation, Pepper considers whether to hold this remarkable paper aloft right now, to wave it triumphantly underneath the steady stroke of the ceiling fan, or whether to keep it in its place, inside the folder marked HARRIS, for the private eye tracking somebody down for Mrs. Annabelle Dommerich. Somebody she must have known well, or at least well enough to be quite certain he (or she!) would never put down roots in the nation's heartland, far from the sea.

Of course, there are other letters. Pepper skims. They have all been arranged in chronological order, oldest to youngest, beginning in January of last year (now, when, exactly, did Mr. Dommerich ascend to the great tobacco shop in the sky?) and ending—Pepper licks her thumb and shuffles to the back of the folder, hoping and praying, because she could use a little excitement here—

November 6, 1966.

4.

"I'm going with you," says Susan. Her bottom lip is fixed stubbornly beneath the upper.

Florian puts his hand on her arm. "Sue, you're much better off down here. I'll telephone and let you know how it goes."

"But I can help!"

She gazes upward, and Pepper thinks, My God, you're better at this than I am, aren't you? The three of them are standing rather intimately in Florian's bedroom, neatly made, while Florian packs his toothbrush back into his overnight bag. He's already dressed for the ride, in a comfortable cotton shirt and dungarees, beaten-up loafers fitted snugly to his feet. Outside, the afternoon light is yellowing with age.

He smiles down at Susan. "That's sweet of you, kid, but Pepper's the one who knows the most about what's going on."

"Pepper's going?"

"I'm going?" Pepper says.

Florian turns to her, eyebrows raised. "Aren't you?"

"No, no, no." She gestures to her belly. "Pregnant lady. A cripple! I can't handle another all-night car ride. Take Susan instead. I'm sure she can see to your needs much better than I can."

"I don't know about that," Susan says modestly.

"Sure you can, honey. He seems like a simple enough man to me."

"Pepper," says Florian, "can we step outside for a moment?"

5.

They stop under the shade of a lemon tree, and Pepper turns to face Florian, crutches braced under her arms.

"Before you say a word, just consider for a moment. You can't possibly be thinking of keeping poor Sue-Sue at home while you whisk another woman off in your T-Bird."

The astounded look again. "But there's nothing going on with the two of us. It's strictly platonic."

"My God. Do you know nothing about women at all, Dommerich?"

"I know a lot about women."

"So you say. But don't you know that dear Susan will spend the next week imagining us pulling off the road every five miles to have screaming fog-up-the-windows sex in the back-seat?"

Florian's gaze drops down to her belly and back up again. "You're kidding, right?"

"My goodness. How flattering."

"I'm not saying you're not attractive. Christ. I think I already made that clear. But—well, for one thing, the logistics—"

"Where there's a will there's a way."

A slow shade of pink rises up Florian's neck and over his cheeks.

"Not that I've actually tried it," Pepper admits. "But I do have an imagination."

"Well, that's not the point. It's none of Susan's business who I'm sleeping with or not sleeping with."

"Really? Because I get the feeling she wants it to be her business. And don't even try to tell me you're not aware of that little fact."

He had the grace to look embarrassed. "Maybe so. But she also knows me better than that."

"Does she?"

"Yes. I may be a lawyer, but I'm not a cad. Anyway, I've got other things on my mind. You're coming along because you're familiar with the car Mama's driving, you're familiar with her state of mind and all that, and you're just—well, you're just a little more—I don't know. Resourceful."

"I think you underestimate Miss Willoughby."

"She's not that kind of girl, that's all."

Pepper curls her fingers around the handles of the crutches. "Oh? And what kind of girl is that, hmm?"

Florian holds up his hands. "I'm not going to let myself fall in that trap again, believe me. You're just two different women. Not bad or good. Just different. And if I need someone to back me up while I track down my mother somewhere on the Georgia coast, someone I can count on, I want *your* type of woman."

"And if you're going to get married and have pretty babies, you want her type?"

"What are you talking about? Who's getting married?"

Pepper puts her hand on Florian's arm, just above the elbow. A lemon branch, heavy with fruit, brushes her shoulder. "Look. Take my advice. Bring Susan with you, okay? She's stronger than you think. Besides, this way you really *can* pull off the road and have sex with her, if you feel the itch."

"Actually, the thought didn't cross my mind."

"Now it will."

6.

From the grateful look on Susan's face, Pepper knows she did a Good Thing. She hopes God is taking note, assuming He hasn't given up on her long ago.

Susan hurries home to pack a few things (she says). Her family's house is about a quarter-mile down the road. That's how they met, Florian says, as they watch her car pull away in a puff of dust. They played in the ocean together as kids. The girl next door, says Pepper. Just like the movies.

She heads back to her room to rest, tosses her crutches in the corner, lies back on her neat bed, and watches the ceiling fan rotate above her. The baby, awakened by the stillness, begins to squirm inside her. You did a Good Thing, she tells herself, though she doesn't feel particularly good. She feels as if a hollow has opened up in her chest, occupying a space she didn't know existed. It interferes with the businesslike beat of her heart.

A few minutes later, there's a knock on the door. "It's me," says Florian, through the crack.

"Haven't you left yet?"

"Are you decent?"

"I'm never decent, or so they tell me."

He opens the door. Pepper sits up.

"Are you sure you won't come?" he says, filling the doorway, framed by the growing blue twilight.

She shakes her head. "Third wheel."

"You wouldn't be a third wheel. Anyway, what are you going to do? I can't let you stay here alone."

"I won't steal anything, I promise. Throw any wild parties and drink up your liquor."

"That's not what I meant." He sits down carefully at the end of the bed, sinking the mattress, and stares down at his knitted hands. "You should go home to your folks."

"Wouldn't that be a delightful Thanksgiving surprise! Pepper waddles in on her crutches, looking unnervingly like the turkey on the table. No, I'll wait just a bit longer. Like they used to do it, you know. Sending the shameful daughter off to Switzerland for a six-month walking holiday with a trusted female relative."

"Except you don't have one of those around here."

She snaps her fingers. "Oh, damn. Well, modern times."

"This is stupid," he says. "You should be with your family."

"My family's not the same as yours, darling. We're better off without each other, in times of trial. Otherwise the arsenic bottle gets uncorked, and the police have to get involved."

"Pepper," he says, shaking his head.

"Off you go, now. I'll be all right. I have Clara to run for the doctor, if anything goes horribly wrong." She reaches over and pushes his shoulder, because she can't resist, just once.

Florian lifts his large hand and places it over hers. "I'll telephone and let you know what we find out."

"Do that thing."

She slides her hand away. He climbs to his feet and scowls down at her. His waist is right at the level of her eyes: his trim stomach, his brown leather belt pinning the dungarees in place.

"Take care of that foot, all right? Use your crutches."

"Would I never?"

And then his hand is cupping her chin, and she has to look down at his blurry wrist, because the two of them combined—his gaze and his touch—create way too much firepower for the hollow in her chest to contain.

"Off you go," she says again, and the hand falls away.

He makes it to the door and stops. "Oh, hold on. This is for you."

She looks up. He's holding out a small envelope between his fingers.

"What's that?"

"Letter for you. Clara sent it along."

When she doesn't get up, when she doesn't even move, eyes frozen on the white rectangle in Florian's paw, heart frozen inside the black hollow, Florian shrugs and sets the envelope down on the lamp table near the door.

7.

Pepper's heart starts again, at a brisk hand gallop. But she's not the kind of girl who avoids bad news, is she? She's not the kind of girl who sits and stares for an hour at the Ominous Object, before she finally gathers up the strength to pick it up with trembling fingers.

Not Pepper.

She doesn't bother with the crutches. She hops ungracefully across the rug and snatches up the envelope. The light has faded fast, the way it does in November. She switches on the lamp and rips open the flap.

The handwriting. How could you possibly rage at the familiarity of someone's messy black handwriting? But she does. She wants to rip it to pieces. She reads it instead.

We need to talk. Forget the lawyers. I'm waiting on an airplane at the Melbourne Municipal Airport. Let's work this out together.

It was unsigned. Of course.

Lawyers. What a hoot. If Captain Seersucker has a law degree, she's Marie Antoinette.

Pepper rips the note to pieces, and when she's done, and her heart is once more cold in her breast, shooting frozen blood all over the place, she finds her toothbrush and a clean dress and a change of underwear. She throws them in a linen laundry bag, tucks her pocketbook over her shoulders, grabs her crutches, and hobbles out the door of the guest cottage, through Annabelle's soft-scented courtyard and toward the driveway.

8.

They haven't left yet. Florian is putting Susan's bag in the trunk of the Thunderbird. Susan's in the passenger seat, touching up her lipstick.

"I've changed my mind!" Pepper says, tossing the laundry bag to Florian.

He grins, catches it handily, and closes the lid of the trunk.

Fourth Movement

"The supreme art of war is to subdue the enemy without fighting."

SUN TZU

ANNABELLE

Germany • 1938

1.

In the pasture nearest the tennis court, Johann was teaching Florian how to ride a pony, using a longe line and an enormous amount of patience. I sat on a picnic cloth, with Frieda and Alice and my new baby sister, and watched them circle under the hot sun. Frieda was giving little Margot her bottle. Above the waving grass, I could hear Johann's bass voice, giving out instructions in German, though I couldn't make out the words.

"Is it perfectly safe, do you think?" said Alice.

"The younger the better, Johann says."

"Oh, yes," Frieda said. "We all started when we were two. I think Frederick is more horse than boy, sometimes."

"He looks as if he's enjoying it, at any rate." Alice drew her knees up under her chin. She wasn't wearing a hat, and her blond hair, streaked by the persistent sunshine, was gathered into a chignon. She wore a dress of white eyelet and looked like a daisy. When Margot began to fuss, she turned her head and stretched out her long arm to tickle her daughter's chin. "What's the matter, darling? Are you keen to be off riding horses, too?"

Frieda laughed and put the baby to her shoulder. "She just needs to burp, I think."

Alice lay back on the cloth. "You're far better at this than I am, aren't you? Perhaps I should let you adopt her."

"I like babies, that's all," Frieda said.

I gazed across the hot meadow grass. Florian looked so grown-up in his riding clothes and leather boots. I could tell by the set of his shoulders that he was concentrating fiercely on Johann's words. He was always desperate to please his father.

His father.

And there it was, just like that: the knot of pain in my chest, which had become smaller and appeared less frequently as the months passed, but which never quite disappeared. I imagined it was a permanent condition, a chronic illness to be managed in the privacy of my own brain. It helped, perhaps, that I hadn't heard a single word from Stefan himself since we parted on that hot July day a year ago. He had walked out of the Paris Ritz and vanished. Not even Charles knew where he was, or maybe he wasn't telling me. A clean break, like an amputation. Eventually, you realized you could survive without all your limbs, that you could function and even thrive, because human beings were designed to take a battering. And though you weren't whole, you at least had a son. And though it sometimes seemed as if your heart had stopped beating, you at least knew that somewhere in the world, another heart was beating for you.

Margot burped daintily, and I shifted my gaze to my baby

sister and marveled at the difference between her and Florian. Her delicate lips, her perfect tiny fingers. If I leaned in to smell her hair, I knew she would be puppy-sweet. How was it possible that my sturdy son, rising and falling in his stirrups as the pony moved to a trot, had been nursing at my breast only a year and a half ago? My baby was gone forever. I wouldn't get him back. I had this new Florian, this walking, talking, pony-riding Florian, a swaggering miniature image of the man who had created him inside me. But my baby was gone.

"Are you all right, Mother?" asked Frieda. "You look a little ill."

I rose to my feet and shook the crumbs from my dress. "I'm fine, darling. I think I'll just take a walk."

2.

We sat down to lunch an hour or so later. The sunshine poured through the long French doors, and as I took my seat at the end of the table and picked up a glass of water, the housekeeper came up behind me and told me that a woman had been here to see me.

"Who?" I asked in surprise. I had no friends here in Germany, only a few neighboring acquaintances who didn't approve of me at all.

"She did not leave her name, Frau von Kleist, but she gave me this note for you and explained that it was urgent."

Alice and my father were already in place, drinking their wine and talking animatedly about tennis. The smoke from their cigarettes drifted to the ceiling. The boys scraped back their chairs. Johann looked expectantly across the table, which was fragrant with a profusion of red roses I had cut just that morning.

I tucked the note under my plate. "Thank you, Hilda."

3.

For a house so large, Schloss Kleist offered little privacy. Actually, it wasn't the house itself, it was the inhabitants. You could not be called to the telephone without everyone wanting innocently to know who had called; you could not play tennis without at least a pair of spectators. It was easier at night, when I could retreat to my cozy rooms at the end of the east wing without some request bouncing my way every four minutes. During the day, I could achieve a quiet moment only in the lavatory, which is exactly where I opened the note Hilda had delivered to me at lunch.

It was written on a leaf of cheap notepaper, the kind you might pick up in a hotel or a train station. The words were English and neatly printed, as if the writer wanted to be sure I could read them properly.

I need your help. Wilhelmine. 23 Marktstrasse

I folded the paper and put it back into my pocket. Just before I opened the door, I remembered to flush the toilet and run the faucet, so I could pretend to wash my trembling hands.

4.

I found Johann upstairs in our bedroom, changing into his tennis clothes.

"Isn't it a little hot for tennis?" I said.

"Your father made me a challenge. One does not turn down a challenge from the father-in-law." He reached for his shirt. His chest was pink and enormous, like a side of beef. "Will you come to watch?"

"Thank you, no. I thought I might motor into the village for a bit of shopping," I said.

"Shopping?" He stopped and lifted his eyebrows. "But you do not like to shop."

"I need to order a hat for the festival."

"Have the milliner come to us. It is what Frieda would always do."

"I'm not Frieda, remember?"

He set the shirt aside and smiled. "No. You are my beautiful Annabelle. I almost die to look at you."

"Johann, stop."

"Come here, beautiful Annabelle." He snared me around the waist and slipped his hand inside the opening of my blouse.

"Johann! What's gotten into you?"

He kissed me, and when he lifted his face away, his eyes were soft. "The sunshine, I think. It is so good to have the sunshine again."

5.

I waited until the tennis balls had actually launched into the air before I slipped into the garage and started up the Mercedes.

The village was a few miles away, down a meandering road that glared white in the sun. I had put the top down, and the draft pulled at my hat, smelling of ripe hops and sunshine. I concentrated on keeping the car steady, on breathing just the right amount of oxygen into my lungs: not too much, not too little.

Marktstrasse was almost deserted; everyone had done her shopping early and gone home to enjoy the summer afternoon. I pulled up in front of number 23—a small hotel I'd never noticed before—and a slim figure stepped out of the shadow of the eaves.

"Frau von Kleist?" she said.

She was pretty, I thought, in a cold wash of jealousy. She stood taller than I did, and her curling dark hair bobbed about her ears. She looked more modern than I had imagined. She wore no makeup, except for a bit of lipstick, and she didn't need to. Her silk blouse and wide trousers were well made and a little mannish, almost like a movie star's, suiting her the way Alice's deep V-necked dresses suited Alice. I could well imagine Wilhelmine as an elegant new bride in a hotel bed, making love to Stefan, making a daughter with Stefan.

"Wilhelmine," I said. "I'm sorry, I don't know your last name."

"It's Himmelfarb," she said in perfect English. "May I get in?"

"Of course."

She got in the passenger side and shut the door. "Let's drive somewhere, if you don't mind. I have already taken enough risk."

I released the clutch and we set off down Marktstrasse in a little spurt of white gravel. She leaned her elbow on the door and turned her head to watch me, as if she was waiting for me to start the conversation.

So I did. "It's Stefan, isn't it? Something's happened to Stefan."

She went on regarding me, without speaking.

"Tell me, please. At least tell me he's alive, for God's sake."

"I'm sorry," she said. "I was just trying to see if you were sincere."

"What the hell does that mean? For God's sake, tell me what's happened!"

"He's alive," she said, and my shoulders slumped. The car swerved to the edge of the road, and Wilhelmine gripped the edge of the doorframe and pressed her right foot into the floorboards. When I had righted the car, she said, "All right. So you don't know anything about it."

"I haven't heard from Stefan in a year. Not since he walked out of the Paris Ritz last July."

"Ah. Then I suppose you don't know he was taken by a pair of Gestapo agents as soon as he turned the corner into the rue Cambon to fetch his automobile, and he has been held like a dog in the Dachau camp ever since."

I stuffed my hand into my mouth and swerved to the side of the road—this time deliberately—slamming the brake with my foot, until the Mercedes bumped to a stop alongside a weathered fence. The engine coughed and died. I opened the door just in time to vomit into the grass.

6.

"It was a month or two before we realized he was actually missing," Wilhelmine said, "and it was several more months before we found out for certain where they had taken him. He is a very special prisoner, you know. They would not let me see him. I managed at last to get a message to him, and he sent a reply that he was fine, but I could hardly recognize the writing."

"Oh, God," I said, holding my fist to my mouth. I thought of my tranquil autumn and winter, settling Frieda into her school, resuming my cello studies, a recital Johann arranged at a music conservatory that was very well received. He said he was proud of me. Christmas in Paris, surrounded by my new family. A pile of decadent presents under the tree, including a breathtaking necklace of black pearls from Johann, which he fastened around my neck himself. Plenty of food and wine, plenty of music and warm fires. At night, Johann would hold me close to his chest, because a Paris apartment, however grand, is always drafty in winter; and as I drifted to sleep, safe and warm, I would say *Good night, Stefan* in my head, and wonder if he were keeping some woman warm in his own arms while she drifted to sleep.

Sometimes, when the bitterness ebbed in my heart, I even wished he were. I wished he did have a woman in his arms, because no one should lie alone in the middle of winter.

"That was in May," said Wilhelmine. "The officials refused to tell us any more, only that he was being held indefinitely for crimes against the state. So I demanded to know what crimes, and after many weeks of letters and telephone calls, they at last sent me this." She handed me a piece of paper, folded twice into a square.

I stared at the paper between my fingers. "You said *us*. Whom do you mean?"

"His family, of course. His parents cannot sleep for worry."

"Of course."

"I have not told my daughter. She loves him so much. She draws pictures of him and hangs them in her room."

The tiny indentations of the typewriter were like Braille under my fingertips. The paper was crisp and thin and terribly official. I unfolded the page: not in the easy flips by which you opened the morning news, but by brute force, the individual grasping of each leaf requiring dogged concentration.

"As you see," said Wilhelmine—I did not see, actually; I could not comprehend the German script before me—"this is an arrest order for one Stefan Silverman, for the crimes of murder and treason and various other infractions, according to evidence and sworn statements."

"Murder," I said. "Did he really commit murder?"

"Does it matter?"

"No." My back rested against a fence post. Someone was mowing a field nearby; the drone of the engine floated along the motionless summer air. If I closed my eyes, I could smell the wholesome brown scent of newly cut hay. I said, "How did you know about me?"

Wilhelmine's arms were folded across her silk chest. Her breasts were small and lean, like the rest of her. I thought she wasn't wearing a brassiere. She was practical and stylish all at once; she was indomitable. "Do you have a cigarette? I left mine in my motorcar."

I said I didn't.

She crossed one leg over the other. "I knew he had a mistress in Paris, a married woman, and he had gone to see her during the summer. So in May, after I got this arrest paper at last, I went to France. I went first to the Ritz, because he always saw his women there; it was such a great pleasure to him, to screw some beautiful woman in the bed of the Imperial Suite." She paused. "I'm sorry, that was rather cruel, wasn't it? I have always said I would not be bitter. I did love him, you know. I still admire him very much. It is impossible not to admire such a man as that. He has such qualities." She made a circle in the dust with the toe of her elegant shoe.

"Please go on," I said.

"So I went to the Ritz, and at first Alfonse would not tell me anything, though I could see perfectly well that he knew all about you. I am old hands with Alfonse, you see. He prizes discretion above everything. I had gone there to murder my husband a few years ago, and Alfonse stood very firm, even though I was Stefan's lawful wife. He would not let me disturb the bastard." She laughed. "But this time I told him it was a matter of life and death, that their precious client had been arrested and thrown in a prison when he walked out of the hotel last July, and that he was now in great danger. So Alfonse gave me the note you left for Stefan."

I squeezed my eyes shut and contemplated this. "But I only signed it *Annabelle*. There was no surname."

"Oh, that was the easy part. Everyone knew that the Baron von Kleist had made a fool of himself over a young French wife named Annabelle."

Across the road, the cows were on the move, wandering slowly across a tender green pasture. "I don't understand," I said. "What does my husband have to do with any of this?"

Wilhelmine straightened her lean body away from the fence and turned to me. "Are you serious? You are this ignorant?"

I looked up at her helplessly, into the full glare of her contempt. The air around us seemed to be cracking into pieces, preparing to shatter. "Yes," I said. "I am this ignorant."

Her small dark eyes traveled over my face, taking my inventory: forehead, brows, eyes, mouth, chin. "I suppose that is why he fell in love with you, of all of us. You are so fucking innocent. It must have been a relief." She laid her thumb against my cheekbone, like a lover's caress. "Sweet thing. Look again at the paper. Tell me if there is any other name that springs from the page."

I lifted the paper and stared at it. The gothic script had always confounded me; I had learned a great deal of German during my marriage, but I seemed to lose the meaning when I saw the words written in that dense medieval lettering. But now my eyes, as if knowing what to look for before my brain did, traveled down the page and fastened on the words *Johann von Kleist*.

"You do not know that the two of them, they are like Javert and Valjean? They are immortal enemies. It all made sense to me, when I saw that Annabelle von Kleist was Stefan's lover. Why your husband would not let him go, like the bloodhound tracking down the fox. Why there is now no possibility of Stefan's release."

I slid down the fence post and came to rest in the dusty grass. "It's not true."

"You know it is. You are ignorant but not foolish."

"But Johann's a general in the army, not Gestapo."

She snorted. "This is Hitler's Germany, Frau von Kleist. No one is what he seems. Do you know what your husband did in

Berlin last year? He oversaw the reorganization of the prisons, the prisons in which they put the people who do not agree with the Nazis, so that now they go to the rehabilitation camps, these beautifully designed camps, even bigger and better than before."

"My God."

"But it is more than that. There has always been a grudge. I believe Stefan pinched his nose a few years ago, intercepted some papers or some matter like that. And then there was this murder of a police agent, who was sent to catch him and put him in the prison. And I think you understand your husband, Frau von Kleist. I think you understand he is a man of rules and consequence. He is dogged in pursuit of his goal."

"Yes, I understand that." At the word *understand*, the shattering began at last. The fatal tap on the cracked glass. Stefan and Johann. Johann denouncing Stefan, having him arrested and thrown into Dachau to be tortured, and then going home to our Paris apartment and playing horses with Stefan's son. Taking Stefan's lover to bed, the final stroke. *We are man and wife again.*

I wanted to crawl out of my revolted skin. I wanted to vomit again, but there was nothing left in me. I took off my hat and let the sun bake into my hair.

Wilhelmine sat down next to me, Indian-style. A wooden slat creaked as she leaned her back against it. Her knee was sharp and bony against my thigh.

I whispered, "He never said anything. Stefan never said a word."

"No, I am not surprised. Stefan has his faults, but he plays fair. He does not turn women into pawns."

I tilted my head back into the fence post and stared at the hot sky. A few small clouds sat against the blue, not moving. I waited for them to splinter and break apart with the force of my shock, but they did not. The sky stayed in place, the clouds stayed in place. The sun kept burning, white and distant. The same objects, except the world was now utterly changed, a different universe from the one in which I had existed an hour ago.

"So, then, Frau Himmelfarb," I said. "What do you propose we do to save him?"

7.

When I returned to Schloss Kleist an hour later, the house was in uproar. Frieda flew across the entrance hall and wrapped her arms around me. She was my height now, almost taller. "Oh, Mother! There you are! It's so awful!"

"What's happened?" I touched her blond hair and my ribs ached.

"It's Papa! They were playing tennis, and it was so hot, and he must have had a dizzy spell. He fell and hit his head."

I stepped back. "Where is he now?"

"He's upstairs in bed. The doctor is coming. Oh, Mother, will he be all right?"

I was already climbing the stairs. "I certainly hope so," I muttered.

The bedroom was dark and smelled of lemon and vomit. Someone had closed the curtains. Hilda sat by the bed, holding a cloth to Johann's forehead. His eyes squinted open when I entered.

I let out a sigh. At least he was awake.

"Thank you, Hilda," I said. "I'll take care of him until the doctor arrives."

"But Frau von Kleist—"

"Don't worry, I've had some training as a nurse."

She rose from the chair and handed me the cloth, which was cool and damp and lemon-scented. I lost my breath, thinking of Monte Carlo, and dropped into the chair.

Before me, Johann tried to smile. "Hello, *mein Liebling*. Not quite so heroic a pose, I am afraid."

I picked up his hand and tried his radial pulse. A little rushed, but steady and sharp. I placed the cloth against his forehead, where a large purple bump had already risen. "You'll be all right, I think. A concussion."

The door closed behind Hilda.

Johann whispered, "You were right about tennis—"

"Never mind the tennis, Johann," I said crisply. "I am leaving you this afternoon. As soon as the doctor comes, I'm packing my things and Florian's, and I'm leaving with a friend."

Johann's eyes flared. He tried to raise his head from the pillow. I pushed him back.

"Don't. You'll hurt yourself. There's nothing you can do. Stefan's former wife came to see me today, after lunch."

"Stefan?"

"Yes, Stefan. My lover, Florian's father. But you knew that, didn't you?"

"*My* son."

"No, he's not. I spent three days with Stefan in Monte Carlo, the three happiest days of my life, and we made Florian there. And then you had Stefan arrested, and you gallantly married me while he was safe in prison, and you never said a word." I paused.

"What a triumph, to take Stefan's lover and his baby, too. You must have felt so triumphant."

Johann struggled against his foggy brain. His head moved from side to side. "No. No. This is not true. I love you, I saw you first, I loved you *first*, before I even knew—before he—" He made a grunting noise.

"Don't upset yourself, Johann. You'll only make your injury worse."

"No. No. I love—love you both. Not because—Stefan—"

"Don't lie to me."

"True. Stefan is a criminal." He said that clearly, at least. "A murderer. Broke the *law*."

"If you weren't hurt, I would smack you. I would bloody murder *you*. Do you know what you've done?"

"He broke the law!"

"Stop it. Just stop it. He may have broken the law, but his cause was just. At least he was *doing* something about this horrible situation, while you sat back and said, *Ja, ja, the people will come to their senses*. You had him arrested and thrown in prison, and then you went home and tucked Stefan's baby son into his crib, and then you took me to bed and you screwed me good and hard, didn't you? What a goddamned thrill that must have been for you."

He removed the cloth from his head and dropped it on the rug. He said, in his thready, stunned voice, "What is this? What are you saying? *You*. You went back to him. My heart broke."

"No, I didn't. We hardly even touched each other, did you know that? I admit, I went to see him, but we never even kissed. I loved him so, and I never so much as kissed him. And then I thought about running away with him, and I came home and you were there with Florian and darling Frieda, and I knew I couldn't do that to you. You asked me to forgive you, and I was so full of guilt and shame. I thought it wasn't your fault, and you had tried so hard, you had given me so much when I needed you, and now you needed me. So I gave him up and went back to you. My God, what a fool, what an utter fool. I actually said to myself, *It's not his fault, he's a good man, I have to find a way to love him.* To *love* you!" I was crying now, beating my fist on the counterpane next to Johann's beefy leg. "I am such a fool."

"Annabelle. Please." He started forward and I jumped back from the bed, wiping my face.

"Don't you dare. It *is* your fault. It *was* your fault, and I'm leaving you. I'm taking Florian and going to find a way to get Stefan out of prison, and if you dare to stop me, I'll find a way to ruin you. I'll tell Frieda what you did. I will blacken your name across Europe. Florian will curse you all his life. Do you understand me?" I shouted.

Johann's head fell back. The door rattled with a loud knock, and an instant later it flung open to reveal the shocked doctor. "Frau von Kleist!" he hissed.

"I'm sorry." I swiped my cheeks. "I will leave you to your examination, Herr *Doktor*."

PEPPER

A1A • 1966

1.

The backseat of a Ford Thunderbird isn't designed for a heavily pregnant woman to lie back and take a nap, plaster-wrapped foot and all, but Pepper's too pooped to care. Besides, up front are Florian and Susan, and Susan's resting against Florian's shoulder, and that's really not a sight for sore eyes, is it?

So she curls on her side, facing the slick leather back of the front seat, and enjoys the disembodied rush of the automobile as it consumes forty miles an hour of the black highway, the old faithful A1A that connects the extreme barrier coast of Florida with the rest of the Eastern seaboard. Florian looked at the map and said they should be there by morning, and Pepper believes him. He said they could pick up the interstate in Daytona Beach, save a lot of time. Pretty soon the interstate would reach all the way down to Miami, imagine that. You could drive the length of Florida in less than a day.

Florian's voice drifts over the seat. "How are you doing back there? Asleep?"

"I'm all right."

"Comfortable?"

"I've slept in worse places."

He laughs, nice and throaty, and Pepper just closes her eyes and enjoys the male sound. The car hums underneath, a reliable American engine, eating the open road. If only she could fall asleep.

"Is Susan awake?"

"Nope. Out like a light. My arm went numb a few miles back." He pauses. "You should try to sleep."

"Can't. You know how it is."

Another handsome chuckle. "Yeah, I guess so."

The leather sticks to her cheek. She licks her lips and thinks about telling him the whole story. Getting this fear off her chest and onto his. After all, she's concerning herself in *his* beeswax, isn't she? It's only fair.

Because it's not as if his opinion of her morals can sink any lower.

But her lips remain closed, and it's Florian who speaks into the midnight quiet, almost as if he heard her regardless.

"I've got another personal question for you, Schuyler."

She sighs. "Some men never learn."

"Is everything okay with you?"

Pepper licks her lips again. "Peachy keen."

His shoulder has apparently had enough of its tender burden. He shuffles about, adjusting Susan's weight to a more convenient location. She murmurs protest and then goes quiet. "I've been thinking," he says.

"Not that again."

"Pepper, if you're in trouble of some kind . . ."

Pepper laughs.

"I mean other than the obvious. Are you?"

Her foot hurts. She forgot to take the painkiller before they left, and now there's a dull ache that surrounds her like a bandage right at the arch, and is now starting to creep its way into her ankle. She tries to move the foot more comfortably, but the cast is too heavy, and she's too tired. "What makes you say that?"

"Oh, I don't know. The letter I gave you. The way you changed your mind about coming along with us."

"Oh, that? I just decided the two of you needed a responsible chaperone."

"So listen," says Florian quietly, so she has to strain her ears to hear him. "I'm going to make a little confession here, because I want you to trust me, all right? That's how it works, according to the shrinks. An exchange of trust. I tell you something I'd rather keep secret, and then afterward you maybe feel like you can do the same."

"What if I don't trust shrinks?"

"That's all right. I'll say it anyway." He pauses, and Pepper guesses they're passing someone, because his dark head moves and his profile appears as he checks the road behind, and then the engine roars happily and the car makes a lateral shift. He continues, when the machine returns to its ordinary purr: "I guess you could say I had a little thing going for you, this past year."

As declarations go, it's a simple one. Once, when Pepper was in college, a boy sent her a bouquet of roses attached to a love sonnet attached to a diamond bracelet. She sent back the flowers and the poem but kept the diamonds. (No, she didn't! But she was tempted.) This is no bouquet, no handwritten sonnet, no string of costly jewels. But the clean and simple lines of *I had a little thing going for you,* spoken in Florian's assured voice, achieve what no passionate paragraphs did before: they make Pepper cry. Just a little, from the corner of her left eye, dripping past the bridge of her nose and into the no-man's-land of what-might-have-been.

"Only a little one? I must be losing my touch."

"Look, considering you didn't know I even existed, you should be grateful for what you've got."

"Fair enough."

"Anyway, that was my fault. The thing is, you knocked me off the rails when I first saw you. I'd heard about you before—everyone was raving about Pepper Schuyler—and to be honest, I take a little pride in not falling for the girl that everyone else is falling for. But *you.*"

"But me?"

"You. You have a way of casting a spell. I guess you know that. You're like one of those attractor beams."

"Oh, that's right. Leading all you poor helpless men to your doom."

"No, but it wasn't just that." A pause. "You know, the thing about sirens, they make you think there's this extraordinary creature behind the lights and music, but when you yank away the drapes there's nothing to see. But you were the opposite. You were at a party, holding court, and I swear I heard you quote two or three different Enlightenment philosophers in a single fucking sentence, and not one of those idiots listening to you had any idea what you just did."

"Well, you know what they say. Law is wasted on the lawyers."

"Yeah, well, that's what I thought. That you were wasted on that crowd."

Pepper doesn't reply. Susan stirs a little, maybe at the animation in Florian's voice, and then drops back off. When he speaks again, his tone is softer.

"Did you ever think about going to law school yourself?"

She lets out a sharp laugh. "Daddy wouldn't let me. Well, specifically, he wasn't going to pay for it, and I didn't want to have to earn my degree on my back."

"Neanderthal."

"Now, now. That's my father you're maligning." She props her head up on her elbow and studies the back of his head, a round silhouette in the glow of the headlamps ahead. "So if you were so crazy about me, why didn't you try your luck?"

He shrugs. "Because you were already in love with someone else. But I *was* crazy about you. I admit it. I thought, That girl is throwing herself away. She could do so much better if she just . . ."

"Just what?"

"Slowed down for a moment. Realized there's more to life than sex appeal. More to *you* than sex appeal."

"Well, you're wrong there. Not much inside."

"The hell there isn't," he snaps, and Susan grunts. He repeats it more softly. "The hell there isn't, Pepper."

The car finds a bump on the road, and Pepper's heavy body jolts against the cushion. She puts out her arm and braces it on the front seat.

"Sorry," says Florian.

"No harm."

"Anyway, I guess I'm just trying to say that I know a little more than you think. That maybe I could help you, if you let me."

Pepper asks, "What made you stop?"

"Stop? Stop what?"

"Being crazy about me."

Florian drives silently, without replying. Pepper reaches for the crank and rolls down the window a couple inches. The breeze is chillier than she expects, but it's a small price to pay for some goddamned air. The draft ripples loudly in her ears, but she still picks out the words when Florian finally speaks, maybe because her ears are a little bit in love with the sound of his voice.

"I don't know. Maybe I didn't."

2.

At one point, they stop for gas, right about the time Pepper has finally managed to drift off to sleep. She wakes in terror, heart smacking, breath choked, and sits up to the anemic glow of a pair of streetlamps leaking through the blackness, exposing Florian as he stands underneath, leaning against the pole, watching the sleepy attendant as he pumps the gas.

There's no sign of Susan. Pepper peeks over the edge of the seat and there she is, the little darling, still sleeping, a tiny smile suspended on her rosebud mouth. Pepper crawls out on the driver's side, so as not to disturb her.

As she approaches Florian, she realizes she's dying for a cigarette. She hasn't smoked since the third day in Cocoa Beach, when the carefully rationed pack ran dry, and she misses not so much the delirious hit of nicotine but the smell, the taste, the lazy ceremony of lighting up and drawing the smoke down your throat and into your lungs. The curls of white billowing upward, like your own thoughts traveling to heaven for inquisition.

"I don't suppose you have a smoke," she says.

His face is sallow under the lamp, his eyes deep-set and hollow, and his hands are shoved into the pockets of his dungarees. "Sorry. I quit the day my dad got diagnosed."

Damn it, Pepper thinks.

"You were pretty close?"

"Yeah. Best friends. I could tell him anything, things I couldn't say to Mama." He pauses. His eyes haven't shifted from the pimply young attendant, as if he's making sure the kid doesn't take off in the shiny blue T-Bird himself, sleeping Susan and all. "I have this memory of him, my earliest memory. I think it must have been when we were still in Germany. We're making paper airplanes and flying them into the fireplace, and they burst into flame. I thought it was the greatest. I thought he was the greatest."

"How old were you?"

"I guess I couldn't have been more than two." He shakes his head. "It's just a brief memory, like a flash. But vivid, you know? I can still see that fireplace. The puffs of flame."

"Pyromaniac."

"That's what boys do. Make stuff and then destroy it." He laughs.

"You must miss him. Your father."

"Every second." He pushes away from the lamppost and digs his wallet out of his back pocket. "Looks like he's done. Is Susan awake?"

"No. I'm beginning to think that woman can sleep through an artillery bombardment."

"You can stretch your legs for a bit, if you want."

"No, I can't." She gestures to her foot.

An outraged look fills his face. "Wait a minute. Why aren't you on your crutches?"

"They're in the trunk."

He swears and reaches down to pick her up, and Pepper doesn't complain. She just holds her head virtuously away from his shoulder and thinks, This is the last time ever, scout's honor.

Hardly worth mentioning, really, but the Girl Scouts kicked Pepper out after a month. Something about sassing the scout leader.

3.

They are headed to Cumberland Island, off the southern coast of Georgia. Pepper's not quite sure what Florian expects to find there. That last letter from Harris, P.I.—the one dated November 6, three days before Pepper arrived in Cocoa Beach—informed Annabelle Dommerich that she might find the contents of the enclosed newspaper article of interest as a possible lead, and he would be happy to travel to Cumberland Island to investigate in person, with her written authorization, expenses billed according to the usual arrangement.

The article itself had been removed, though the small silver paperclip remained, attaching the letter to nothing.

"It's not exactly proof," Susan said doubtfully, but Florian said it was the way the facts fit together. The only logical conclusion.

So here they are, climbing onto the brand-new interstate highway near Daytona Beach at half past two in the morning, while the Thunderbird's three hundred horses whinny in unison. Susan wakes up suddenly, lifting her head against the glow of the streetlights on the onramp. She asks where they are, and Florian says they're heading onto the interstate, they'll be in Georgia around sunrise.

All right, she says, and her head disappears again, behind the flat ledge of the front seat.

4.

When Pepper wakes up a few hours later, she's aware of two facts, and that's all: she's lying on the backseat of a car, and the car has stopped.

Her hand goes straight to her belly and finds—with relief—the strong little ball, still in place. Still there.

And then she remembers there's nothing to fear. She's escaped into the night again, just in the nick. She's headed for Georgia. A vagabond. Pepper on the run.

She sits up and looks out the window at a salmon-pink sunrise rising above the distant marsh grass. On the other side of the car lies a wide street, silent as the grave, studded with tombstone cars. Beyond, a pillared white building glows hopefully in the dawn. The Riverview Hotel, the sign says.

"I guess we're in Georgia," she says, to no one in particular, because the front seat is empty. Which rather offends Pepper, because who leaves a pregnant woman asleep on an unknown street at dawn?

She stretches, runs her fingers through her unkempt hair, and opens the door.

Outside, it's chillier than she expected, as if they've crossed some invisible line from the endless summer of Florida into a world in which seasons existed. Pepper tucks her cardigan about her shoulders and inhales the Georgia morning. A suggestion of smoke lingers in the air, mingling with the fishiness of the nearby sea, and Pepper realizes she's standing at the edge of a glassy tidal river, that the distant marsh is actually the opposite shore, and that a modest white boat lies moored to the railing, next to a sign that reads CUMBERLAND ISLAND FERRY. A figure leans back against the rightmost edge of the ferry sign, covering the last three letters. One arm crosses beneath a round bosom, while the other operates a cigarette in short and furtive strikes.

Well, well. Not so squeaky-clean after all.

Pepper reaches back in the car for her crutches and hobbles toward Susan. Her limbs are stiff and ungainly after the rocky night, and her tongue is coated in fur. Dollars to doughnuts, she looks like hell. But then Susan looks remarkably like hell, too. The skin actually sags beneath her lashes, an effect made worse by raccoonlike smears of black mascara, and her blond curls have expired. Two pretty women brought low by a night in a Ford Thunderbird.

Susan waves her cigarette. "Don't tell."

"Wouldn't dream of it."

"Want one?"

Pepper nearly says yes, and then she thinks of Florian quitting cold turkey the day his father got cancer. "I'm laying off the smokes right now. But I might just huddle around your lighter for a second to warm up."

Susan laughs. "I almost forgot what cold felt like. Florian told me to pack a jacket, but it slipped my mind. Serves me right."

"Speaking of which, where is the little devil?"

"My jacket?"

"Florian."

"Oh, he's just getting rooms, so we can rest and freshen up before the ferry leaves." The cigarette is nearly finished. She holds it between her thumb and forefinger, sucking every last drop into her pale mouth. Her skin is pink with cold, her eyes excessively blue inside their charcoal circles.

"I could use a little freshening." Pepper watches longingly as Susan drops the final crumb into the turf and crushes it under her pristine white sneaker. "And then the fun begins."

"The fun? You mean looking for Mrs. Dommerich?"

"Well, maybe *fun* isn't quite the word. Fireworks is more to the point, when Florian finds out that his dear mama is tracking down an old flame."

Susan hesitates. "Do you think so?"

"You don't agree?"

A look of wariness enters Susan's young forehead. "It could be an old school friend," she says.

"Come on, honey. We both know you're not nearly as naïve as you let on."

"Oh, I don't know." She looks down. "I guess it doesn't matter anymore, now that Mr. Dommerich is gone. I'd just hate to think she was . . . you know, that it was anything . . ."

Pepper braces the crutches under her arms and clasps her hands together. She's warmed up a little, thanks to the miniature furnace burning away inside her, but her fingers feel like numb little sausages. "You never know what's really going on in someone else's marriage."

"My mother didn't like him," Susan says. "Mr. Dommerich. She said he wasn't very pleasant. He didn't like to talk about himself. But I thought he was nice, once you got to know him. I think he was just quiet because of what happened, you know, back in Germany."

"What happened back in Germany?"

"I don't know exactly, but I always got the feeling it was something terrible. Because he wouldn't ever talk about it, wouldn't even allow any photographs in the house. Like he thought someone might, I don't know, recognize him, or something like that."

"But they got out before the war even started."

"I know. But that was just the feeling I had." She pauses. "He used to teach me German words, until my mother got upset. I think maybe they were vulgar; he had this naughty sense of humor, though you wouldn't think it at first. He seemed very proper. I called him by his first name once, Rudolf, and he looked at me like I was crazy. I was so sorry when he got sick." She eyes her pocketbook, as if considering another cigarette. "He about worshipped the ground Mrs. Dommerich walked on, and you could tell she loved him back. The way they looked at each other, like they were sharing a secret. They had all these kids. Stepkids and half-siblings and full siblings. I couldn't tell half of them apart sometimes. Keep straight who was who. They were mostly older, except for the twins. They had twins after they moved to America. Margot and Lizzie. They're in college now. I only have one sister, so I loved going over there, everybody crawling over each other. She just loved taking care of them all,

Mrs. Dommerich. She's one of those mother hens, you know? I don't know how she found the time for her music."

"Or anything else," murmurs Pepper.

"What's that?"

"Nothing. And you and Florian?"

"Oh, him." Her cheeks are already blushing with cold, but Pepper imagines a little more color. "Don't tell him, but I had a crush on him since I was a little kid, when he saved our beagle Molly after she got caught in the surf. He came up out of the water—it was a horrible riptide, there was a storm offshore—all dripping and handsome, and I was a goner. Isn't that the most? And he never paid the slightest bit of attention to me. I was just Margot and Lizzie's friend."

"Oh, that's just boys. Trust me, he had his eye on you, a pretty thing like you."

"Well, if he did, he didn't let on for years." She casts a hairy eyeball at the hotel entrance. "Not until last summer. He was back for a week or two, and he finally noticed I existed. Asked me to dinner. I had a date with Billy Fielder—"

"Oh, who's Billy?"

"Just a boy." She looks away. "I called Billy up and canceled, and—well. We had a real nice time. He kissed me good night."

"Better late than never."

"Yes, I guess so." Again with the hesitation. Susan's such a good girl, she hates to hurt anyone's feelings, even when they're not around. She opens her mouth, closes it, and discovers her pocketbook again. "It's funny," she says, rummaging for the cigarettes, "nothing's ever quite what you expect, is it? Even something you've wanted for years."

"That's life, honey."

She lights up and draws in deeply, eyes closed. "But what am I saying? He's terrific. He's the best. He always opens the car door for me and gives me his jacket when it's cold out. He said his mom made him take her out on a date when he turned sixteen, so he would know how to treat a lady. Don't you love that?"

"It sounds like Annabelle, all right."

"He called me a few times when he went back to Washington, wrote me a couple of letters. I missed him like crazy. I thought about moving there to be with him, but Mom said no, you make them come to you. Like dogs, she said. Or was it sheep?"

"Mom is probably right. But it's easy for her to say, isn't it?"

"I'll say. Oh, shoot!" She snatches the cigarette from her mouth and drops it on the ground. "Here he comes."

"You know, he can still smell the smoke on you."

"Oh no. Do you think so?"

Pepper shrugs. "Don't worry. I'll say it was me. Just don't let him get too close until you've washed your mouth out with Listerine."

5.

But sneaky cigarettes are the last thing on Florian's mind. He strides across the parking lot like a warrior advancing over enemy territory, and from the wattage of his eyes, Pepper guesses it's news. Good or bad?

"She's here," he says. "*Was* here. Right here at this hotel."

Pepper scans the street for a vintage black Mercedes, a pearl among swine. "*Was* here? So where is she now?"

"On the island. Cumberland Island, like we guessed. She took the ferry out yesterday."

"And she's still there?" Susan's words emerge in a cloud of guilty cinnamon Dentyne.

"They don't know. That's the thing. She never checked out of the hotel. She didn't take a suitcase or anything. But . . ." Florian holds his hand up to his brow and turns to stare at the boat moored beside them, and he looks like he's forty years old, just like that. He looks as old as God.

"But?" Pepper says softly.

He turns not to Susan, but to Pepper, and his eyes are like two brown stones. "But when the last ferry came in, she wasn't on it."

ANNABELLE

Germany • 1938

1.

At the top of the entrance gate to the prisoner's camp at Dachau, the iron formed into the words *arbeit macht frei*.

"In English, it means, literally, *Work makes freedom*," said the man next to me, with conspicuous pride. "Though perhaps it is more usefully translated as *Work will make you free*. You will find, Frau von Kleist, that all our prisoners are kept occupied with honest and wholesome labor, for the great progress of the Reich."

"So my husband tells me."

The September sun shone white on my face. Underneath my neat suit of light blue wool, I was dripping with perspiration, though the morning was still cool. I followed the officer through the gate, past the barbed wire and the ominous empty strip of land overlooked by the tower. The officer was explaining how perfectly secure the camp was, how I had nothing to fear. There were sharpshooters in the top of that tower, guns already cocked, eyes and muzzles trained on any movement. A prisoner had no chance of escape.

"What if he were to dig a tunnel of some sort?" I asked.

The officer shook his head and told me this was impossible, that every prisoner was required to strip naked and relinquish everything in his possession upon entry into the camp. He was then issued a striped uniform and a number. Unless this prisoner were to dig with his bare fingers—here the officer laughed—he would have no capability for such a project.

"Besides," he went on, "that is why we keep them occupied with physical labor during the day. They have no thought of anything but sleep at night."

Of course, I said. How clever.

2.

We toured the various buildings—the infirmary, the canteen, the camp offices—and saw the gray-striped prisoners shuffling about the laundry. The interiors were spotless and smelled of lye and disinfectant. Lieutenant Helmbrecht repeated at intervals what an honor it was to have the general's wife inspect the camp, and how he hoped I appreciated the genius of its design and operation, its remarkable efficiency. While the SS were of course in charge, the prisoners actually ran the camp themselves, organizing into work details and operating the laundry and the library and the infirmary. Work and responsibility, sobriety and industry: these were the pathways to rehabilitation. The new complex had just been opened last month, a model for future camps. The lieutenant was young and fair and high-pitched with enthusiasm, a bit like Frieda describing the day's tennis. I complimented him on his exact knowledge of the camp, his thorough attention to his duty. He blushed and consulted his watch.

"It is nearly time for the midday prisoner muster, Frau von Kleist," he said. "May I have the honor of presenting this spectacle to you? I assure you, it is perfectly safe. The prisoners would not dare to step from line."

I said I would enjoy that very much.

3.

"Tell me more about your prisoners," I said, as we walked toward the beaten rectangle of the assembly area. Lieutenant Helmbrecht's leather boots had taken on a film of dust, dulling their shine, but they still struck impressively on the ground. He kept his hands folded behind his back as he walked.

"They are divided into two groups at present," he said. "The political prisoners, who are classified by a red badge, and the criminal ones, who wear green. Here we have mostly the political prisoners, because that is the purpose of building these camps: a place to hold these dangerous men without overburdening the state prisons."

"Are they ever released?"

"Very rarely, I am afraid. The tendency to sedition and agitation is a chronic condition. If released, they will simply continue their criminal activities against the state." Lieutenant Helmbrecht shook his head in a way that suggested profound regret. "I have often wondered if there is some mental weakness or disorder associated with this tendency."

"A fascinating theory, Lieutenant Helmbrecht. I shouldn't be at all surprised."

We came to a halt at the edge of the assembly ground, where long lines of men in striped clothes were filing into order, a strange sort of convict army. Like soldiers, except they were not. Like trailing ants, except they were men.

I thought, He's here, Stefan is here. One of these men is Stefan.

At the outset, I had conveyed to the lieutenant and the camp authorities that my German was limited, but this was a lie. In fact, I'd spent many hours dedicating myself to the study of my husband's native language since our reconciliation last year. Johann had been so pleased. He helped me practice, pointed out the nuances of *Sie* and *Du*. He said that he hoped I would be able to converse with his friends, to see that there was nothing to fear, that good people and good intentions prevailed in Germany. I never had that opportunity, but I could listen now as the commands rang around the muster grounds. I could understand what was happening. The prisoners stood in line, wearing identical striped uniforms and caps. The ones with the green badges stood to the right, and the ones with red badges stood to the left; the red badges far outnumbered the green. Each row lay in a precise line, separated from the others by the same distance. I gazed across the rows of gray-striped limbs, the expressionless faces beneath the caps, and I thought, in panic, I will never find him; this is impossible.

Lieutenant Helmbrecht turned to me. "There are four thousand two hundred and five prisoners in total, of which—"

"May I walk down the rows? My husband is a humanitarian, Lieutenant Helmbrecht, and he instructed me specifically to examine the condition of the prisoners."

"But Frau von Kleist, I assure you we take the strictest care of these men. The prisoners themselves are in charge of their own governance. We watch continually for signs of infection, and sickness is quarantined at the first symptom. There is an infirmary, staffed by the prisoners themselves, those who were employed in the medical profession—"

"And I confess, I'm a little curious about these incorrigible criminals, and how thoroughly you have managed to subdue their dangerous tendencies. I'm eager to report to my husband how brilliantly Dachau fulfills its mission, and whether any of its techniques can be copied at the other camps."

Lieutenant Helmbrecht's young cheeks turned a little pink. "Of course, Frau von Kleist."

He shouted a command to one of the guards, who stepped forward and accompanied us down the first row of prisoners. The red badges were vivid against the gray and white of their uniforms, as if an artist had tinted some aspect of a monochrome photograph for visual effect. Each face was fixed with the same expression of neutral hatred, and as I walked down the row, sweeping my gaze along the procession of cheekbones and gaunt eyes, I realized that the Nazis had won: I could not tell these men apart. Everyone was thin, everyone was striped, every face matched the other. You hardly noticed who was tall and who was short. You didn't see the cropped hair hidden under the striped cap. You saw no difference in complexion between one sunburn and another.

"Excellent," I said to Lieutenant Helmbrecht, as we came to the end of the row.

"Thank you, Frau von Kleist."

I looked again across the rows and columns, which were so

exactly spaced that from where I stood, at the diagonal, the men formed yet another straight line. They must have drilled them this way, all day in the hot summer, until they got it right. And Stefan had lived here for a year. All year, last summer and autumn, the bitterness of winter and spring and summer again, he had worn his striped uniform and stood out here while the sun shone and the wind blew and the snow fell.

Where was he?

Do something, I thought. Show me where you are. You must know it's me. You must know why I'm here.

And as I gazed across the motionless lines of men, doing my best to appear pleased with what I saw, I realized that he would not. Of course he would not. Stefan would open his own veins before he would allow me to risk myself for his sake.

I put my gloved hand on Lieutenant Helmbrecht's shoulder and let out a little cry.

"Frau von Kleist!"

"I'm just—oh, dear—the sun—"

I sagged to the ground, and as I did I caught the motion of one single man stepping reflexively out of line, some distance to the left, at the edge of a row about halfway down the column.

4.

I protested that I was quite all right, just a passing dizziness, but Lieutenant Helmbrecht insisted that we head to the infirmary and see the doctor. He took my elbow and led me down the center aisle, and I clutched my hat to my head and watched the faces stream by, until we had gone halfway down and I saw them, as if they were magnets: a pair of hard caramel eyes trying not to find me.

"Lieutenant Helmbrecht! Wait a moment!"

"Yes, Frau von Kleist?"

"That man there! I think—I'm not sure—"

"Is something wrong?"

"No, no." I went on, stopped, and turned again. "No, I must examine him."

"Why, what's the matter?"

"Has he been seen by a doctor recently?"

"All our prisoners are under the close supervision of the barracks government. If any symptoms of sickness are detected, they are immediately referred to the infirmary." He trailed just behind me, grasping at my elbow, but I was marching like a nurse now and would not be grasped. Stefan's neck beckoned ahead, sunburned instead of white, dark hair cropped so short it was only a shadow at the bottom of his cap, but this time it was really his. It was Stefan, really Stefan, a few yards away. In a few seconds, I would be touching him.

"I am a trained nurse, Lieutenant Helmbrecht, and I am quite sure I saw symptoms of typhoid in that man."

At the word *typhoid*, the lieutenant stopped short. I went on, turning down the correct row, and then I stopped before Stefan. Or rather, an apparition who resembled Stefan: too brown and bony and empty to be the man who had faced me on a fourth-floor bed of the Paris Ritz and laid his finger across my lips. The scar shone white against his sunburn. On his chest, the red triangle-shaped badge bore a number I couldn't quite read.

"How lucky I am wearing my gloves." I touched the corner of his eye, which was pleading with me.

"Frau von Kleist!" exclaimed the lieutenant.

"Oh, dear," I said. "This is very serious. How are you feeling, prisoner?"

"Get the hell out of here," Stefan muttered in English.

"I see. Very bad indeed. Let me see your palm."

I took his hand and turned it over. His palm was scarred and blistered. I ran my finger over the lines. "Have you had any episodes of rash, prisoner? Dizziness and headache?"

"Please go."

I gave him back his hand, but not before I had slipped a capsule from the inside of my glove and placed it in the center of his palm. His fingers swallowed it at once. "Take this at once," I said in English, and then I turned to the lieutenant, who stood at the end of the row, barking at the terrified prisoners to get back in line.

"Lieutenant, it is as I feared. He can hardly stand. He is almost delirious. He must go the infirmary at once for treatment, before he infects the entire camp."

"My God!" said Lieutenant Helmbrecht. He turned to the guard who hovered next to him. "Take that prisoner to the infirmary at once."

The guard, horrified, stepped down the line and took Stefan's elbow. He threw me a last look of shocked understanding and staggered forward. As he did so, his hand came up to his mouth.

"You see?" I said. "He is falling on his feet. You may need an orderly and a stretcher." I bent down to help him up and whispered in English, as we rose together: *Be ready.*

The guard took back Stefan's elbow and forced him down the row. The prisoners stepped back in horror as we went, covering their mouths. I walked a pace or two behind and watched the back of Stefan's neck as it bobbed and slumped like the neck of a man on the brink of collapse. I thought for an instant of Tosca, instructing her Mario to play his part well, to convince the guards he had really been shot, and then I remembered that this was real, that I had actually done this, that I was actually walking down this row of prisoners at Dachau under the September sunshine, hoping I had not just given Stefan a death sentence.

"Well," I said to Lieutenant Helmbrecht, when the prisoners were dismissed and the assembly ground returned to peace, "how very fortunate for you that I am a trained nurse. Of course, these gloves should be burned at once."

5.

The rain arrived at sunset two days later, and by the time we reached the crossroads and parked the car on the grass, it rattled against the windshield as if it never meant to stop. Wilhelmine opened her window an inch or so and lit a cigarette. "Now we wait," she said.

I turned my head to glance into the backseat, where Florian lay in a deep sleep underneath his favorite blanket. We had left the Himmelfarbs' house near Stuttgart an hour ago, when the telephone call had arrived at last, and had bundled Florian inside without even waking him. He had stirred but never opened his eyes, having spent the entire day playing outside with his half-sister, Else. At one point I had gone out to take him in for his nap, but Wilhelmine had stopped me. Let them play, she said. They may not get another chance.

"Don't say that."

She had shrugged and leaned forward to wipe the mess from Henrik's mouth. He was sitting in his high chair, and she had been feeding him peas. "Matthias refuses to leave. He says he will not let Hitler drive him away like a dog."

"It's common sense, though. You can't keep fighting when everyone is against you."

"Not everyone in Germany is like Hitler, Annabelle. Most of my neighbors, they are disgusted."

"But they won't speak up, will they? Which is worse, I think. Look at my husband. He never believed in all the Nazi propaganda, but he went along with them, he did everything they asked, because he's afraid to do anything else."

She laughed. "Can you blame him? Did you not see what they have done to Stefan?" When I didn't reply, she went on. "Anyway, I think you are wrong about von Kleist. He is not bad. He is simply a man of duty, that is all. I mean, there is no doubt that Stefan broke the law, that he killed a Gestapo agent and all these things. He killed that agent with his bare hands, and maybe the man was a bad man, maybe he wanted to arrest Stefan and put him in prison, but he was still a man who had a wife and three children, I believe. So it was your husband's duty to hunt down the man who had killed this agent, and by God he did."

"You can't possibly be excusing him."

"No, not exactly. But I think I understand him. And I will tell you this: I even think, if I were you, I would rather be married to a von Kleist than to a Stefan. I would pick the steady sun over the starburst."

"But he *is* the sun. Stefan is the sun."

She shook her head.

I put my hand on her arm. "Wilhelmine, you've got to leave. You can't stay here."

"And where would we go? Germany is our home. Everywhere it is like this, really. There is nowhere we are safe. There is no country on earth that will open its arms and shout, *Welcome, Jews!* Even in America, you cannot get a visa anymore unless you are a millionaire or a personal friend of Mr. Roosevelt, or I suppose if you are Albert fucking Einstein."

How could I answer her?

We had sat in silence, except for the sound of Henrik eating his peas, until Wilhelmine removed the bowl and lifted him out of his chair to rest on her shoulder. "So we will take our chances, as always. Like our fathers and mothers did before us."

I had muddled over her words for hours, and I muddled over them now, watching the rain track down the windshield. There was just enough moon to see the road nearby, to see the shadows of the trees and mountains around us. Wilhelmine tucked her feet up underneath her on the seat and smoked quietly, tipping the ash out the crack in the window. She had been to university in Stuttgart—that was where she met Matthias—and studied English and history, and she carried about her an air of trouser-wearing worldliness that saturated her skin. I thought Stefan was a fool for letting her go, and that maybe he loved me because I was her opposite. I did not believe in a perverse universe. I didn't believe in fate, except for the one that bound me to Stefan.

"I think you are right," Wilhelmine replied, when I said this thought aloud, a little more delicately. "He was never in love with me. We had some attraction, but I could not satisfy something in him. And he drove me crazy. Always restless, always wanting to change things. *Why can you not stay home with your wife and your daughter?* I shouted to him. *Why do you have to go out and pinch the nose of the fucking Gestapo?* And he said that someone had to." She dropped the cigarette stub outside the window and put her arms around her legs. "I said there was no object. He was going to get killed for no object at all."

"Then why are you risking yourself for him now?"

"Because I am an idiot, Annabelle." She picked up her cigarette case from the seat between us. "Anyway, it is the last time. He is your problem now."

"But what about Else? He'll want to see her."

"Then he should not have got himself arrested by the Gestapo, should he?"

I asked if she would let me have a cigarette, and she laughed and lit one for each of us. The smoke burned my lungs, but after a minute or two I noticed my nerves settle, one by one, as if they were being put to bed by a comforting hand. I held the cigarette in front of my eyes and examined it. "It's not so bad."

"I expect they will kill me one day, but I don't care enough to stop. Just don't have a second one, and you will be safe."

A light appeared in the darkness ahead. Wilhelmine straightened in her seat. "Okay, now. If that is not the ambulance, you let me do the talking, all right?"

I coughed, put out the cigarette, and said: "You know, your English is really very good."

"Eh. I used to watch a lot of American movies."

The light resolved through the gloom into a pair of headlamps. "It's big enough," said Wilhelmine. Her fingers tapped the steering wheel. A few more damp seconds passed, and then: "It's them."

The air inside the car was like a cigarette fog. I realized I couldn't breathe. I opened up the door and set my foot into the soggy turf. "Wait," said Wilhelmine, but I was already walking through the rain to the approaching headlamps, waving my arms, sucking the wet October night into my lungs.

Wilhelmine caught up with me an instant later. "You fool," she said.

"You told me it was them."

The glare grew larger and hurt my eyes. I stepped back and she caught my arm. "I might be wrong."

The brakes squeaked softly through the drumming rain. A man jumped out of the gray cab almost before the truck stopped. Wilhelmine called to him: *Bellende Hunde!*

Beissen nicht, he replied.

Wilhelmine turned to me. "All right. Let's get the bastard out."

The driver set the brake and opened the door, swearing at the rain. Wilhelmine and I were already dashing to the back of the truck with the first man. He swung the doors open and I hoisted myself onto the bed, slipping and streaming, calling out Stefan's name.

"It's no use," said the driver. "He's either asleep or delirious, or both."

I flung out my arms and found a warm body on a stretcher. *Stefan,* I said.

He muttered a word.

I ran my hands up his torso until I found his hair, hot and dry, like kindling. I fell to my knees next to the stretcher and cradled his head in my palms, brushing his shorn hair, kissing his cheeks. I whispered to him that I was here, Annabelle was here, he was safe, I would never leave him again.

6.

Stefan's fever broke two days later, right on schedule. He opened his eyes and asked first for a cigarette and then for coffee. I put the cigarette in his mouth and lighted it, and his eyes widened with pleasure.

"Where did you get these?"

"I wired my father in Paris and had him send them."

"You will go to heaven one day."

"I'm already there, Stefan." I kissed his forehead and went to make coffee.

7.

When I returned with the coffee, I led in Florian by the hand. Stefan turned his head toward us, and his face, already stark, went rigid with shock. He stubbed out the cigarette.

"I was going to wait," I said, "but he's really too young to leave alone."

Stefan took a long time putting out his cigarette. When he lifted his eyes from the ashtray, they were wet.

I set down the coffee and lifted Florian into my arms. "He's yours," I said.

"I know."

Florian held a biscuit in one hand. His hair, always unruly, spilled into his forehead. He stared curiously at Stefan and then turned to me. "Is he sick?"

"Yes, darling. Stefan is a little sick. But he'll be up and about in no time, and you two will have such fun together."

Florian turned this over in his head and looked back at Stefan. "Ride horses."

"Yes, you can ride horses if you like."

"Papa ride horses."

"Yes. Papa rides horses, too."

In the bed, Stefan held very still, watching his son's lips as he spoke. His knuckles were white around the edge of the blankets. I carried Florian with me to the chair next to the nightstand and sat down.

"I thought it was so obvious," I said, "but everyone just thinks he looks like me, because he has dark hair and brown eyes."

"Yes, I know."

"How do you know?"

"Because I would watch you two in the Tuileries, when you went for your walk and your ice cream."

"*What?*"

Florian struggled in my arms. I set him down and he ran to the window, zooming his toy airplane in an arc above his head. Stefan watched him go. "That was why I came to Paris, Annabelle. The real reason. I could keep myself away from you because I knew this was the right thing, but I had to see my son. I had to know what he looked like."

"You *knew?*"

"I am not stupid, Annabelle." He was still watching Florian zoom about the room on his sturdy legs, and the expression on his battered face was so warm and tender I had to look away. "I never meant to disturb you, I swear it. But then I saw you together, and you were so beautiful, and he was so beautiful, and I thought this very dangerous thought. I thought, Please

God, let me just speak to her once and set us both to rest. I swore to God I would not fall into temptation." He shook his head. "Obviously I am not to be trusted."

I took his hand. "I am so glad you did. If you hadn't, we wouldn't be together now."

"No, this is true."

"So you see? I was right after all."

"About what, Annabelle?"

"The perverse universe."

He would not stop looking at Florian, following Florian around the floor, and his eyes were still warm and tender, but a little mournful, too, turned down at the corners like a dog that doesn't hope for much. "Yes, you were right," he said softly.

8.

Stefan drank his coffee and watched Florian play, while I made some toast and brought a few toys into the bedroom.

"I suppose I should ask where we are," he said.

"We're on Lake Konstanz, in a house owned by Matthias's family. Wilhelmine's husband, though he wasn't very happy about it."

"Ah. I suppose Wilhelmine helped you with all this."

"Yes, she did. She found men to forge papers and then find an ambulance. I came up with the plan, though."

"A very good plan. You almost had me fooled. Maybe a little risky, though."

"I'm sorry you had to suffer, but we had little choice except to trick them somehow."

"May I ask what was in that capsule you gave me?"

"It was a weakened form of the typhoid bacterium. One of Wilhelmine's university friends got it for us. He works in a medical research laboratory. I think it's an experiment of some kind, but I had to take the risk, and he assured me it wouldn't kill you."

"Ah, very clever. So you gave me this pill and waited for the symptoms to take effect, and then you waited until they made the decision to transfer me to a hospital?"

"No, that was the clever part. Charles helped me with that. He knew a doctor at the military hospital in Frankfurt. He had him call up the camp and say that they'd heard there was this case, and could they please send you over for trial of an experimental medication? And of course the doctor in the infirmary said yes, because first of all he is a prisoner, too, and second, we had sent him a message in a shipment of aspirin, and third, he gets along very well with the camp commandant."

"My brilliant Annabelle. This must have taken a great deal of planning. How did your husband never suspect?"

I glanced at Florian and lowered my voice. "I left Johann in August, Stefan. You see, I didn't know. I had no idea he was the one who had you arrested. Wilhelmine told me, and I took Florian and left him that day."

I delivered this information like a thunderbolt, but Stefan only gazed back at me with quiet eyes, unmoved.

"And all this time, he has not tried to find you?"

"No. He had a concussion playing tennis, that same afternoon. He couldn't stop me."

"Not then, no. But he could have sent somebody. He commands an army, not just the official one but an unofficial army, too. You have no idea how much power he has. He could at least have told the officials at Dachau to be prepared for a possible escape by me."

I opened my mouth and closed it again.

Stefan leaned back into his pillow. His face was pale beneath his sunburn. He must have lost fifty pounds since I saw him last; the bones were so prominent on his face, everything sharp and drawn. I had seen bruises and scars on his body, as I washed and dressed him, and I had cried over them. But what alarmed me most was the expression in his eyes. The hollowed-out glassiness, as if he were staring into another universe.

"So," he said. "It seems the good Johann has let us both go."

"But that's impossible."

"On the contrary. It is the only possible reason I am lying here in this bed next to you and my son. I wonder whether he has discovered a tender spot for me after all, or whether I owe all this to his love for you."

I seized Stefan's hand. "He doesn't love me, not the way you do. Not the way I love you. He loves me as an object, as an ornament. As a substitute for his first wife."

"No, he is very much in love with you for yourself, Annabelle, and I have never blamed him for that. I am guilty of the same crime."

I laid my head next to his on the pillow and stared at the white scar that trailed down the side of his face. "What have they done to you?" I whispered.

"My dear and innocent love. You do not really want to know."

9.

I brought my cot into Stefan's room and slept with Florian there, so we could be a family. By the next day, Stefan was taking a few steps out of bed. He went to the window first, and looked across the autumn trees to the distant lake. "I presume we are on the German side still," he said.

"Yes. I didn't dare cross over while you were unconscious, and anyway, Matthias said it would be better to wait a few weeks, until the alarm fades. But I have papers for you. We can cross whenever you like. Or we can take our chances with a boat on the lake, but Matthias says it's risky, there are guards everywhere these days."

"Very wise of Matthias."

For some reason, he looked taller in his new gauntness. His wide and fleshless shoulders stuck out like the arms of a clothes hanger. I hadn't shaved him, and his beard bristled from his chin. I put my arms around his waist. "We'll go to Monte Carlo and take the *Isolde* to Capri. We'll have our vineyard at last. We'll give Florian a sister and a brother and teach them how to press the grapes and the olives."

"This is a tempting picture."

"It's our picture, and it will be real. I'm going to drown you with my love, Stefan, and make you all better."

He braced one hand against the windowsill. "I had better return to bed, then, and get my rest."

10.

The weather continued warm. Back in America, they would have called it an Indian summer, but here in the Alpine foothills it was just a pleasant warm autumn, crisp in the mornings, bright with foliage. After a few days, I brought Stefan outside, where he played with Florian on the lawn. I told Florian not to be rough, that Stefan had been very sick and needed his strength.

"What have you told him?" Stefan asked, lighting a cigarette as Florian went off to play with the croquet set he'd unearthed in the shed.

"Nothing, yet. He was very fond of Johann. I don't want to confuse him, and anyway, if we tell him you're his father instead, he might resent you. We'll know when the time is right."

"You are a good mother."

"You'll make a wonderful pair, once you get to know each other."

"I already know him. I know him like I know my own palm. Whether he will appreciate *me* is another matter." He lay back on the grass and stared at the blue sky. "It is a lovely autumn."

"Yes, it is."

I lay back next to him and took his hand.

"Thank you for my son," he said.

"You're welcome."

11.

Matthias Himmelfarb's summer house was not especially large, but it was comfortable and well loved, smelling of pine and a hint of camphor against the moths. There were four bedrooms upstairs—we slept in the largest one—and two ancient bathrooms, one of which connected to the master bedroom. Downstairs, there was a kitchen and an informal dining room, a living room, a small library, and a sunroom. A pair of small bedrooms communicated with the kitchen, for the use of the maids. They were both empty, of course, and twice a week I took the car into the village and collected groceries, which I cooked myself, not very expertly. *Eat,* I told Stefan, and he ate, but as a matter of duty, not because he was hungry.

You don't understand, he told me. I do not know what to do with a large meal anymore.

I threatened to hire a cook if he didn't eat more, and so he did eat more, mouthful after mouthful, a forced march of nutrition. His face filled out a little. One evening he asked if there was any wine, so I brought back a few bottles from the village the next day, and we drank them both together that evening, after Florian was in bed, and promptly fell asleep on the sofa. When I woke up, he was gone.

I sat up in panic, but he was only standing by the window, staring at the lake, which was pregnant with a whole silver moon. *You frightened me, running off like that,* I said, and he told me not to worry; he couldn't sleep, that was all.

"Why not?"

"There is too much in my head now, love."

"Then push it out. Let me inside instead. I can make you sleep."

"Ah, Annabelle."

We stood next to the silver window, staring and staring.

"You are such a fool, Annabelle. You should have stayed with him."

"What are you talking about? I couldn't stay with him."

"You deserve better than me. I smoke and drink and fornicate, all to excess."

"Yes, but only with me. Our covenant, remember?"

"Yes, I remember. And all this time, I have been true to this covenant and its commandments. Can you believe that?" He laughed. "But then I have not had much opportunity, and we have seen how little I am to be trusted with a beautiful woman."

"Only with *me*. You can't be trusted with *me*."

He sighed, as if acknowledging a religious truth. "Only with you, Mademoiselle. If that is what you want from me."

I knelt before him and pulled the drawstring of his pajamas.

This is what I want from you.

Annabelle, no, he said, but his hands went to my hair and he leaned back against the window with a sigh that was more like a groan. After a moment, he whispered, *You have not ever done this thing before, have you?*

I said I hadn't, that he would have to show me what to do.

Ah, no, you will kill me, he said, but his hands were already guiding me, his bony hips were already moving in rhythm with me, and it was like the dream I had, the first night I spent in his bed, except that the adulterous woman kneeling between his legs at the window, enjoying the clutch of his fingers in her dark hair, was me. Was Annabelle von Kleist.

He lasted only a minute or two, and when he finished, he

could not stop shuddering. He sank onto the hard floor with me and wept into my hair, and we didn't say anything. Not a single word. Just holding each other, until we fell asleep.

12.

I woke up the next morning in bed, nestled inside the skeletal curve of Stefan's body, and his smell and touch were so familiar, it was as if the past three years hadn't existed. I opened my eyes in joy, expecting to find a Mediterranean sunrise.

Instead, I saw Florian's empty cot.

I bolted upright. "Florian!"

"He's all right. I gave him a little breakfast. He is reading some books in the library. I can hear him from here."

"But he can't read yet."

"He does not seem to accept this limitation."

I smiled. "Like his father."

"I would say, like his mother."

Stefan lay flat on his back, watching me from the pillow. His pajamas were buttoned primly to the neck. He had begun shaving his beard as soon as he could walk to the bathroom, and the flesh on his jaw was now a little thicker, a little more substantial. I touched it with my finger.

"We have a son."

"Yes, Mademoiselle. A wonderful son."

I lay back down on my side, pressing against him. "Don't look so somber. It's over. We're safe."

"Not quite safe. We are still in Germany."

"We can cross the border whenever you like. You should

grow your beard or a mustache first, though, and maybe let your hair lengthen a bit."

"I suppose that is sensible."

He reached for his cigarettes, but I lifted myself across his chest and stopped his hand.

"How busy is Florian?" I said softly.

"Not busy enough, I think."

"We can be very quiet."

He reached again for the cigarette case. "You are a very reckless woman, Annabelle von Kleist, and always have been."

I took the case from his hand and plucked out a cigarette. They weren't like ordinary ones you bought from a drugstore or a newsagent; they were long and wrapped in brown paper, like a cigar. I slipped one between his lips and lit him up myself. "I won't let you do this, Stefan."

"Do what?"

"I won't let you barricade me outside your skin."

"I am not barricading you."

"Yes, you are. You don't want me in. You think I'll be appalled at what I find there, and you're wrong. I already know what's inside you. I've already been inside your skin, remember?"

"You have no idea, Annabelle, no possible idea what is inside me now."

"It doesn't matter. That's the point of having this thing, this rare and perfect thing we share. Whatever is in you, it's mine. You're mine. You can't resist me, so you might as well stop fighting and let me back in."

He turned his face to one side and let out a long stream of Turkish smoke, but his eyes didn't leave me. He was thinking about the night before—I knew he was, I could see the tiny reflection of the memory as it reeled behind his eyes—and what I had done to him before the window. The brief moment of his resurrection, the instant of hope.

I took his face in my hands. "You see?"

"Yes, Annabelle. I am yours. That was never in doubt. But you see, I am not now perfectly certain that you belong to *me*."

I turned on my back and pulled him over me.

"Then let me convince you."

13.

We made love without speaking, almost without moving, listening for signs of Florian through the doorway. Stefan's hips ground carefully into mine. At the end, I stifled my cry into his shoulder, and he bent his face into the pillow while his body made a series of rapid convulsions and then went perfectly still, except for the tiny stroke of his thumb against my temple. The room was so quiet, I could hear the last of Stefan's cigarette sizzle to ash in the tray. I could name each individual bone of Stefan's body, each rib, each breath like a bellows, each section of brutalized skin. The scent of tobacco and sweat, the soft reek of sex. Stefan, lost and found.

For God knew how many minutes, we lay just like that, transfixed by the audacity of what we had just done, by the fact of Stefan's intimate flesh inside me, as if in obedience to some natural law. The slow crash of his heartbeat against mine. Over and over. Again. And again.

Until life returned to us. Until the small sound of footsteps climbed the staircase and we broke apart, straightening our nightclothes like guilty lovers. I swung my feet to the ground just as our son appeared in the doorway, looking so much like his father that I couldn't say a word.

Florian didn't seem to notice this curiosity, that he had found me here in Stefan's bed, flushed and disheveled. He hoisted an enormous illustrated book onto the white counterpane, next to my legs, and pointed to a painting of Frederick the Great on horseback. "Papa!" he said, and his face shone with hope.

14.

November arrived suddenly, in a gust of cold new wind that made the roof shriek and left six inches of surprised wet snow across the landscape. Florian jumped on our bed at half past six with the news, and Stefan valiantly rose from beneath the covers to bundle his son in an inadequate coat and take him outside to make snowballs.

They came stomping in half an hour later, red-skinned and shivering and identical, and I directed them to the old stove and the hot cocoa as if we'd been doing this for years. "To think it was sixty degrees and sunny yesterday," I said, when we were curled up together on the sofa, mugs in hand, watching the fire. "Maybe it's time to fly south."

"Like birds," said Florian.

"Yes, darling. Like birds, to Stefan's ship. He's going to sail us to a beautiful island, where the sun is always shining and warm, and we can grow grapes and olives." I turned to Stefan. "What do you think?"

"I think you are right. It is time to move on, before we are found." He disengaged from us gently and rose to put another log on the fire. He had gained weight, but he was still too thin, and he no longer moved with the fluid grace I had loved. He moved like a marionette, or rather like a man who was trying not to move like a marionette. He straightened from the fire and put one hand on the stone mantel. A cigarette dangled from the other.

"Do you think they might find us here?"

"Frankly, I am surprised they have not found us already. But then, we seem to be the children of good fortune at this moment." He turned and smiled. "Florian, how would you like to go into the library with me, and I will show you how to make a paper airplane."

Florian jumped from the sofa and took Stefan's hand, and they came back an hour later with their arms full of paper airplanes, which they flew into the fireplace, one by one, to the screeching delight of Florian as each one burst to its spectacular end.

15.

"Are we really in danger?" I whispered to Stefan, when we crept into bed that night.

"Of course we are in danger."

"Then why haven't we left already?"

"We are in danger wherever we go, Annabelle, and this place is as good as any. Besides, I like it here. The peace, and the lake, and no people at all."

"Except me and Florian."

"Except the two of you."

"Are you happy? Would you rather be alone?"

A long pause, and then: "Annabelle, I am grateful to God for every day he allows us together."

"There will be thousands more days to be grateful for. Years and years."

Stefan was lying on his back, while I curled around him. His arm lay around my shoulders; mine crossed his concave stomach. "Yes, of course," he said.

"That wasn't very convincing."

He shifted around me and quietly kissed my neck, while his hands found the edge of my nightgown and drew it up my legs. "Then let me convince you," he whispered.

The action caught me by surprise. We had made love often as October bled quietly away, but always it was Annabelle who first laid her hands on Stefan, always it was me who led him, inch by inch, past the possibility of resistance. He seemed to act under the conviction that God had allotted the two of us, Annabelle and Stefan, only a finite amount of sexual consummation, like coins in a purse, and he didn't want to spend them all too quickly and be left with nothing. *Ah, Annabelle,* he would whisper, the sign of his capitulation, and we would mate in silence, under the covers, slow as tar, hot as blazes, straining to maintain the perfect tranquility of the bedsprings, so that release came like the smothered hiss of a blowtorch, and we would fall asleep exactly as we were, too depleted to move, while Florian turned in his sleep and snored innocently in his cot nearby. (It was unthinkable to us that he should sleep in another room.)

But this time was different, as if a shallow but significant tide had turned between us. This time Stefan was the one who urged me along, who pulled back the covers and lifted my nightgown to my waist; Stefan who trailed his lips up my legs until I had to stuff my fist into my mouth; Stefan who then turned me on my stomach and entered me with lazy grandeur, like the unfurling of a giant canvas; until he could give no more and sank down to cover me, flush against my back, breathing in my ear.

I am inside your skin, he whispered. I am reading your thoughts.

What am I thinking?

That you have fallen in love with me all over again. That you love my scars and my sinful habits, and my loyal heart that beats for you. That you want me to make another baby inside you, so there is no chance God will put us asunder again.

(I shut my eyes.)

Very good. But you didn't mention the rest. You forgot your beautiful eyes, and your skin, and—and—

Don't cry, Annabelle.

Let's not talk anymore.

(He lifted himself on his elbows and began to move inside me.)

If that is what you want, *mein Engel*.

16.

The next morning, my period arrived.

"Don't say it's God's will," I told him. "Don't say it's a sign of a perverse universe."

Stefan held up his hands. "I am not saying anything. I am only here to give you what you want."

"I just want *you*, and Florian, and the three of us together, and nothing to pry us away from each other, ever again!"

"Shh. Calm down." He held me close against his chest. "Then I will find a way to hold the three of us together, Annabelle. If I have to take on the entire universe, I will do it. I will give you what you want."

I listened to his heartbeat beneath the pajama shirt.

"But what do *you* want?" I whispered. "Do you want another child?"

"I want you to be happy. That is all. That is all that is left."

17.

That night, I dreamed about Johann.

Probably it was Florian who planted the seed. The two of them had grown so exceptionally close over the past year. At times, it sickened me to remember how Johann had chased Florian around the nursery floor, pretending to be a great bear, while Stefan's son squealed in delight. Other times, I thought how peacefully they had sat together in a sunlit window, reading from a book, and I marveled that Johann could have loved this boy so profoundly, this Jewish boy sired by his great rival, and whether that love was born of perversity or generosity. I alternated between rage and pity, hate and wistfulness. I would focus my brain on his duplicity, I would recall every scar on Stefan's body, and then into my head flashed Wilhelmine's words—*He killed the agent with his bare hands; he had a wife and three sons*—or Frieda's blond head under Johann's huge and gentle hand.

Mostly, I tried not to think of Johann at all.

But Florian thought of him for me. Florian played happily and affectionately with Stefan, but he hadn't forgotten the man who had once cradled his purple newborn body in a pair of thick palms. That afternoon, Stefan chopped wood while Florian and I carried the split logs across the dying grass to the woodshed, and Florian said in German, "Where is Papa?"

"He's back home, darling."

"When do we go home, too?"

We set the wood into the pile and I fingered his hair. He was bundled in his warm coat—I had found a new, thicker one in the village—and his cheeks were pink. "Aren't you happy here?"

"I want Papa," he said, and he started to cry.

Stefan paused in his chopping and turned to look at us. I gathered Florian against my chest and picked up his hand to wave at Stefan, at Stefan's jacket made of rusty wool, and asked Florian if he could count the number of logs Stefan had split with his ax. It was that easy, distracting Florian, because he was not quite two and a half years old, but when you are twenty-two years old and have lived with a certain man as your husband for three years, more or less, you cannot banish his memory so easily, even when you want to, even when you now sleep heavily beside the man who owns your heart and your blood and the marrow of your eternal bones. It takes strength to hate that husband, the relic of your former life, and when you fall asleep, your brain's fortifications fall away.

You realize, in horror, that there is a small but inevitable hole in your heart, a hole you never wanted but perhaps deserve. A man who is no longer your husband, and a child who will never be born.

18.

Stefan had stopped shaving his upper lip two weeks ago, and his mustache was now a sinister thing, dark and thick: longer than Hitler's, but not by much.

"What do you think?" he asked me, turning from the mirror, waggling his eyebrows.

"I think it's monstrous, but if it helps us across the border, I'll worship it forever."

"Then let's leave tomorrow."

"Tomorrow." I went to the library and read the calendar on the wall. "That would be the ninth of November. An auspicious date?"

Stefan bent down to grasp Florian and hoist him on his shoulders. "What do you think, little man? Are you ready to sail away?"

Florian squealed with pleasure and reached for the brass arms of the chandelier. "Sailboat!" he said.

"Not quite." I stretched to my tiptoes to kiss the dimple in his knee. "But I think you'll like Stefan's ship even more than a sailboat."

19.

We woke up before sunrise the next morning, into a hard frost beneath a massive fall of leaves. Florian was still asleep. I washed in the bathtub while Stefan stood in a towel before the mirror and shaved carefully around his new mustache, dangling a cigarette from his lips. I parted the curtain and stepped from the tub and found my own towel, and when I glanced at the mirror I saw he was watching my reflection. I let the towel drop to the floor.

"You are so perfect." He wrapped his hands around my waist and examined the meeting of his thumbs. "You are so small and round and warm and full, all at once. Like the buns they make in England, at Easter."

"Hot cross buns."

"Yes, those. They always looked so delicious, when I saw

them through the window of the bakery, making the glass fill with steam."

"Forbidden bread?"

He laughed, and the sound was magnificent. "Yes, very much."

I put my arms around his neck. "And now you have a bun of your very own."

"My own delicious hot cross Annabelle bun, to be gobbled up each morning with hot coffee and a good smoke."

20.

"You see?" I gasped, several minutes later. "It's beautiful. The universe is so beautiful."

"*Gott im Himmel*, Annabelle bun. At this moment, the universe is whatever you say it is."

21.

We packed up the old blue Opel Matthias had lent us and tucked a sleepy Florian between us on the front seat. I watched Stefan as he locked the door of the Himmelfarbs' house and stepped back for a last look before tucking the key beneath an empty flowerpot.

When he climbed inside the car and started the engine, I said, "We've been happy here, haven't we? In spite of everything."

"I think we have been happy here *because* of everything," he said, and he backed the car out of the drive and onto the narrow and curving road toward Lake Konstanz.

PEPPER

Saint Mary's • *1966*

1.

The first ferry doesn't leave until half past nine, and the fishing fleet is long gone. Not a boat in sight, for love or money. Florian's ready to swim out to Cumberland, but Pepper convinces him he's better off eating breakfast instead.

"She's fine," Pepper says, over coffee and bacon.

"How can you possibly know she's fine? She's gone missing!"

"She's not missing. We know exactly where she is."

"With a stranger."

"A stranger to us, maybe, but not to her. Because I don't doubt for a second that she knows this person on Cumberland. In fact, I'd go so far as to say that they're probably good friends."

He sets down his coffee cup and stares at his plate. "What makes you say that?"

"An educated hunch. Putting two and two together." She taps her nose. "The old female intuition."

"You don't know anything about it."

"Maybe not. But I'll bet you do, if you're willing to admit it."

He looks up. "What the hell does that mean?"

Now, Pepper's always been a breakfast kind of girl, even when breakfast falls somewhere between lunch and dinner. She likes her coffee and her sun-bright orange juice, she likes her smoky rich bacon and her scrambled eggs, she likes her toast hot hot hot with butter on top, and maybe a little strawberry jam, too, and she likes all this even more now that she's growing another human being on the strength of that feast. If she were in Pompeii, and the ash were raining down, she would still insist on wiping her yolks clean with the last of the toast before evacuating the city.

But as she takes in Florian's beleaguered face, his ravaged eyes and his jaw composed of honest right angles, she discovers that her stomach is already occupied by a pair of eager butterflies. She discovers that her heartbeat isn't in need of a further dose of the hot black stuff. All she needs is more of what's sitting across the table from her, turning to her in his hour of need, treating her not as an object of irresistible sexual allure—God knows she's no longer *that* Pepper—but as a comrade.

She sets down her fork and thinks about laying her hand on his. Then she does. She tries not to sound too throaty as she purrs: "You said something, back in the car, about being honest with each other."

"I've been nothing but honest with you."

"Well, then maybe you're not being honest with yourself."

He frowns. She pats the hand.

"Look, I'm not going to tell you what I think your mother's doing on Cumberland Island, and why I think she's in the best of hands. I want you to tell me what *you* think she's doing. Tell me what *you* know, in your heartiest heart of hearts."

He stares at her slender hand on top of his thick brown paw, and then he finds her face. "Are you actually suggesting Mama's having an affair?"

"Not at present, maybe. But you're a lawyer. Look at the evidence." She ticks her fingers. "Mama drops a fortune on a sentimental car from her Germany days. Mama hires a gumshoe on the sly to track down a person or persons unknown. Mama gets news of said person and bolts off like a schoolgirl for a Beatles concert. It adds up to something, by anyone's math. Even yours."

He shakes off her hand. "I can't believe you're even suggesting this."

"Tell me something. Was it ever hinted at any time, by either of them, that maybe someone left something valuable behind, back in Germany? Something that, once the faithful spouse is honorably buried, might possibly be reclaimed?"

"What the hell gave you that kind of crazy idea?"

Among her other skills, Pepper knows when to beat a strategic retreat. She withdraws to her coffee, which isn't quite as strong as she likes it, but coffee is like doughnuts: even a bad batch is better than no batch at all. Susan's still upstairs, fixing her hair after a long hot shower, probably finger-curling the way her mama taught her. Pepper knocked on the door fifteen minutes ago. *You go on without me,* Susan said absently. *I'm just freshening up.* Pepper shrugged and said, *Suit yourself.* Who was she to judge? A woman involved in the intricate choreography of getting her man: you didn't second-guess her choice of steps. You let her be to get on with the dance. Pepper, now, she was ready to trot downstairs for breakfast after only a two-minute shower, a slathering of Pond's, a swipe of lipstick and a ponytail, but Pepper wasn't looking for a husband.

But. This man. This Florian. Bemused and angry and worried,

the more so because he knew Pepper was probably right, and this pretty story he'd constructed around his parents' marriage— true love and abiding faithfulness and unchecked adoration—was just a pretty story, after all. It always was. Pepper knows. You have the rush of falling in love, the chemical combustion of mutual attraction, *Oh, he's The One* and *We'll never stray* and *Eternity isn't long enough for us, praise God.* And then there are babies and cracker crumbs left in the sheets, there is stomach flu and flatulence and hangovers, there is the way he always eats his peas by spearing them one by fucking one with the leftmost prong of his fork, there is the way she leaves smears of beige makeup all over the washcloths by the sink. There is the pretty young secretary at the office, there is the handsome new tennis pro at the club. And you find a way to smile and kiss and pretend everything is blissful, when in fact you've only learned the secret of mutual tolerance.

"Sweetheart," she says, as kindly as she can, "this doesn't mean your parents don't love each other. Mine do, in their way, against all odds and affairs. But your mother said something to me, while we were driving up from Palm Beach. She said—first of all—that she'd been in my position once, and everything turned out all right."

"What? *Your* position?" He looks in horror at the edge of the table, where the top of Pepper's pregnant belly forms a ski jump into the butter.

"She also said that she had left a piece of her heart behind."

Florian's cheeks turn pale. He sets his fingers on the table and rises to his feet. "This is bullshit," he says, and he walks straight out of the empty dining room, leaving behind a plate still criminally full of breakfast.

And Pepper, who sighs and reaches across the salt to capture Florian's bacon.

2.

She gives him twenty minutes. Twenty minutes should do the trick, right? Enough time to settle the angry red blood cells back in his veins, so he could see the cold blue light of reason.

She finds him on the side of the porch facing the river. His hands are braced on the railing. She leans back next to his right forearm and crosses her hands demurely under her bump.

"Ferry leaves in an hour. Are you sure you want to be on it?"

"If only to prove you wrong."

"Frankly, you should be hoping I'm right."

"Why's that?"

"Because what's the alternative? You want her to spend the night with a total stranger, possibly not at her own request?"

He swears quietly.

"You know what?" says Pepper. "It's her life. You're all grown up. Your father's been dead for a year. Let her have some happiness, if this is what makes her happy. Let her go."

A blanket of clouds has unrolled overhead, while the three of them were cleaning and dressing and eating breakfast, and now it's begun to drizzle. Pepper listens to the soft drum of the rain and tilts her head just enough that she can see the side of Florian's grim head, the tension in his jaw.

"You know, it doesn't mean their marriage was a lie," she says. "I asked Susan. She says they loved each other. It's not the world shattering around you. She left a piece of her heart behind, not the whole thing."

"All my life," he says, "I've wanted what they had. All my life. I mean, I won't lie. I dated some girls, I had some fun. But all that time, I was waiting. That's why I never asked you to dinner. I knew if I did, I was a goner. I was going to fall straight in love with you, and my odds weren't great, were they? My odds weren't great that you were going to fall in love right back. Settle down with one lucky guy."

"Don't be so sure."

Florian's body is still next to hers, and so close she can feel the flex of the tendons of his arms, the muscles of his waist. There is a competent trimness to him, as if he could change shoes and hike straight up the Appalachian Trail, all the way to Maine, and she wishes to God she could remember. Remember the moment they first met, in a Washington living room. Why can't she remember? If only she could remember, if only she could locate that critical instant, maybe she could go back and change it. Move the pieces around, so the game ended differently.

But then, poor Susan. Stuck with Billy Whatshisname.

"That's all right," she says, when he doesn't reply. "You made the right decision. Susan's a terrific girl. She's crazy about you."

"I know that."

A car edges into view around the corner, a long flat hood, newish and bluish. It rolls to a stop on the opposite side of the road, parking just behind Florian's Thunderbird. The chrome-tipped tailfins rise into the drizzle. The driver switches off the ignition but doesn't get out.

"So maybe I was an idiot," Florian says. "Maybe you don't worry about true fucking love, or a happy marriage with the nice house and the nice kids. Maybe you just ask the girl out to dinner."

"Unless it's too late." Pepper caresses the side of her belly and watches the blue car. "Unless the girl's already got herself in too much trouble."

"Pepper," he says warmly, and he lifts himself from the railing and turns to her, covering her hand, and for just the sweetest instant in the world there are no blue cars and no Susans and no missing mothers.

But then there are.

"Florian! There you are," chirps an unnaturally cheerful Susan, beautifully coiffed and impeccably dressed for a dune-swept barrier island in November, pressed Levi's and short rubber boots and a crisp white blouse unbuttoned all the way to there.

Susan. Unmarried, unpregnant, unimpeachable.

3.

Pepper waits until the ferry is out of sight before she turns to the man on the bench. "I appreciate your patience," she says.

He puts his hands on his knees and rises slowly, as if he's had a hard night of his own. Maybe he has. His cheeks are a little ruddy, his eyes heavy. "I wasn't in the way, was I?"

"Not at all. I don't think they even knew you were there."

"Good, good." He smiles. "It's not so easy to be inconspicuous, with a face like mine."

"Don't flatter yourself. They have more important things to think about." She gestures to the front door. "Shall we go inside? They've got a cozy little sitting room off the lobby. Just the thing for clandestine shenanigans, but well within screaming distance if you try any funny business."

"All right. Lead the way."

Pepper stops by the front desk on the way and asks for coffee. She could use a little something warm, to heat the chill in her blood at the sight of this man's familiar face, his thick waving hair and his eyes that look as if someone has tugged the ends downward.

So very like his big brother.

Only not quite. A bit fresher, a bit round-cheeked still. Give him time, Pepper thinks, leading him into the parlor. Trying not to waddle.

The room is old and charming, the fire crackling in the fireplace. Really, it's a lovely little hotel, neat as a pin, polished to a mellow gleam. The smell of woodsmoke lies pleasantly over the beeswax and the nearby tide. He waits for her to sit first; he was raised that way. She chooses the extreme end of the sofa. He finds a nearby armchair and offers her a cigarette, which she refuses. No, she doesn't mind if he smokes anyway.

When the cigarette is lit, he tells her he's glad she agreed to see him.

"I didn't have much choice, did I? You've cornered me, fair and square."

"That wasn't my intention. We just wanted to talk with you."

"Then you shouldn't have sent your goons to threaten me in a stairwell in Palm Beach."

"That was a mistake. That was the lawyer's gig; we had no idea."

Pepper leans her elbow on the sofa arm, props her head on her hand, and thinks about this little word *we*. Two innocuous letters, so much stronger than *I*. That's the trouble with this family of his, isn't it? You're never dealing with just one of them. You take on one, you take them all. You stood no chance against a front like that.

"Well, the whole affair wasn't what I'd call gentlemanly."

"Nor would I. But we—"

But he's interrupted by the coffee, which is carried on a tray with a plate of gingersnaps. The owner doesn't seem to recognize him, or maybe she's just being polite. The hotel is family run, seeping at the seams with the spirit of southern kinship. She pours them both coffee from an old silver pot and directs them to the cream and sugar. When she's gone, Pepper reaches for the coffee and selects a gingersnap, the largest one.

"You're looking well," he says. "Seeing a doctor?"

"Of course I'm seeing a doctor. Saw one two weeks ago, right before I came down to Florida. I'm fit as a fiddle. Both of us are." She crunches her gingersnap in two. "Absolutely blooming, the doctor said."

"Well, good. That's the most important thing." He rests his cup on his knee. "We do want what's best for you, Pepper. No one's trying to evade responsibility here."

"Oh, God, no. The cost in lawyers alone must be crippling you."

"You could have avoided all of this by taking a phone call or two."

"There wasn't any point. Your brother wants me to give up the baby. I'll see him in hell first. What's there to discuss?"

"Nothing, I guess, if you're going to be stubborn and un-reasonable. If you're going to get greedy and vindictive instead of doing what's right."

"What's right for *you*, you mean. You and your family."

"What's right for everyone. Including you. Including the baby." He leans forward to rest his elbows on his thighs. He's a big man, football big. The cigarette looks tiny between his meaty fingers. "I know you think we're just trying to cover up a mistake here. But we're not. This is my brother's child we're talking about."

"A child he wanted me to get rid of."

"Well, you didn't, and now he wants—we all want—for that baby to have the best possible life."

"Then we have nothing more to talk about. Stay out of my life, stay out of my baby's life, and I promise you we'll stay out of yours. I have a family of my own to make sure this baby is well taken care of."

He sighs and crushes out his cigarette into the ashtray on the coffee table. His briefcase sits upright next to the chair, just a few feet from the fire. He takes a drink of coffee and lifts the briefcase onto his lap, unsnapping the fastenings in two loud cracks.

"Is that really true, Pepper? Is your family really prepared to take this baby into its heart and give it the love and care it needs? Do your parents even know you're pregnant? Because I don't see them here anywhere. I don't see your sisters or your aunts and uncles lavishing you with love in your time of need."

"We're not the lavishing kind of family, but we muddle through."

He withdraws a sheaf of papers from the briefcase, shaking his head as he goes. "You're a single woman, Pepper. A child needs a secure home with a mother and father."

"He has a mother. Me."

"But what about a father? Every kid needs a father. And who's going to marry you, Miss Schuyler, in your present state? Or saddled with a newborn? Who's going to take you on?"

"Plenty of men."

"That's exactly what we're afraid of. Plenty of men. Because that's who you are, right? You're not mother material. Let's be honest. You're Holly Golightly, nothing wrong with that. Everyone's different. You'll be much happier if you give this baby up and continue with your life, free and clear. And the baby, too."

He hands her the papers. She closes her hands on her lap and stares him down, keeping her mouth shut, afraid of what the hell she might say if she opened it.

"When exactly are you due, Miss Schuyler?"

"Ask your brother. He can do the math."

"January? February?"

Pepper presses her lips together and sits back in the sofa, sipping her coffee, any old pregnant housewife entertaining a guest in her living room.

"Let's say February," he says, glancing at her belly. "Let's say you have the baby in the middle of winter. Do you know what it's like, living with a newborn? And you're on your own, you're bored and cooped up, you can't have any fun. You like to have fun, don't deny it. Newborns are no fun, honey. Trust me."

"Like I said, I'll muddle through."

He lifts the papers an inch or two from the leather surface of his briefcase. "Expensive, too."

"I have money."

"Listen to me. You don't have to do this. We've got papers all drawn up. We have a couple ready to take the baby, as soon as it's born, and care for it like it's their own."

"Have you, now? John and Jane Smith from Long Island, loyal Democrats?"

"No. Me. My wife and I. We'll take the baby."

"Like hell."

He holds up the papers. "See for yourself. We've discussed this at home. My brother came to us with the idea, actually. I think maybe you know my wife's had a couple of miscarriages. She'd welcome this baby with open arms."

"Sure she would. Did you tell her whose it is?" Pepper laughs. "What am I saying? She'll probably think it's yours."

The ruddiness in his cheeks spreads to the tip of his nose. "Don't be an idiot, honey. You're not a fit mother. That baby will be loved and cared for, far better than if you tried to raise it yourself. And you'd be free. No more worries, no more responsibility. You can live your life." A delicate hesitation. "We'll compensate you, of course."

Pepper knots her hands around the coffee cup so he won't see the rage inside them, shaking like a volcano on the verge of eruption. She freezes her mouth in a smile and says idly, like it's a game, like there's nothing in the world at stake: "You seem to think I'm one of your bimbos. You seem to think I'm just one of your usual girls."

He drums his fingers on the briefcase and smiles. "You know, that's the funny thing about you bimbos. You all think *you're* the one who's not the bimbo."

Pepper sets down her coffee cup. "Off you go. Discussion's over."

"I'm not leaving."

"Then I am."

She sashays . . . well, not exactly. She waddles elegantly down the line of the chintz sofa, between the chairs and to the door, and she's just about found the knob with her trembling volcanic fingers when his hand takes her by the elbow.

"You're not just walking away from this."

"Watch me."

She yanks the door open, and guess who? Black-robed and elegant.

Annabelle.

ANNABELLE

Germany • 1938

1.

We had stayed only a month in the Himmelfarbs' house, but I felt as if we were emerging, drowsy-eyed, from a Rip van Winkle hibernation. The world seemed to have changed somehow: not just the fallen leaves and the cold air, but the constitution of the physical universe. The atoms and molecules had realigned on a different axis.

By nine o'clock, we had reached Konstanz, on the rim of the lake. We had our story polished and ready: We were the Dommerichs, Rudolf and Annabelle and our son, Florian, skiing enthusiasts, visiting friends in the mountains near Verbier. Stefan was going to do all the talking. If the guard asked me a question, I was to answer in one word if possible, and if he questioned my accent, I was to say I had been brought up by an aunt and uncle in Geneva because my parents died when I was little.

"But he won't ask you any questions, I think," Stefan said. "You have your big, innocent eyes. He will think you are nothing but a sweet little hausfrau and I am a lucky man."

"Little does he know."

The streets were quiet. Stefan parked the car outside a tobacconist and went inside for newspapers and cigarettes. "You poor thing," I said. "They don't have your favorites. That will be something to look forward to, when we get to Monte Carlo."

He lit himself up and sighed in relief. "Do you know what I am looking forward to most of all?"

"Safety? Being on your ship again? Making love to me in your splendid stateroom?"

"Yes, all these things, and especially the last one. But mostly I am looking forward to hearing you play your music again."

"But I left the Amati at the hotel in Antibes."

He shook his head and picked up the newspaper. "I had it taken back to the *Isolde*. It is waiting for you there, in my cabin."

I caught my breath and said, "Our cabin."

"Yes. Our cabin." He frowned at the headline before him.

"What's wrong?"

He swore under his breath. "They have shot vom Rath."

"Who's vom Rath?"

"He is no one, just a diplomat in Paris, at the German embassy. Your husband probably crushed him under his heel on his way to work each day and never even noticed the mess. But now some stupid Jew has walked in and shot him in his office."

"Is he dead?"

"No. Not yet." He swore again and tossed the newspaper into my lap, next to Florian's sleeping head. "But you will never guess. The fucking Nazis are calling for blood."

2.

At the crossing, a long line of automobiles stretched down the road. Nobody was moving; most had shut down their engines and gotten out of their cars, smoking and talking. Stefan opened the door and said he was going to find out what was going on.

He came back half an hour later, and his face was grim. Florian was awake and eating an apple. "We're going to find a hotel," he said. "They have closed the border temporarily. No one knows if they will open it today."

"Can't we just wait and see?"

"I don't want to give them any chances."

We found a plain but comfortable hotel on the outskirts of town, overlooking the main road, so that Stefan could watch for any signs of activity. The weather was too cold for Florian to play outdoors for long. We kept to our room and ordered our lunch, while the line of cars grew along the road outside. Stefan smoked and paced the wall, glancing out the window from time to time, until I asked him to stop and read Florian a story. All right, he said, stubbing out his latest cigarette, and while he was explaining about the three little pigs, room service knocked on the door.

Because he had slept so long in the car, Florian didn't want to take his usual nap after lunch. He ran around the room, firing an imaginary gun at imaginary pirates, while I chased fruitlessly after him and Stefan stood perplexed at the end of the bed.

"Go," I said at last, brushing my hair from my face. "Go downstairs and see if you can get any news."

Stefan, looking relieved, grabbed his coat and hat and cigarettes and hurried from the room.

By three o'clock, Florian had at last fallen asleep, and Stefan hadn't returned. I pulled a chair next to the window and sat there, pretending to read in the fading autumn light. The line of cars had shortened, but I couldn't tell if this was because the border had opened or because people had simply given up. A large number of men milled about on the sidewalks and streets, some of them in uniform. I felt the waves of their restlessness rippling upward through the window glass, like a field of visible energy, and for the first time my blood began to quicken. One man stopped right under the window and looked up, as if he knew I was watching, and the look he sent me was so full of blank hatred I startled up from the chair. The book spilled to the floor. The man spat on the sidewalk and moved on.

When Stefan finally opened the door at half past four, I rushed to his arms. "What is this?" he said, taking me against his chest.

"What's going on out there?"

"A damned mess." He gave me a last squeeze and tossed his hat onto the writing desk in the corner. "There is no word yet on the border."

"What are all those men doing out there?"

"Waiting for a fucking riot, I think." He glanced at Florian, who was stirring on the bed, though his eyes were still closed. "We had better hope that fool vom Rath stays alive."

"A riot? Here?"

"My dear, they are waiting for it. They are waiting for a damned excuse."

"Who are they?"

"Hitler, Goebbels, every man down the line. The pretext, it doesn't even matter. I went to the newsstand for a paper, and do you know what? The Jewish papers were not there. They have stopped publication, by order of the Reich, because they say there is a great Jewish conspiracy afoot, but really because they want to strip us of everything we have left, every possible means of protest and information. Meanwhile, they are expelling Jews who were not born here. They are sending them to Poland by the trainload, and Poland sends them back. That is why this man Grynszpan shot vom Rath, because his family had been expelled to Poland with hardly the clothes on their backs."

"My God."

"There is nothing left." He was speaking in a hushed voice, pacing, lighting a cigarette. "They are ready to strike. The Gauleiters are waiting for the signal from Goebbels, I have no doubt. Waiting to hear that vom Rath has died, or not even that. They will send the local party members to attack every fucking synagogue in Germany, every Jew they can lay their hands on. I must telephone Wilhelmine."

"Wilhelmine?"

"Because of Else, Annabelle." He turned to me, and his eyes were wide and shocked and exhausted. "They are not letting Jewish children in the schools anymore. My daughter, she is not even a human being here anymore."

"Of course, of course. Call her now."

There was a large black telephone on the writing desk. Stefan sank down in the chair and picked up the receiver. I had borrowed clothes for him from Matthias, who was an inch or two shorter and perhaps fifty pounds heavier, so that gray wool jacket hung from Stefan's shoulders and exposed his wrists. I thought, We will have to go shopping for him in Monte Carlo and buy him several fine new suits and white shirts, and this time I'll iron them for him myself with a bit of starch, the way he likes them.

Stefan flicked the ash from his cigarette and told the operator that he was making a long-distance call to Stuttgart, gave the exchange and the number, and tapped his heel against the floor while he waited for the connection.

Florian stirred and sat up on the bed. "Mama?"

"Right here, darling." I sat down next to him and cuddled him against my side.

Stefan straightened and spoke into the receiver, in German, asking for Mrs. Himmelfarb. There was a pause, and a crease opened between his eyebrows. "I see," he said. "Perhaps Mr. Himmelfarb is available? No? Can you tell me when she is expected to return? I see. Then will you please tell Mrs. Himmelfarb that Rudolf Dommerich called from Konstanz, on the border, and to please return my call at once. The Nazarene Hotel"—he glanced at the paper on the writing desk—"room number 209. Thank you."

He set down the receiver and said to me in English, "They're out, it seems."

"So I gathered."

"Your German has improved, at least." His smile was forced.

Florian shook off the last of his nap and wriggled down the bed to the floor. Stefan looked at him and his mouth softened. He held out his arms and Florian ran tipsily into them, to be swung up on his father's knee.

"She'll be fine," I said. "Else will be fine."

"Yes."

Stefan brushed his nose in Florian's hair, the way I always did, inhaling his little-boy smell, and my ribs hurt as I watched them, identical hair and identical eyes, the son giving comfort to the father in his ill-fitting suit, his gaunt Dachau frame. When I closed my eyes, I could still see every detail, and I thought, I will never forget this, I will always remember the two of them sitting on the chair in the dull November afternoon, in the hotel room that smelled of Lysol and cigarettes and dread.

3.

The telephone rang at half past ten o'clock, waking the three of us like the sting of a wasp. Stefan stumbled from the bed and grasped the telephone receiver, while I gathered Florian against me and stroked his damp hair.

"Wilhelmine! Where are you? Yes? Yes?" He cursed. "No, we can't anyway, the border's closed. No. Just stay where you are, do you hear me? Stay where you are, and I will come to get her. For God's sake. You must come, too." A pause. "Tell him he is a fucking idiot. Tell him Stefan said he is a fucking idiot. God damn it. All right. I'm leaving now."

As he spoke, I thought I heard the distant sound of something shattering.

Stefan slammed the receiver into the cradle and turned to me. I couldn't see him very well in the darkness, but I felt the angry energy that rippled from his body.

"I have got to go to Stuttgart at once," he said. "Vom Rath has died. The Gauleiters are already at work with their minions. Wilhelmine says she can hear the smashing and screaming from her window. She wants me to take Else. She wants us to take Else with us, out of the country, to safety."

"Of course, of course. My God." I scrambled out of the covers. "Of course we'll take her. But what about Wilhelmine and poor little Henrik?"

He shook his head and turned on the lamp. "That idiot Matthias won't leave, and Wilhelmine knows he is an idiot and still she will not leave him. It is a nightmare." He was tearing off his pajamas and reaching for his suitcase.

I climbed out of bed and ran to my suitcase.

"What are you doing?"

"Getting dressed."

"What? No. You are staying here, Annabelle. You are staying here with Florian."

"And let you go off by yourself? Are you kidding me?" I lifted my nightgown over my head and reached for my blouse. "Not a chance."

"Don't be stupid, Annabelle. I will be there and back by morning. You will wake up and find me, you will hardly even know I left."

"Do you think I'm a fool? I've spent the last three months trying to save you and keep you safe, and I'm not going to let you out of my sight. Tonight of all nights."

He seized my arms. "Annabelle, no. Please don't do this. You've got to stay here. You'll be safe in the hotel, you and Florian."

"I don't want to be safe if you're not."

"But Florian!"

"Don't you *dare*. Don't you *dare* blackmail me. We are a *family*, Stefan, we are not going to break apart. Do you hear me? I'm in your skin, remember? We're a *family*. I swore it when I found you again, I swore I'd never give you up. Stefan, please, you have *got* to understand, you have got to take me with you."

"You are killing me, Annabelle."

Florian began to cry.

I put my hands on Stefan's cheeks. His bones fit into my palms. "I won't let you. I won't let you walk out of this room alone. You are not allowed to do this alone anymore."

"Annabelle, please—"

Florian slithered from the bed and ran to Stefan's legs. "Don't leave. Don't leave."

"You see?" I whispered. "This is all there is. This is all we have. The three of us."

Stefan closed his eyes. His hand dropped to Florian's head, to the sobbing face that stuck to his knees and wet the legs of his pajamas.

"Stefan. I gave you my own blood, remember?"

It was a cheap plea, and he must have known it. That pint of blood had entered his veins three years ago, and by now it was gone, churned over and converted into Stefan's own. But as I said the words, I recalled the drone of the tender's engine, the slap of waves against the hull of the *Isolde*, the briny smell of the sea and the reek of gasoline exhaust. I remembered Stefan's brave and lugubrious voice, telling me not to be stupid, and the giddy plunge in my belly as I fell in love with him. The sight of my red blood flowing through the tube and into the vein on his wrist, to bring him back to life.

Stefan said, in a defeated voice, "You will do exactly as I say, is that understood? You will hide in the boot if I tell you to hide in the boot. If there is the least trouble, I will deposit you in the nearest hotel and you will wait there quietly with our son, is that clear?"

I fell on his chest.

"Yes. Yes, that's clear."

4.

We reached the outskirts of Stuttgart just before two o'clock in the morning. A lurid yellow-orange glow hung over the rooftops, like a bank of fog. "They have started burning," Stefan said.

"What are they burning?"

"Whatever they can, probably. Synagogues, businesses. Maybe houses."

"My God."

"What did you expect, Annabelle? They want to destroy us, don't you know that?"

"Destroy? You don't mean that."

"What do you think I mean? I mean destroy. I mean obliterate, I mean they want us blistered from the face of the earth."

"But how could they do that, while good people are watching? While the world is watching? They can't possibly think they can get away with it."

"That is the point. They want to see what they can get away with. The entire history of the past five years, they have been seeing what the world will let them get away with. And the world is so sick of everything, it doesn't care."

"It will have to act now."

"Just watch, Annabelle. Just watch and see what the world does and doesn't do."

I stared at the lurid sky.

"It's impossible. They just want to get rid of you. They just want you out of Germany."

"You do not understand a thing, Annabelle. Not a fucking thing."

"But you're talking about murder."

He tossed his cigarette out the window. "Do you want to know how many times they tried to kill me at Dachau? They called it punishment and rehabilitative labor and all kinds of nice, clean things. But they just wanted to kill me, that is all, neat and simple. Only I would not give them the satisfaction."

"Then why did they agree to let you out to go to the hospital?"

"A very good question, Annabelle. I have asked this myself many times."

I looked down at Florian's sleeping head in my lap. "You think it was Johann."

"I do not think anything anymore. I just want to get the hell out of here with my wife and my son and daughter. I want to get the fuck out of Germany while we are all still alive. What is it?"

"You called me your wife."

"And you are crying about *this*?"

"Yes, damn you. I am crying about this."

5.

Everywhere you could hear the sound of smashing glass. Stefan drove quickly, past throngs of young men whose faces were yellow under the streetlights and the glow of the fires, whose eyes were lit by something else, but you couldn't outrun that sound. It shattered the ends of your nerves; it made your heart explode and explode in your chest. *Hurry*, I said to Stefan, pressing my feet on the floorboards, but it was a stupid thing to say. He was already driving as fast as he dared.

He knew the way, which was fortunate because I didn't

recognize anything in this strange glow that had overtaken the city. The Himmelfarbs lived in a residential neighborhood, lined with trees, and as we approached the district the crowds of young men seemed to thin out. Maybe we're past the worst, I said, and Stefan didn't reply.

We turned a corner, and I recognized the street. My gaze traveled down a few houses to the right, and there it was, the familiar low iron gate, the tiny garden, the five steps leading to the stoop. The sidewalk was empty and still, except for the distant sound of shouts and breaking glass, a radio play of destruction. All the lights were out in the houses. Stefan stopped the car and jumped out. He went around the passenger side, took Florian from my arms, and grabbed my hand. We hurried up the stoop and banged on the door.

"It's me, Wilma! It's Stefan! Open the damned door!"

The door sprang open over the last two words, and Wilhelmine Himmelfarb stood gray-faced in the entry, her hair lank over her forehead, holding Henrik on her hip.

"Thank God," she said.

1.

Pepper stares downward at that Audrey Hepburn neck, ending in the crisp triangles of a black collar, a trench coat belted chicly at the waist.

"There you are," Annabelle says brightly, holding out a black leather hand.

"Here I am."

Annabelle turns her attention to the man at Pepper's elbow. "Good morning. I don't believe we've been introduced. My name is Annabelle Dommerich."

The hand again. He takes it, shakes it briefly, mumbles his name.

"Enchanted," says Annabelle.

"I thought you were on Cumberland Island," says Pepper.

"Yes, I expect you did. Well, I'm back now. As you see."

"But Florian and Susan are on the ferry out, the one that just left. You've just missed them." It occurs to Pepper that this remarkable failure might not necessarily be a coincidence.

"Yes."

"I'm sorry, Mrs. Dommerich, but if you don't mind, the lady and I were having a discussion—"

Annabelle turns and gives him the blinding smile. "As a matter of fact, sir, I do mind. I need to speak rather urgently to Miss Schuyler. I'm afraid your little discussion will have to wait."

He gives her an amazed look, the look of a man unaccustomed to hearing the word *wait*. The astonishment lifts his thick eyebrows almost into his hairline.

Pepper links elbows with Annabelle. "Poor dear," she says. "That's twice in one morning."

"Twice what?"

"Refused."

2.

"I don't believe that man means to leave," says Annabelle, staring down from Pepper's second-floor window to the blue Lincoln parked outside. The drizzle has let up, but the blanket of gray remains, deadening the chrome on the bumpers and the tailfins.

Pepper stretches out on the narrow single bed and props her foot on a pillow. "It's a genetic disease that runs in the family. They can't hear the word *no*."

Annabelle makes an irritated noise.

"Anyway," Pepper continues, hardly missing a beat, "enough about little old me. What the hell are *you* doing here?"

"Hmm." She turns from the window and leans against the sill. "What do you think of my son?"

"I think he's delicious. So does the fair Susan. They'll make you some beautiful grandkids, those two."

Annabelle frowns, but it's not the ordinary kind of frown. It's a flat-browed, purse-lipped kind of frown that says, *Not on my watch, sister.*

"If Florian marries that girl, I'll disown him," she says.

"What's this? You don't like Susan?"

"I like her enormously, but she's not marrying my son." Annabelle pauses. "She's tone-deaf. I won't have Florian living without music."

"That seems a little unfair. It's not her fault, is it?"

"And she'll let him walk all over her. Florian can be a little bossy, like his father. He needs someone who'll stand up to him." She gazes innocently at the ceiling.

"And yet you let them sail off to Cumberland Island together, without any adult supervision." Pepper holds up her hand. "Don't even try to tell me you didn't know they were on that ferry. I just want to know how you gave them the slip. And maybe why."

Annabelle turns back to the window. The overcast sky is flat against her face, ironing out every possible sign of age. She could be twenty years old. "He's taking something out of the trunk," she says.

"Never mind him. You said you had to speak to me."

"That was only to rescue you."

Pepper sits up. "What happened out there?"

"On the island, you mean? Nothing. I went, I came back."

"And the part in the middle? Did you find what you were looking for?"

"Yes. Oh, now he's coming back inside. There's something

under his arm, a large envelope. My God, the look on his face."

"I said never mind him. I want to know what happened last night. Why you came back, looking like a chocolate éclair that's had all the cream taken out."

Annabelle walks to the fireplace and holds out her hands to the flames. Pepper admires her fingers, long and beautifully shaped. Her head is bowed a little, examining the nails. "Like I said, nothing happened. I went to see if I was right, if an old friend of mine was living there."

"An old lover."

"I suppose you could say that."

"Well, was he?"

"Yes, he was. It was him, all right." She rubs her hands together, and with her right thumb she twiddles the slim gold wedding ring on the fourth finger of her left hand.

"Well? Did you say hello? Throw yourself in his arms? Spend the night in bed?"

"None of those things." She picks up the silver candlestick on the mantel and studies the base, like she's looking for the hallmark. "I managed to find out where he lived. It was a bit of a trek. I took a bicycle. I waited outside for a bit, gathering up my courage. It's a bit frightening, you know, seeing someone again after such a long time. You don't know how they've changed, or how much you've changed, or whether they forgive you for everything. So I waited."

A knock sounds on the door.

"Ignore it," says Pepper. "You waited?"

"I waited until midnight, and then I turned around and went

back to the inn, and this morning I found a fisherman to take me back to the mainland. And now I'm packing up and going home."

Pepper stands up, grabbing the sofa arm for support. "What? You gave up?"

Annabelle looks at her sharply. "Why do you care?"

I have no idea.

"I just do, that's all."

The knock sounds again. A thick masculine voice: "Miss Schuyler! I need to speak with you."

Annabelle lifts her eyebrows. "We could sneak out the back way and leave in my car, if you don't mind leaving your things behind for Florian to bring later."

"No, I'm going to settle with him, believe me. But you first. I need to know why you gave up. You of all people. You gave up on his doorstep."

"Gave up what?"

"Everything! Claiming him back."

"Claim him back? But that wasn't the point, darling. That wasn't the point, after all these years. He has his own life now. I just wanted to see if it was really him. I just wanted to make sure he was all right."

"You went to all that trouble, just to look at his house? You didn't even knock and say hello?"

"No. There was no point."

"Why not?"

Annabelle smiles and spreads out her hands. "Because he wasn't alone."

3.

Pepper plants her crutches into the rug. "This had better be good. I'm heading upstairs right now to pack up."

His face is a picture of anger, all grim and highlighted in red. He strides right past her and tosses the long manila envelope on the coffee table, next to the remains of the gingersnaps. "Come here."

"I'll stand right here, thanks."

Pepper can still hear the click of Annabelle's shoes on the stairs, making her defeated way to her room, where she will pack her things for the drive back to Florida, to the big empty villa by the ocean. Or maybe she will just go straight to her son's house in the Washington suburbs, for Thanksgiving? The widowed matriarch, presiding over her sprawling family. Someday Pepper will have to get the whole story out of her. The car, the man she left behind. The man she married.

"All right," he says. "Have it your way."

He unties the fastening on the envelope and draws out a thin stack of papers. "Please understand, we don't want to have to use these. Your family, they're an institution in New York, they've given this country some of its finest citizens. So we'd really hate to have to send this information to the press."

He spreads the papers out on the coffee table, pushing the plate with the gingersnaps into the corner. Some of them are typewritten pages; some are photographs. A nice little collection. Pepper recognizes her father in one of them. He seems to be naked.

"We did a little research," he says, in an apologetic tone, as if to say, *You left us no choice, honey, no choice but to dig up all this dirt from under the carpet.*

Well, every family has its dirt, doesn't it? But Pepper's family is so old and distinguished, so sprinkled with rebellious and eccentric characters. The dirt accumulates gradually in a family like hers, but it's a rich and fertile kind of dirt: the kind that, if you plant a seed, will grow a whole goddamned garden of scandal. And maybe that kind of thing doesn't matter anymore. Maybe it won't get you struck from the Social Register, or blackballed from the Knicker-bocker Club, or (shame of shames!) ostracized from the best Fifth Avenue drawing rooms.

But maybe it will.

It all depends, doesn't it, on what's contained in that little array laid out on the coffee table, next to the gingersnaps.

Pepper hobbles across the old rug and stares down at the field of white rectangles. She picks up one of the typewritten pages and reads about Uncle Freddie, whom everybody knew had gotten his oil contracts the old-fashioned way, but really. To see the whole affair in black-and-white.

He clears his throat. "The attorney general may have to prosecute."

She looks up. "The irony here is that *your* family's done worse."

He shrugs. Because it hardly needs saying that if a man smuggles in a bottle or two of whiskey from Canada and the cops are paid not to hear him, it didn't really happen.

What a nuisance, Pepper thinks. What a damned nuisance. I'm going to have to be a hero, aren't I?

After all this, I'm going to have to take the fall.

4.

He lets her go upstairs to pack. It's not as if she's going to try any funny business, is she, not when those papers still lie in their manila folder, under his arm. He even takes the laundry bag and carries it to the blue Lincoln himself, what a gentleman, dropping it into the trunk like a sack of refuse. Then he opens the door for her.

"Thank you," she says, removing her crutches from under her arms and tossing them inside. The seats are pure virgin white, not a single smear, reeking of cigarettes. She pauses with her hand on the top of the doorframe and stares at the generous porch of the Riverview Hotel, the empty ferry landing to the side. The river, leading out to the wide blue sea.

He swings around to the driver's side and puts the key in the ignition. The engine takes a few turns to get going, but then it lets out a nice handsome roar, eager to be off, eager to drive right out of this damp and sleepy town and head back to Washington in time for Thanksgiving.

"Stop!"

A lithe black figure leaps down the front steps toward the street.

"Pepper, no! Don't get in the car with that man!"

"Get in," he says to Pepper. "Now."

Pepper braces herself on the door and swings inside, and the Lincoln lurches forward, away from the curb, racing back up the street toward the brand-new interstate.

5.

After a block or two, he glances in the rearview mirror and turns on the radio. Roy Orbison. "Who the hell was that, anyway?" he asks.

"You've never heard of Annabelle Dommerich? The cellist?"

He whistles. "No kidding. How do you know her?"

"We met in Palm Beach."

He glances again in the mirror. "She's a very attractive woman. Married?"

"I don't think you're her type."

"They all say that at first."

She looks out the window. The town still looks asleep. Each block blurs past her eyes, doors closed, sidewalks empty. Maybe it's the drizzle, which has begun again, pattering against the windshield. He turns on the wipers. *Swish, swish,* into the dull drone of the engine, the rattle of rain.

He reaches across her and unlatches the glove compartment. "Mind if I smoke?"

"Suit yourself." She rolls down the window a pair of inches and thinks, I'll probably have to kill him. Kill him and steal the envelope and disappear somewhere, start a new life in Canada or Mexico or Australia, all by myself, assumed name, the works. Maybe they'll write a book about me one day. *Pepper: She Really Was That Bad.*

All right. Not kill him. She's not *really* that bad. But knock him out. How? Well, somehow. Knock him out and steal the envelope and . . .

But they probably have copies somewhere, don't they? This is not a family that leaves things to chance. This is a family that lays its plans with care.

Damn it. Damn it all. She's stuck.

She'll think of something.

She's stuck.

Breathe, Pepper. The baby needs oxygen. You'll think of something. You always do.

You're stuck.

He fumbles with the cigarettes. The buildings thin out, the turn in the highway approaches. Somehow he juggles it all: cigarettes, lighter, turn. Pepper puts her hand on the door handle and braces her feet against the floorboards. He's taking it a little fast, isn't he? But the blue Lincoln can handle it.

They straighten out, and a black shape appears before them, stopped in the road: a beautiful swooping Mercedes-Benz Special Roadster, stretched out like a shiny black panther, and a woman slamming the door and turning to face them, arms crossed, eyes fierce.

"Stop!" shouts Pepper, and he looks up from his cigarette and slams the brakes.

ANNABELLE

Germany • 1938

1.

The house was dark, except for Wilhelmine's feeble flashlight jiggling ahead. My eyes picked out the familiar details: the newel post at the bottom of the stairs, shaped like a pineapple; the worn oriental rug; the elegantly cluttered mantel of the parlor fireplace, as we flashed past the doorway. She led us downstairs to the basement. A child's whimper floated upward. Stefan pushed past us both and vaulted down the rest of the stairs. When I turned the corner, he was holding Else up to his chest. She was fully dressed in a thick wool cardigan and plaid skirt. His face was buried in her dark hair.

"Else!" cried Florian, and I shushed him, but Else was already wriggling out of her father's grasp, as Florian struggled from mine.

"They played together so happily when I was staying here," I whispered to Stefan.

"Thank God," he said, and his voice was like the crunch of fine gravel. He turned to Wilhelmine. "Where is Matthias?"

"He is upstairs, closing all the shutters. Henrik is asleep."

"Get him. Get him dressed. You've got to come with us, the both of you."

"But Matthias—"

"Damn Matthias! He is an idiot. There is a mob three streets away. Do you hear me? A mob. They are smashing windows and taking people from their homes." He spoke in English, crisp and raging.

Wilhelmine's mouth parted.

"Go!" thundered Stefan, and she turned and raced up the stairs.

"This is unreal," I said. "I can't believe this is happening."

He was pacing along the wall, running a hand through his dark hair. "It is perfectly real. It is exactly what I have been saying for five fucking years. God damn it!" he shouted, and turned to drive his fist against the wall.

Else and Florian stopped playing and stared at him. The light from the single bare bulb cast a harsh shadow along the side of his face, making him look a little mad. "Stefan, the children," I whispered.

He lifted his eyes to me. "I need a gun. I need a gun to protect us, I need two or three. And do you think the civilized Matthias has a single gun in his civilized house? Of course not. We are left to defend ourselves with our bare hands. Because right is on our side. We can put that on our tombstones, eh? *Right was on our side.* How—what is the English word?—how very poignant."

The sound of urgent voices drifted down the stairs, arguing in German. The soft wail of Henrik, awake now.

"Stefan, please." I knelt down and gathered the children

against my legs. "It will be all right. We'll drive all night if we have to."

"And how are we going to get across the border, hmm? We will have to swim down the Rhine."

"I'm an American. We can go to the consulate."

"But I am a fugitive, remember? There is nothing your Roosevelt can do for me, even if he wanted to."

The voices were getting louder, strong and male. Stefan and I locked eyes and realized, at the same precise and horrified instant, that the sound came not from Matthias and Wilhelmine, arguing about whether to flee their home or to ride out the storm, but from outside the house. From the street outside the window.

"Stay here," Stefan said.

"Don't go up!"

Booted footsteps thundered up the front steps, just above our heads. An instant later came the crash of fists against the door, the shouted demand: *Öffnen!*

Stefan reached for the chain dangling from the light socket and turned off the bulb. Else cried out. "Shh," he said, and in the faint light from the stairs he bent down and kissed her head and then Florian's. "Stay here with your mother," he said in German. "I will be right back."

A crash, as the door came open. A flurry of shouts. Wilhelmine screaming.

Stefan was heading for the stairs. I grabbed his arm. "Don't go up there!"

"Just stay here, all right? Listen to me. If they come down to search, if you hear them coming down, you take that back door into the garden. There is a hidden gate at the end, behind the shed. Do you know it?"

"Yes."

"Take the children out that way. Find a house somewhere, somewhere to spend the night, and then go to the consulate."

"Not without you!"

He gripped my shoulders with his hands, strong enough that the tears started in my eyes. "Take the children! Please, Annabelle. They are all there is left."

His face was lurid and anguished. The sound of his whisper was so hoarse, I could hardly understand him.

"I can't leave you here," I said.

"I'll find you. I swear to God I will find you." He leaned forward and kissed me hard, so I knew without doubt he was lying, that there was no chance I would see him again in this life, and then he ran up the stairs and into the light, and closed the door behind him.

2.

"All right, children," I whispered in German, because Else's English was not very good. "We are going on a little adventure. We are going to sneak out through the garden and play hide-and-seek with the rest of the grown-ups."

My voice was shaking, my hands were cold. I couldn't see them, because Stefan had closed off the door at the top of the basement stairs, leaving us in a thorough darkness that was both velvety and ominous, a black paradox. I found their woolen shoulders, their silken heads, and herded them to the back of the basement. From upstairs came shouting. Wilhelmine screamed.

"Mama!" said Else, breaking free.

"No, darling!"

Shuffling, pounding. A gun fired, a crack of manufactured thunder unlike any sound I'd ever heard, and then the authoritative thump of a human body falling against a wooden floor.

No. Please. Not this.

Hail Mary, full of grace, the Lord is with thee . . .

"Else, come here." I scrambled after her.

Someone wailed, a voice that was neither male nor female, rising up above the scuffle and the pounding.

. . . Blessed art thou among women . . .

Another shot, rattling the floorboards above us.

. . . and blessed is the fruit of thy womb, Jesus . . . Please, please, God, no, not this . . .

My hands found the shoulder of Else's woolen sweater. I dragged her from the bottom of the stairs.

. . . Holy Mary, mother of God . . .

Crack. Crack.

. . . pray for us sinners . . .

Crack.

. . . now and in the hour of our death . . .

I hauled Else back across the basement floor, kicking and wailing. I held my hand over her mouth, trying to stifle her agony so they wouldn't hear us. Wouldn't come downstairs and find the children, too.

Crack. Crack. Crack. Now I felt the sound, rather than heard it. My ears had gone as numb as my fingers.

Hail Mary, full of grace . . .

Florian flung himself against my leg as I reached the back of the basement. I fumbled for the doorknob, but my hands were so numb, and I couldn't see.

. . . full of grace . . .

The door, the door. Smooth brass. The knob. Turn.

. . . pray for us sinners . . .

Crack.

A rush of cold, clear air. Shouts drifting out from the upstairs window. Set down Else, grab her hand, grab Florian's hand.

. . . pray for us sinners . . .

Running across the damp grass, fighting the moonlight, Else sobbing. The garden wall. Where is the gate? To the right, the right. Lift the latch.

. . . pray for us sinners . . .

Push the children through the gateway, into the empty alley behind the house. Running down the pavement. Which house? The friend, the children we played with that hot August day, which house? Turn the corner. Smell the smoke. Shouting.

A group of men. Uniforms. My God. Stop. Go back.

I turned, saw more soldiers, turned back to the first group, which had rattled to a halt next to a streetlamp, five or six yards away.

Nowhere to go. I clutched the children to my skirt. "Mama?" said Florian, like a question.

Somewhere in the middle of that throng, a figure staggered downward, was hauled up again by a pair of soldiers, flailed, shouted my name.

"Stefan!" I gasped.

A man at the front of the pack stepped forward, immense and dark-coated, into the light from the streetlamp. Beneath the brim of his cap, his eyes were such a pale shade of blue, they were almost white, and I gasped in recognition.

"Frau Silverman," he said, "you must come with me."

Pray for us sinners, now and in the hour of our death.
Amen.

3.

The butt of a rifle guided me into the back of the truck. I gripped the children's hands and helped them up and inside, onto the benches lining the sides. Stefan was thrown in right behind us. I tried to lunge toward him, but a pair of arms jerked me back. In the next instant, something warm and wriggling shoved up against my chest in a shriek of outrage: Henrik. I hadn't even heard him.

The gears ground, the truck lurched forward. There was now no sign of Johann. Perhaps he was riding up front. I was too sick to feel anger, too desperate to keep the children steady on the bench as we bounced down the road. Too drenched in relief and fear at the sight of Stefan, slumped on the opposite side, his feet a few inches from my feet, prodded upright from time to time by a rifle.

It will be all right, I thought. We will find a way out of this.

I thought, He's alive. Stefan's alive. We will live.

In a day, in a week, in a month, we will be safe and free, we will be sailing through an empty blue ocean in the *Isolde*, pointing out the dolphins to the children, making love all night in the wide white bed in Stefan's stateroom.

I closed my eyes and whispered in English: "Are you hurt?"

"A little."

I laid a hand over Florian's ear. "Where is Wilhelmine?"

"Dead, my heart. They are both dead."

The children grew magically quiet in the rhythmic bounce of the back of the truck. I wedged the four of us into a corner, to give my arms a rest, inhaling the sweat of the soldiers and the dirty mildew of the canvas top. I thought, I hope it was quick. Dear Wilma. I hope it was quick. Please, God.

Hail Mary, full of grace. The Lord is with thee.

Was that right? But it was the only prayer I could think of.

Blessed art thou among women, and blessed is the fruit of thy womb, Jesus.

I said aloud: "I'm sorry."

"The fault is mine, Annabelle. They were looking for me."

"It's not your fault. It's their fault. It's Johann's fault."

Holy Mary, mother of God, pray for us sinners, now and in the hour of our death.

I asked, "Did Johann kill them himself?"

"No. He came at the end. To make sure they took me alive."

The truck squealed to a halt, and then made a sharp turn to the left. Henrik nearly fell from my arms. Henrik, the orphan baby Jew, motherless and fatherless. He began to cry again, and I cradled him up against my shoulder and hushed him softly.

Amen.

4.

The children slept, as children will. The air inside the back of the truck grew humid and stank with human occupation. I nearly fell asleep, too—my brain was so stunned—but I kept awake by pinching myself and by staring at Stefan's shadow a few feet away. Sometimes a little light came through the canvas, and I saw there was a stain of blood on the shoulder of his jacket, but I didn't know if it belonged to him or to someone else. It was a large stain, and very dark, almost black.

I didn't count the hours. How could I? But the night went on forever anyway. We had arrived in Stuttgart sometime after three, and spent no more than twenty minutes inside the Himmelfarbs' house. Let us say it was four o'clock when we left. Shouldn't the sun have risen by now? Yet the canvas remained black, the interior of the truck filled only with shadows, the suggestions of men. No one spoke. Just grunts and shuffles, the occasional broken wind. I couldn't even see what uniforms they wore. Which particular tentacle of Germany's monster had snatched us.

The truck lurched and then staggered to a stop, in a series of squeals from the naked brakes. Stefan straightened, slumped, and straightened again. I brought the children close. Henrik was damply asleep against my shoulder; Else's head lay on my lap. Every muscle ached. I couldn't feel my arms, because of the pressure on the various nerves. My shoes hurt my feet, too tight and too hot.

Could I move, if I had to?

Florian stirred against my ribs.

A metallic bang, and the back of the truck opened up to reveal a forest clearing, trimmed faintly in the pink of a rising dawn. A white young face appeared in the gap.

Aussteigen! he shouted.

Out we stumbled from the back of the truck, blinking and bleary in the gray-pink light. Else ran to Stefan and clutched his leg, and he tried to kneel and comfort her, but the guard wouldn't let him. So she went on clinging and sobbing, *Papa, what's happening? Papa!*, while his large hand cupped the side of her head. The guard turned to me and motioned angrily. I shrugged and gave him a helpless look. I was carrying Henrik in one arm and holding Florian's hand with the other. The guard's face compressed with anger, but he let Else stay.

I came up to Stefan and breathed in the sticky scent of his neck. "Where is Johann?" I whispered in English.

"I don't know. Not in the truck."

Ruhig! said the guard.

I thought, If I can just speak to Johann. If I can just reason with him.

But I knew, even as I hoped, that this was impossible. That I never would have stood a chance: Annabelle against Johann's rigid professional duty. I never had. Not even when we were living as man and wife.

So when he appeared through the rose-colored mist, dressed in full uniform, flanked by a lanky adjutant, even more giant than I recalled, I looked into his pale heavy face and my lips moved in prayer.

Hail Mary, full of grace, the Lord is with thee.

Johann stopped and took us in, the five of us, Stefan and me and the three children who clung to us.

"Papa?" said Florian, and I tightened my hand around his, and for some reason, perhaps Johann's splendid uniform, perhaps the faintness of the early light or the stern lines of Johann's face, my son stayed right where he was, next to my leg.

Johann's gaze flicked down to Florian, but I saw not the slightest softening of his stiff expression. He turned to the adjutant and muttered an order, and the adjutant turned to the guards and barked in a high and crackling voice, the German words so shrill that I had to pick through them one by one to understand.

By then, the men were already scrambling to obey. One of the guards took Florian by the arm and yanked him ahead, while another prodded his rifle into the small of my back. We stumbled forward. Johann turned smartly and led the way; the adjutant stayed behind with the truck and the other guards. Stefan walked a pace or two ahead of me, limping a little, holding Else's hand. Her ribbon had come loose, and her dark hair spilled about her shoulders. She clung to Stefan's hand with both of hers.

"Johann, please," I called. "The children. For God's sake. Have mercy."

But Johann's massive legs marched on, his field-gray shoulders remained square and polished in the soft dawn. To the right, I spied the familiar lines of the black Mercedes, parked in the mist at the edge of the clearing. The sight made my stomach contract. Henrik's heavy body slipped downward on my hip. "Please, slow down," I said, and Johann stopped and, without even turning, pointed to the car and ordered the guard at my back to put the woman and the children inside.

"No!" I shouted, but I couldn't fight the guard, not when Florian hung from one arm and Henrik lay heavily on my hip. And then I thought, Yes, why not, put the children in the car where they will be safe. Where they won't see what happens. The guard jerked the door open and pushed the small of my back. Florian crawled onto the seat and found the steering wheel. I set Henrik down with my shaking hands and turned for Else.

But Else wouldn't leave Stefan. She wrapped her arms around his leg and clung, like a sobbing burr, impossible to extract. The guard, exasperated, grabbed her small shoulder, and Stefan, without warning, swung his fist into the guard's face. The man stumbled back with a cry. The blood flooded downward from a cut under his left eye. Stefan pressed forward, hitting him again, hitting his jaw and nose, knocking the rifle from his hand, and the attack was so swift and vicious that the other guard was only just turning, only just setting his rifle to his shoulder by the time the other guard fell to the grass and Stefan swooped the dropped rifle into his hands.

The gun, at last, that he needed.

As soon as Stefan's fist had connected with the guard's jaw, I ran to Else, who stood stunned a few feet away, her red mouth open in a frozen scream. I lifted her in my arms and tossed her into the car, and when I whipped around, slamming the door behind me, the second guard fired his rifle at Stefan.

"No!" I screamed, but it didn't matter, the bullet whistled past and hit the car instead, punching a perfect hole in the rear bumper.

In the same instant, Stefan fired back twice, *bang bang*, and the guard's head snapped back, and then his entire body staggered and flew, like a man kicked by a horse, and the pieces of his skull and his brain splattered the damp grass and the gray wool of Johann's left arm in tiny pink chunks, while a crimson flower opened over his chest. His feet twitched and then went still, and I thought, as I compressed my cheeks between my two shocked hands: Now he will kill Johann. My God, Stefan is going to kill Johann.

5.

The day after our wedding, the morning after our wedding night, Johann and I had driven down to Italy along a southern route, because the Alpine passes were already covered in snow and Johann did not want to take such a risk with his beautiful car and his new wife. We reached Nice by evening and Johann asked if I would like to stay overnight or to drive straight through, and I glanced at the glassy dark Mediterranean and the red sun dropping below it, and I said I would like to drive straight through, if he wasn't too tired. So we did.

Johann telephoned ahead to the hotel in Florence, so they were expecting us when we arrived just before dawn. He carried me up to the room, which was old and decorated with beautiful stuccos, and the sleepy bellboys followed with our luggage. We were to stay in Florence for two weeks, and I remembered thinking, as I lay on the bed and listened to Johann's exhausted snoring, it would be lovely to stay forever.

I had slept for an hour or two before the bells of the cathedrals woke me. There was some light creeping between the slats of the shutters. I turned my head and for an instant the sight of Johann's sleeping face shocked me. Then I remembered: we were married.

I rose and went to the suitcases, which had been left unpacked because we were so tired. I opened up mine first. I hung my dresses in the wardrobe and my underthings in the drawer; there were not many, and I thought perhaps we would do a little shopping. Italian clothes were supposed to be beautiful. When I had emptied my own bags, I turned to Johann's single brown leather-covered trunk, plain and ancient, and I hesitated. But we're married now, I remembered. He's my husband, and a wife is supposed to unpack her husband's things, to make his life more comfortable for him.

So I opened the trunk and discovered a miracle of precise and efficient packing, no more than I supposed I should have expected. I put his shirts and underclothes in the drawer, and I hung his suits and his single dress uniform, which he had worn for our wedding. At the bottom of the trunk I found his pistols.

There were two of them, exactly alike, made of cold black metal and utterly forbidding. I stared at them for a moment, not quite sure what to do, and then Johann's voice came to me from the bed.

"Annabelle? What are you doing?"

"Unpacking. What would you like me to do with your pistols?" I said it casually, as if cold black service pistols made an everyday appearance in my life.

"Bring them here."

I picked up the pistols, one in each hand, and brought them to Johann, who was sitting up in the bed, a little blurry still, his bare chest dusky in the shuttered light. He took the pistols from me and explained that these were Lugers, the Pistol 08 manufactured by the Mauser works, a very fine example of German engineering and craftsmanship. He showed me the mechanisms and let me hold one and lift the safety on and off, so there would not be any tragic mistakes. A pistol like this was not a toy: it was a tool, a weapon of extreme lethality. Did I understand? Because the thought of some accident occurring to his Annabelle, of any harm at all coming to his beloved wife, was too much to bear.

I said I understood, and he placed them in the drawer of the bedside table, next to his head.

I sat on the edge of the bed, a few inches away, and nudged him playfully. "What kind of man brings pistols along on his honeymoon?"

"A man who is ready to protect his wife at all times," he said, and his face and voice were so serious that I lost my smile.

"But surely we're safe here," I said, gesturing to the dark and elegant room around us.

He shrugged and said you were never completely safe in this world, that the threat always came when you least expected it, and his words reminded me how his first beloved wife had died without warning. How a wicked invader had stolen into their bedroom and killed her, and Johann had been helpless to stop it.

I leaned down and kissed him deeply and honestly, almost passionately, and he lifted me into his arms and told me that he would take me out to the shooting range when we arrived home in Germany. He would show me how to use a pistol properly, so I could protect myself if such a thing ever became necessary, God forbid.

As it turned out, the snow had already fallen by the time we reached Schloss Kleist, covering the shooting range in a thick blanket of virgin white, and the secret of firing a lethal black Luger pistol remained unknown to me.

But I had been assured, over and over, by those who knew my husband well, that I had nothing to worry about, because Johann was an expert.

6.

By the time Stefan had fired his rifle, by the time the guard's body had hit the ground, already dead, Johann had drawn his pistol from the belt at his waist and stood calmly, oblivious to the gore around him, pointing the barrel at Stefan's chest.

Perhaps fifteen yards of grass separated them, no more. At such a short distance, even the thick yarns of mist were no impediment. The burnt scent of saltpeter filled my nose and stayed there. I couldn't breathe it in, could not even draw the air into my lungs to scream or plead or reason. My feet stuck to the ground, planted side by side in front of the closed door of the Mercedes, where the children sat waiting. I wanted to run out, to stop them, to throw myself on Johann's pistol. But if I moved, I would distract Stefan, and Johann would fire.

Or the other way around.

I heard Wilhelmine's voice. Wilhelmine, who now lay dead in the hallway of her house in Stuttgart.

You do not know that the two of them, they are like Javert and Valjean? They are immortal enemies.

Neither man spoke. Each mouth sent regular white plumes into the November air, but no words. There was already so much between them, a long and tangled history of which I knew almost nothing, incidents and encounters that had occurred before I met either man. Dark-haired Stefan holding his stolen rifle, fair Johann with his pistol. Like a duel, like a pair of Regency rakes, except that it was real. Except that one of them would actually kill the other.

Which one?

Holy Mary, mother of God, pray for us sinners, now and in the hour of our death.

So intent was I on the two men standing across from each other, still as volcanoes, pointing their weapons, that at first I didn't notice the other guard when he stirred from the grass behind Stefan.

I didn't see him place his hand on the ground and hoist himself up, shaky and enormous and silent. Only when he leapt toward Stefan's back did the sight of him register in my brain, and I knew, even as my mouth opened, even as I screamed *Watch out!* that I was too late, that I had failed, that Stefan was the man who would die this November morning.

Crack.

A puff of smoke drifted from the tip of Johann's pistol, and the guard dropped from Stefan's back, leaving half of his forehead behind.

Stefan staggered sideways under the impact, and set his knee on the ground. My feet moved at last. I ran across the grass and took Stefan's weight on my chest; I wrapped my arms around Stefan's back and gasped, *Are you hurt? Are you hurt?*

No, he said.

He looked over my shoulder. I turned, too.

Johann, face impassive, put his pistol back in his holster. He walked toward the second guard, examined him for a second, and turned to the two of us, Stefan and Annabelle, sitting stunned in the bloody grass.

"Get in the car. We must leave at once, before the border closes."

Fifth Movement

"When a man steals your wife, there is no better revenge than to let him keep her."

SACHA GUITRY

PEPPER

Georgia • 1966

1.

Bed rest, the doctor says, and Pepper's not pleased.

"But there's nothing wrong with me," she says. "I'm fine, the baby's fine."

"By the grace of God. You're lucky that lovely Mrs. Dommerich found you and brought you in, after a fall like that." He peers at her over the clipboard. He has nice blue eyes, she thinks. Maybe a little too blue. Could you trust a man with eyes that blue? He says, like it's her fault: "I still don't quite understand how it happened."

Pepper considers telling him the truth. There's no reason she shouldn't, really, except that he wouldn't believe a sitting United States senator would behave so ignobly at the scene of a traffic accident. Certainly not in a humble seaside town like Saint Mary's, Georgia. She holds up her hands helplessly. "My crutches slipped."

"Hmm." He pats her foot. "We've reset the bone, and this time there will be no more walking about until it's healed.

Especially not on slippery November sidewalks. Is that understood?"

"Yes, sir," Pepper says meekly. "Whatever you say, sir."

He leans forward over the bed. "It's not going to work."

"What's not going to work?"

"That pretty face of yours, darlin'." He straightens, winks, makes a note on the chart, and walks to the door.

"Doctors these days," says Pepper.

"I heard that. And you're lucky I don't tell your father."

"Tell me what?" says Dadums, walking through the open door with two steaming cups of coffee.

2.

As Thanksgiving dinners go, Pepper's had worse. You wouldn't believe how many Schuylers could fit in a single Georgia hospital room, holding plates of rubber turkey and canned gravy, just like Mums didn't used to make, ever. Pepper's little nephew Lionel listens to her stomach with a stethoscope and announces it's twins. Maybe triplets.

"Good," Pepper says. "You can adopt one of them."

Daddy avoids looking at her stomach at all, but at least he's there, blaming everything on her mother, dodging volleys of returning blame. The water in his glass is probably vodka. Her sister Vivian's husband reads Pepper's chart and assures her that the—what had she called him?— goddamned hayseed country doctor out here really does know what he's doing, no matter how many times he drops his *G*'s and calls her darlin'.

"He's rather handsome, too," says Mums.

"Give it a rest, Mums. You've already got a dishy young doctor for a son-in-law. You don't need another."

"Just an observation, that's all. If you'd taken more of my advice, you wouldn't be in this little fix, now, would you?"

"If I'd taken more of your advice, I'd be keeping the drunks company in the church basement."

In short, another festive holiday with the Schuylers.

3.

Daddy remains behind, after an exchange of eloquent glances with her mother that ends in a resigned sigh. He drops down in the chair next to the bed and asks her what the hell happened.

"It's a long and sordid story."

He doesn't take her hand and say, *Try me.* He really, truly doesn't want to know the details. He strokes his chin a few times, and then he lights a cigarette and blows the smoke out to the side. His face is gray and heavy. "Well," he says at last, "at least you're all right now."

"I'd say that's a matter of opinion."

He stares at her ankle. "Next time, come to us a little earlier, all right?"

"Now, why didn't I think of that?" She smacks her forehead.

Her father says to the ankle: "I just—I didn't know what to do with you. Whether to let you make your own mistakes or step in. You were always full of trouble. I was damned if I did, damned if I didn't. Maybe that's no excuse, but it was true." He turns back to her face, the seat of her trouble. "And I didn't want to hurt your spirit. I loved your spirit."

She can't say a word.

"You'll understand when you have one of your own."

She nods.

"We'll take care of you. Everything's going to be all right."

"But what if it's not?" she says. "What if you open up the newspaper tomorrow and someone's leaked out some story about Uncle Freddie, about how he bribed that senator to get his oil contracts?"

There is a small silence, during which Daddy's eyes grow small and hard, like a pair of agates.

He says quietly: "Who? Who's leaked out some story?"

She shrugs. "Someone might."

He stubs out the cigarette in the ashtray next to her bed and finishes the water in his glass. He rises from his chair, all paunchy and once-handsome, smelling familiarly of hair oil and cigarettes and just a hint of booze, and he pats the top of her head, as if she were eight years old again.

"I'd just like to see the honorable gentleman try it."

4.

Pepper's not prepared for the feeling of relief that drenches her when Florian Dommerich's dark head appears through the crack in the door.

"Am I allowed inside?" he asks.

She sets aside her book, taking time with the tasseled bookmark and laying the volume just so on the blanket next to her thigh. "I don't suppose I'm in any condition to stop you."

He smiles, and the rest of him unfolds from behind the door, just as capably handsome as she remembers. His hands are full of coffee. Pepper's chest seems to have run out of room for her vital organs, pushing them upward into her throat.

"You're looking well," he says. "May I sit down?"

She gestures to the chair.

"Mama'll be along soon. She's talking with your doctor. I understand it's bed rest for you, young lady." He gives her a stern look and hands her a foam cup of coffee. The other one remains in his palm, looking small.

"That's what happens when your mother blocks the street with her three-hundred-thousand-dollar car and causes an accident." Pepper blows across the surface of the coffee. "How's the car, by the way? I almost wept when I saw the damage."

"Oh, it'll be fine. We found a good mechanic in Washington. He about lost his jaw when he saw it." Florian chuckles, and Pepper's a goner. That chuckle.

"Did you have a nice Thanksgiving?"

"Sort of. Two pregnant sisters-in-law snapping at each other, one nephew with pneumonia, one brother quit his job to become a musician and move to California. The usual. You?"

"Vodka in the aspic, arsenic in the cranberry. The usual."

He grins. "I told you so."

"Told me what?"

"Your family would take care of you, if you gave them a chance."

"Trust me, Dommerich. I liked it better when I was on my own."

"Liar, liar." He drinks his coffee and smiles at her, a little goofy. There's something relaxed about his face, something pleasant, and she wonders if it's relief, and whether her face looks the same way.

"How's Susan?" she asks.

He runs a hand through his hair. "Susan's back with her folks in Florida. Had a nice Thanksgiving, she says."

"You talked to her?"

"Called her up this morning. We talked for a bit." He swishes the coffee in long waves along the side of his cup, staring down intently, like he's calculating sine, cosine, and tangent. "She thinks Hobbes is a brand of shoe."

"No, she doesn't."

He looks up. "Yep."

Pepper puts on a grave face. "She was probably just kidding you."

"Maybe. Anyway, I'm glad you're all right. I was a little panicked when I got the message at the hotel."

"The Mercedes got the worst of it."

He was shaking his head. "I'd never have forgiven my mother if something happened."

"It wasn't her fault. It was that idiot driving the car. There was plenty of time to stop if he hadn't been trying to light a cigarette. She just wanted to stop him, that's all."

"Well, at least she did that."

"Yes. You should have seen her." Pepper looks at the ceiling and smiles. "She stripped him bare. Flayed him like he was eight years old. I couldn't get a word in edgewise. I was so mad I hopped out of the car and forgot all about the crutches."

He gestures to her foot in its outsized cast, lying in state on the pillow. "You won't forget now."

"No."

"And now he's out of your life for good. His brother, I mean. Both of them."

Pepper looks back down at the gentle mountain of her pregnancy, this foreign salient of her once-lithe body. For maybe the thousandth time, she thinks, My God, I'm going to be a mother, and for the thousandth time it doesn't quite sink in. Maybe it won't sink in until the baby's born, until it's alive and kicking in her arms, until it's nursing at her breast, further ruining her perfect curves. Maybe not even then. Maybe the sonofabitch was right, when he spoke to her there in the parlor of the Riverview Hotel; maybe Pepper isn't mother material.

"That depends," she says. "I mean, it's his baby, too. I can't just say never, can I? I'm kind of stuck with him."

"That's generous of you."

"It's not for his sake, or his family's sake. It's for the baby's sake. The baby deserves a father, if his father decides he wants to be a father."

"Or she."

Pepper looks up.

Florian's smiling. "Might be a girl."

"Might be. God help her."

Florian goes back to swishing his coffee. "So I was thinking . . ."

"You could use a haircut? A decent necktie?"

"Probably both of those things. But mostly I was thinking we might have coffee sometime."

"Unless I'm hallucinating, that's what we're doing right now."

"So maybe we could have coffee more often. A regular thing."

"Don't you have to go back to work on Monday morning?"

"I could visit on weekends."

"That's a hell of a drive."

He leans in close, so she can smell the flavor of his shaving soap. "I could fly."

Maybe she banged her ribs in the accident. Maybe it's pneumonia. A heart attack. Whatever it is, there's definitely something wrong with Pepper's chest. She'll have to ask that nice doctor for an X-ray, the next time he comes around.

"It's a dumb idea," she says. "The dumbest idea I've ever heard. I'm not much fun at the moment."

"That's okay. I happen to like you when you're not much fun."

Jesus. Now her eyes.

"I guess I'm not in any condition to stop you," she says, and then, without thinking, "even if I wanted to," and thank God the door opens right then, before she can go on to say something even more stupid, and Annabelle Dommerich marches into the room, carrying a big bunch of fragrant pink roses.

"They're really from Florian," she says, planting a kiss on Pepper's forehead, "but he was too shy to give them to you himself."

"Mama, for chrissakes," says Florian.

5.

"Thank God you're all right," says Annabelle. "I'd never have forgiven myself."

Pepper lets out an aggrieved sigh. "You were trying to help."

"Well, I did, didn't I? All's well that ends well."

"Speak for yourself." Pepper gestures to the whole lot: belly, bed, cast. "And now I've got my family crowding half drunk around my bedside every second, thanks to your meddling."

"Yes, I was right about that, too," Annabelle says smugly. "I just had to pin you down, nice and helpless, so you could see for yourself. And the car will be fixed by the end of the week. *And* I got rid of Susan."

"How did you manage that?"

"Oh, I may have hinted that Florian was conceived out of wedlock, or something like that." She leans forward, woman to woman. "He likes you, you know."

"I know."

"So don't you go around breaking my son's heart. He's really very tender inside, though he hates to show it."

"Trust me, I wouldn't dare. I saw what you did to that son-ofabitch outside."

"Good, then. You'll be very happy. I can see you're already in love with him. I'll have that Cartier watch on my wrist by Christmas." She winks. "Our bet, remember?"

Pepper rolls her eyes and reaches for the cherry Jell-O.

"By the way," Annabelle continues, examining her fingernails, "I'm taking your advice."

"I beg your pardon? When did I ever give *you* advice?"

"About my friend on Cumberland Island. I realized you were right, that I was a coward. And I suppose my pride was hurt as well. Every woman likes to dream that a man will pine for her eternally, when the reality is that the poor dears just need some company. They can't manage on their own forever." She smiles brightly. "So I'm off on the afternoon ferry. Finish off that unfinished business and brush my hands clean."

Pepper scrapes her spoon around the sides of the Jell-O cup, wondering if it would be bad form to lick it clean. "I'm glad to hear it. Tell me how everything goes. I hope you kick the bitch out."

Annabelle laughs. "I'll do no such thing. I'm just going to say hello, give him something back, and wish him well."

Pepper looks up. "But don't you want to wait until the car is all fixed?"

"The car?"

"I mean, what are you going to say? *I've bought back the Mercedes, please don't mind that crumpled mess in the rear wheel well.*"

Annabelle's face clears. "Oh, my dear. I'm not bringing him the car. Why would I?"

"But I thought it was his. His car."

"No, no. The car belonged to my dear husband, God rest his soul. And it's a beautiful car, and my husband loved it very much and was sorry to see it go, and I'm sure he's very happy, wherever he is, to know that I've found it again. No, for this man, I have something far more valuable." She looks at her watch, starts, and picks up her gloves and pocketbook, which are made of rich blue leather in contrast to her neat black trousers and cashmere turtleneck sweater. She picks up her coat, made of beautiful aubergine wool, and slings it over her shoulder. "I'm going to be late."

"But wait! I'm confused. I thought—"

But Annabelle is already slipping through the door into the bright hospital corridor, an elegant blue-tipped bird among the antiseptic white walls.

Pepper sets aside the empty Jell-O cup and says aloud, to the baby: You know, one day, we have really got to make her sit down and tell us the whole damned story.

ANNABELLE

Germany • 1938

1.

In the interior of the Mercedes, nobody spoke. Johann drove intently along the dirt road, glancing into the mirror every so often, while Stefan and I occupied the other seat, covered with sleeping children, staring like corpses through the windshield, too shocked to say anything at all. To ask a single question.

Until Florian woke up. Florian lifted his head from Stefan's chest and saw Johann driving keen-eyed, both hands gripping the wheel, washed clean by the morning light, and he shouted, "Papa!" and flung himself on Johann's thick arm.

Johann had already taken off his jacket that was covered in brains, and he opened up his arm and pressed Florian to his shirt, without saying a word.

Next to me, Stefan closed his eyes and stroked Else's dark hair, and a minute later his breathing relaxed, and he seemed to have fallen asleep.

2.

Johann lit a cigarette and asked if I wanted one. I said no, thank you.

"Are you well?" he said. "You are not hurt?"

"No."

He adjusted Florian in his arm, so he could smoke and drive at the same time. "Good. I had some concern, when I saw them putting you in the truck like that."

"You didn't show it."

"I couldn't."

The air was close inside the car, despite the late autumn chill. I found myself wishing we could open the top. I leaned across Henrik's sleeping body and turned off the heater. "Where are we going?"

"To the border crossing at Neuenbürg, about a hundred kilometers away, south of Freiburg. It's a smaller one, in case we have any trouble."

"I don't understand."

He maneuvered around Florian to tap his cigarette into the ashtray. "Listen to me. If we are going to get you across in safety, you must do exactly as I say, all right?"

"All right."

"We are husband and wife. These are our children. We are going south to Italy, to spend the winter there for your health. You've been sick, okay?"

"Yes. What about Stefan?"

"We will stop shortly, about a mile from the border, and put him in the boot."

"The boot? Won't they look?"

"No," he said, "because I am a general in the German army, you understand. I am a senior official; I am a confidant of the Führer. I outrank any idiot officer at the Neuenbürg crossing, at least until they find out what I have just done."

He took in a long draft from his cigarette, which was nearly finished, and then he pulled the pack from his shirt pocket and lit another one from the end of the first, which he stubbed out in the ashtray.

"And what have you done?" I asked softly.

"I have committed an act of treason, I suppose."

"You have saved us. You saved Stefan."

He shrugged.

"Why?" I asked.

"Not for his sake, certainly. Not even wholly for yours."

"Then whose?" But I knew the answer.

He drove on silently for a moment, negotiating a series of curves in the road. There were no other cars, an eerie absence of other people, and I remembered the riots last night. The riots that had started all this, and now seemed like another age. The smoke was so thick, I couldn't breathe. I rolled down the window a couple of inches.

"I was in Munich yesterday," he said. "There was a great meeting, a celebration, actually, a commemoration of the—oh, what is it in English?—I believe it's called the Beer Hall Putsch. When they sent Hitler to jail, many years ago, and he wrote his book. We were all expected to be there. A very nice dinner, a big dinner, and then we got word that vom Rath had died, the poor bastard. And instead of giving his speech, Hitler left, and Herr Goebbels spoke instead."

"What did he say?"

"He said that the party wouldn't instigate any demonstrations, but that they wouldn't stop them, either. If the people wanted to kill Jews in revenge, no one would stop them." He cracked open his own window and blew out the smoke. "And all I could think was Florian. This enemy, this animal they were talking about, was my boy. They want to kill my boy." His voice broke. "They will kill my dear boy because he is a Jew."

I waited while he struggled. My eyes blurred, so that I couldn't quite see the road ahead, and turned my head to the window instead, where the smudging of the passing trees was a normal optic effect.

Johann went on: "So I left, before anyone could see what was in my face, and returned to my hotel, and there was a message there that they—the Gestapo agents, these men I have worked with many times—had discovered who was involved in the escape of Stefan Silverman a month ago and that they were planning a raid that night on the house of the Himmelfarb family in Stuttgart. Why tonight? Of course, because the demonstrations would lend them the perfect cover; they could do what they wanted this night."

"Oh, God," I whispered.

"I got in my car that instant and left. By then, I think I had gone a little mad. I thought, I have been wrong. I have been wrong about my country. I have been what I believe the Americans call a stooge . . . is that the word? Stooge?"

"Yes, I think so."

"A stooge for these men, these selfish men who will commit any crime to win themselves another gram of power. I have got to do this, I have got to stop them. I have got to do this for my boy."

He wiped his face and dropped his cigarette out the window.

"In the event, I arrived too late. They had already shot the Himmelfarbs like dogs in their own house. I saw the wife there on the rug, shot through the forehead, here, and the stomach." He gestured. "But then I saw Silverman. He was fighting like a madman. I thought, My God, what the fuck is Silverman doing here, when he should be safe in Switzerland? The goddamned bastard is more a hero than I am, he is fighting for his people instead of enjoying his new wife and his son and his freedom. And I realized in that second what God was asking me to do."

He started another cigarette, and the sun, now fully risen, darted out from a cloud, blinding the windshield. Else stirred and groaned, and I put my hand over her brow to shield her.

"How are the girls?" I said. "How is Frieda?"

"She was distraught when you left. She is a little better now. She is with my sister."

There was a low ache in my gut, like the removal of some vital organ. I stroked Else's hair and said, "And you? How are you?"

He glanced down at Florian's head, and then he lifted his hand, the one with the cigarette, and rubbed his forehead with his thumb. "For some time, I wished I would die. Not to kill myself. But that God would take me in the night, so I would not wake up and find you both still gone. I thought He must be punishing me, and yet what had I done? I was only doing my duty. I had done what I supposed was right."

I thought, His face is so lean. His big frame, there isn't an ounce of extra weight. He hasn't been eating. He is smoking too much.

I thought staunchly, But he deserves that. He deserves not to eat, for what he did to Stefan.

"Now, of course," Johann went on, in a quiet voice, "I see why God allowed me to live."

He slowed the car, and we turned from the smaller road onto a large paved highway. A signed passed by: FREIBURG, 78 KILOMETERS. In a hundred kilometers we would be out of Germany.

A thought occurred to me. "So what will you do?" I exclaimed. "You can't go back, can you?"

"No, they would probably arrest me if I tried. I sent a telegram to my sister before I left Munich. She was to pack up everything she could and bring the girls to Paris. I hope to God she has succeeded. The boys are still at school in England."

"Thank God."

"Yes." He paused. "They will confiscate my estate, however."

"I'm sorry."

"Don't be sorry. Maybe it is what I deserve." He pulled out another cigarette. His voice was rough, as if he were choking on glass. "You must take care of Florian. You must take care of my dear boy. He will not remember me."

"He might."

"No. He is too young. If he were three or four, perhaps. But this is for the best." He lost himself a little on the last word, and covered it with the cigarette. With his thumb he rubbed the inner sockets of his eyes.

I couldn't think of anything more to say. Thank you? My limbs were tired and aching from holding the children, from the long night without sleep, from the avalanche of fear and dread piled on my shoulders.

All at once, I couldn't hold my head up any longer. I leaned my heavy cheek against Stefan's shoulder, and as I listened to his breathing, the rhythm of his respiration that I knew more intimately than my own, I realized that he was awake.

3.

We passed Freiburg just before noon, and a few kilometers later Johann pulled over into a field by the side of the road. The children were awake by now, restless and hungry and confused.

"Let them stretch a bit," said Johann. "Then we must go into the village for a little food and to clean up, so we look like a civilized family. Silverman, it is best if you wait here, I think."

"Of course," said Stefan.

"I will need napkins for Henrik, and milk," I said.

"Yes, we will get all these things." He looked up at the sun, or the spot overhead where the sun would be, if the clouds hadn't moved in the way. "I have been thinking that we might wait until it is closer to dusk. Dusk is a good hour—harder to see details, but there is not so much suspicion as at night."

Stefan nodded. "Very well." He was watching the children in the field.

In the village, Johann visited a barber for a shave. I took the children into the market and bought food and milk and cigarettes. The atmosphere was deeply subdued; hardly anybody was out. There were thick black headlines on all the newspapers, but I didn't read them. In another shop I found a bottle for Henrik, and napkins. I bought five, enough to last a day or two, until I could find a way to wash them. Johann was waiting for me at the car, freshly shaven, jacket miraculously cleaned. He took the packages from me and put them in the boot.

"How did you get the jacket cleaned?" I asked.

"I had the barber do it. I explained that we had hit a deer along the road."

"Did he believe you?"

Johann shrugged. "He didn't ask any questions."

We drove back through the eerie streets to the field where we'd left Stefan. I let the children out of the car and stepped out after them to look around. There was no sign of Stefan's dark hair, his gaunt brown shoulders. I turned to Johann. "Where's Stefan?"

Johann was unwrapping the food. "He'll be back."

"But where has he gone?"

"For a walk, I think. She was his wife once."

"I've got to find him."

Johann put a hand on my arm. "Let him be, Annabelle. He'll be back. He will be back for you and the children."

There was an unsettling normalcy to it all, eating lunch with Johann and Florian and Wilhelmine's children. The air had warmed a bit, so we sat in our seats in the car and kept the doors open. Henrik insisted on sitting in the grass. Else and Florian chased each other. My brain was still so numb; I could hardly comprehend the past twenty-four hours. I had focused on the necessary details, hygiene and food and sleep. But the great truth sat behind it all, the awfulness, like a gorgon waiting for night. And this man, sitting next to me. Johann, my one-time husband, lost and found. Soon to be lost again, this time for good.

It's a damned thing.

"I don't know what to tell Else," I said. "How do I tell her?"

"Wait until she asks, and then tell her the truth. You will

know what to say. She is very young still. It's much easier when they are so young. Once they have turned five or six, they understand what has happened. They know enough to grieve."

I rose and brushed the crumbs from my skirt. "Could you watch them for a moment? I'm going to find Stefan."

4.

I found Stefan on a fallen tree, in the woods at the perimeter of the field, not far away, after all. He was smoking a cigarette and drinking from a bottle of Scotch whisky.

"Where did you find that?" I asked.

"In the car, before you left."

I sat down beside him. "Are you all right?"

"No, I don't think so. Not at the moment."

I laid my hand on his thigh. "We'll raise her children. That's all any mother wants, that her children are safe."

"We left her lying there in the hallway. You did not see her face, Annabelle, but I will see it always." He looked at his hands, the one with the bottle and the other with the cigarette. "You are a good mother. It was the last thing on my mind, on the yacht, when I was going mad for you, lying awake and imagining what it would be like to have you. But now I'm grateful."

"Listen to me." I turned his face toward me. "We have each other, and the children. We'll learn to be happy again."

"Listen to you. There is no one in the world like you."

"That's what you said when you kissed me, that first time."

"Yes, I remember."

I put my hands on his cheeks and kissed him, the way he

had kissed me three years ago on the Île Sainte-Marguerite, and I ended the kiss the way he had, sliding my lips across his cheek to his ear.

"The damnedest thing about all of this," he said, "is that if I hadn't wanted to do the right thing, it would have been all right."

"What do you mean?"

"I would have taken you to Paris, instead of going to Germany to finish things with Wilma first. I would have slept by your side through the long winter, watching the baby grow. Maybe it would have been a sin, living with you like that, but it would have been better than prison, and no one would have died. God in Heaven, how happy we would have been. I would have held my son in my two hands. So where is the nice moral here? I should have been a scoundrel instead."

"Don't say that. Don't talk as if this was your fault."

"But it is. Their blood is on my hands." He dropped the cigarette into the leaves and squashed it under his heel. "Though I suppose my original sin was to seduce you in the first place, instead of leaving you for von Kleist to marry."

"No, because I seduced you. And there would have been no von Kleist if there had been no Stefan."

"Then some other worthy man, as God meant for you."

I put my arms around his neck. "God didn't mean me for some stupid worthy man."

He set the bottle on the wet ground and kissed me, because he had no choice, because when you are covered in death you crave life. He kissed me feverishly, there in the quiet woods, and tucked his hands inside my coat, covering my breasts with his hands. "In prison, I dreamed always of this, your breasts in the

August sunshine. We had only a few days, didn't we, but when I dreamed, I swear it was like the whole of my life."

"Because it will be. It will be the whole of our lives, from now on."

He bent down and buried his face in my chest. His hands crept under my dress, and I felt something wet against my feet, as the bottle of whisky spilled over my shoes. We sat there quietly, while his breath warmed my breasts and his hands warmed my hips. "What are you doing?" I asked softly, even though I knew the answer.

"Listening."

"What am I saying to you this time?"

"Ah, the usual absurd things. That you love my hands on your skin. That you want me to make love to you, even here in these wretched cold November woods. That, in your stupid American optimism, you are already counting the children we will have together, and the olives we will grow, when we finally reach our island."

I nearly laughed in relief. "Yes, exactly."

He stroked my thighs with his thumbs. "That your heart still beats for me."

"Yes, always. And yours?"

"Do you need to ask?"

I tried to lift his head and kiss him, but he wouldn't let me. "No, please, a moment more, Mademoiselle. Just another moment like this, with no more talking."

There were no birds to sing for us. The last leaf had already fallen. I stared up at the bony tops of the trees, at the gray sky above, and listened to Stefan's heartbeat against my belly. The air smelled of whisky and rotting leaves. In Capri, I thought, the sun will be shining, and it will smell like lemon and eucalyptus.

"You're shivering," he said at last.

"Not from the cold."

He lifted his head. "We should get back to the car."

5.

We stayed in the field for a few more hours. Stefan played with the children while Johann slept in the car. When it was time to go, Stefan took the passports and papers from the inside pocket of his jacket, the ones that Wilhelmine had had made for us, and he gave them to Johann. "You can use these to cross the border," he said, "in case the guards have already been alerted. It will be safer this way, if you don't wear your uniform."

Johann stared at the papers, turned them over, and nodded. "These are good forgeries," he said, and he took off his uniform jacket and asked if he could trade with Stefan. The sleeves were too short, and the wool strained against his shoulders, but only if you looked closely. He tucked the papers into his pocket, lifted the lid of the boot, and made an apologetic gesture. "It will not be too long, I hope."

Stefan climbed obediently into the boot, a little stiff and trying not to show it. He had to bend his body to fit inside. When he was comfortable—or at least as comfortable as he could make himself—I leaned inside and kissed him, and I didn't care if Johann saw us. "Everything will be fine," I said.

"It seems your husband is a decent chap after all."

"He's not my husband anymore," I whispered, kissing him

again, holding his cheek. "I'm Mrs. Annabelle Dommerich now, and I'm married to you."

"As you say."

Johann stepped in and closed the lid. He leaned against the metal and said, "Okay?"

"Okay," came Stefan's faint response.

We drove the last twenty kilometers in silence. Johann smoked cigarette after cigarette, holding each one close to the crack in the window, checking the mirror from time to time as if wary of pursuit. The children clustered on my lap, restless and bored, poking at the gears and the dials. Else asked for her mother. The sky had already begun to darken by the time we reached the signposts for the border, for the bridge across the Rhine into France.

"Here we go," said Johann, rolling to a stop, and I looked ahead to the striped metal pole across the white pavement, while my stomach turned sick with fear.

Johann glanced at me. "Don't worry. Smile, okay?" A face appeared in the window, and he turned. "*Guten Tag, mein Herr.*"

The man's eyes took in the interior of the car, the size of the passenger inside, and his face registered surprise, which he smothered quickly. "Heil Hitler. Passports, please."

"Of course." Johann reached inside his jacket pocket and produced the papers. "Here you are."

The soldier took the passport from Johann's fingers. He cast another curious glance at the elegant Mercedes, the beautiful polished wood inside, and then he looked down at the first passport and fumbled through the pages. "Mr. Dommerich?" he said.

"Yes, sir. My family and I are heading to Italy before the

snow falls. My wife is in poor health, I'm afraid. These northern winters."

The soldier's gaze traveled respectfully in my direction. I tried to look wan, as befit an invalid. Henrik whimpered and shimmied down my lap to rest at my feet.

"Frau Dommerich?"

"My wife is ill," said Johann sharply.

"Let her speak. I am required to verify her identity."

"Her identity is obvious."

So much natural authority, packed into so bass a voice. The young soldier actually hesitated. "Herr Dommerich, you've surely heard—that is, because of the demonstrations last night—"

"I have no knowledge of these so-called demonstrations," said Johann, "and what is more, I don't care. I am concerned for my wife's welfare. We have hotel reservations in Lyon, and it's already late."

The guard peered inside again, at this mysterious invalid who inspired such passionate devotion in her husband. "Yes, sir. I quite understand. I'll just—"

"Papa," Florian said suddenly, "where is Stefan?"

Else looked up from the map, which she held upside-down on her lap. "Stefan's in the boot, silly."

The air froze. There was no sound at all, except for the slight crackle of the map between Else's small fingers and the knock of my pulse in my throat.

The guard looked at the children, and then at Johann. "What did the child say?"

"Nothing."

"She said something about someone in the boot, sir."

Johann knocked the ash from his cigarette into the dust outside the car. "Soldier, I assure you, the only thing in the boot of my car is my wife's baggage."

"But the girl said—"

I lifted my head and spoke in my best German. "Do you mean Stefan?"

"Yes. The girl said someone named Stefan is in the boot of the car."

I smiled. "Stefan is my son's teddy bear."

Florian opened his mouth, and I moved my hand over his lips in a gesture that looked like a caress.

"His teddy bear?"

"Yes. Doesn't your son have a teddy bear?" I looked at the soldier with my most enormous round eyes, and he began to stammer.

"I—I don't—that is—"

"What's this? Your wife hasn't given you a big strapping son?"

"No, she—that is, I'm not married—"

"Well." I looked tenderly at Johann and reached out to stroke his arm. "A fine handsome young soldier like that. I think every soldier deserves a pretty German girl to marry."

The guard's face had turned the color of a radish.

"I quite agree, my dear," said Johann, "and now I'm afraid we must be off. Are we through here, soldier?"

"Y-yes, sir! Heil Hitler, sir!" The guard stepped back and waved us on.

"Heil Hitler, soldier. I shall be sure to write a letter to your commanding officer, praising your efficiency."

6.

On the other side of the river, the French guard was half drunk, and hardly even glanced at our passports before he stamped them at a sloppy angle. We drove on down the darkened road for perhaps fifteen minutes, watching the beams of the head-lamps as they swept over the pavement, until Johann seemed to spot something on the side of the road and pulled over. A barn, made of crumbling yellow stone. I nudged the children off my lap and opened the door almost before we had fully stopped.

Under the lid of the boot, Stefan made a little groan. Johann grabbed him under the shoulders and helped him out, and he knelt into the grass and vomited. I had no handkerchief left. I waited anxiously until he had finished, and then I sat on the ground and pulled him against my chest.

"We will stop here tonight, then," said Johann. "I'll sleep in the car, you can have the barn. You can leave in the morning. Here are the keys." He handed them to me.

I stared dumbly at the metal in my palm. "You're giving us the car?"

He shrugged. "You can leave it in Monte Carlo. I will pick it up later. You *are* leaving from Monte Carlo, aren't you?"

"Yes. Help me get him up."

But Stefan shrugged us both off. The children had spilled out of the car and stood there, blinking, as he rose to his feet. "Let us have a little dinner," he said, "and then we will rest for the night."

7.

The straw was old and musty, but I had never known anything more comfortable. I settled the children a few yards away and covered them with my coat, and then I collapsed next to Stefan.

"I'm sorry," he whispered. "I smell like the devil."

"I don't care. We've done it, we're safe, we're free. We're in France."

His arm closed around me. "Yes, by God's grace."

"We'll telephone my father from Monte Carlo and let them know we're safe. They'll be worried."

"Yes, of course."

"And your troubles will be over. You will rest and recover."

"I am very fortunate, Mademoiselle, to have you watching over me."

"Yes, you are. And I was just thinking, in the car, that maybe this horrible night will wake up the world to what's going on. Maybe Johann can speak to the embassy in Paris, and the whole nightmare will be over, and Wilhelmine won't have died in vain."

He kissed my hair. "My dauntless American girl. Go to sleep. We will save the fucking world in the morning."

"I can't sleep."

"Try."

I closed my eyes and pulled him closer, until his breath was warm in my hair, and that was all I remembered until I woke up some unknown hour later, and he was gone.

"Stefan?" I whispered, into the dusty silence of the barn.

"Over here."

I lifted my head and saw his shadow, sitting by the hollow in the straw where the children lay sleeping. What lucky children,

I thought, to have Stefan for a father, and then I pictured Johann, bent uncomfortably on the seat of the Mercedes outside, covered by his gray uniform jacket, and for an instant my heart hurt.

But I will thank him one day, I thought. I will return to him and thank him for the gift he has given to me tonight, to Florian and me. That he loved us both so much, he gave us back to his immortal enemy.

I settled back in the musty straw and closed my eyes again. In a moment, Stefan would come back to bed and put his arms around me, the way he always did, and in the morning we would drive down with the children to the sunshine of Monte Carlo, to the life we had dreamed together.

"Thank God," I said softly. "I thought you'd gone away."

Coda

"The sea does not reward those who are too anxious, too greedy, or too impatient. One should lie empty, open, choiceless as a beach—waiting for a gift from the sea."

ANNE MORROW LINDBERGH

STEFAN

Cumberland Island • 1966

1.

The knock arrives at sunset, half an hour after he stomped back, damp and chilled, from feeding the horses. He has showered and shaved and put on the teakettle, and at first he thinks the telephone wire has come loose again in the November wind, and is now flapping against the roof.

He pauses, fingers still wrapped around the handle of the kettle, and turns his cheek to the ceiling, listening. The sound comes again, three imperative knocks, knuckles against wood.

He doesn't have many visitors, and they usually mean trouble of some kind: horses loose or fences down or hurricanes on the way. That's surely why his pulse crashes against his neck, as the knock echoes about the empty rooms. Why his blood turns buoyant in his veins. Because there might be trouble.

He wipes his hands on the dishcloth and heads for the front door.

He doesn't have far to walk. The house is small and simple: living room, dining room, and kitchen on the ground floor, along with a small office and plenty of bookshelves. (He has too many books to count, the natural consequence of solitude.) Upstairs, two roomy bedrooms and a bathroom. One of the bedrooms has a sleeping porch, and he really does sleep there in the summer, when the heat billows up from the tall marsh grasses to merge with the smoldering sky, and you almost can't breathe the air, it's so wet. He puts up the screens with the netting to keep the mosquitoes away, and he sleeps in a pair of cotton pajamas with no blanket. In the morning, he's covered in dew.

He walks across the living room to the entry hall, past the signs of his recent visitor. If he stands still and closes his eyes, he can still smell her in the air: a hint of perfume, the soap she uses. He can almost hear the trace of her laughter, like an echo trapped in the furniture she has touched. Right there, in the corner of the living room, just two days ago, he showed her how to waltz to the "Blue Danube." Something every woman should do with a man who loves her.

When he reaches the entry hall, he pauses, because he hasn't heard the knock again, and maybe he was mistaken. Maybe he'll open the door and there will be nobody there. It's happened before, usually after his visitor leaves. He'll think he hears something, some sign of human love and habitation—maybe she's turned back after all, maybe she'll stay this time—but when he opens his eyes, he knows he's alone again. That this promising sound was just a delusion, after all.

Knock, knock.

Well, not a delusion this time.

He draws the cool air deep into his lungs, reaches for the knob, and opens the door, and there in the light from the porch stands a dark-haired woman in a coat of soft aubergine wool, full and delicate both at once, whose eyes open wide at the sight of his face.

"Stefan," she whispers.

His hand sticks to the knob. His chest fills up with quicksilver and runs over. He thinks, Hell, I remembered her face all wrong, I forgot the shade of her eyes, I forgot her cheekbones and her pointed chin, I forgot how beautiful she is. How could I forget that? When she lives inside my skin.

"May I come in?" she asks, and it seems he forgot that, too, the sound of her voice.

Somehow, he steps back and opens the door, just wide enough.

"Would you like some tea?" he asks.

2.

The next morning, it's so much easier. He opens his eyes from a velvet sleep, and for a moment he thinks he's in Monte Carlo, at the scorching end of August, and a tantalizing future still beckons outside his window. He can almost smell the lemon trees in the courtyard, and then he remembers it's Annabelle's skin. Her skin smells like lemons. What kind of miracle is that?

The light is still gray and hushed through the shutters. Annabelle is deeply asleep. It seems to him that he'll wake her if he stays in bed—wake her with the force of loving her—so he untangles her from his arms instead and slips downstairs to make coffee, the way she likes it.

The teacups still sit on the kitchen table, half full, and the sight makes him smile. The way they talked awkwardly—*How are you?* Fine, fine. *How do you like Cumberland Island?* It is marvelous, except for the terrible heat in July—and took their tea in tiny nervous sips.

The way Annabelle had crashed down her cup into the middle of another calcified sentence and said, *Don't look at me like that,* and he had said, *Like what?* and she said, *Like you want to kiss me.*

The way he had stared at her, hammering heart, thinking, God in heaven, what does she mean, can it be true, and then thinking, Of course it's true, it's Annabelle, Stefan, it's your own fucking *Annabelle* walking in your front door three decades later, out of the clear blue sky, wanting you to break the ice and everything else, and you are just going to sit there with your cock in your hand while the clock ticks and the house groans and the minutes bleed irretrievably away, the dwindling minutes remaining to you both?

The way she had risen from her chair like a princess and said, *Unless you don't want to kiss me, after all,* and he said, *But of course I want to kiss you,* and she had given him a look both defiant and vulnerable and turned to climb the stairs, and he had thought how very like Annabelle this was, like no one else in the world.

The way he had then run after her and hoisted her over his shoulder and taken her up the rest of the stairs before he could doubt himself. The way she had laughed and put her soft palms on his skin and kissed him, and somehow it had all worked perfectly, being inside Annabelle again, losing himself inside Annabelle, drenching himself in the purity of her heart, his skin inside her skin, her skin inside his, in a thoroughly imperfect way.

The way it had worked again, even more perfectly imperfect, an hour later.

And Annabelle was right, as always: the awkwardness dissolved at the first touch, poof, like magic. You know where you stand with a woman, when you have just made love to her after a long absence. She knows where she stands with you. You can go to sleep happy, listening to each other's heartbeats, because you know her again and she knows you, because you are no longer strangers, and you will work everything out in the morning, over hot coffee and a good smoke.

3.

When he returns with the coffee, she's awake, propped up against his pillow. Her breasts are heavier than before, darker at the tips, a woman's breasts. Just looking at them makes his ribs hurt.

She takes the coffee and sips. "So who's the woman?"

He's busy lighting a cigarette, and nearly spits it out of his mouth. "What woman?"

"The woman you were dancing with the other night. I saw you through the window." She gives him a challenging look. "Does your heart beat for her, too?"

He resumes lighting the cigarette, takes a good drag, and blows the smoke out slowly and with profound enjoyment. Then he crawls up the bed and starts kissing her breasts. "Yes, as a matter of fact. My heart beats for her, too. The two of you beauties, you are the great loves of my life."

She pushes his head away. "Bastard."

He's laughing and kissing her. He's so full of relief—that quicksilver in his chest last night, it turned out to be relief, of an elite and highly distilled grade—and so full of Annabelle. He takes the coffee from her hand and puts it on the bedside table. He sticks the cigarette in the corner of his mouth and grasps her two hands, so she will the hell stop hitting him with them. "That was Else," he said. "Else visits me here."

As if her limbs have turned to butter. "Else?" she whispers.

"Yes. Didn't you get a good look, when you spied on the two of us through my window? She tracked me down a few years ago. I made her promise not to tell you." He removes the cigarette and resumes kissing her. "Johann was still alive."

"I see." She lies against his pillow without moving, accepting the kisses. "And when he died?"

"I thought I would wait for you to come to me. I didn't know if you wanted me, after everything. After so many years."

"Oh, Stefan. Don't be stupid." She moves finally, threading her hands in his hair.

He stops kissing her then, just lies on her soft body with his lips in her neck, smelling her lemon smell, letting the shock settle in his bones, letting her skin become his skin. He is in bed with Annabelle, and it's not a dream. He opened the door last night, and she was there, genuine hot cross Annabelle bun, warm and round in his arms.

"I brought your cello," she whispers.

"My cello?"

"The Amati you gave me. I played it everywhere for you. I played it in Carnegie Hall and the Boston Pops, I played it on every single recording I ever made. Did you hear any of them?"

He wants to say *Every one*, but his lips won't move.

"So I thought I would bring it back to you. That was my excuse, that the instrument really belonged to you, and I was

ALONG THE INFINITE SEA · *511*

just playing it for you, all these years. That was how I worked up the courage to come here."

Holy shit, he is going to cry.

"I mean, I couldn't just walk through the front door and throw myself at you," she adds, very reasonable, as if she hadn't done just that in the kitchen last night, over two cups of anemic Lipton.

So he starts to laugh instead, helpless gusts of laughter. He loses the cigarette in the pillows and has to go scrabbling for it, still laughing, shaking with goddamned unstoppable amusement, until at last he puts the cigarette in the ashtray and springs from the bed and opens up every single shutter over every single window, filling the room with a salmon-pink sunrise.

She looks at him like he's crazy. "What are you doing?"

"I am admiring your breasts in the sunshine," he says.

"Oh." She settles back in the pillows and spreads her arms. "If that's all."

And that is one of the things he loves most about Annabelle, what has not changed about her in all these years: her joy. Like the first time he made love to her, on the cliffs at Antibes, the delight that seeped from her pores, the transparent love with which she drenched him, the wanton absence of any shame, even though she was a virgin who had been kissed only once. That was why he couldn't resist her then, and he can't resist her now. She turns his sorrow into joy.

4.

When he's finished making love to her a third time—and it takes a while, make no mistake, he's not the young man he was, not that she seems to mind the additional effort one bit—they lie boneless on the bed, drunk and sated as a pair of new lovers, surrounded by twenty-eight years of questions.

He tells her about the war, and working for the French Resistance, the bullet in his chest that nearly brought him to a bad end. He shows her the scar. Thank God for penicillin, he says. He talks about wandering aimlessly through Europe after the war—the worst years, he says, because there was no purpose anymore, no friends left alive, nothing to do but despair over the six million lives he had failed to save—until he crashed into some sort of bottom (wasn't that the phrase?) and moved to America. He says, I thought I could at least be on the same continent as you, the same continent as our children. I could see what they were up to, what fine young people they were becoming. She says, in a breaking voice, You said *our* children, and he strokes her hair and says, Yes, I was their father and you are their mother, and you cannot possibly know how I left my heart on the floor of that barn for you to keep for me, how much my heart was in your hands.

Then why did you do it? she says. Why did you leave us like that?

Because I had no choice, my Annabelle. Because I had a profound debt to repay, a fucking world to save. Because he was the better man. Because he loved you so well.

So she tells him about the early years, how they waited in Monte Carlo until the boys arrived from England, until Margaret reached them with the girls; how she and Johann and all the children sailed to America in the *Isolde*, how they left the Mercedes in a shed at her aunt's house in Cape Cod, so no one would connect the Dommerich brood with the Nazi general who committed subversion and treason and then disappeared. How she couldn't bear him at first, because he wasn't Stefan, and then gradually the shared parenthood brought them together—he was such a good father, she had to love him for that alone—and the shared secrets, too. And then Henrik started nursery school, and she wanted another baby so badly, she would have slept with Stalin if she had to. So we finally went to bed together, she says, and I got pregnant with the twins two seconds later, let that be a lesson. He laughs and says it was no more than she deserved, sleeping with someone else, and then she goes quiet and he knows what she's thinking.

He says, I came close a few times, I admit. I came damned close.

But you never?

No.

Ever?

(He sighs.)

Not even once, Annabelle, though I thought sometimes it would kill me, I was so lonely.

(There is a long silence, laden with awe.)

Why not?

Because we had a covenant, remember? And because you were raising the children for me, all the way across the ocean, and I had nothing else to give you in return. I had nothing but that.

The wind is picking up again. A shutter bangs against the side of the house, because he forgot to latch it, in his haste to see the sunshine on Annabelle's skin.

He says, And there is another reason.

What was that?

Because there was a time when this fidelity was the only virtue I had left. The only vow I hadn't broken.

(She lies quietly in his arms, until he thinks that maybe she's gone to sleep.)

Then:

Do you know what I think?

What do you think, Annabelle? (And isn't that the best part of all? Just saying her name aloud.)

I think you're just like your son.

5.

They watch the sun sink from the shelter of the porch, curled up in the old rocking chair Stefan repaired himself, covered by a thick plaid horse blanket. There's a cold snap coming. It's maybe even going to freeze tonight, he can smell it in the air. A good night to share a bed with the woman you love.

"Two more questions," he whispers in her hair.

"What's that?"

"The first one. How did you find me?"

She laughs. "It took months. I hired an investigator. I figured you would have a new name of some kind. I gave him a list of possibilities. And a couple of weeks ago he sent me an article about Cumberland Island, and a man named Stefan Himmelfarb who was caring for the wild horses who were injured or sick, and I knew it had to be you. I read that article and I could feel you behind the ink. But when I arrived at the hotel in Saint Mary's, I lost my nerve."

"*You*, Annabelle?"

"Yes, me. I'm not the nubile young maiden I once was, in case you hadn't noticed."

"This is nonsense. You are still the most beautiful woman I have ever met, despite the immense crookedness of your toes."

She snorts her very practical American disbelief. "And besides, you had three decades to fall out of love with me and find some other woman to warm your heart."

"Don't be stupid." He tucks the blanket around her shoulder.

"Well, that's my answer, like it or not. So what's your second question?"

"In fact, since you ask, I have a great many questions, and we will have to spend long weeks answering them all. This may take until the new year at least. But the most important question is this."

He pauses, for effect. The sun drops another millimeter, just touching the tips of the marsh grass, illuminating the backs of the horses as they saunter habitually across the meadow to the lean-to he built with his own hands, and the hay he has just laid out for them, with Annabelle's help.

And wasn't that almost as good as saying her name aloud? Sharing the evening chores, side by side, in the manner of a couple married for years. Maybe she will stay until the new year. Maybe she will stay all winter, and they will share this routine every night. He hardly dares to think about the spring. There is such a thing as too much joy, and the perils of tempting fate.

"Well?" she says.

He turns her face toward him and fixes her sternly.

"What in the hell did the two of you do with my yacht?"

A few years ago, I came across a short article in the newspaper, concerning a vintage automobile—a rare 1936 Mercedes 540K Special Roadster—that had been discovered in a shed at an inn in Greenwich, Connecticut, where I then lived. According to the article, a German baroness had driven this extraordinary car around Europe in the years before the Second World War, having various affairs (including one with a Jewish Englishman) and generally making herself unpopular with the ruling party in Germany. Eventually, she fled to America with her Mercedes, and at the time of the car's rediscovery in 1989, it hadn't been touched in two decades. A cigarette stub still rested in the ashtray, stained with lipstick, and a single leather glove inhabited the glove compartment. Fully restored, the car sold at auction in 2012 for nearly twelve million dollars. I couldn't resist.

But I'm a writer of novels, not biographies, so I wanted to make up a story of my own and weave it into the overall narrative of my fictional Schuyler family, which now stretches over several books. I also felt I had something more to say about the journey—physical and moral—undertaken by the people of Europe between the two world wars, and the discovery of a rare 1936 Mercedes in a Cape Cod shed seemed like the perfect springboard into this world.

Most of the characters in this book—and all of the principal ones—never existed in real life, no matter how vibrantly they live in my imagination. There was no Johann von Kleist in the German high command, and no Jewish nemesis by the name of Stefan Silverman. While the Himmelfarbs did not exist, nor did they die on the night of 9–10 November 1938, millions of German Jews were not so lucky. Kristallnacht saw the destruction of a thousand synagogues and seven thousand businesses; over thirty thousand were sent to camps like that at Dachau, and the number of dead and injured will never be known exactly. Despite the horror expressed in the foreign press in the days following the pogrom, the world—"weary of everything"—responded more or less as Stefan imagined it would. Only the quiet heroism of individual Germans emerged to redeem humanity that night.

As a writer of historical fiction, however, I try to keep the history as my background, and my characters at the center of the stage. This novel isn't intended as a textbook on Nazi Germany and the politics of prewar Europe; for those interested in learning more about this crucial year in Hitler's consolidation of power, I highly recommend Giles MacDonogh's engaging and exhaustive *1938: Hitler's Gamble*, to which I referred again and again.

As for the identity of the father of Pepper's baby, I have no comment.

ACKNOWLEDGMENTS

The book you hold in your hands is not the original version of *Along the Infinite Sea*. Writing swiftly on a tight deadline, I tried to open the file one evening—the night before April Fool's Day, ahem—and had no luck. Neither did the assembled geniuses at the Apple Store. I sent the file to Putnam, where it was referred to the ominously titled Forensics Department. The cadaver could not be dissected, and neither could any of the copies I had saved earlier.

So I started over. I rewrote those first 250 pages—the writers among you will now proceed to throw up—and the story took an entirely different turn. Go figure. I could not, however, have decided exactly how the love triangle of Stefan, Johann, and Annabelle would play out without the emergency help of my immensely talented friend Karen White, who took my phone call and walked me through my very complicated plot until I realized what I had to do. In her own wonderful novels, Karen is an expert at moments of emotional impact, and I might not have had the courage for that final resolution on the German border without her clear vision and her assurance. I hope she enjoys reading the result.

Beyond Karen and her creative assistance, I have many more wonderful people to thank for their help in putting the finished book into your hands. Alexandra Machinist, my irreplaceable literary agent, has held my hand and walked me through a fireworks year, and I am deeply grateful to her and to her hard-working colleagues at ICM for all their support. As for the talented and enthusiastic team at Putnam—my wonderful editor, Laura Perciasepe (whose name alone gives me joy); my publicist, Katie McKee; my whiz-girl marketing mavens, Lydia Hirt and Mary Stone; the ridiculously talented art department that delivers me cover after stunning cover; and a host of other superb professionals—I simply can't say enough. You have taken me on a marvelous journey, and I can only hope it's been as much fun for you as it's been for me.

I have so many people to thank in the book world—writers, bloggers, booksellers, readers—I can't even begin to list them here, but you know who you are. Your bookish enthusiasm keeps me writing, even on those days when I'm in a muddle, and I thank you with all my heart for your kind words, your emails and tweets and Facebook posts, and your energetic company when we meet at book events.

I owe special thanks to my lovely friends at the Putnam Restaurant on Greenwich Avenue—my diner of choice, and that's saying something—who fry my bacon just so and keep the coffee coming generously while I frown and stab at my laptop all morning. It's amazing how much you can write when someone keeps stopping by to refill your coffee cup.

And finally, as always, to my family—friends, in-laws, outlaws—and most especially my beloved husband, Sydney, and our four crazy kids. I love you all.

Two Women on the Beach, in 1936 © Else Neuländer-Simon, Yva

When we were researching the provenance of the photograph on this cover, we discovered a heartbreaking story that seemed very relevant to the book.

The photograph was taken by a German-Jewish fashion and portrait photographer, Else Neuländer-Simon (known as Yva) who worked in Berlin in the 1920s and 1930s. Yva was a popular photographer and her work was published in many well-regarded newspapers and magazines, such as *Die Dame, Berliner Illustrierte Zeitung* and *Münchner Illustrierte Presse*. One of her young apprentices who later attained fame under his own name often cited her as a strong influence: Helmut Newton.

By the mid-1930s, due to changes in the law by the Nazi regime, Yva was no longer allowed to run her studio, and by 1938 she was forced to give it up entirely. On the outbreak of war, she was initially sent to the Jewish Hospital in Berlin to work in the X-ray department, then in 1942 both Yva and her husband, Alfred Simon, were arrested and deported to the Sobibor concentration camp. They were both killed, probably on arrival at the camp in June 1942, although the judicial declaration of death is December 1944.

Due to Yva's tragic death, her photographic works are not held by an official estate, but by the various libraries and publications in which she was published. We are very grateful to the collection of F.C. Gundlach at the House of Photography, Deichtorhallen Hamberg in Germany, for allowing the use of this image, and for the opportunity to share Yva's story.

'I wish I could remember more. I wish I had taken down every detail, because I didn't see him again until the summer of 1938; the summer the hurricane came and washed the world away...'

Lily Dane has returned to the exclusive enclave of Seaview, Rhode Island, hoping for an escape from the city and from her heartbreak. What she gets instead is the pain of facing newlyweds Budgie and Nick Greenwald – her former best friend and former fiancé.

During lazy days and gin-soaked nights, Lily is drawn back under Budgie's glamorous and enticing influence, and the truth behind Budgie and Nick's betrayal of Lily begins to emerge. And as the spectre of war in Europe looms, a storm threatens to destroy everything...

OUT NOW